ADVANCE PRAISE

"This contemporary story, humorous and moving by turns, follows a young woman, Pattianne Anthony who, in the tradition of American travelers, finds she has nothing to keep her home. Her travels take her from urban New Jersey to a small town in Minnesota to little more than an outpost at the edge of Western Canada where she finds happiness among the people who have also found a life left of center. It is also a tale of the impossibility of becoming someone that someone else wishes you were (that you thought you could be), with an ending that is nothing but joyful."

—Whitney Otto, author of *How to Make an American Quilt*

"Despite my natural pessimism, this book broke down my defenses and set me up to root for a well-earned, conventional kind of happy ending. But then it took a turn and became an altogether different story, leaving me to sputter along with the characters, 'Unfair—this is not what I was expecting.' I was crushed. And then it found its way to another kind of happy ending, a richer, more satisfying one than I'd wanted in the first place. Last year Lily King's novel *Writers & Lovers* won deserved acclaim for its heartfelt, realistic portrayal of a woman's intellectual and emotional development. If *A Small Crowd of Strangers* doesn't generate at least as much, it'll be a crime."

—James Crossley, bookseller, Phinney Books

"In *A Small Crowd of Strangers*, the profoundly talented Joanna Rose creates a generous, compassionate, and vivid world. We drift along with Pattianne Anthony, newly married but barely tethered to her own choices. When the truth about her marriage gains an unexpected and inexorable momentum, it both explodes and saves Pattianne's life. Piling detail upon shining detail, Rose builds her story of political strife, spiritual awakening, and feminist reclamation to a climax that made me laugh and cry and long for more. An important meditation on how our supposed missteps often create as much life as they destroy, Pattianne's final destination rewards the reader as much as it does the character."

—Michelle Ruiz Keil, author of *All of Us With Wings*

"*A Small Crowd of Strangers* is a lovely story about a young woman whose unchecked yearning leads her somewhere true—even if she takes the long path in getting there."

—Michelle Anne Schingler, *Foreword Reviews*

"As a fan of Joanna Rose's groundbreaking novel, *Little Miss Strange*, I was eager to read the next, *A Small Crowd of Strangers*. Lucky readers— this novel, too, is buoyant, tender, and it's so easy to invest in her lively characters and the gorgeously described landscape. At the center of the novel is Pattianne Anthony, a quirky reference librarian who is smart and witty, but who also tends to make major life choices on a whim. One of those is to marry a charming schoolteacher, Michael Bryn, and move from her childhood home in New Jersey to St. Cloud, Minnesota. It's Pattianne's discovery of self that most captivates through these pages— her budding realization that she has let life lead her instead of her leading life. As Pattianne ventures out, we witness her profound discoveries about love, family, faith, and the abiding strength of an eclectic community, and in this way Rose's novel becomes sweetly intimate, a joy to read."

—Debra Gwartney, author of *I Am a Stranger Here Myself*

PRAISE FOR LITTLE MISS STRANGE

Winner, Pacific Northwest Booksellers Association Award
Finalist, Oregon Book Award

"An extraordinarily powerful first novel in which what is not said often seems infinitely more important than what is."

—*Kirkus*

"This is a wondrous, uncanny book, like few others you will have read. . . . A story so assured and accomplished that it seems the work of a seasoned novelist at the peak of her talent."

—Floyd Skloot, *The Oregonian*

"An amazing book."

—*Richmond Times-Dispatch*

A SMALL CROWD OF STRANGERS

JOANNA ROSE

FOREST AVENUE PRESS
Portland, Oregon

ISBN: 9781942436430

Library of Congress Control Number: 2020941492

Distributed by Publishers Group West

Published in the United States of America
by Forest Avenue Press LLC
Portland, Oregon

Printed in the United States

Forest Avenue Press LLC
P.O. Box 80134
Portland, OR 97280
forestavenuepress.com

For Tony,
with love

A SMALL CROWD OF STRANGERS

I. MONTCLAIR

1: THEY WERE CALLED PEEPS

IT WAS THINGS LIKE reading all of John Updike, and all of Elmore Leonard, and doing the crossword in the middle of the afternoon when she didn't have to work, with the all-classical station pouring out the windows of her apartment over the dry cleaner's. That's what being thirty was about. That's what finally being finished with graduate school was about.

Pattianne kept her part-time job in the library of the education lab, which paid just enough, and technically made use of her shiny new master's degree in library science. And she kept her sometimes-boyfriend, Steven. Even-Steven, she called him, because he was so even-tempered, which was really him not caring very much one way or another about her being his girlfriend, or them being a couple, or really anything besides arguing about almost everything.

"The only good book ever written was *Under the Volcano*," he might say, or something like that, after about the third scotch. He loved that book.

"Yeah, if you're a depressed drunk looking for a good reason to commit suicide," she'd say, or something like that, after about the third vodka tonic. Pattianne hated that book.

He also liked having just enough drinks to have really nice sex.

"Nice?" he would say. "Nice?"

He owned a tavern with a bunch of guys who had dropped out of law school together, a laid-back, uncollege type of place called the Truckyard.

On a breezy afternoon in early March she stopped by the Truckyard on her way to work with a new find, Requiem in D Minor. She was discovering she loved Mozart. Even-Steven had played violin in high school and fancied himself a musician, even though all he played now was the stereo. He poured her a glass of chardonnay, and then he put Mozart in the CD player. He leaned against the back bar and stared through his smudgy glasses at the ceiling. It was the beginning of the part of the requiem mass that was called the introitus, coming on so low that she wondered if something was wrong with the CD player. Even-Steven leaned against the bar and ran his fingers through his thick dark hair. It stood up in a sexy mess. She got that dreamy, damp feeling and thought about calling in sick. Library jobs are like that, a little too easy to call in sick, but, at twenty-eight hours a week, also easy to catch up on work.

About three minutes later, though, Even-Steven took the CD out and slipped it back into its case. He set the case gently on the bar in front of her and tapped his finger on it, leaving it smeared with grated cheese. He leaned over the bar and whispered in her ear, "That's a shitty orchestra."

Two guys at the end of the bar watched.

Even-Steven took out another CD and slipped it into the player. Same music, coming on so achingly slow.

"This," he said, with a grand gesture toward the stereo, "is the greatest recording of the Requiem in D Minor you'll ever hear."

The guys at the end of the bar applauded. Pattianne sighed in what she hoped was a melodramatic way and picked up her CD.

"You got cheese on my Mozart," she said. She slipped off her barstool. "Off to work."

Even-Steven winked at her, cute and annoying at the same time, amazing how he could do that. As she went out the Truckyard door, Mozart blared behind her, Even-Steven jacking up the volume.

The spring breeze blew grit into her eyes, along with the smell of the Passaic River. When she got to the library, she took the CD out and looked at it.

"Alas," she said to Melissa.

Melissa was the intern at the table next to her, and she loved hearing Even-Steven stories. Melissa also loved black roses, had several, in fact, tattooed on her left arm, and she had a big plastic one pinned to her messenger bag. This one she now unpinned and handed over, saying, "Requiem for an afternoon of lust."

Pattianne made a shrine in her in-basket with the CD, its case with the blue-and-yellow painting of Mary and Jesus propped up reverently behind the black rose.

And then, not an hour later, on a warm, windows-open-for-the-first-time kind of spring day, he came in to the North Jersey Regional Education Lab, wafting on a scent of soap. She'd seen him around. Him with his pretty face and black hair. She didn't know his name until she saw it written there, on the pink request form, in perfect cursive. A breeze started to lift the request form off the desk, and they both reached for it. He touched it first and held it down with two fingers. "Hello?" he said. "They told me at the front desk that you could help me access this database. Are you Patty Anthony?"

"No," she said.

He had red lips shaped like a bow.

"I mean, yes. Database, yes, Patty, no. It's Pattianne."

She was thinking, *Access is not a verb, it's a noun.*

She said, "Let me set you up with an access code."

If she moved her hand one inch, their fingers would touch.

Michael Bryn. The neat peaks of his capital *M*. The round loops of the *B*. Michael. Not Mike. They probably knew some of the same people. Montclair was a small town. There were nodding acquaintances, people to say hello to or perhaps to avoid, if they'd been at certain parties where there had been too much to drink maybe. There was that argument about Genesis and penises. There was going home with the wrong guy and then his real girlfriend dropped by with bagels and flowers to make up in the morning.

Mostly Pattianne stayed kind of invisible, sitting at some bar on the end stool and chatting up some bartender, eavesdropping on witty people telling witty stories, the way some people could hold all the words together until it was time for everyone to burst into laughter like applause. Michael Bryn was like that. She never even really followed his stories when she'd see him with some group of people from the Ed School who stood around him, waiting to laugh. She'd watch his mouth, the way he flicked the tip of his tongue across his lips.

Melissa's message appeared on Pattianne's computer screen: *Ask him out!*

Pattianne copied the access code on the pink request form and slid it toward him.

"Thank you," he said. "This is all I need?"

There was chardonnay in her head, and warm spring air. She pulled the pink slip back and wrote her phone number under the access code. "You need this too."

"I do?"

A tiny crease appeared between his eyebrows.

"Well, and this." She wrote *Pattianne Anthony.* Not quite perfect cursive.

"Oh." He looked at the form, then looked up at her. He had blue eyes, dark blue.

Her face got warm, and she just knew it: those two round blushing spots were showing up on her cheeks.

"We should get together," she said in a rush. "Sometime."

Her cheeks felt that special shade of chardonnay pink, and she was just thinking *Oops, wrong move* when his wide forehead smoothed out.

"Well," he said. "There's a film festival at the State Street Cinema. Tonight is the last night."

She loved that place. It was a funky little movie house with an actual curtain that opened and closed. They showed cartoons before the feature film.

"Great," she said. "I could meet you there. I get out of here at six."

"Okay." He stood there and looked at her. She wondered if she had brushed her hair lately. She tried to remember what earrings she was wearing.

"Well, good. And, well, so, I have to print out some grant applications," he said. "How easy is this database? I need numbers on state test scores from Bergen and Passaic Counties, from the last five years. By grade."

"Graphs," she said. "Simple."

He laughed. "You think graphs are simple? Awesome."

He had a nice laugh, kind of quiet. And so what if he used the word *awesome*?

"Melissa?" Who was of course paying close attention. "Can you put together some numbers? Test scores? By grade?"

"How soon?"

"Now?"

Melissa kicked her messenger bag under her workstation and came over. "Now works."

MICHAEL BRYN LOOKED BACK and forth at the two of them. Melissa had pierced eyebrows as well as many tattoos. He avoided looking at Melissa's tattoos. It was harder to not look at her pierced eyebrows.

"Follow me," she said.

"See you around six," Pattianne said.

He said, "Okay," and followed Melissa into the maze of cubicles.

He didn't often get asked out by girls, mainly because he usually did the asking. When it got to that point in a conversation, or an encounter, where it seemed the logical next thing to do, he just did it. It wasn't like it was an issue with him. Although now he wasn't sure about who should buy the tickets. He'd get there a little ahead of time and just buy them.

Melissa set him up and left him at a desk. He took out the pink piece of paper. Pattianne. Not Patty.

She wasn't at her desk when he left. The Melissa girl was, though. She said, "Bye-bye now."

He said, "Thank you." The little picture of the Pietà on the CD in the in-basket with the Lenten rose was the one by Van Gogh. His mom had sent him an Easter card with the same picture his first year away from home. His mom loved the Pietà.

SHE WAS WALKING UP to the theater just when he got there. She was wearing red sneakers. She said, "I love Harvey Keitel," a little out of breath, and handed the six dollars for her ticket through the ticket window. He could handle that, really. She had asked him out, but when they hit the concession stand, he gave a twenty to the girl behind the counter before Pattianne had even gotten the straw out of the dispenser.

Then they went into the popcorn-smelling dark of the funky theater. He'd wanted popcorn, but popcorn on a first date could turn awkward—how much salt, or butter flavoring, and then there was the actual sharing. Who holds the bucket? And that thing where you both stick your hands in at the same time.

If this really was a date.

"Halfway okay with you?" she whispered.

And actually, it wasn't. He liked sitting in the very back. But she headed down the aisle, and it was a little repertory house, small screen, so really, it would be fine.

They settled in to the seats, and he unwrapped his Snickers bar.

The beginning of any movie was one of the great small moments of life. It was all there before you. All you had to do was sit, and it would begin. Especially a movie you'd seen before, that you knew you liked. He settled back, took in a deep breath.

That's when he smelled it. Cigarettes. There were no people within four of five seats, or in the row in front of them. He glanced behind. No one there.

Damn. A smoker.

Halfway through, she got up to go to the bathroom. When she came back, she didn't smell like she'd slipped out for a smoke. In fact, there was a perfume smell. Maybe she had gone out for a smoke and had doused herself with some spray or something. But no. The trace scent of cigarette was still there, like before. Then she got up to get a drink of water. Finally she whispered, "I'm going to go hang around in the lobby for a little bit." Then he got it. He liked Harvey Keitel, too, but *Reservoir Dogs* was pretty gruesome, even among Harvey Keitel movies. He got up and followed her. She was reading the framed obituary of Gene Siskel hanging on the wall by the bathroom. He stood behind her for a minute, reading it too. She was quite short. And she actually smelled good. Flowers.

"So," he said when they were outside. "Sorry about the movie."

She said, "Didn't you like it?"

"Well. Yeah."

"Then you don't have to be sorry," she said, "I'm sorry I saw it, and one of us being sorry is enough."

He couldn't think of anything to say except to apologize again, but then she laughed, so he did too. She kind of bumped him with her hip. He bumped her back, and they started along the sidewalk. She was smooth. She was easy. But you don't say that about girls. Smooth. And that flower smell was lavender. They stopped at the corner of the park where there were four lanes of traffic. She looked up the street one way and then the other. She took a step away from him and looked up at him. He felt tall. Then she took out a pack of cigarettes. Either he was going to say something or he probably wouldn't see her again. She pulled a cigarette from the pack, then put the pack back into her jacket pocket, which is when he realized she didn't have a purse. She said something about *Little Nicky*, which was one of the dumb Harvey Keitel movies. This was it. He took the cigarette out of her hand.

"Here," he said. "Instead."

He kissed her, on the mouth. A small kiss.

She tasted like Red Vines and root beer.

She tilted her head back and kind of peeked up at him through her bangs, which were curly and blowing around.

"Well," she said. "I guess I wasn't expecting that." But she was smiling.

He said, "You taste like root beer."

She laughed a small laugh, and he said, "And Red Vines." The laugh got a little bigger.

Then he said, "Want a ride home?" It just came out.

"No, I just live down that way. But I hope you call me sometime."

"Okay."

"Okay."

Another kiss, this one on her cheek. His sister had told him once how fun it was when guys did that. Then she kind of backed away, said, "Bye, thanks," and she turned, walking down State Street.

He headed up State Street the other way. He turned around once. It was just when she was turning around, and they waved. Then she kept walking, in those red sneakers.

Two blocks away, reaching into his pocket for his car keys, he realized he still had the cigarette in his fingers.

PATTIANNE HAD BEEN TELLING herself, and her sister, and her parents, and even Melissa, that she was going to quit smoking when she finished grad school. And here was this pretty boy who thought she tasted like Red Vines and root beer. There was something friendly about a pack of cigarettes, though. It was the last part of giving them up, reaching for that familiar square pack in a jacket pocket. How you could go into any convenience store or gas station or grocery store, anywhere, any country, "Pack of cigarettes, please," and there they'd be. To quit smoking was to become aware of desire. After the first week or so, reaching for a cigarette every eight minutes, it's what was left. Desire. At first, her whole body wanted something every minute (actually every eight minutes, she'd looked it up), but still, pretty much always. To say she was filled with desire might not be true, but her hours were punctuated by it.

Give them up she did, though, and call her he did. They walked by the river, and in and out of record shops hunting for used Mozart CDs. He walked her home from work, home from a movie about migrating geese, from a walk along the riverfront, and, each time, they kissed— one long kiss out on the front step, a kiss that left her too shaky to say, "Why don't you come in?" When she got in her bed and reached down for herself she would be wet and ready for her own fingers, and she thought about that mouth. She thought *yes*.

The kisses were getting longer each time.

Sometimes at work, she sat and stared at a piece of paper, and she would be empty of thought but filled with sex. She felt lightheaded, like she was getting a cold, and she would realize that she'd been away, not thinking of fucking or of his mouth or anything at all, just slipping off into this breathless place of desire. She thought of breaking it off with Even-Steven. She was completely distracted. Her underpants were always damp.

She found herself drinking espressos from little stands on Silver Street with Michael Bryn instead of vodka tonics at the Truckyard, waiting for Even-Steven to get off work. The grass growing between the sidewalk cracks was adorably green, and she found herself leaving her jacket at home so she could feel the soft air on her bare arms. She quit reading Elmore Leonard because she couldn't pay attention to the story.

MICHAEL WAS DRIVING THE O-bug north on the turnpike, window rolled down, the air a little too cool, and he was whistling. Not just whistling, but whistling a Frank Sinatra song he didn't even know. He immediately stopped whistling and rolled the window back up. He was going to tell his mom and dad about Pattianne.

He was done being messed up about Corinne Mullins. She was gone from his life, and she'd been gone for a year. He'd been on lots of dates, and he didn't even really like dating. It got a little crazy.

Like the Saturday his father had arrived early to pick him up for a ball game. The screen door was open, and he'd knocked on it and opened it partway, didn't even come all the way in. A girl from the night before was still there, in the living room, barefoot, her hair wet from the shower. His father had said hello to her and then he said, "I'll wait in the car," and backed out, shutting the screen door gently.

He didn't say anything when Michael got in the car, just shifted into drive and drove. Michael crossed his arms over his chest and tried to lean back in the seat. His head pounded from rum and Cokes. There was a fun run through Edison, and they had to wait at Plainfield Avenue while people in costumes and hats ran across the intersection. Tutus. Balloon hats. A guy with a what looked like an actual live monkey on his head.

Michael said, "Was that a real monkey?"

His father said, "So, who was that young lady?"

A lot of rum and Cokes.

"Diana," Michael said.

Sunlight glared on the straight black edge of the dash.

"I mean Donna," he said.

It wasn't until they pulled into the parking lot that his father spoke again.

"You're a better person than this."

For an insane moment, Michael felt tears sting at his eyes. He stared hard at the chain-link fence in front of them. He'd met her late in the evening, at the bar. It hadn't even been a date. After his father had left to go wait in the car, she sat on the couch, pulling on those cowboy boots, and said, "I'll be slipping out the back, sweetie."

"He's early," Michael said. "I'm sorry."

She just said, "You do have a back door, right?"

At least his father hadn't seen the cowboy boots.

Now there was Pattianne. She was funny and fun. A little anxious. A pickup truck raced past him on the right and honked the horn, Michael doing fifty in the left lane.

"Sorry, dude," he said, and put on his blinker, checked behind him, and got over.

His mom was folding towels on the dining room table when he walked in. She did that sometimes, when it was sunny like this. Michael kissed her cheek. Claire came through the doorway from the kitchen with two drinks in her hands.

"This is for you." She handed him a bourbon and ginger ale with a twist of lemon. "I heard your car a block away."

She slurped the other drink, and their mother said, "If you can't drink that like a lady, you don't get it," and she took the drink out of her hand and slurped it herself.

Michael Bryn Senior came through the doorway then with two more drinks. He handed one to Claire, said, "Sláinte!" and they all clinked and sipped. Chitchat. Sunshine. Basketball. Claire's new haircut. A little of this, a little of that. Michael still couldn't get used to seeing Claire with a drink. His mom picked up a stack of kitchen towels and headed into the kitchen. He followed her.

"So," he said.

She stacked the towels into a drawer by the sink, except one.

She said, "Yes?"

She draped the towel over the small rod on the end of the counter.

He laughed. It felt fake. She turned to him, and her face eased into its mom smile, the one where her eyebrows did that funny thing.

"What's up, oh kiddo of mine?"

"I've been seeing someone."

And then she did that other thing she always did. She turned away from him, gave him a little space. She opened the oven door and peeked in. He smelled stuffed peppers. He didn't like stuffed peppers. He wondered if he would ever be able to come right out and say that to her, that he really didn't care for stuffed peppers. She closed the oven door.

"She's a librarian. Her name is Pattianne." He took a sip that was more of a gulp. "Anthony."

What to say? That she quit smoking for him. That she was an amazing kisser. That she wore red sneakers.

"She loves Mozart." Then he felt like a fool. "And I want you to meet her."

His dad and sister laughed at something out in the dining room,

Claire saying, "I'm sure," and laughing some more. His mom looked at him. There it was—the mom worry. But just for a second.

"You could invite her to church with us on Easter. The choir will be singing the Coronation Mass. How does that sound?" She slipped her arm through his. "That's Mozart," she said. She steered him back to the dining room.

It sounded great.

THE SHOPS ALONG SILVER Street had window boxes full of daffodils and early tulips, the whole street lined with cherry trees, and the pink petals drifting in the air made Pattianne feel like she was in some romance cartoonland.

Michael stopped at one shop window that had dresses on hangers pinned up, as though the dresses were dancing, and he said, "I like that one," pointing to a dress of light green rayon, or maybe silk, with dark shell buttons down the front.

"Pretty girly," she said. "I think you'd look better in the blue—match your eyes."

"Silly bones," he said, and when she pulled him along, he didn't move. He said, "I'm thinking of your eyes."

"My eyes are hazel," she said. "No particular color at all."

He turned her by her shoulders and looked down into her eyes.

She said, "Don't," and tried to find something else to look at. She said, "Let's go get coffees," wanting to be moving, standing still suddenly unbearable, and Michael trying to look into her eyes was why, but he held her by the elbows, warm fingers on her bare skin.

"Your eyes are green, Pattianne Anthony," he said. "That color green, like that dress."

To stand very close to someone and let them look at your eyes will cause the sidewalk to drop away. "They're hazel," she said. "No particular color at all." And she closed her eyes just long enough to feel ridiculous, and when she opened them, everything, the cherry petals, Michael's face, everything around her, jumped a little brighter. Michael Bryn, his pretty-boy face when she opened her eyes, there he was.

He whispered, "You have no idea how pretty you are," and he turned her around and pushed her toward the glass door, Tessa's Dresses in gold curlicues.

She was thinking, *I am not pretty. I am plain. Good teeth, good skin. Otherwise ordinary.*

His whispered voice behind her, "Let's you go try on that dress."

She tried to not go in the door.

"Michael." She tried hanging on to the sidewalk with her feet somehow. "This is a Silver Street dress shop. I am a part-time librarian. I can't buy a dress here. And if I could buy it, I couldn't wear it, not that little tiny thing." This is what she said instead of what she was thinking. Which was, *He thinks I'm pretty.*

He said, "Just try it on."

She turned to him. "No," she said. "You do realize I'm a thirty-year-old woman."

The blue eyes blinked. "Thirty?" he said. "You're kidding."

It was her height, or rather the lack of it, being five feet two inches tall. She had never looked her age. She still got carded regularly. She said, "Why? How old are you?"

"Twenty-five."

That felt awkward. Five years.

She said, "You're kidding," and he laughed a little, and the awkward moment passed.

"Well," he said. "I mean, don't get me wrong—thirty is impressive. But what's that have to do with that dress?"

"I'd look like I was in eighth grade or something. Girls who wear that kind of dress have basically no internal organs."

"Come on," he said. "Don't you need a new Easter dress?" He pushed her through the door, his hands on her shoulders, the carpet inside so thick that she thought there was a step up, and she stepped up, to that surprise landing of a step up where there is none.

"Can we help?" A girl with big painted-on eyes and no internal organs stepped out from behind a flower arrangement.

Pattianne said no and turned around face-first into Michael's shirt, blue, pinstripes, laundry soap, starch. Starch. A warning tried to sneak into her brain.

He said, "She wants to try on that green dress."

A warning about guys who starched their shirts and said *Easter dress.*

"No," she said.

"Excuse me," Michael whispered to the girl, his arms around

Pattianne, who was staring at the blue pinstripes and breathing the clean smell of him, and not even thinking of a cigarette. He said, "Do you have a dressing room we can duck into for just a sec? I can talk her into anything if I can get her kissing."

The girl's lollipop-pink lips went into a round O and she stared at Michael, and Pattianne got loose and went back out the door.

He came out right after, lollipop-pink laughter trailing out the door of Tessa's Dresses. There was a painted iron bench by the door, and she sat down, and Michael sat down next to her. He leaned forward, his elbows on his knees. "Okay," he said. "No green Easter dress," his easy laugh kind of bubbling up around his words. A woman walked by pushing a little girl in a stroller, and as they passed close, Michael pointed a finger out to the girl, who reached her fat baby fingers out to him, and the mom kept pushing, not seeing Michael flirt with her cute little girl. They pushed on down Silver Street. He folded his hands together and did not say a word, just watched them, the little girl's hand waving in the air. Pattianne watched them too. Silver Street was always full of young matrons, wearing their cute children like diamonds. The hair salons had childcare. The kids all had stuffed penguins. "So," Michael said, and he scooted closer. "Do you want to go to Easter Mass with me" — the pink petals raining down on them gently — "and my family? You could meet them." Tall baskets of white lilies crowded both ends of the iron bench.

Pattianne touched the waxy petals to see if they were real. She couldn't tell.

"Christ the King, in Edison," he said, close to her ear, whispering. "Latin high Mass. Easter service, choir. My mom and dad. And my sister, Claire."

Even if she had her jacket on, there would still be no pack of cigarettes in the side pocket. She touched the center of a lily and the orange powder smeared on her finger. She wiped it on her jeans.

"That stuff really stains," he said.

She turned and faced the top button of his shirt, where it was open, where there was white skin and that soft angle of bones coming together.

She kissed him. Slipped the tip of her tongue across those lips.

If they could go home right now and fuck, she'd wear the green Easter dress, she'd go to Mass with his parents. But she didn't say that.

She said, "It sounds a little . . ."

Michael Bryn put his arm around her shoulders and squeezed ever so softly.

"It sounds a little intense," she said. Which sounded idiotic even to her. "I mean, we don't know each other very well really."

"It is intense," he said. "They'll be singing the Mozart Coronation Mass. It's amazing. They're brilliant. They went to Rome and sang for the pope."

"Mozart," she said. The air in the shade had a slight chill, and his arm around her shoulder suddenly felt just right. It didn't have to be about meeting his family. It didn't have to be about going to church. It could be about Mozart.

"So"—feeling her way through this—"your parents are Catholic?"

"Well, yeah," and he laughed.

"Mine were," she said. "I mean, I was raised Catholic. I never went to Catholic school though. I mean, I don't really go to church. Anymore."

That arm, light and easy across her shoulders, his palm warm on her arm. "Why not?"

Maybe he really wanted to know, or maybe there was a judgment there, or maybe this was just conversation, like all their few times together were full of, just wandering conversation. Do you like basketball games, no, have you ever been out west, yes, what do you want to do now that you've finished grad school, nothing. Did you know that Mozart's full name was Johannes Chrysostomus Wolfgangus Theophilus Mozart? He'd said wow.

The squeeze, this time her elbow, which was a little bit ticklish.

"I don't know how to put it," she said.

She had walked down the aisle at First Communion behind Victoria Pidoto, and all she remembered was Victoria's amazing dress, with tiers of lacy ruffles and a wide sash that tied in a big satin bow. Her parents just quit going to church after her sister Jen did First Communion. She noticed they didn't go anymore, and she kind of thought they hadn't been going for a while.

She wanted a cigarette, wanted a vodka tonic.

"I should get going," she said. "I'll think about the church thing. Want to walk me home?"

That time it wasn't such a long, long kiss.

Pictures of Jesus with his long hair and sad eyes made her feel the way she felt about Johnny Depp and Abraham Lincoln. She went for years without thinking about God at all, ever, dreaming along as if she were a flower or a dog or a stone in a creek. Freedom from religion was a sort of religion in itself.

Religion meant the religious right.

She went over to the Truckyard. Even-Steven wasn't working. He was sitting at the bar. He leaned back and looked at her through those dirty glasses.

"What are you up to?" His usual bullshit bar banter. "About five-two?"

She sat next to him. Lisa was behind the bar doing the crossword. Whenever Lisa made Pattianne's drinks, she made them big. Like now. Tall glass, heavy pour. Vodka tonic, extra lime. Even-Steven lit a cigarette and offered her one out of his pack. Camel straights. She shook her head.

He said, "You're a lightweight." Then he got up and went behind the bar and got a pack of Marlboro Lights from the cabinet. He looked at her as he tore the cellophane and opened the box, the master of the desultory gesture. He shook one cigarette up and she took it. He flicked his lighter and lit it. It tasted awful. He came back around the bar and sat back down.

Church. There was an old, old understanding between her and whatever it was that used to happen those Sundays when she was little, between her and the chanting, between her and the candles, her and the early morning light through the stained glass. It was an understanding that was so old, so private, so much a part of her that it had never even been important.

Even-Steven said, "So, chatterbox, want to come over?"

Pattianne shrugged.

He said, "Do whatever you want. I won't charge you for the cigarette."

The smoke from the cigarette floated between them and he nudged her.

She said, "Sure."

"Here, then, you can have the whole pack."

Ha, ha.

Lisa said, "Below the kingdom."

Pattianne said, "Phylum."

She drank the vodka tonic, and then another, and he drank his beer, and another. Things just kind of went on around them—drinks, cigarettes, drinks, cigarettes—and it got dark out. There was an old *Saturday Night Live* on the TV above the bar.

Even-Steven had the most beautiful long throat, that soft white skin. She'd put a hickey there once. Really pissed him off.

Finally she got up, and he got up. She headed for the door. He followed. No one would ever accuse Even-Steven of being romantic, although as soon as they were outside he fell in beside her and they walked toward his apartment, leaving her car parked by the Truckyard.

He said, "I haven't seen you for a while. What did you do, get a life?" And he pulled her by the elbow until they were touching.

His apartment was a funky messy place, mostly music stuff, and a big TV and books stacked up everywhere. There was only the light from the streetlight, and he took off his jeans and his sweatshirt and stood there tall and naked and easy. He went to the CD player and put on Miles Davis. But he took another CD from the shelf and tossed it to her. Requiem in D Minor, still all wrapped up tight in its shiny plastic—the best version of the Requiem in D Minor ever recorded.

"For your very own," he said. He got onto the bed. "Come here, I missed you."

And then he fucked her so nice, kind of slow and lazy, just like he always did.

With Even-Steven there were orgasms, strange little tickly ones at the very end that she would hold her breath and reach for somehow. The first time it happened she was so surprised, she said, "I came."

"Congratulations," he said.

She remembered he didn't even open his eyes. "Well," she told him. "That doesn't usually happen."

"Oh, what," he said, "now you're going to expect it every time?" That was his idea of compassion, or humor, she was never sure which with Even-Steven, and it didn't really matter with Even-Steven.

Then he said, "No, really, I'm glad," in a flat, embarrassed voice. He hated it when he had to be sincere.

"Fuck you," she'd said. "And yes, every time." And it did, almost, with him, happen every time.

And now, with Miles Davis playing on and on, with Even-Steven lying on his back, quiet, his long body white in the streetlight light, she wanted him again, but she didn't wake him. She just lay there, wanting.

Sometimes she slept but dreamed she was awake and lying in bed, wishing for sleep. It was one of those nights.

The light finally came into the sky outside his window, and she slipped out of the tangled sheets, found her clothes, tiptoed around piles of dirty jeans and T-shirts, picked the new CD up off the table, knocking a paperback book onto the floor. Cormac McCarthy. Of course. It landed on a sweatshirt and didn't make a sound. She headed for the bathroom where Even-Steven's old yellow cat, Tangent, was sleeping in the sink. Tangent always slept in the sink, curled into the round basin. His ears twitched, but he didn't wake up and look at her. Her throat ached, but she couldn't run any water. She didn't want to face Even-Steven's kitchen. Her head pounded gently. She got dressed and went down the stairs and out into the day.

The sky was gray, a fine haze of clouds high up, and the air smelled damp, the stink of cigarettes in her hair. She walked back to the Truckyard to get her car, parked under a maple tree and covered in pale green dust, her poor old Volvo, which made a lot of noise starting up. NPR leaped from the radio, and a fair amount of static, and she snapped it off. This was her favorite part of being with Even-Steven, sneaking away early, the city not awake yet. Today, however, her head was intensely hungover, and empty. She just drove. She was a bad driver when she had a hangover. Bad reactions. Too jumpy. She was very careful, and drove the side streets of sleepy Montclair, avoiding the early traffic on the river-front drive.

When she got home, she put the CD on, loud enough that she could hear it in the shower. It didn't really sound any different from the other one. She was all clean and shampooed and wrapped in her long chaste fuzzy bathrobe when the phone rang. She turned the music down. It was Michael.

"I didn't wake you up, did I?" It was only seven fifteen, but he didn't even sound sleepy. "I just got back from a run. It's beautiful out. How are you?"

It was not a question she wanted to answer, but she loved it that he was asking.

He said, "Want to meet for breakfast?"

And she said yes, not that breakfast really sounded like a good idea. Her stomach was a little lurchy. But she got dressed, chose her green sweater, pulled Mozart out of the CD player, and headed back out the door. The sun was lighting up the sidewalk, with its black polka dots of old chewing gum amid the sparkles of whatever it is they made old sidewalks out of. A sheet of newspaper blew along like it was a tumbling tumbleweed right here in Montclair, New Jersey. Gold pollen shimmered on the Volvo. She slipped the CD into the CD player and took off up the street, along the river-front drive where sprinklers were sprinkling and runners were running, and if she hadn't been marveling at the whole of creation, she would have been mindful of the fact that, although she felt a little better, she was still hungover, and when the red light suddenly appeared, complete with a kid on a skateboard in the crosswalk, she slammed on the brakes. The kid leaped away from the front bumper, his skateboard flying up, and he started yelling.

"I'm sorry," she yelled back. "I'm so sorry," waving her hands.

He stomped out into the intersection. Righted his skateboard with his toe. Skated away. Pattianne didn't move. The light was red, for one thing. She turned Mozart off. Sat there through the green and then another red. Breathing. The skateboard had flipped all the way across the intersection. She wondered if she was going to throw up. Finally she drove the last three blocks to Violet's Bistro and parked, taking up two parking places. Got out and walked toward the door. Her knees were shaking.

Michael was at one of the picnic tables under the purple striped awning. He stood when he saw her. His face looked so pink and bright. Not like someone who had been out drinking late and having sex and sneaking away at dawn and almost killing a child.

"I almost hit a kid."

"What?"

"Just now."

She stood still.

"I don't know." She felt a kind of fizz, a nervous giggle. "I had the music blasting and I guess I just almost hit this skateboarder."

"Oh my god, are you all right?"

"It was Mozart," she said. "Requiem in D Minor," and he put his hand on her arm.

"I'm all right, really," she said, not all right. "It was a red light."

He put his arm around her. He wore a blue sweater that was scratchy and soft at the same time, and there it was again, that arm, that comfort, and suddenly she was crying. She was horrified, and she said, "I don't know why I'm crying. I'm all right, the kid was fine, he just skated away on his skateboard—it was one of those really long ones," and then she was laughing again, and shaking.

"Sit down," he said, and she sat down. "Here," and he handed her a paper napkin.

"Thank you."

He sat on the bench next to her. "You really love that music, huh?"

She tried to blow her nose without honking.

He said, "You want to eat out here or wait for a table inside?"

"I don't know. What do you want?"

"I want you to go to Mass with me, hear the choir sing."

His arm around her shoulders, the purple striped awning, a skinny kid all in black skating safely away on a skateboard. A waitress in yellow overalls came up to the table, and Michael said, "Hi—two coffees with cream, and waffles." Little chuckles all around.

SHE CALLED JEN THAT afternoon. Jen still lived a couple towns away from their parents. It was a long messy drive down the New Jersey Turnpike for Pattianne, an easy couple miles, past fields, a Girl Scout camp, and an office park for Jen.

"Hi, this is Jen. I'm on a need-to-know basis, so you should probably just call back later instead of leaving a message."

"Just pick it up, Jen, it's me."

"Hey there, hi."

"So," Pattianne said.

"Hi. What's up?"

"Nothing. Well. Actually, when was the last time you went to Mass?" Jen took their grandmother to church sometimes, Nana Farley.

"Is this a conversational gambit, or do you want, like, a specific date, like a year or a Holy Day or something?"

Jen and Pattianne were close and loved each other and all that—

pretty sisterly, she'd have to say—but Pattianne wasn't in the habit of sharing the intimate details of her life with her sister. Like boyfriends. Jen liked Even-Steven, though.

"Conversational gambit," Pattianne said.

"Bullshit."

A garbage truck inched along the narrow street outside the window. All the colors of the rainbow were smashed up together in its maw, plus a lot of black plastic.

"I want to go hear this choir," she said. "On Easter Sunday."

"Well, there are no Easter bonnets."

Jen would be staring out her own window, looking down on the busy toy main street of the toy town of Jamesburg, where she lived in a shiny new condo unit across from the colonial post office that was still the post office.

"They haven't done that since like 1963 or something," Pattianne said.

"You can if you want to, though."

"It's a high Mass." She wandered back to her bedroom and flopped on the futon. "Latin."

"Ah," Jen said. "Wear a dress."

"Oh, good. That's just what I needed to know. Thanks so much."

"Are you really going to Mass? Or is it a concert in a church?"

"Mass. With a friend. And his parents."

That quieted things down for a second. Then Jen said, "You're technically still a Catholic, I think. Until you commit a mortal sin. Like never going to church anymore and all that, but I think you have to be officially ex-communicated to set the alarms off. They have them installed in the doorways now, you know. Retinal detectors. Are you dating a Catholic guy?"

"Well," she said. "His parents are Catholic. But we're not really dating."

"Right. Have fun. Don't drink the water."

"It's wine."

"That either."

Not much help. But she loved talking to Jen, and afterward she always wondered why they didn't see each other more often, and she told herself they would, especially now that she was finished going to school and all. And she knew they wouldn't. And thought maybe they would.

But for now, Easter. She looked it up on the internet, and the first thing she got was all about *alleluia*, which was the buzzword of the day apparently, a Hebrew word adopted by the Christian church, *Hallel* being the greatest all-time expression of praise in Hebrew, combined with *Jah*, the shortened form of the name of God, JHVH, which is *Jehovah* with the vowels taken out, meaning "I am." It becomes *hallelujah*, *alleluia* being a Latinized spelling.

There were suggestions for starting the day with the phrase and the lighting of an Easter candle, and ways to celebrate, but Pattianne was distracted: the vowels taken out?

She wandered around in Hebrew for a while, this site and that, until she learned that the Torah didn't have vowels because the vowels were the breath sounds, and it was something about the Hebrew religious texts needing to be spoken aloud to be interpreted truly, and so no vowels in the written version. She wasn't sure she had it right, but then it was time to go to work.

As well as black roses, Melissa wore a lot of religious symbols on her jean jacket, her messenger bag, her arms, so Pattianne asked her what she knew about Catholics.

"That they have rules," Melissa said.

"Like what?"

"Like you aren't allowed to go to Communion unless you join the club. And if you don't join the club, I guess you are consigned to the fires of hell, or a Democratic regime that finances abortion clinics."

She should get Jen and Melissa together. "Seriously."

"Seriously."

So she called Jen again.

"Hello, this is Jen's answering machine."

"Jen? Pick up, it's me."

No pickup.

"I have another Catholic question—do you go to Communion?"

She got a message back on her phone later that afternoon.

"Sure. It makes Grammy happy."

Pattianne did what seemed like the next logical thing. She dropped her good dress off downstairs at the dry cleaner's. It was longish, a flower print, kind of gray and blue. Some green. No particular color at all.

Church music. The chanting sound of the liturgy. The stained-glass windows. That people have believed this or that for so long, struggling with some idea of eternity. What it must have been like, to live in the time of miracles. That there are no miracles anymore. There are logical explanations and media hoaxes, but no miracles. Even God hasn't appeared in person since somewhere late in the old testament. People talked about Jesus being their personal savior, but God himself doesn't show up like he used to. No burning bushes, no wanderers in the desert.

She just wanted some Mozart. A little Mozart, a little Michael Bryn.

He picked her up in an orange VW, and the first thing she noticed was how good he looked in a navy blazer and white shirt and lavender tie. She shut the door of the VW and he said, "Happy Easter, egg."

Adorable. She said, "You too. Alleluia."

The next thing she noticed was the beige plastic Madonna on the dashboard.

"This is the first time in a long time I've been to church," she said. "I mean, is this your car?"

She was kind of hoping he would say no, but he patted the steering wheel and said, "This is my O-bug."

"O-bug?"

"Orange," he said, and they were off, down the interstate to Edison. She held a small gray leather clutch with tissues and her wallet and a comb, and as they drove, Michael weaving in and out of traffic, the O-bug rattling like a roller skate, damp fingerprints appeared on the gray leather clutch. It seemed too noisy to talk. It seemed dangerous to distract him, too, or maybe it was just the way the steering was, kind of slippery. Her tights itched.

When they got off the freeway and it was a little quieter, a little calmer, she said, "So, I'm not really a practicing Catholic."

He reached over and touched her leg, moved his palm on the rayon, or whatever it was the dress was made of, and he asked, "Does that bother you?"

"No. I just want to be sure. I mean, things change, I might not know what to do. During Mass, I mean."

"There they are." He pulled into a parking lot. She couldn't see who he was talking about. There were a lot of people heading up the steps of the white stone church, Christ the King, which was a modern, low kind of church, and that made her feel a little relief for some reason. She got out and brushed at the seat-belt wrinkles in her dress. It was sunny. It was a little cool. She wished she had a sweater or something. She wished she had a cigarette. Michael took her elbow, and they joined what seemed like a throng, crossing the parking lot, crossing the street, and he pointed to the rest of the Bryns waiting in a small neat group on the stone steps of the church, looking around. They reminded her of nature photos of meerkats, standing on their hind legs, looking around, all hyper-cute. Mrs. Bryn saw them first and said, "Here's our Michael," and they all turned.

Pattianne hung back as Michael kissed his mother's cheek, his father's cheek, and then Claire, who was bouncing in little lavender shoes, as pretty as Michael—Claire, not the shoes, although the shoes were very pretty—and they were all saying hello at once—the Bryns, not the shoes. Claire and Mrs. Bryn both wore silver crosses, each set with a purple stone, glittering at their necks. Claire lit up like the sunrise looking at Michael. They all had the same blue eyes.

"This is Pattianne Anthony," he said, and he put his warm, navy blue arm around her shoulders.

Mrs. Bryn was smiling with her mouth, her shiny lipsticked mouth, but not with her eyes, and for the instant Pattianne dared think about it, she was glad she and Michael hadn't had sex yet. His mother would know.

Mrs. Bryn reached out a hand and said, "Hello," in a voice smooth and low. A quick clasp and then she let go, and Mr. Bryn was next. He looked like Michael but there was gray in his hair and wrinkles at his eyes. Smile wrinkles. Warm hands, and he took both her cold hands in his and said, smiling, "Hello Pattianne. How are you? Besides cold?" and he rubbed her hands. They became instantly warm.

Then he steered them all into the doors, letting go of her hands somewhere along the way, and then there she was—in church, Michael's mother and sister and then her and then him and back there, shepherding them along, his father. Soft organ music overhead. She sniffed for the smell of incense but all she could really smell was the perfume Michael's sister wore. The altar far to the front was crowded with white Easter lilies at the feet of a huge statue of Christ, who seemed to be standing in front of a cross instead of hanging up on it. The murmur of voices, *hello, hello, happy Easter*. No one saying *alleluia* as recommended on the website. There was the familiar thump of the kneelers landing on the floor. And pastels—lavender, pink, baby blue, peach, rose, on dresses and ties and shirts—she had forgotten about the pastels of Easter. The throng of pastels shuffled down the center of the main aisle, and to either side people genuflected and slid into the pews.

Genuflect. One of her favorite words. She tried to think what it would take to play it on a Scrabble board, and then she panicked, being a nonbeliever, about the genuflecting, did she or didn't she, and she only had a moment to panic and the decision was upon her as Michael's mother chose their pew and in they all went, one at a time. Pattianne tried to make it some blend of perfunctory and respectful and mostly unnoticed. Got in. Sat down. She could feel her heart in her fingertips.

She set her purse on the pew between her and the sister—Claire, Claire—and then Michael's father dropped the kneeler to the floor, and they all knelt forward. She did too. A woman right in front of her wore a dress with apple blossoms on shiny material. She was fairly wide, the apple blossoms printed across her back in symmetrical rows. The woman had finished her pre-Mass praying and was sitting back in her pew, the rows of apple blossoms, eight to a row, inches away. Pattianne shut her eyes and felt like a phony and opened them again and concentrated on trying to remember the words to the Hail Mary. She peeked down the row at the Bryns. Mr. Bryn had wrapped one arm around Claire, his hand cupping her shoulder, and Pattianne looked away.

The music swelled then, and goose bumps rushed over her body, front to back, even her nipples rising up, and they all stood, the entire place, as one. Michael squeezed her elbow, and she was afraid to look at him but she did. He was about the prettiest boy she had ever dated. The procession moved down the aisle all in white. Altar boys, one of them holding the tall gold crucifix, and four lesser priests, one of them swinging the smoking gold globe of incense, and the main priest holding a big red book.

Her nose started to drip, and she got a tissue out of her purse and wrapped it around her finger and dabbed, her Grandma Anthony's saying *A lady never blows her nose in public*. Ladies didn't eat in public either. Smoking never came up.

Celebrants. They're called celebrants, those other priests.

The choir filled the high space.

The music was loud and it soared, and so did the rushing of air in her chest, and then the rushing to her eyes. She dabbed and dabbed, but by the time the processional got down the aisle the first tissue was a goner. Everyone sat, pastels rustling, pews creaking. She got another tissue and tried to breathe through her nose to calm herself like they said in yoga class, but her nose was clogged now. And a lady never blows her nose in public, and she was pretty sure a church counted as public.

It was beautiful, the Latin, and the priest was a tenor. She had tried to learn Latin. Took it one year and had to drop or she would have significantly lowered her undergrad GPA, and she'd tried it again, audit, and dropped it that time, too, but it was beautiful, and she heard the words of it now like native language, its syntax informing her sentences, the music of her wordless thoughts.

The crucifix was a regal cement statue, Christ with a crown, standing before the cross, his hand with its hint of stigmata held up in front of the sacred heart. Not quite as gory as the standard crucifix.

The choir broke into song again and she jumped, and the word *swoon* came into her head, she felt like she would swoon, and she dug out another tissue. The main priest seemed to be doing all the stuff up there, all the other celebrants sitting and standing and kneeling on either side of the altar. To the right was a smaller altar, Mary with robes of sky blue and a crown, Queen of Heaven, stars around her feet. And then familiar music, she even knew some of the words: *In nomine patris, et filii, et spiritus sancti*. It felt wrong for her to actually sing them, though. Not a member of the club. Besides, she couldn't carry a tune. Her mother used to tell her to just mouth the words. Besides, she kept tearing up. Besides, Michael had a gorgeous voice and he was singing right next to her, a little weird, his face raised, his eyes closed.

And then came the small bells, and the silence, and then the big bells outside somewhere, and row by row in front people got up and headed down the center aisle to Communion. Entire rows emptied. No one remained. If she didn't go up to the Communion rail, she would be sitting completely alone in the middle of a sea of empty pews.

Like a neon sign over her head flashing *Apostate Apostate*.

She sat. Michael moved past her. Then three women. Pink flowers, candy-yellow plaid. Mint-green flowers. Perfume.

Peeps. They were called Peeps, those spongy candy chicks.

The pastel dresses moved slowly up the aisle. Then they all came back. Michael's father and mother and sister moving past her and kneeling. Michael next to her kneeling. She sat. Wished she were kneeling too.

Standing, sitting, kneeling again, the music rising and rushing around. It kept pushing her to the edge of tears, the choir so big back there above them all. She wanted to turn and watch them. She didn't. She stood, knelt, sat, so stiff that by the time the priest said, "The Mass is ended, go in peace," every part of her body ached.

Her face got red and blotchy when she got teary, even if there weren't actual tears involved. By the time they all shuffled out to the impossibly sunny Easter morning, bells ringing, her head pounding louder, she just wanted to get away.

Mrs. Bryn had a small twist of a smile on her face. Maybe it meant, *Are you sleeping with my son?* Maybe it meant, *This is just the way my beautiful face always looks.*

It turned out to mean, *We're so glad you could come.*

"We're so glad you could come, Pattianne," she said, and held out a hand, took Pattianne's, held it an extra moment.

"Alleluia," Pattianne said, hearing the chirpy sound of her own voice. "It's a Hebrew word adopted by the Christian church. *Hallel* was an expression of praise in Hebrew, and *Jah*, the shortened form of the name of God, JHVH, which is *Jehovah* with the vowels taken out, meaning 'I am.'"

Michael's mother said, "Really? The vowels taken out?"

"Breath," Pattianne said.

They all nodded, waiting.

And then Michael kissed his mother on the cheek and told her, "I'll catch up with you at Aunt Alice's." Mr. Bryn said something, and Claire did, too, and Pattianne was sure she did too. She had nice manners after all, as well as straight teeth and good, if sometimes blotchy, skin.

The ride home was quiet. She took one quick look in the visor mirror and wished she had not, her eyes wet and red and glassy. She was exhausted.

Michael kept his eyes on the road, Sunday traffic heavier now.

She'd never even known she liked Mozart. She couldn't really listen to music, always had to have it quiet when she read or studied, and got in the habit of just not turning any music on. She would hear classical music at Miss Mimi Stein's house, though. Miss Mimi Stein lived in her parents' neighborhood in Cranbury, and Pattianne would be there, in Miss Mimi's pretty gray house, music playing, and sometimes she would say, "Who is that?" Or, "I like this music," or something, and Miss Mimi would say, "That's Mozart." Finally she pointed out that Pattianne only ever asked about it when it was Mozart. "You love Mozart," Miss Mimi told her.

They pulled up in front of the dry cleaner's, and Michael parked without turning off the car, which choked to a stop anyway. He kissed her cheek.

"Thank you," he said, and when he smiled, she could see where he too would have smile wrinkles around his eyes one day.

"Thank you. Call me, okay?" She slid out, snagging her tights on the seat. The O-bug was a breath of ease driving away up the street. Inside she pulled off the tights and the dress, put on her overalls, her flip-flops, the stretched-out black turtleneck. The sartorial equivalent of junk food. Then she went to the nearest dark theater. Popcorn with butterlike flavoring. A peguin movie.

It was too cold for flip-flops really. She sat there with her feet tucked under her butt, tucked into herself. The penguins all survived except for one egg.

During what she figured to be dinnertime at Nana Farley's, she called her parents' house and said Happy Easter into their answering machine.

"In the classic tradition," she said. "Alleluia. Which, I learned, means 'I Am' in Hebrew, which is the name Jehovah with all the vowels taken out." She always tried to fill in a little extra space on their answering machine.

Then she opened a bottle of Barefoot chardonnay. Somewhere toward the end of the bottle she fell asleep.

MONDAY WAS A LITTLE rough, but she had her hangover routines. Stay in bed a little long with an ice pack on the forehead. Drink lemon-ginger tea with honey. Take a bath with lavender bath salts. She washed her face with lemon and yogurt and patted a touch of rosemary under her eyes, an old trick of beautiful Frenchwomen to get rid of puffy eyes, which she saw on an interview with Catherine Deneuve, and which may work or may not, but by ten thirty she was ready to face the day when the doorbell downstairs rang.

The sun was blinding. It was Michael. He pulled her into his arms and it was not a chaste kiss, and he whispered, "I have chocolate bunnies," and he led her by the hand upstairs and then kissed her again and said, "I was lying about the bunnies."

And kissed her again. There were hands then, and tongues, and there went her overalls, and then his shirt. The smell of lavender bath salts everywhere.

2: UNCHASTE, UNMARRIED SEX

JEN WAS DOUSED WITH perfume, which she only ever did when she'd been hitting on her purple pot pipe, which used to be Pattianne's purple pot pipe. Pattianne had given up smoking pot when she'd figured out it made her ears ring, which Jen said was ridiculous but, nonetheless, she happily took possession of the purple glass pipe and seemed to use it fairly often. It was the last Sunday of the month, and she and Jen were at dinner at the parents'. Their father was snoozing in the maple-and-patchwork den, sections of the Sunday paper all around him, basketball on TV, their mother in the living room with her own copy of the Sunday paper. They were in the kitchen.

"Hey, stoner." Pattianne set a bottle of Barefoot on the counter. "Get down those wine glasses."

She didn't let Jen know it was the perfume that gave her away. She let her think it was that she was acting stoned. That made her just a touch paranoid. Jen handed the glasses over one at a time, saying "So," and then taking the lid off a pot of ham and green beans and potatoes all boiling away. She put the lid back on and turned to the refrigerator. "So," she said again, and she took out the jar of mayonnaise. "What's up?"

"Nothing."

She said, "Easter Sunday and all."

"The choir was amazing. I cried."

"What about this new Who's-It?"

"What are you doing with mayonnaise?"

Jen put the mayonnaise back. Pattianne handed her two glasses of wine and called out, "Hey, Mom, you want a lovely glass of Barefoot?" Their mom said yes. Their father stirred in the den.

They drank the wine, they ate ham and beans, and Pattianne got itchy and wanted to drink the second bottle of Barefoot that was out in her car. Her father and mother maintained their hold over the empty space that existed somewhere above the center of the table, which she and Jen talked under and over and around.

Her father asked Pattianne how the job search was going.

"Dad," she said. "I have a job."

"Is it full-time yet?"

"I'm staying part-time for now."

Same conversation every time, although sometimes her mother thought to ask if she had benefits yet. *No, Mom. I pay my own health insurance.* Her mother would nod. She would pass the butter.

Her father said, "Your hair is getting long, Pattianne." This was more a comment on Jen's short haircut, though.

Pattianne had had really long hair growing up, hardly ever got it cut, except for getting the ends trimmed, or there were bangs every once in a while. Their father liked long hair. In grade school, Pattianne could sit on hers, and the other girls always wanted to undo the braids her mother braided every morning, and brush her hair and measure it. "Look at that mess," her mother would say when she came home from school, hair loose and flying around, all rippled from braids and snapping with static electricity. She would rebraid it, pulling the braids tight against Pattianne's head, so it was neat when her father came home. When she was thirteen, she went to a beauty salon and got it cut short. Her neck was naked, and the ends of her hair were thick and soft. It felt like she was going to throw up when she walked into the kitchen and waited for her mother to turn around.

When she finally did, she said, "What is your father going to say?"

And, "Where did you get the money?"

Her father came home from work. He hung his suit jacket on the back of his dining room chair, and he stared. He didn't reach down and rub Starla's curly spaniel ears, and she sat at his feet, waiting. He loosened his tie and he stared. Then he turned away. He went in the den and turned on the news.

Pattianne whispered, "Starla," and the spaniel followed her out of the dining room and upstairs into her bedroom. She sat on the floor and cried until dinner, hugging Starla around the neck. Starla licked her fingers. She was always licking her fingers. "I hate him," she told her.

That's how the parents were. The worse it got, the quieter they got. Unless they were happy about something. Then they just didn't say anything.

Now it always seemed like they were just really waiting for the girls to leave.

They each drove their separate directions when they did, and Pattianne's cell phone rang as soon as Jen's car was out of sight. The ringtone was the whistle part of "Sitting on the Dock of the Bay," which Jen put on there so Pattianne would always be happy when the phone rang even though she hated phone calls for the most part.

"So," Jen started right in. "Why didn't you mention the Catholic? Didn't you say he was an ed major? You know that would have thrilled her to her toenails." Their mother had been particularly unresponsive when she'd learned that Even-Steven owned a tavern.

"Hey," Pattianne said. "Do you know if anybody does a whistle version of Mozart?" Jen was good at devising personal ringtones.

"I'll get right on that," she said.

"I gotta go, there's too much traffic to talk on the phone."

"Can I tell her?"

"No."

"Why not?"

"'Cause it isn't anything to tell."

"You mean you guys aren't sleeping together?"

"What, *that's* what you want to tell her?"

"Are you?"

"Jen, I have to hang up."

Pattianne really couldn't talk and drive. She turned up the radio. The classical station was playing a march. The only thing she disliked more than a waltz was a march.

SHE NOTICED HE DIDN'T go to Mass every Sunday. He slept late on Sunday, at her house eventually. He slipped a box of condoms in the drawer of the table next to her futon. June came on cloudy and rainy, and there were long Sunday mornings of having sex and then not having sex and then having sex again before he went out into the rain to buy a *Washington Post*, because he hated the *New York Times*, and she would slip in whatever CD she had found lately, Concerto for Flute and Harp, Piano Sonata, and take long, perfumey showers and make coffee while he was gone. He came back with bagels, or merendine buns, and the *Washington Post*, and he sometimes said, "Mom says to say hello." He could go from being with Pattianne to talking to his mother on the phone just like that. Pattianne would be in the shower, shampooing her tender parts, and he'd be walking along the sidewalk talking to his mother. She wondered if he let her know that they had just spent the night together.

She asked him once, "What exactly did your mom say?"

He said, "She said, 'How's that new girlfriend of yours? Tell her I said hello.'"

She supposed Even-Steven had a mom somewhere, but it had never come up in the conversation.

She liked being by herself for a while after all that Sunday-morning sex. Sometimes she stayed in bed when Michael left, especially if it was raining hard. She listened to the rain instead of Mozart. She liked to stretch out over the whole futon and get herself off. That didn't happen when they were actually together, but afterward, as soon as he was gone, it was almost like she was still really making love to him, the wetness and the slipperiness all still there.

Once he asked, "Don't you have, you know, orgasms?"

"Sometimes," she said. "Don't worry."

AND FINALLY, ON A warm, cloudy afternoon in June, she went down to the tavern and sat at the bar. She waited around until Even-Steven was finished with the lunch rush, and they were leaning against the bar, and she was sipping on some nasty, bitter imported beer. The gray sky made the day seem timeless, and so did drinking beer in the afternoon.

He said, "The reason you don't like beer is that you don't drink it right," and he held his bottle up to the light. "Watch." Then he tipped the bottle up and drank down what was left in it, big swallows that moved down his throat, the white skin of his throat, the Adam's apple.

"Listen," she said. "I have to tell you . . . I don't know how to say this, but I won't be coming around anymore."

She didn't look at him when she said it. She wanted to say *I'm sorry*, but she resisted.

"Okay, drink your beer any way you want," he said finally. He slid his empty bottle to the edge of the bar, and the guy who was bartending grabbed it by the neck and set another full one down.

She said, "I'm serious."

He was quiet, didn't say anything until the new beer was half gone, and then he set the bottle on the bar. He pushed his glasses back up on his nose—they were always slipping down his nose—and he leaned back in a farsighted kind of way, looking at her. He said, "I thought we had a good thing."

There was a bit of a flutter in her throat. "Me too."

He looked right at her for a long minute, his eyes small and round and pretty, his long, lazy body. He turned back to the bar. He said, "Damn."

BY MID-SUMMER SHE AND Michael were as coupled as you can get, and he didn't even know it. He was in Minnesota on a fishing trip with his father. Michael had an interview at a private school, and they flew there together, then went wandering around in the creeks with hip boots on. Michael called it hassling trout that were smarter than him.

She knew she was pregnant even before she went to the clinic, but she didn't believe it. Michael was so careful, such a gentleman with the condoms, checking the box with a little shake when he left sometimes, and she just thought *no no no* the whole time the doctor at the clinic was explaining to her *yes yes yes*. When the doctor asked her about the dates of her last period, she tried to remember, and what she remembered was tickly little orgasms with Even-Steven and the beginning of Sunday-morning sex on Sundays.

She had to get it done by herself, before Michael got back from Minnesota.

There were three appointments on hot, blue, sticky summer days. She signed pieces of paper at the clinic, and the women there were kind-faced and patient, *what's your group insurance number, do you have a middle initial*. The doctor said, "This is seaweed"—something small and stiff that felt like a tampon, late in the afternoon before the last appointment. She said, "It will dilate your cervix. It will cramp a little bit." And then the next morning she said, "This will hurt a little bit." Pattianne lay on her back with her feet up in the stirrups, and it was like having a pelvic exam. There was that speculum they use to open you up wide, except there was a loud noise, a machine sound. She took two days off work, and then there was the weekend, and she lay in front of the fan in a T-shirt with a thick pad between her legs. She read two mystery novels that she had read before, drank limeade. There was a postcard of a sunset over Lake Superior from Michael, and she set it on the bookcase without even reading it.

He called on Sunday afternoon. "Dock of the Bay," courtesy of Jen. When Otis Redding finally stopped whistling, she left. She walked down to the river. The sidewalk was cracked and patched with tar that stuck to her sandals like gum, and sprinklers were cutting off and on in the commons, and kids ran around screaming in the spray, and the people on the river walk were slowed way down, like they all had thick pads between their legs, and finally she just sat on a bench that was empty except for a couple pieces of the *Times*, which she couldn't read because she kept running up against this blank wall of Michael in her head. She thought of lying, and she wondered what it would be like to tell him the truth, explain to him exactly why they weren't supposed to have sex for two weeks. She couldn't imagine what words to use, or what his face would look like, shocked, or disgusted. Or relieved. Gulls out over the river were screaming louder than the kids in the sprinklers. She just couldn't get her brain to do it, to try to come up with some words.

She ended up just not saying anything. She ended up ignoring the doctor's advice a week later, and made love with Michael, watching herself from somewhere in the room, watching her own face, the face with the closed eyes, the face that Michael kissed and kissed until his long body arched and arched and then he fell on top of her and she couldn't see her face anymore, just her hands, him holding her wrists down against the blue-striped sheet. After a while, a few days, a couple weeks, she felt lucky, it all seemed to happen quietly and then go away. Sometimes she would find herself holding her breath for no reason, and there it would be, and then the thought she wasn't thinking would just go away on its own.

They'd had Starla until she was so old she peed everywhere and couldn't walk anymore. Pattianne was there with Jen, crying herself breathless, touching Starla's soft Spaniel ears, while the vet gave her the shots. Starla's brown eyes opened, and stayed open, and she stepped off into somewhere else, on her own.

MICHAEL'S BIRTHDAY WAS AT the end of September, a Saturday this year. Twenty-six, and he thought about how that was closer to thirty. How the gap in their ages was narrowing, if only for a few months until her birthday in January. He went to his parents' house for breakfast, with flowers for his mom, yellow ones. He gave his father a set of power golf balls. He gave Claire a pair of socks with monkeys on them. Giving each other gifts on their own birthdays was a tradition. It had started when Claire was about four or five and had a birthday party. She didn't understand how things worked, and kept trying to give her presents back as the kids left.

During breakfast, in the middle of mimosas and French toast with strawberries, his aunt Alice called. She was his godmother.

"Thank you for the card," he said. "And the check." She sent him a check for ten dollars every year. His parents had started a savings account with the first one. There was $250 in it now.

His birthday present sat on the dining room table, a sweater. His mother always got him a sweater. Except one year, when he first started grad school, and she gave him a tie. That made him feel a little weird, and the next year she went back to giving him sweaters. This one was blue.

When he was a little kid there would be a blue sweater vest each for him and his dad under the Christmas tree. They opened them on Christmas Eve and then wore them to Midnight Mass, where they both took off their heavy winter coats and laid them neatly on the seats. The dark church lit with candles. The Christmas songs he knew the words to. When they got home, he and Claire were hustled off to bed, and he would lie awake for a long time, singing Christmas songs.

In the morning Michael would put his sweater vest on over his pajamas. Lots of cute pictures, Christmas pictures of them all, and it wasn't until second grade that he realized his mother and Claire wore matching Christmas outfits too. Then one year Claire wore a red dotted dress and his mother's was dark green. The next year they went to Aunt Alice's church for Midnight Mass. It was up in Tarrytown, and they'd left early in the evening, without opening any presents, and come home very late.

They went to Mass on Christmas Day the next year. His dad had become a deacon, and served at Mass, wearing a dark suit and tie. Michael was nine, old enough to be an altar boy. He'd been nervous. His mother and Claire were out there where he couldn't see them, and everything was different.

After Mass, he had to put out the candles with the long-handled snuffer. He loved that snuffer. The church slowly emptied, making him feel a kind of panic, but he was careful not to smash the wicks. When he was finished, he went into the vestry and removed his alb, hung it carefully in the closet, took out his coat and put it on, and they would be waiting in the vestibule, ready to go home. He soon was allowed to wash the priest's hands and ring the bells.

Looking back on it, he couldn't remember when he had stopped getting sweater vests. He couldn't remember when he had started imagining getting small sweater vests for his own son one day, or when he had started picturing a little girl and a wife in matching Christmas dresses.

AFTER HIS BIRTHDAY BREAKFAST he drove back to Montclair, to Pattianne. He didn't know why he was so nervous. He was sweating on the back of his neck.

Saturday was busy in the neighborhood around the dry cleaner's, and he had to park two blocks away. He took the package out of the glove box. It was a little painting from a shop in the town where he and his father had stayed when they went fishing.

He'd tried to call her from Minnesota. He couldn't get ahold of her. He knew she didn't usually carry her cell phone with her. When he went into the little shop with his father to get postcards, Michael had fingered the turquoise necklaces.

"Just a little souvenir for Pattianne," he said.

He tried to remember if she wore necklaces, but he didn't know. He knew she wore earrings, sometimes dangling ones, sometimes the other kind.

"I don't know," he said.

The dangling ones hung there in that space under her ear, where he could kiss her and she'd give out a little sound.

His father cleared his throat gently, flipping through the postcards on the rack, and he said, "Something a little less intimate than jewelry might be more appropriate."

The necklace slipped through his fingers, onto the glass counter, and it slid to the floor. He bent quick to grab it, feeling his cheeks flush. He bought the little painting. The woman in the shop had wrapped it for him in brown tissue with a straw ribbon.

He hadn't given it to her right away, when he got back, in August. She had asked him about the fishing, and Minnesota. When she asked him about the interview, he saw that now there was a future to be considered, and that she saw it, too.

"I think it went well," he said. "I'll hear about it by the end of September."

Neither one of them seemed to know what to say next. Making love to her, he felt the distance of just that two weeks of being away. He saved the painting for his birthday.

Now he ran up the stairs to her apartment, getting even sweatier. She was waiting at the open door, in the funny striped shirt and her big overalls. Dangling silver hoop earrings in her ears tangled with her hair. There was so much to know about her.

He held the present out to her. "It's a birthday thing we do. Give each other presents."

She wandered back into the room, pulling opening the straw ribbon. It floated to the floor, and he picked it up, following her in.

"Claire started it. She kind of didn't get it when she was little, and now we always do that."

And now Pattianne would do it, too, be part of this birthday thing.

She unwrapped the brown tissue paper, and it floated to the floor too.

"We give each other presents," he said. He picked up the tissue paper. "On our birthdays."

He was out of breath. The oil painting was no bigger than a postcard, smears of color like the dark sky over the lake.

He said, "It's the lake."

There was a strange silence there between them. He wanted to pull the long curl of hair loose from the intimate silver earring.

IT WAS A SILENCE she had become attached to. Michael Bryn could chat up a storm. He talked to her landlord about deferred maintenance, he talked to the waiter about running shoes. He seemed to have an unending supply of details in his head that he could come up with at will and match to any person. But sometimes he ran out of details with her. They were uncomfortable together sometimes. She thought about marrying him.

She took the oil painting when she went to visit Miss Mimi Stein in October. Every year, on Columbus Day weekend, they drove together in Miss Mimi's Oldsmobile to Pigeon Swamp State Park, feasting their eyes on the fall foliage.

Miss Mimi had been the first person she'd met when they'd moved to Cranbury, when she was ten. She was the Avon lady, and she came to their house, not to sell Avon, but to say hello, since she knew they were there, because she had her polished fingernail on the pulse of the neighborhood. Her lipstick matched her fingernails. Pink. Not red, like Pattianne's mother.

Miss Mimi had said, "This shade is called Buttons 'N' Bows."

She talked about the neighborhood, about the boys who used to live in their house, how they used to hide behind the barberry hedge and throw crab apples at cars. She said, "Those boys were the dickens," and she winked at Pattianne, and leaned against the kitchen counter, black patent leather pocketbook hanging from one elbow, while Pattianne's mother measured coffee into the Mr. Coffee. Miss Mimi drank her coffee black. They took their cups into the living room, a quiet beige-and-gold room.

Her mother said, "You have homework."

Miss Mimi said, "Come and visit me sometime, Pattianne Anthony."

She went into Jen's room and listened, kneeling on the floor at the heater vent. They talked about playing bridge, about tulip bulbs, about being allergic to cats, about blue eye shadow. Miss Mimi didn't believe in blue eye shadow.

"I have a nice charcoal gray," she said. "It's very subtle for daytime wear. A frosty pearl gray for evening. I'll bring you some samples."

When Miss Mimi left, everything was quiet except for the sound of the cups and saucers, her mother taking them into the kitchen. Pattianne got up off her knees and waited a minute. Her knees had flat red circles from kneeling, and she rubbed at them before she went down to the kitchen.

She said, "She lives in that house with the white flowers."

Her mother said, "Don't you go bothering her."

Miss Mimi's cup had a pink kiss mark on the gold rim. Buttons 'N' Bows.

"She said come over and visit," Pattianne said. "She doesn't have any kids."

"That's because she doesn't like kids."

Pattianne felt bad about that. But Sundays were long and boring, her mother in the living room with her copy of the Sunday paper, her father reading his in the den, Jen off somewhere making friends. Miss Mimi would be working in her flower garden. She would wave. She wore lavender gardening gloves. Pattianne finally leashed up Starla and walked along the sidewalk to the small gray house with the shrubs and white flowers.

That first day, she asked her, "Why do you have so many white flowers?"

Miss Mimi pointed to a patch of thin lily leaves shivering in a breeze outside the window. Tall shoots of orange flowers hung above the leaves.

"That color breaks my heart. I wait for those lilies to bloom all spring. One year they bloomed late. Or maybe the delphiniums bloomed early. Anyway, they bloomed together that year. Blue and orange. It changed my life. I had been a white person until then." She laughed, her wet laugh, her flowered handkerchief. "Moonlight gardens had been my favorite. All white flowers, with some dark purple to look black, some lavender to look silver. But then that blue and orange happened to me. Lord."

"How did you know?" Pattianne asked another time. The white flowers were like pillows of lace everywhere. "About a moonlight garden?"

"There's a famous moonlight garden in England," she said. "It's called Sissinghurst. I saw pictures. So I bought a book. Come here."

Miss Mimi's books were her treasures, and they filled up a whole room at the back of her house, a room she had built just for her books. If the dark green drapery was pulled back from the wide window, there was the window seat.

"Window seats," Miss Mimi said. "Are not good places to sit and read."

She was right. It was uncomfortable to sit and read there, for very long anyhow, and besides, there were two chairs and a small sofa, all cushioned and upholstered, and lamps here and there everywhere, and a library table in the middle of the room at one end. The library table was long and had a single wide drawer that held sharp pencils in a black wooden tray, a perfect gray eraser, a magnifying glass, a small pad of lavender note paper. Pattianne wanted a library table at home instead of the blue-painted desk where she did her homework.

There was a dictionary stand, too, with a huge Oxford Dictionary that had pages like tissue paper, an amazing dictionary, a whole story for each word. Pattianne was in love. She wanted to look up words in a dictionary so big it would have its own stand.

Her mother said, "Don't be ridiculous."

The walls of Miss Mimi's library room were floor-to-ceiling books. They were in order. Grouped by subject, except for the fiction, which wasn't even in there, it was in the apricot- colored guest room, where it took up two walls of shelves.

"Fiction," Miss Mimi said. "Alphabetical by author. Easy."

Poetry books were thin, and a hundred of them could take up no more space than the half-high book case that ran along the wall of the hallway leading back to the library. The anthologies were the fat books along the bottom shelves.

"Poetry," she said. "Easy."

But the books in their groups in the library were stacked up and lined up and piled up and stuck in here and there. There was religion and nature and history, and a lot of books about books and books about words. There were big books about art and architecture, and there were atlases. There were books about how to take photographs and how to grow gardens and how to drink tea and how to name the birds.

The window seat with cushions changed over the years, from blue velvet to green stripes and even Black Watch plaid for a while, and beyond the window seat, out the wide bay window, the sloping yard was all smooth green with smooth green shrubs here and there along the edges. Or a perfect smooth slope of snow. A tall slender pin oak scattered red leaves that curled palms-up in the grass every fall.

THEY HAD COFFEE IN the dining room before they left on their foliage tour, and Miss Mimi held the tiny painting in her hands, tipping it sideways, looking across the surface. "Exquisite," she said. "A lot of paint on here, such brush strokes on such a small piece."

She handed it back.

"So," she said. "What kind of young man gives a lady a small painting as a gift?"

"He's a teacher."

And he's careful about being sweet, and sweet about being careful. When he calls, he asks first if it's a good time to talk, and he never calls at work. He has neat fingernails. He holds doors open.

"He's polite," Pattianne said.

Miss Mimi had a laugh that always ended in a cough. "What about the barkeep?"

"Alas," Pattianne said, and they both laughed.

The Oldsmobile was like riding a couch. Gray velour seats, and the utter quiet of a new American car. Miss Mimi hardly ever drove it anymore, and she seemed to be getting too small for it. She turned on the CD player as they pulled out of her driveway. Mozart.

"Symphony number 40," she said. "Maybe not for today," and she turned it off. "So tell me what you've been doing."

And as they drove along the rolling and winding roads of southern Jersey, along gold grass fields with rows of red oaks lining far-off creeks, past stands of dark red maples in yards, and golden honey locusts and purple sweet gums, Pattianne talked about Michael.

He won't wear new corduroy pants until they have been washed and washed and washed. He wears blue sweaters. He likes having his teeth cleaned. He was a summer-camp counselor for seven years straight until this year. He likes to drive to strange neighborhoods and park his Volkswagen and go walking around looking at the houses and the yards. He guesses at what kind of families live there. He likes spy movies, although he will go to any movie anytime, really.

"We go to the movies a lot."

He hasn't found a teaching job yet, still living by tutoring and subbing. He'd hoped to get a job in Minnesota, but hadn't.

"Lucky for me," Pattianne said.

He likes to take pictures of churches, but they're just snapshots with a funky digital camera. He emails them to his grandmother in Pennsylvania.

"He looks just like his father," she said. His father has warm hands and smiles with his eyes, which she didn't say.

"Even my sister likes him," she said, and Miss Mimi said, "Ah. But what about your parents?"

They had offered him a drink and then they all went in the living room and sat together on the couch. Michael started a conversation about golf, about gas prices, about the new bridge over the Raritan River.

"Hard telling," Pattianne said.

THE PARENTS MET AT Christmastime. Mrs. Bryn had a party every year, the Saturday before Christmas.

"But Christmas is on Sunday."

And Michael said, "Silly bones," which was apparently a meerkat expression of endearment. "We wouldn't have it on Chrtistmas Eve."

So the Saturday before the Saturday before Christmas, Michael picked her up. He wore his blazer of midnight-blue corduroy and a white, pressed dress shirt, and the snow came down in a fine soft fall of "Silent Night." He opened the car door.

"Look in there," he said. "It's for your mom."

A waxy white box was propped behind Our Lady of the Bug. Inside, within a fold of white tissue, was a small white orchid, wrapped at the stem with a curl of silver ribbon that held a silver bell.

He said, "She likes bells, right?" Pattianne heard herself telling that to Miss Mimi, how he'd noticed the collection of bells in the beige-and-gold living room.

"You got my mother a corsage?"

"My mom's idea," he said.

The meerkat matriarch as gracious hostess. Pattianne wondered if she knew they were sleeping together. Maybe she assumed they were, or maybe she hoped they weren't.

Michael got onto the Turnpike and into the left lane. He reached over and touched her wrist. "This is special," he said, looking over for a second and then back to the snowy highway. A semi rushed past on the right and he was saying something else, and she looked at the speedometer—they were only going about forty-five. The lights of another semi behind lit up the O-bug. She folded the box back up and held it. She couldn't take her eyes off the road, as if she could drive them herself if she stared hard enough.

"Never," she heard him say.

The semi pulled around them on the right, a moving wall of noise, a wash of slush across the windshield, and behind the Madonna the tiny Volkswagen windshield wipers slapped back and forth.

"Always," he was saying now.

"Michael," she said.

"I love you," he said.

"Get over in that lane," she said as loud as she could without shouting, and then the semi was past, and in the sudden quiet of its passing, she said, "Please."

Michael put on the blinker and got into the right-hand lane. Then he slowed even more and pulled onto the shoulder, shifted to a stop, and into park, and turned to her.

"Okay," he said. "Now. Is it okay with you? For me to say that?"

"That's not what I meant," she said. "I just meant we were going too slow for the left lane."

"Pattianne," he said.

He touched her ear, and then he tugged her earlobe, pulling her toward him, his fingers warm, and so was his breath, and he smelled like Dentyne gum. She was freezing, short dress, thin tights, little dressy shoes, and the damn heater didn't work.

"I love you," he said. "Do you love me?"

"Yes."

"We spend a lot of time together." He took in a breath, let it out. "At your house."

His apartment was boring, and single-guy trashy. He did keep up with the dishes.

"I know," she said.

"I just love you," he said. "That's all."

"I do too," she said. "Love you."

It was intense, there on the side of the highway, and all she knew for sure was she wanted him right there, right then. He loved her. She loved him. And now tears and mascara, and she hated parties.

"I mean, that's okay, right?" she said. She didn't know why she was all weepy. It had been coming at her all of a sudden lately, this weepy thing.

"Silly bones," he said, and he kissed her on the nose, which was often the second part of this silly-bones thing.

He took a small white box out of his pocket and he handed it to her. She opened it. A small silver cross set with an amethyst. He took the silver chain and he fastened it around her neck and then he tucked it under her hair. A man who could fasten one of those tiny clasps in the dark. He unbuttoned her top button and tucked the cross under her coat collar. He started back onto the highway. He sang "O Holy Night," his voice that loud, beautiful tenor, and he kept singing, more verses than she knew there were to that song, and then he sang it in Latin, and he drove straight to her parents' house in Cranbury.

Her mother wore a black velvet suit and a white blouse. Her father pinned the orchid to her lapel while she stood still, her hands held in front of her, her chin lifted slightly.

"Very nice, Michael," he said, and he touched her mother's hair with one finger, tucked a stiff gray curl behind her ear. Her earrings were small gold bells.

"It's very pretty," she said. She smiled once, and then again.

"My mom's idea," Michael said, smiling smiling smiling. "You're going to love my mom."

"We're very much looking forward to meeting them," her mother said, two more small smiles, and they all stood in the middle of the living room, and her father said, "Well, then." The TV was on, a laugh track laughing back there in the den. They stood in the living room with the bells, in the china hutch in the corner, and arranged on the tables on each side of the couch, and on the windowsill of the bow window. Thousands of bells.

"Well, let me turn off the television," her mother said, "and get my purse."

Her father turned to the mirror by the door and touched the perfect knot in his tie, a silk tie of white-on-white paisley with threads of red running through the design. She had given it to him for Christmas last year. His eyes in the mirror looked at hers for a second. Then her mother came back into the living room with her black wool coat over her arm. The curl of hair was once again in front of her ear.

The idea was for her parents to follow in their car. Once they got off the turnpike there were a lot of twists and turns. Michael watched their headlights in his mirror, reaching over to touch her leg, her hand. Once he kissed his fingers and touched them to her lips. He pulled into a subdivision.

"My parents kind of don't know," he said. "How much time we spend together. At your house, I mean."

It was more nights than not. His lovely pinstripe shirts were starting to take up space in her closet. There was a razor and shaving cream in the bathroom.

He had the extra key.

Maybe he wanted them to live together.

He drove slowly, guiding them all through the winding roads, the treacherous cul-de-sacs.

NANA FARLEY HAD JUST come right out and said it.

"Are you and this Michael Bryn having relations?"

"Nana."

She said, "Is he going to marry you?"

It was in her kitchen, after church on the Epiphany. Nana Farley was measuring ground coffee from a canister into her ancient percolator, and the parents and the uncles and their wives and about fifteen cousins were all over the rest of the house, and Michael too, somewhere in all that noise. Uncle Bert's loud cigarette laugh, thumps from the little kids going down the stairs on their butts. Some kid rang the long golden chimes that hung on the wall under the box of the doorbell, and Aunt Maureen yelled out, "You kids get off of those stairs."

Nana Farley held the red plastic scoop midair above the coffee canister and looked into the percolator.

She said, "What number was I on?"

"One for the pot."

She dumped in the last scoop. Plugged in the cord. Then she leaned on the counter. Shorter than Pattianne. Her white hair wisped out from her ancient, feathered, pillbox hat, and her chin, that Farley chin, stuck out. A dish towel was looped into the belt of her dress.

She wasn't even her favorite grandmother, but she was the Catholic grandmother, and Grandma Anthony was in a home since her stroke and didn't talk anymore, didn't even know them, and when she used to go to church, years ago, she went to Roselle First Presbyterian. Today, Michael had gone to Mass with the Farleys. On the Epiphany, her parents went to Mass with her mother's family. Nana Farley, the uncles, their wives, and as many little kids as possible. Michael had looked at her with a question when she stayed seated in the pew next to the parents while everyone else received Communion, all the pews around them empty, except for one very small, very old woman sitting up very straight and sound asleep. Even Jen received Communion. Now Nana Farley tapped her fingernail on the counter.

She said, "You were baptized and confirmed, Pattianne Anthony."

Baptized, tap, confirmed, tap.

She said, "This boy is Catholic."

Catholic, tap.

Pattianne poked her finger through the plastic wrapper on a store-bought coffee cake.

"You can cut that and set it out on that plate." Farley pointed her chin up to a platter on a top shelf. "Are his parents Catholic?"

"Yes."

"Here," she said. She took the dish towel out of her belt. "Wipe that off."

Pattianne wiped the china platter, wiped its pink roses.

Nana said, "What parish?"

"Christ the King"—wiping the gold edge—"in Edison."

"Are you trying to scrape the roses off the plate?" She took the dishtowel back. "How long has it been since you received Communion?"

"Nana."

"Do you do your Easter obligation?"

"Nana," shouted Luke, and there he was, running into the kitchen, with an even smaller cousin, his brother Stephen maybe, right behind him, Sunday shirttails untucked from Sunday pants. "Nana," Luke shouted. "I get to feed the goldfish."

Nana pinched the long sleeve of Pattianne's blouse, and Luke wrapped his arms around Nana's knees, and Stephen grabbed the back of Luke's shirt and pulled, and Nana leaned close to Pattianne.

"Listen," she said. "You two get yourselves over there to Christ the King, and you talk to that priest, missy." Her dentures hissed. And, "No," she said to Luke and Stephen. "I already fed the fish. Here, take these spoons in and put them on the dining room table. And here, Stephen, take these napkins."

Luke took the spoons in both hands. Stephen put his hands in his pockets. Aunt Betsy came to the doorway with a baby in her arm and a small shoe in her hand, and she said, "Stephen James, put your shoe back on."

The boys ran out the door. Stephen grabbed the shoe on the way by, and Aunt Betsy shifted the baby to her other arm and she said, "Mother Farley, come sit down. I'll bring that pot out when it's perked."

Nana Farley handed the neat stack of paper napkins to Pattianne, and she limped to the doorway and put her arm through Aunt Betsy's arm, then turned back once more.

"That cake cover, missy," she said, pointing her chin at the pink glass cake cover on the top shelf. "Bring that cake cover."

"I JUST LOVE YOUR grandma," Michael said later, back in Montclair, cutting lemons at Pattianne's kitchen counter, the back of his shirt crisscrossed with creases, half untucked. "This knife isn't very sharp," he said, and she said, "There's a cutting board under the sink," and he said, "I like olives."

He was making vodka martinis. He'd found a bottle of vermouth in one of the cabinets and got inspired by the martini recipe on the label. She had no idea where that vermouth had come from, it was dusty, and way up in the back behind some Tupperware.

"Vermouth doesn't go bad," she said. "I don't think."

"It was the training pants," he said.

She tried to burp quietly. She was full of coffee and store-bought coffee cake and bacon, and she kept burping.

"Well," he said. "That and the purple ducks."

Kid stories were like sitcoms, or like dreams—you had to be there.

"Poo-poo ducks," he said. "Do you have a hammer?"

The wind blew icy bits, and it was three o'clock on the Sunday after Christmas, a timeless time if ever there was one. The icy bits were the only real indication that there was anything alive anywhere out there. Even the traffic on the turnpike had been sluggish and bored with itself. Not one car passed the O-bug, driving all the way home in the left lane.

"No hammer," she said.

Now the wind hit hard at the side of the building, and the thin, white curtain on the window moved, the window by the big chair, where she was all wrapped up in her quilt, her nose dripping from the cold, and not paying attention. Her elbow poked through the hole in the quilt, and she wanted her sweater. She could move the chair away from the window, but her feet tucked under her were just getting warm, and getting up, moving the chair, going to get the sweater, rewrapping herself, getting warm again—it was too much trouble.

Michael held a blue dish towel up in the air. "Clean?"

"Yes, probably."

He dumped the tray of ice cubes into the towel and wrapped it all into a bundle.

"Your Aunt Betsy is a doll." He whacked the bundle on the counter.

"And that Luke"—he whacked again—"what a terror."

"That was Stephen. Luke's the one he was terrorizing. I think. There's about fifty of them."

Michael picked chunks of ice out of the dishtowel and dropped them into a glass milk bottle. "I like this milk bottle."

"That was from Grandma Anthony's house. My other grandma. My nice grandma."

"Nice grandma?"

He poured vodka into the milk bottle, stopped, held the milk bottle up, looked, poured more vodka.

"Why is she nice?" Then vermouth.

How to explain that happy kind of being together, how it was always okay, no matter what they did, how Grandma Anthony would just smile at her, for no reason at all. "Because she liked me."

He shook the milk bottle just a little bit and then poured the martinis through his fingers into wine glasses. He twisted a lemon peel over each glass.

"Voila," and he walked in and presented her with the martini. His khakis were baggy and wrinkled at the knees.

The martini didn't taste like a good idea, but then the warmth of it started down her throat, and after a second sip, it seemed like a better idea.

He said, "Nana Farley likes you, doesn't she?" He held his martini up to the light. "Good martini? I think it tastes basically like a martini, I guess, anyway. Not quite like a bar martini. Maybe it's the milk bottle. It skewed the presentation."

"Skewed?" she said. "Hey. Why don't you get me a tissue from the bathroom?"

He set his martini on the edge of the bookcase and went in the bathroom, and came back with the whole box.

"I love how you say tissue instead of Kleenex," he said. "Tissue sounds like a little tiny sneeze."

He picked his glass up and sat on the chair in front of the couch. His hair stuck out all over his head.

"Cheers," he said. "So what's wrong with Nana Farley? You don't think she likes you?"

"I don't think she likes anybody," she said. "I think she's cranky from all those years of having kids."

He worked one shoe off, then the other. "There are seven of them?" One dark red sock had the beginnings of a hole in the toe.

"Eight. She started out with ten. One girl died of appendicitis when they were kids." She picked a wet blue thread out of her glass. "There was an Uncle Martin who was killed in a car wreck."

Michael slurped at his martini. "Wow. Ten kids. How many kids in your dad's family?"

"Two. Uncle Frank. I never knew him. He died of cancer."

"Ten kids," he said.

She swallowed the rest of the martini in one swallow. The icy alcohol hit the back of her throat, no taste, just heat and a hint of danger, and she held the empty glass out to him. He reached across the space and took it and then leaned back against the couch.

"My mom's family had five," he said. "There are twenty-two cousins on her side, mostly in Pennsylvania, some here, Aunt Claire and Aunt Christine, and I think eleven cousins on my dad's side, mostly up in Massachusetts, western Mass. He has three sisters."

He sat there on the floor, holding the empty martini glass by the stem, turning it a little bit in his fingers, staring out the window, the boring, lifeless light of January in his face.

She said, "How about another martini?"

He said, "All this time I guess I thought you came from a small family."

"I do," she said. "I mean, our part of the family kind of keeps to itself."

Which bumped him out of his reverie, and a frown appeared and disappeared between his eyebrows.

He said, "What do you mean, keeps to itself?"

"I don't know," she said. "We don't see them much. Holidays, you know. When I was little, I used to get to stay with Grandma Anthony, in her house in Roselle. How about another martini?"

He got up and stood there, bounced his knees. "They all seem to get along." The window glass shook, and he stepped close to the chair.

"Freezing rain," he said. "There's a draft coming in here."

"I know," she said. "I'm cold."

He touched her nose with one finger and he said, "You are," and then he kind of pinched. Cute move. His fingers smelled like lemon peel. "How about another martini?"

He took both glasses to the kitchen counter and filled them up, emptying the milk bottle. There was vodka left in the vodka bottle, but the vermouth bottle was empty.

She said, "Have you ever had a smoky martini?"

"Ten kids," he said. He sneezed. "Damn. What did your grandfather do?"

He came back with the two glasses, gave her one, stood there, sipped. He sneezed again.

"I think I'm getting a cold."

"Steel," she said. "Pittsburgh. I don't know."

"I don't think your grandma seemed cranky," he said. "It seemed like she was getting off on all those kids. I mean, all those grandchildren, that's so, I don't know, just so cool, all those kids running around. That Stephen, he's really something. He tried to make a noose out of my tie."

"A smoky martini is made with single-malt scotch instead of vermouth."

He said, "She asked me what parish I belong to."

"And vodka," she said. "Good, premium vodka."

He said, "I kind of evaded the question."

"Lemon twists."

He said, "I don't really belong to Christ the King anymore."

He stared. Squares of window light in each eye.

Pattianne said, "Blink."

"I go there to Reconciliation with Father McGivens," he said. He picked a blue thread out of his teeth. "But sometimes I go to Saturday Mass at Blessed Sacrament, or Saint John the Apostle. 'Cause they're here, in Montclair."

And she thought *When?* When did he go to Mass on Saturdays?

She said, "Reconciliation?"

"Confession," he said, blinking now. "I need a Kleenex."

Michael in the confessional at Christ the King, confessing the sin of spilling his seed on her breasts, one of his favorite sins, how they discovered it the first time they ran out of condoms. She wondered how he said it, whispering in the dark confessional, kneeling there, like he knelt over her? What did the priest say to absolve him, to make him believe he could receive Communion and then come to her bed and have unchaste, unmarried sex that was definitely not open to God's intervention for new life?

He said, "I liked being at Mass with you today, you know," and he closed his eyes. "That's a nice church, St. Albans." And this would have been the moment to ask about why she didn't go to Communion, but he seemed to miss it.

The cold vodka hurt the back of her teeth, and the next burp came up vodka flavored instead of bacon flavored.

She said, "I used to get to stay at Grandma Anthony's house for two weeks every summer, just me and her."

The tiny frown came and went between his eyes again. "She's in a home now? In Roselle?"

She fished out the lemon twist and chewed on it and drank down the rest of the martini through the chewed lemon twist, and the next burp was pure lemon flavor.

She said, "No more bacon."

Michael said, "No more bacon?"

She said, "Why don't you pass that milk bottle over here?"

He walked on his knees over to the counter and back with the milk bottle, and shook the melting ice into her glass.

"So," she said. "We should make smoky martinis next."

He wiped his fingers on his shirt and he said, "With bacon?"

"Smoky because of scotch. Not bacon, it doesn't have anything to do with bacon."

"I ate a lot of that bacon," he said. "Bacon-butter sandwiches."

"If you can eat it on bread with butter, my grandmother serves it," she said. "Poor cake—did you ever have poor cake?"

"What's poor cake?"

"White bread and butter. Sprinkled with sugar. A lot of sugar."

He said, "Like a sandwich?"

"Open-ended," she said. "No. You know. Open-faced."

"Wow." He up-ended the milk bottle, dripping a couple last drops into his glass.

"Ten kids," he said.

He went to the kitchen counter and picked up the vodka. He poured some into the milk bottle, and then he looked at what was left and poured it all into the milk bottle and then he looked into the cabinet over the refrigerator.

"There's this J&B—that's scotch, right?"

She said, "It's supposed to be single malt."

"Mavis's is the only place we can get liquor on Sunday that's close by," he said.

He opened the J&B.

"Very dry," she said. "Smoky martinis are supposed to be very dry."

"Gotcha." He drizzled a little scotch into the milk bottle and looked at her.

He said, "More?"

"Don't know. Maybe just a touch more."

He poured in just a touch more and then he brought in the milk bottle and sat cross-legged on the couch.

He said, "What church do your parents go to?"

"They don't."

He said, "Lapsed? Would you say they're lapsed?"

Abortion, and now sex that has nothing in the whole wide world to do with new life. Once, when she was ten or so, she went to Confession on Saturday morning, stole a Milky Way bar from the Banner Mart in the afternoon, and received Communion the next day. It was easy.

"I guess they are."

He picked at the hole in his sock. "And you?" He tugged at a long red thread and pulled the hole in his sock down around his toe. "Look. These are brand-new socks. What would you say you are?"

"Drunk," she said. "I would say I am drunk. How about you bring that bottle over here?"

"You get kind of bossy when you get drunk, don't you?"

"My feet are finally warm," she said. "Come here and get the rest of me warm."

THE NEXT MORNING HE went to his apartment early, before going to work. He shut the door behind him and stood there. He'd lived here for three years and could still remember the first day. His first place of his own, no roommates, a bedroom with a bed instead of a futon on the floor.

The blue curtains his mother had put up were all closed. The place was dark and cold. He hadn't turned the heat on in days. He picked up the clutter of mail that had dropped through the mail slot and sat on the couch. Junk mail, a gas bill, a credit card bill. His cold was worse, and he wanted to go back to sleep. He didn't feel good about being here. He liked her apartment better. It was bright and always warm, and she was always there. They were always there. Together. He dropped the mail on the couch and got up, went into the dark bedroom. His closet doors were open, showing empty hangers. A pile of laundry was on the bed. He sneezed three times in a row, and he went in the bathroom. The Kleenex box was empty. He blew his nose with toilet paper. The roll was almost empty too. He couldn't even remember the last time he'd taken a shower here.

He had to get to work. He felt like crap. He stuck the toilet paper roll in his coat pocket.

There was no way he could be doing this. His parents would freak. Almost everyone he knew started out their lives as couples by living together, and he tried to imagine telling his parents. He couldn't. He couldn't even imagine saying it to Pattianne. She seemed so willing to just go on as they were.

He tried to imagine marrying her.

Maybe he could call Father McGivens. He was more than just the priest who had given him First Communion and confirmed him. He'd been part of Sunday dinners and graduations. He came over on Saturday afternoons to watch football. Sometimes Michael watched with them. Father McGivens had played running back at Fordham. He would pound his big fist on the arm of the chair and yell at the games and act very unpriestly and make them laugh.

Father McGivens had talked with him about Corinne Mullins, who got so angry about the child-abuse scandals that she said she would never enter a Catholic Church again. A quiet, steady example of faith is what Father had advised. So Michael had started going to Mass every Sunday again. He and Corinne broke up anyway.

Maybe he could help him figure out what to say to his parents.

Father McGivens said, "Come on by after work."

HE GOT TO CHRIST the King and sat in the car, mumbling out loud.

"I met a girl."

"I know how they'll feel about us living together."

"She isn't into church."

His nose was running, and he pulled off another piece of toilet paper and blew it. His throat ached a little. He looked at his watch, stuck the toilet paper roll back in his coat pocket, and got out. It was colder now.

The wind was sharp and got right inside his coat. When he pushed open the door to the rectory office, there was a fire in the fireplace, and Father McGivens sat at the big desk, leaning back in the chair. A football game was on the radio.

"Michael," he said, sitting up, standing up, coming around the desk. He gave him a quick embrace. His sweater smelled like cigar. "Always good to see you. How's the new year so far?"

He was square-shouldered, tall, and straight. Michael stood up straighter just being near him.

"Great," he said. "Good."

Father McGivens went to a sideboard. "Cup of coffee?"

"Yeah, thanks, yes, please."

"Have a seat." He waved his hand at the arrangement of chairs and the half-couch, away from the desk. Michael took off his coat and draped it over the arm of the chair. He sat down and leaned back. The chair felt too soft, and he sat up. Father McGivens poured the coffee and handed him a cup. He turned the radio off and sat on the couch, resting his arm along the back of it.

"I don't suppose you've come to sign up for the CYO basketball team?"

"No," Michael said. "I have a pretty chopped-up work schedule, and I'm doing some subbing. Wish I could."

Michael sipped at the coffee. It was black. He usually put cream in his coffee, but coffee with Father McGivens was always black. Wind blew the branches of a tree against the window, and the heat kicked on with a nice rush of air. Father McGivens crossed one leg over his knee, the knee cracking.

"Well, we can always use another body when it comes to stuffing envelopes. There's still a chance to get the Family Life bill on the ballot."

"I wanted to talk to you. You might remember Pattianne?"

Father McGivens straightened his leg and it cracked again. He pushed up the sleeves of his sweater and leaned forward, resting his forearms on his knees. "I do," he said.

Michael gulped the coffee. It was too hot, and his eyes watered.

"Your mother tells me you've been seeing quite a bit of each other."

A sneeze tickled his nose. He set the coffee on the table. "We're kind of at a point," he started. "I kind of need to make a decision."

Father was nodding just slightly. Michael took in the whole of him. Big. Open. Easy. He'd known this priest as long as he could remember. Father McGivens had helped him talk to his parents about his decision to be a teacher instead of going to law school. He'd reassured Michael when Corrine moved away, saying that it was her journey to make.

"And you're thinking of becoming" — Father clasped his hands and looked at them — "sexually involved?"

Oh God. Suddenly the chair Michael was sitting in felt huge. He felt small. He felt his pulse hammering. His neck was hot. His throat ached. He wondered if he had a fever. He had to say something.

"That's not it."

"I'm glad to hear it." Father leaned back. "It's a big step, one most young people take far too lightly."

Then Father McGivens said, "She isn't active in the church?"

"No," Michael picked up his coffee and saw that the cup shook. He blew on it and set it back down.

"Are you thinking of marriage?"

"I don't know."

Father McGivens stood up and went to the sideboard. Poured himself a cup of coffee. He stood there for a moment, his back to Michael.

He said, "If you were sexually involved, the easy answer would be to disentangle. Separate. Cool things off. The issues would become clearer. But that's not the case, right? So why don't you and the folks stop by for coffee after Mass some day soon, and bring this young lady along? We can begin by all getting to know each other a little better."

"Good." Michael stood up. "I'll ask her." He suddenly couldn't wait to get away. He felt creepy. He was a liar and a sneak. "I'll call you. I'll check with Mom and Dad."

He picked up his coat. The toilet paper roll dropped out of the pocket and rolled across the carpet. Father McGivens picked it up and looked at it.

"I need to buy some Kleenex. I have a cold."

"Well, take care of yourself," Father McGivens said. He handed him back the toilet paper. "Flu going around."

"Thanks," Michael said. "Thank you."

His eyes were watery, and he just wanted to get away.

3: STRAIGHT ON TILL MORNING

PATTIANNE SAT AT THE kitchen table and watched Michael peel a small onion.

He said, "I believe in chili in January."

He said he had never noticed anything odd about January before he met her, and she would point things out to him, like how people tend to wait a little longer after the light turns green, the whole world sleepy and slow, and he would say, "My gosh, you're right."

"So," she said, "you're having January opinions of your own now?"

He took a wooden kitchen match from the box and put it between his lips, the match tip sticking straight out. He talked around it.

"The sulfur in the match," he said. "It absorbs the onion, whatever it is about the onion that burns your eyes." He blinked. He chopped at the onion. His eyes watered.

Her eyes did not water. Mostly her eyes blinked and mostly on the side of closed.

January was always time out of time. Pattianne felt like it just happened without anyone even noticing. Everyone was home writing their thank-you notes. People forgot to call, or visit, they didn't notice that you didn't call, or visit. They saw enough of you over Christmas, you saw enough of them.

Michael had a regular job now. He was a life-skills coach. It was a life-skills program, mandated by the state as a certain condition of parole.

"Not parole," he said. "Probation."

He hung out after school with juvenile delinquents.

He said, "They don't call them that anymore."

She said, "Little monsters."

"Not so little. Middle school."

Worse. Middle monsters. All the energy and bad judgment of little kids with a budding sense of irony and adventure. She'd interned once in a middle-school library. All she could do was laugh at those kids. They were funny and impossible. And sad.

Ten to six, his work schedule, noon to five, hers. Long, easy hours to sit inside, stay warm, read. She bought paperback mystery novels by the pound at the Goodwill. She waited for him to come home to her at night.

His Volkswagen rattling down in the street was a sound her body heard before her brain. She would close her book, close her eyes, listen to the rattle stop and choke and then stop again. She would get up from the chair and let the blanket fall away from her warm legs and look out the window, down to the street, to the orange hump of the Volkswagen under the streetlight. Go to the door and open it, more cold air from the hallway coming up the wide wooden stairs. Go into the kitchen and open a bottle of red wine. She was a careful opener of wine. Nonflourishing. By the time the cork gently popped, there he was, closing the door, dropping his coat on the chair.

They drank chianti from glasses, he drank the taste of chianti from her tongue, she sucked the red of it from his lips. They had red, swollen mouths from kissing and sucking. Drunk on red wine, sucking Michael Bryn's lips was time out of time. And they fucked, sometimes on the couch, once on the floor, once on the kitchen counter.

And he would say things like, *God, you wouldn't believe this kid today.* Or, *I have to do something about this kid's brother.* Or, *Why do some people even have kids?* And she would say something like, *I have braunschweiger and zwieback.* Or, *There's a Harvey Keitel movie on the movie channel.* Because Michael loved braunschweiger and zwieback. Because Michael loved Harvey Keitel. Because she didn't know why some people had kids.

The fifteenth of January was her birthday. It was the same day as her father's birthday. January was all around her. January without a cigarette was daunting. Her New Year's resolution was to have one. One.

Michael dumped the chopped onion into the pan, where the butter was already sizzling and, actually, burning.

She said, "Next Sunday at this very moment we'll be sitting at my parents' house at the dinner table."

They would all sing "Happy Birthday," and her mother and Jen would get to that third line, and sing "Happy Birthday, dear Daddy and Pattianne," cramming both names in there, and she herself would just sing "Dear Daddy," and he'd sing "Dear Pattianne," and everybody would watch each other to do it right. It was the only time they even said *daddy*. *Daddy* seemed like a word for families that made popcorn or went to theme parks or played Chutes and Ladders around the kitchen table. They always just went off in their corners to read. They always called him Dad.

"Maybe we should go out to dinner," she said. "Just us. Instead."

The smell of frying onions was one of the things in the whole world that she loved. "Let's go to dinner in the village."

Two bulbs were burned out in the ceiling lamp, leaving one, and the flames under the frying pan were a small blue light.

"The village?" Michael said. "Instead of you and your dad's birthday party?"

The streetlight outside was sodium orange, and it made the kitchen darker instead of brighter.

"Mulberry Street," she said. "Fettuccine con gamberetti."

"Where's that new can opener I got?"

"Tiramisu." She closed her eyes. "Gattinara."

He pulled open the silverware drawer.

"It's in the spice shoebox," she said.

He said, "Let's get him some of that whiskey."

"What whiskey?"

"That whiskey you gave me for my birthday."

He said, "Hey, there's chili powder in here."

"Hey," she said, "that was Irish whiskey. And hey, my dad drinks scotch."

"Do they have that brand in scotch?"

Ed School boys were rookie drinkers.

• • •

LEMON CAKE WAS HER father's favorite kind of cake, and since she was his birthday girl it was automatically hers, too, and so her mother always made lemon birthday cake. She decorated it with frosting flowers and letters, *Pattianne & Daddy*, in neat cursive, blue this year. There were seven candles in a circle. Pattianne didn't know why seven, no reason, except to have candles to blow out. She and Michael stood side by side, viewing the cake as it sat on the sideboard on its china pedestal. Jen leaned against the doorway, watching them watch the cake.

Michael said, "It's a beautiful cake."

Their hands touched secretly.

He said, "My mom always buys our cakes from Greene's Bakery."

There was a soft, shaky moment in his voice.

He said, "This is so sweet."

Jen reached out and swiped her finger around the frosting at the bottom of the cake.

"Not sweet," she said. "Lemon."

"Cue the laugh track," Pattianne said.

"Bada-bing," Jen said, and beat her fingers in a drum roll on the stack of china dessert plates and then stopped and waited for her to say *bada-boom*. She reeked of perfume.

"Bada-boom."

The table was set with the good china, white with a gold stripe around the rim. The regular china was just plain white with no gold stripe. Michael had a grocery bag with party hats, each a different color and a feather sticking out the top, and he went around the table setting one by each plate.

Jen put hers on and stood by her chair. She said, "Standard seating configuration."

Which was Jen, their mother, Pattianne, their father, around the table, same seats, always. Tonight, however, there were five chairs, and Pattianne pointed to the fifth chair, and said, "What do you call that?"

Jen pulled at the elastic strap of her party hat and tilted it so it stuck out the front of her head like a unicorn horn. "New standard?"

Jen couldn't stand not knowing—*are you moving away, are you going to marry this guy?*

"Wouldn't you like to know?"

One side of Jen's mouth smiled more than the other side, resulting in a look she was often advised to wipe off her face as a child. Pattianne pushed the two chairs on the one side closer together.

Michael took a tall silver box out of the grocery bag.

He said, "I'll just set this in the living room for now."

Jen pushed her party hat down to her chin so that it stuck out like a party hat sized zit.

"Dad and I went bowling this afternoon," she said. "I let him win."

And there was finally that moment after dinner, when the plates were cleared, when Jen jumped up and turned off the light, and their mother came in from the kitchen with the cake. The dark room, the lit candles, the moment before singing. There was that moment everywhere at birthday parties. Pattianne always got teary when it was someone else's shining birthday-cake moment. On January fifteenth, though, she had to pay attention to singing "Happy Birthday," getting the both-names thing right. Jen sang loud and off-key, which their mother never found funny.

The parents took their party hats off as soon as the singing was done. Michael left his on, and so did Jen. Hers was a red party hat, which brought out the red in her eyes. Pattianne wanted to take hers off but she didn't. She handed the china dessert plates to her mother, who sliced thin slices of the cake and handed each one to her and she handed it on. The cake was dry and lemony. Pattianne couldn't remember what color her party hat was.

Michael said, "So, great, the same birthday, very cool."

Her father rested his forearms on the edge of the table. He had loosened his tie and folded his cuffs partway up his arms, past his gold watch. He nodded toward them all like a small king.

He said, "She's my girl." He winked at her.

Jen said, "She was born early. Not due till Mom's birthday. Next month. If that happened, she was gonna be Anne. Mom is Anne. Dad's Pat. Get it?"

She had scraped most of the lemon frosting from her cake onto her fork and was licking it like it was an ice-cream cone.

Jen said, "Our gerbil Mike had babies on Mom's birthday when I was in fourth grade."

Their mother took a neat bite of her cake. She laid the fork down next to her party hat.

Jen licked. "My birthday is March 7," she said. "Nothing ever happens on my birthday. I was named Jennifer because Grandma Anthony always wanted to name her daughter Jennifer, and then she never had one."

Their mother took a sip of coffee. She said, "Jen, why don't you get the presents?"

The rooms around the dining room were dark, no lights left on, ever. You leave a room, you turn out the light and you shut the door. Pattianne left lights on in her apartment, and every time she did she felt the pleasure of being a grown-up.

Jen brought in four boxes, two wrapped in pink, and two wrapped in paper with golf clubs on it. She said, "Hmm."

One of the pink boxes was a Lanz nightgown. Pattianne didn't even have to open it to know that. The other pink present was from Jen. Pattianne ripped the paper off, and when she dropped it on the floor, Jen said, "Pattianne, what a mess."

Their mother picked the paper up.

It was a three-volume box set of Emily Dickinson. It was a beautiful set, from the used bookstore, with faded brown leather bindings and a bookplate in the front of each volume, a name, Miss Sarah Keller, in old spidery writing on the faded bookplates. Pattianne had given them to Jen on her last birthday.

"Thank you," she said. "I love it." The truth.

Which sent Jen into a full stoned giggle, which got Pattianne going, always.

Their mother said, "Girls."

Their father opened a navy blue paisley tie and a box of dark-chocolate-covered caramels from the Pennsylvania Dutch shop on the turnpike.

Michael said, "Excuse me," and he went into the dark living room. Everyone stopped, stopped eating lemon cake, Jen stopped sniffling from the giggles. Their mother held her coffee halfway to her mouth. Pattianne took her party hat off. It was the blue one.

Michael came back with the tall silver box and set it in front of her father. It was single-malt scotch. He'd picked it out at the liquor store because of its age. It was thirty-one years old.

"Same as Pattianne," he said.

Her father said, "That's very thoughtful, Michael."

If it were up to her, she'd get out the small crystal glasses from the top cabinet and pour some for everyone. She would force Jen to have some and try to convince her it was good stuff. They would toast. Her father set the bottle next to the box of Pennsylvania Dutch caramels, which were next to the navy blue paisley tie, which was next to his party hat, which was green.

Michael held his hand out. Sitting there on his open palm was a ring-sized box with a gold bow. She had to reach out and take it from him. She had to open it right then and there, with hands that felt shaky, but weren't. It was only red stone earrings, thank God, beautiful red stone earrings.

"Garnets," Michael said. "My mom picked them out. Well, my mom and Claire."

Her father said, "Very nice, Michael."

Jen said, "Very nice, Michael."

Pattianne set the box down next to the blue party hat and took the silver hoops out of her ears. Michael's lips were a small tight bow, a puzzlement there on his face—did she like them, was it okay—and she worked the garnet studs into her ears, turned her head one way, the other, showed him, yes, she loved them. They were beautiful and she would cherish them, even though studs hurt her ears and she never wore them. She tucked her hair behind her ears.

Her father said, "Garnet is the birthstone of January." He cleared his throat.

He said, "I have always loved the name Garnet. I once knew a girl named Garnet."

He straightened his dessert fork across the gold rim of his dessert plate.

He said, "Garnet did the housework at my mother's house, but I think Garnet is a very fine name."

Garnet. Pattianne had never even heard her father say that word before, ever, perhaps, and now he had just said it so many times in a row that it had lost its meaning as a word and become just a sound that caught her mother in a still moment and turned them all into an Edward Hopper tableau, as if he had never spoken before.

Jen caught the moment in its free fall, which was her job in their family.

"And very fine earrings as well," Jen said. "Very nice, Michael."

Her mother's daughter, backing away from that moment.

Pattianne said, "They're beautiful." And she sounded like her mother too.

"Hey," Jen said. "Can I have your silver hoops?"

Pattianne covered her hoops with her hand. "No."

"No," their mother said. "You don't need to wear silver hoops, Jen."

Jen was twenty-five and their mother still tried to tell her how to dress. Their mother also believed only Italian girls wore silver hoops in their ears. She had similar opinions on pierced ears in general. Her father sat back, straight, and both parents looked at some spot in the air over the middle of the table.

Jen said, "How about a small aperitif? There's some Grand Marnier here somewhere."

Jen loved Grand Marnier. She loved to say words like aperitif, especially when stoned.

Michael said, "What's Grand Marnier?"

Pattianne said, "Small aperitif is redundant."

Her father said, "Aperitifs are taken before a meal."

Her mother said, "Pattianne and Michael have a long drive, Jen."

THE BIRTHDAY PRESENTS WERE in her lap, along with two pieces of lemon cake in a plastic container, which she planned on eating for breakfast, both of them. Michael drove fast, topping the Volkswagen out at fifty, singing the Beatles "Birthday" song, two lines, over and over.

He said, "Will you model that nightgown for me?"

Modeling a Lanz nightgown sounded like a good way to not have sex.

"It wouldn't be as much fun as you might think. Besides, it has to stay in its box until next Christmas. Then Jen gets it."

"Your mom gives you a nightgown and then you give it to Jen?"

"My mom doesn't know."

The Madonna of the Dashboard glowed her beige plastic glow.

By the time they got home, the Volkswagen heater was just kicking on. Michael parked and turned to her while the car bucked a couple times. He took the keys out. His tongue slipped across his lips. They had never fucked in the Volkswagen. Impossible, perhaps.

He said, "I think it would be awesome to have a baby on your own birthday."

There could have been a baby almost here by now. They could be sitting at their own dining room table thirty-one years from now, eating cake and trying to speak, or trying not to speak.

She said, "Grand Marnier is orange-flavored liqueur."

The streetlights on the Madonna's head made an orange halo.

She said, "We'll get some. You'll love it. Grand Marnier."

He sucked on his lip, his lower lip, sucking it in with his teeth. When Michael sucked his lip it went straight to her nipples.

"I love my earrings," she said, her voice stopped up back in her throat. "And I love you,"

He said, "I know." A smaller voice.

"And I love lemon cake." The tears let loose.

He said, "Silly bones." A whisper really.

She loved the name Garnet.

HE COULDN'T STAY ASLEEP that night. Usually he conked out right away, especially with her right there next to him. It had been so quiet in that house. They kept turning off lights. Even Pattianne got quiet there.

He got up early and turned on the heater. He made her a cup of coffee with too much cream, the way she liked it. Put it on the table by the futon. She wrapped her bare warm arms around his neck when he knelt down to tell her he was going and tell her it was there. That made him feel a little better. He left the kitchen light and the lamps in the front room turned on. He sat in the car for a while. The O-Bug warmed up. He looked at the windows above the dry cleaner's. She probably was already back asleep. He liked her sister Jen. She was funny. She was like a parakeet that kept going off. What he would call slightly inappropriate. And her dad seemed okay. Dads always liked him. He was the kind of guy they thought was okay for their daughters to go out with. Probably not to live with without being married, though. Pattianne said her parents didn't really know they were more or less living together.

He'd said, "What's that mean, don't really know?" She'd said, "It means don't really care." He kept turning that over in his head now, driving in to Trenton with the comforting flow of the early traffic. It turned into a Beatles song, except instead of "Don't Let Me Down," it was "Don't Really Care." He hated it when songs got stuck in his head. He didn't realize he'd been actually singing it until Johnson, who was working at a table by his desk, said to him, "You know that's not right."

Michael stared at him. "What's not right?"

Johnson said, "In the first place, those aren't the right words. In the second place, there's that," and he pointed to a little poster on a bulletin board by the door. Because We Care.

"That's about not smoking," Michael said. He thought about them not caring, and he decided that simply couldn't be true. He didn't know how they could not care. It made him depressed. And his head ached. He said, "You ever drink Grand Marnier?"

Johnson said, "That shit is brutal."

Father McGivens stood on the steps of Christ the King in the freezing sunlight and smiled a square white smile. He said hello to Mr. Bryn and he kissed Mrs. Bryn on the cheek and then Michael and Claire. Mrs. Bryn wore a dark blue coat dress with a velvet collar. Claire wore a little dark red jacket and a short black skirt. Nobody looked cold.

They all stood on the steps there and smiled, and Father McGivens took Pattianne's hand in his hand. He had huge hands. She felt like she'd stuck her own hand into a baseball mitt. A warm baseball mitt. They only stood there for a little while, the names part of the introduction, and then they went back to the rectory. She walked next to Mr. Bryn, who had a long wool overcoat with a warm chemical smell, like the dry cleaner's.

"Mother," he said over his shoulder to where Mrs. Bryn walked with Michael. "This young lady needs one of Aunt Shirley's scarves," and he looked down at her and he said, "You look cold," and he put his big arm around her shoulder.

She was shocked at the lovely warmth of it. At how much she liked it. At how easy it was to walk alongside someone with his big arm around your shoulder keeping you warm, moving you along.

"Dory's Aunt Shirley crochets and makes lace and knits," he was saying. "I know you kids aren't wearing a lot of that stuff these days, but these are really warm scarves."

When he said you kids she knew that Michael hadn't said anything about her not being a kid, about her being thirty-one, or maybe he had, and maybe she wouldn't worry about it for now. Maybe it really didn't matter. Michael said it didn't matter. Five years wouldn't matter if it were the other way around. It didn't matter to Michael, it didn't matter to her.

Mr. Bryn said, "What's your favorite color?"

She said, "I don't know. Purple, I guess." She heard her voice being giggly and breathless, and she wanted to know what his favorite color was but didn't ask.

They had coffee in Father McGivens's office, white china mugs, no cream or sugar.

Father McGivens said, "So, Pattianne, where are you from?"

"I was born in Reading, but we lived in Newark, and then Cranbury."

The cushion of the chair was old, red turning silver, turning pink, old velvet. Mrs. Bryn and Mr. Bryn sat together on a small couch. Mrs. Bryn crossed her legs. She wore black patent-leather heels that looked high-fashion, expensive, made her legs look long and sexy.

"And your parents are there still?"

She looked up then—this was all about her, she was supposed to be paying attention. She was on display.

"Yes," she said. "We used to go to Mass. I mean, we used to be Catholic."

Surely there wasn't a stupider thing to say.

Father McGivens leaned back in the desk chair and the wood squeaked. "Well," he said. "I guess we can dispense with the secret code words then, can't we?"

He had a smiling face, and white teeth like Chiclets, and he sat back with one ankle crossed over the other knee, like a guy, except he wore his cassock. He said, "I have a cousin at Saint Francis in Cranbury."

"That's where I was confirmed," she said. "Right after we moved there. To Cranbury." Claire was standing neatly behind her mother, and she bounced a little, and she touched one hand to Michael. He sent Pattianne the quickest, most secret look. It said *don't worry*, so she didn't. She just watched him unbutton his blue blazer and didn't even think about how goofy those brass buttons were, and he leaned back in his chair and looked at Claire, and it was like the light from her face lit up his face, like their faces were laughing with each other.

And that was all that happened. They all had coffee, and then they all went back out into the cold, the Bryns to their Bryn car, Mr. Bryn opening the door for Mrs. Bryn, his hand on the small of her back as she got in, and she and Michael to the Volkswagen, Michael opening the door for her.

A tiny puff of warm air came out of the heater vent when Michael started it up.

He said, "I told him you've been baptized."

She said, "I really like your dad."

She did, and she really liked saying it to Michael.

Then she said, "When?"

Michael held the steering wheel like he was wrestling the Volkswagen down the road.

"When what?"

"When did you tell Father McGivens I was baptized?"

"Tuesday. No. Thursday. Last week."

It was not usually good to talk to Michael while he was driving.

When they got back to her apartment, the first thing she did was peel the freezing pantyhose off and put on jeans. She only zipped the jeans partway up.

Michael was spooning coffee into the filter.

She put her arms around his waist. "How about some of that pinot noir?"

He counted four scoops. She pressed against his back, that blue blazer, and slipped her hands into the front pockets of his pants.

"So," he said. "I talked to Father McGivens."

"I liked him," she said. "Why do you always have paper clips in your pockets?"

He turned around in her arms, took the two paper clips out of her hand and set them on the counter, and he took her hands in his and kissed her, holding their hands between them like that, and she reached her tongue into his mouth, and pressed her hips against him, pressing him into the counter.

"He said," Michael said, "no sex," and he let go of her hands.

She pulled him by the butt, pulled right up against him, against his hard-on.

She slipped her hands down inside the back of his khakis.

"You're kidding, right?" she said, pulling his shirt out of his pants, undoing the shirt buttons, rubbing her cheek against the soft hair on his chest. She bit on his nipple, and when he made a sound in his throat, she heard it with her tongue. She unzipped his pants and he made sounds into her hair, into her ear.

"I don't have any condoms," he whispered.

"I do."

Then it sounded like he said they were supposed to disentangle.

"Distentangle?" she said. "Who said that?"

"Father McGivens."

"Yeah, right."

She ended up on the counter, whispering, "Yes, please," Michael's face between her legs.

After, when they were sprawled on the couch, breathless and giggled out, she said, "We're knackered."

"We're what?"

"Knackered. It's a slang thing. English. This after-sex thing like you can't move."

"Mmm."

"So, you think that counts as sex, as the kind of sex we aren't supposed to have?"

"Yes." And he was laughing a little, but he had that dark blue look in his eyes.

"Are you sure?"

He said, "Well, I'm not going to ask."

"Listen," she said. "We need to talk about this disentanglement thing. Because I'm not a Catholic, really."

His eyes closed and he said, "Well, you just be who you are."

The next day she called the clinic to get a prescription for birth control pills anyway. And as for Michael's willpower, it was nil.

SHE HAD LIVED WITH a boyfriend once before, David, a cute potter, and she wasn't sure if her parents had even known. They must have. Michael was still paying rent on his apartment, but he was at her place all the time now. His shirts on hangers in the closet. His pillow, his shaving cream, his blue coffee cup.

His parents didn't know. His mother had suggested Sunday dinner twice, but Michael had had to work both Sundays, and Pattianne was relieved and disappointed at the same time. Once when Mr. Bryn was in town for something, though, he and Michael had met for a beer, and Michael called her and said she should come over, to the Bad Frog Brewpub. When she got there, she stood at the door for a second. There they were at a table at the far end of the room. Mr. Bryn saw her, as if he'd been watching for her, and he smiled and stood up. She got to the table and he reached out and guided her close with a hand on her back between her shoulders, that warm hand.

"Hey there, Miss Pattianne. Michael was just telling me you can beat him at Scrabble." He was laughing. "Well, I have to tell you, anyone can beat him at Scrabble." And they were off on a story of Michael's ten-year-old cousin beating him at Scrabble every time they played, and Mr. Bryn said, "You'll have to play her."

Michael ordered Pattianne a glass of white wine. She never even finished it, just sat there. It was easy, their conversation wrapped around her like a sweater.

"Melissa," she said at work the next day, "do you ever go out for a beer with your dad?"

"My dad drinks red wine."

"Okay, red wine."

"No," Melissa said. "They drink at home."

This was how conversations with Melissa usually went.

"He's into war movies" is what Melissa finally came up with. "So, yeah, I'll pick up a bottle of cheap red, and we'll have one glass of that, and then he'll open a bottle of good red and we'll watch a war movie."

"War movies?"

"*Bridge on the River Kwai*, ever hear of that one?"

VALENTINE'S DAY WITH EVEN-STEVEN had always been something to avoid. Michael gave her a white rose.

Their first Valentine's Day together, and no more talk of disentangling.

Michael's phone rang at almost midnight, out on the kitchen counter where it was plugged into its charger. He jumped out of bed. The ring was just like an old-fashioned telephone. Jen had suggested "Wild Thing."

Pattianne heard him answer, and she heard him say, "Oh my God." She wrapped a blanket around herself and followed. By the time she got there he was saying, "No, I'm on my way."

"My dad," he said to her. "He collapsed. It's maybe his heart." Then his face crumpled and he gasped for a breath. "They don't know what, like a heart attack or what."

His tears hit her like a punch in the stomach.

"Should I come with you?"

He said no, and got dressed fast, and left without looking back at her, saying he would call her.

She stayed up, the apartment getting cold by two when Michael still hadn't come back. Or called. There were shadows in the corners, and she turned on all the lights, which didn't help. She turned on the TV, too, and watched *Casablanca* for a while and then turned it off and tried to read Elmore Leonard, *The Big Bounce*, which she had already read twice, once quite recently. Sometimes reading something she had already read would help her fall asleep. Not this time.

And he didn't call.

She fell asleep around six. He got back at seven.

"How is he?"

"He's got fluid built up."

"In his heart?"

The blanket was tangled around her legs, and she kicked it to the floor.

Michael picked it up. "Congestive heart disease," he said, and he smoothed the blanket out, folded it in half, saying, "Father McGivens said he hasn't been feeling well for a while," and then folding the blanket in half again and laying it on the bed.

She pulled on knee socks. "Father McGivens was there?"

"I have to go back. I have to call work first, and then I'm going to shave. I don't have time to take a shower. Claire's going to pick me up so we can drive up together."

"Claire is coming here?" The dishes were piled in the sink from last night. There were clothes on the living room floor, the wine bottle on the table, a row of empty wine bottles on the counter because she liked the shape, an odd curve, Gattinara, the way she had loved those old heart-shaped Mateus bottles.

"Where is it?" Michael was standing in the bathroom doorway.

"Where is what?"

"You were going to pick up the dry cleaning from downstairs."

"Oh shit, I'll go get it. They open at eight."

"That's okay." He closed the bathroom door.

She started moving, fast, jerky movements—made the bed, grabbed up clothes and put them in the laundry basket in the closet, then out to the kitchen, the colander full of compost, the baking dish crusted with tomato sauce, the wine key open with the cork still screwed onto the corkscrew. She stood there in a pink T-shirt and purple knee socks. Pale winter sun came in through the window without curtains. The window was clean. She loved clean windows. She took a deep breath, blew it out like it was a cigarette.

She turned the burner on under the tea water. She put on Concerto for Flute and Cello, left it playing softly, and went back into the bedroom and pulled on a pair of jeans. Michael came out of the bathroom smelling like shaving cream, and she was standing calmly at the dresser, brushing her hair. Calm. Her heart banging crazy.

"What can I do?"

"I don't know."

He pulled a T-shirt off the floor.

"How's your mom doing?"

"I don't know."

"How are you doing?"

"He was gray. His skin was gray."

The kettle in the kitchen screamed.

"I'm going to wait for Claire downstairs." He put on a sweater. It went on inside out. "I'll call you." And he was out the door.

Mr. Bryn's good, good heart.

HIS FATHER'S EYES WERE oddly bright, and dark. They glittered. There was a thin shine of sweat on his forehead. There was a smell, chemical and sweet at the same time. It was the smell that scared Michael most of all.

His father raised his hand a couple of inches off the sheet. Michael reached for it, but it dropped back down. There was a tube going in the back of it, taped there. The skin around the tape was stained dark yellow. It must have hurt. Michael touched the fingers. They were cold. They curled around his hand gently, and his father's face flickered into a smile. Something white crusted at the corners of his lips.

"Michael," he said. His voice seemed normal. A little low.

"Hey, Dad." Michael heard his own voice, sounding small and scared. He had to get a grip. He cleared his throat.

"How you feeling?" It sounded like he was bluffing.

The machine next to the bed beeped softly. Out in the hallway someone laughed quietly.

"Dad?"

His dad's eyes blinked. They looked straight up, only for a second, and then they closed.

"Dad," he whispered, his lips barely moving, his voice nothing, "Dad, what should I do?"

A deep wet cough shook his dad's chest slightly, and he said, "Are you thinking of marrying her?"

"Who? Pattianne?"

His father coughed the wet cough again and then nothing. His lips didn't move.

"Dad?" Michael said it so softly his father couldn't possibly have heard.

His father let out a breath. His body under the sheet deflated, but he just kept smiling, as if he simply didn't have the energy to stop smiling. Father McGivens appeared next to Michael. He laid his hand on Michael's shoulder.

"Mike," he said to Michael's father, and Michael was shocked at the volume of his voice, so ordinary and loud. "I'm going to take this boy of yours. Dory's turn."

His father actually laughed, a weak chuckle. The fingers on the sheet lifted and dropped. The heart monitor beep was even and steady.

They went out, and Michael's mother was waiting. She looked better than she had when he'd arrived. She'd washed her face and tied her hair back with a red scarf. She had on lipstick. Or maybe it was the red scarf. She hadn't been crying. Nothing to cry about, she'd said, when Claire had gotten teary. He was going to be okay. He was very uncomfortable right now, and he was going to feel a lot better soon.

"Congestive heart disease," she said.

She looked at a piece of paper. It was full of her neat notes in bright blue ink.

"There's no fluid in the lungs," she said. "They have to do liver tests to make sure there is no fluid built up there. And kidney tests."

He had always admired her perfect handwriting.

"There's no edema. Swelling. So far. His hands and feet are okay."

Her fingers had gripped the paper as if it would save them all.

Now he and Father McGivens stopped outside of his father's room. The wide-open area of the CCU nurses' station felt like the bridge of the starship *Enterprise*.

He said to Michael, "There's a prayer service this afternoon with the Family Life Leadership Committee. Your father is scheduled to read lay text."

They were stopped at the edge of the shiny gray floor, where it turned to blue tiles of a hallway. Michael felt himself pulled down the hall. He wanted to keep walking. He wondered if this was feng shui. He and Corrine had argued about feng shui. He said it was superstition. She said it was physics. He stepped onto the tiles, and Father's hand landed on his shoulder, very gently, and even so, Michael startled.

"Michael, are you all right? I know you haven't had any rest, but joining us would be good, for you and your father, and for the others too."

"Yes," he said. He had one foot on the blue tiles and one foot on the shiny floor, and that's when he realized he had on dark dress socks and neon-green Adidas. "I'm sorry, Father, what?"

"I can show you a text that will be appropriate," Father said. He fell into step next to Michael and led him down the hall. "But even if you can simply lead us in the opening prayer, I think it would be important."

"Of course," Michael said.

He didn't think she wanted to get married, but he couldn't say that to his dad. That would make her seem like the kind of girl who'd live with a guy she didn't want to marry. She wasn't that way. She was just dreamy. Out there. Librarians were always spacey in real life.

FATHER MCGIVENS HAD SAID, "We'll be gathering in the Marian Chapel."

Michael heard that, Marian Chapel, and he could feel his brain try to form a question. He tried to think what to ask. *Where is that? What is that?*

Father had said, "The closed door at the side of the altar. Go on back. You'll remember."

Michael didn't remember. There were a few rows of pews. Light-colored carpeting. The windows were clear leaded glass, and it was dark out. The candles on the small altar were lit. If Pattianne were here, she would count the rows of pews. He stood at the back and didn't know where to go. There were five rows. His father's friend Brad, from the office, came in, and stopped right next to him, Michael's hand out, shaking Brad's, before he even knew it. More men came in. More hands shaking his. His father's friends, asking how he was doing in low voices. They asked after his mother. Men who looked familiar even though he only knew a couple names—Jack who played golf, Pete who was a deacon. An older man who seemed a complete stranger shook his hand and placed a broad palm on his shoulder, and that touch stayed after the man went and sat in the second pew, next to Alex Gordon. Alex was his own age. They'd been altar boys together.

Michael felt drawn into their presence. They gradually filled the pews.

He was sweaty. He could smell his pits. He hadn't taken a shower today. He'd been up since midnight. He'd been up since yesterday morning. He hadn't taken a shower since he and Pattianne had made crazy love after their Valentine's Day dinner and all that chianti, and then his mother called. He'd rushed to the hospital.

Damn. He must smell like sex. Father McGivens was right there, and Michael took a step away. They were the same height, but Michael always felt small next to him. Father turned a bit. His eyes were blood-shot. He'd been there all night too. Michael felt again the rush of tears.

"Sorry," he whispered. "I'm kind of wiped out."

"Just the invocation of the Blessed Mother then, eh?" Father put a hand on his shoulder and steered him gently to the pulpit. It was wood, carved like it was lacy. He turned to the men. They all knelt. Father McGivens had gone back to the front pew, next to the guy who was the CYO coach. Basketball.

Michael said, "Thank you all for the kind words."

Then he said, "In the name of the father . . ." It felt good to pray loud. Deep quiet voices joined in around him. *Hail Mary, full of grace, the Lord is with thee. Blessed art thou among women, and blessed is the fruit of thy womb.* Then his favorite part in the middle of the prayer, where the cadence changed: *Holy Mary, mother of God, pray for us sinners, now and at the hour of our death,* and he felt his shoulders drop, he felt his spine straighten, he felt his feet on the carpet.

When he was finished, they all stood, and Father came up to him. Touched him on his elbow.

He said, "Thank you, Michael."

He heard himself say, "Thank you."

He said it to Father, and then he looked out to the group of men standing before him in the small chapel.

"Thank you so much, from all my family."

Father said, "And for the health and recovery of our brother Michael Bryn, oh Lord, we pray."

And all the voices: "Lord, hear our prayer."

Then Father said to him, "Okay, go get some rest. I'll see you back at the hospital."

He wanted to be part of the deep, praying voices. But he went back down the aisle, through the blur of faces, and out the door, closing it gently behind him. He stood there for a second. The voices from within responded again, "Lord, hear our prayer."

He started down a side aisle of the empty, darkened church. Votive candles were glittering in the red glass cups at the shrine of Saint Joseph, and he stopped there, staring at the little flames. He felt like he could hypnotize himself, but the only words in his head were *Holy Mary, mother of God, pray for us sinners, now and at the hour of our death.* He looked around, at the shadows in the back under the choir loft, at the dimmed lamps hanging over the center aisle. The prayer hummed in his head. Not words, just cadence. He pressed his palms into the small of his back and bent back, just a bit. His back cracked. It sounded loud. He was exhausted. He didn't know how he was going to drive home.

Home.

He went outside and called Pattianne. She answered on the first ring.

He said, "Can you come to Edison and get me?"

"I'm out the door right now."

• • •

RYE TOAST WITH PEANUT butter. She cut it into triangles, even using the cutting board, except he didn't see her, him staring out the window, his coffee in his hand, not drinking it. Snow fell. No wind. The radiator clanked, warm. The morning felt big and dark, and not just because it was gray and snowing. She ached for him. And he loved rye toast with peanut butter. She took it to him.

"My dad asked me if we were thinking of getting married."

It occurred to her to drop the plate. Maybe it would smash, and be funny.

But this wasn't funny. She felt her life rushing at her.

Besides, she liked that plate. It was purple.

She said, "Are we?"

He set his cup down and pulled her to him, her face to his chest where the fuzz of his sweater tickled her nose and smelled like soap. She didn't know what to do with the plate of peanut butter toast.

He said, "Yeah, I guess we are."

He kissed the top of her head.

He said, "Is that for me?"

SHE CALLED JEN FIRST.

Jen said, "You're getting married because his dad's in the hospital?"

She said, "No. We're waiting until he gets out."

"Well, why?"

"So he can come to the wedding."

"No, that's not what I mean."

"It'll just be a small wedding. Like in the priest's office, or whatever they call it. Behind the altar."

"Rectory. And that's the weirdest thing you've ever done."

"Really?"

"Well, it's right up there, you have to admit."

FATHER MCGIVENS WANTED TO meet with just her. "Just a little chat, get to know each other" was how Michael put it.

"Is he going to try to get me to rejoin the church?"

"It's okay," Michael had said. "You're a baptized Catholic."

It was just the two of them, Father McGivens and Pattianne. He sat behind his desk, a blotter, a brass paperweight, a cut-glass dish of silver-wrapped candies. She sat in the small chair with a pink velvet seat again and wished she hadn't. She didn't feel like she was going to be able to bluff her way through this, and she felt like she had to. He offered her the dish of candies. She took one. Silver foil with familiar blue stars.

"Thank you," she said. "I don't want to rejoin the church."

He eased back in his desk chair. "Well, that's a place to start," he said, a smile playing across his face, and she remembered liking him on that first visit. "What made you decide that?"

"Um." When they were kids, they weren't even allowed to say *um*, her father making them say "Um, sir" to get them to not say it. "Because I don't believe." Sir.

He said, "You don't believe in what?"

She couldn't really sit all the way on the chair. She wanted to say I don't believe in you, but there seemed like more important things not to believe in. "In all the stories, I guess. The miracles."

"The Resurrection?"

"Yes," she said. "I mean no." It was white and sunny outside the window behind him.

He said, "The Transubstantiation?"

But thinking of red wine made her think not of the blood of Christ, but Michael's lips stained dark. "That too," she said. The sound he made when she sucked his bottom lip. "I mean, that either." Although she used to love that part of the Mass, when the music and chanting fell silent and the small bells rang. She wanted to say that, wanted to explain that she liked going to Mass, but that it was embarrassing, that she didn't want to act like a believer when she wasn't, that there didn't seem to be any place in the church for an outsider to stand. One side of her butt was getting numb on the little chair seat, and she crossed her arms over her chest and sat on the other side of her butt. The chocolate was getting soft in her hand.

He said, "And what do you think of Michael's belief?"

Michael disentangling. Michael kissing her the way he did, where he did. She could feel her cheeks flush.

"I think I can live with it."

Wrong answer. He sat up straight, and then he rose, took up all the bright window for a moment, and then he came around the front of his desk. She slipped the chocolate into her pocket.

She said, "That's not quite what I meant."

He walked around her chair, behind her for an instant, the starchy sound of his cassock, and then he sat in the chair next to her. Square shoulders, square jaw. Dark hair, with a hunk that fell over his square forehead.

He said, "Michael believes in all those stories."

"I know." But she didn't know, didn't know how anybody could really believe, Jesus as magician, playing to the crowd at the wedding feast, feeding thousands with a loaf of bread and a fish. Okay, several loaves and maybe a couple fishes. God in heaven deciding thumbs-up or thumbs-down according to whether or not she went to Mass on Holy Days of Obligation. And Mary. She didn't even want to start on Mary.

"The church is of course much more open to mixed marriage than it once was," he said. "And I'm sure you would do what you can to support Michael in his belief." He was taking a different tack now, his voice shifted to a lighter tone, reasonable. "But what you need to ask yourself is why you have decided to marry into the church. Not why you want to marry Michael, but why you want to marry into the Catholic church. To raise your children in the Church."

He shifted his chair and looked at her the way Starla used to. She'd sit right in front of you if you were eating toast and make you look at her. He had pale blue eyes, nice eye wrinkles.

"Besides all the stories," he said, a smile in his voice. "Which really are the best stories, you must admit."

There had been Mr. Bryn's warm arm around her shoulders that first day in this place, the promise of a purple scarf. Now she stared out the window, sunlight on snow, the black twisted limbs of a bare elm tree.

"The church is her people," he said. Still the smile in the voice. "The Body of Christ means all of us. I suppose I want to ask you what it means for you to join us, in marriage?"

She hated it when people said 'her' when they meant a country, or a boat. Or a church.

"I don't," she said. "Want to join. The church."

He said, "It's much harder to believe than to not believe."

As if it were simply a decision to believe. There was the galaxy in its spiral, and other galaxies, in other spirals, and a universe, and beyond that another. Beyond that there was another, and maybe a certain number more, but there was an end to universes, and beyond that was something. Maybe a god.

"And children?"

She closed her eyes, and the bare elm branches were there in bright red behind her eyelids.

"Of course we've talked about children."

Stephen and Luke and all those cousins, Claire studying child psych, Michael teaching special ed or at-risk kids.

Father McGivens leaned forward in his chair. The elm branches faded across his face, the wrinkles around his eyes that looked tired, the wrinkles across his wide forehead that looked hopeful.

"You are a very honest young woman," he said. "Perhaps not with me, but I think you are honest with yourself. We'll talk again, all three of us."

His breath smelled like chocolates.

SHE CALLED JEN WHEN she got home.

"I met with the priest."

"You guys met with a priest?"

"Just me. Their family priest."

"Family priest? You mean, like, related?"

"It was a chat. Parish priest, I guess. He looks like the guy in that comic strip, what's it called? The one with that country guy, Little Abner?"

"It's called *Li'l Abner*."

"Well, it was okay. He had a dish of Schildermans chocolates on his desk."

"Kosher chocolates?"

"He gave me one but I couldn't eat it."

"I've never seen you resist a Schildermans chocolate."

"He kept talking. Like, about my belief. I told him I wasn't a believer."

"What kind was it?"

"It melted in my pocket." She hadn't remembered it until she was home. "He thinks I am a very honest young lady."

Jen snorted.

AT THE BEGINNING OF the small ceremony in the side chapel at Christ the King, as she and Michael stood side by side before the small altar, Michael's father stood and took both their hands. He wore a gray suit with a silvery stripe that seemed to shimmer. His fingers were cold.

He said, "There are so many days in the life of your child that are the most important day."

His skin was waxy and shiny. There were gray bruises under his eyes.

He said, "You and Michael are making us all very happy today."

His voice whispered. She leaned close.

He said, "Our love for our children is the closest we can ever come to understanding God's love for us."

There were tears in Michael's eyes, looking at his father, and she knew she had never looked into her own father's eyes like that. She waited crazy-long seconds for them to look at her, and they didn't, Mr. Bryn kissing finally both their cheeks lightly, letting go of their hands, sitting back down. Michael still didn't look at her, watching Father McGivens now, his eyes still bright and wet.

He'd gotten teary at the end of *Shane*, too, both times they watched it, right in a row. When he'd thanked Melissa after learning it was Melissa's idea for her to ask him out that first time. When an anonymous donor had pledged fifty thousand dollars during the Jerry Lewis Telethon.

They'd needed the bishop's permission, a signature on what Father McGivens had called a canonical form, along with Michael's promise that he wouldn't fall from his faith, her promise to support him in his faith, their promise to raise their children in the church.

Their children.

Her parents were a blur at the edge of her vision. Actually, everything was. Except Jen, who wasn't smirking or even smiling. Her eyes were big and round. And when she hugged Pattianne, at the end, she whispered, "I didn't think you'd really do it."

• • •

AT THE BRUNCH, MRS. Bryn stayed near her, laughing. Mrs. Bryn, who said to call her Dory, and who had sipped just enough champagne to laugh kind of loud, and Pattianne had sipped just enough to feel happy and stupid. The lovely brunch with quiche, and croissants, a pot of brilliant raspberry jam, silver winter sunlight coming through the sheer drapery of the dining room onto them all, Pattianne's parents and Jen and Nana Farley. Father McGivens, and Michael's aunt Alice, and Claire. There was a small cluster of guys, Michael's friends, hanging out in the kitchen. Mr. Bryn sat on the couch, very still. He had changed from his shoes into brown leather slippers.

Now Mrs. Bryn—Dory—put one hand on each of Pattianne's shoulders and turned her around so she faced the arched opening that led upstairs.

She said, "Through the doorway on the left," leading her up the stairs. "And straight on till morning."

Their bedroom was as big as Pattianne's whole apartment, their bed alone the size of her kitchen. Mrs. Bryn sat down on a folded quilt draped across the foot of the bed, stripes of blue and lavender satin, and patted the spot next to her. Peacock feathers in a tall vase between the windows. A vase so big it was probably called something else. Up close Mrs. Bryn smelled like lily of the valley, her pale blue velvet dress matching the satin quilt, and she took Pattianne's hand in her hand and turned it palm up, open, flat. She set the ring there. Lily of the valley. Blue velvet. Platinum and sapphires.

"It was Michael's grandmother's," she said. "His father's mother." She wore clear nail polish. "I wore it for years." She touched the ring. "She gave it to me herself." The setting was filigree around the round sapphires. "Put it on." She crossed her legs, a sound that on some women said pantyhose and on some women said silk stockings.

"She gave it to me when we were married," she said. "And she told me, this is for the bride of your firstborn son." Champagne on her breath.

Pattianne's fingernails were clipped as short as they could be, a hangnail on the middle finger, mustard on one knuckle, her thin gold wedding band. She slipped the ring onto her left hand, where it was too big, and she held her hand out, the sapphires flashing like they were sending secret messages, out across the galaxies in their spirals.

Mrs. Bryn said, "This is for the bride of your firstborn son."

And maybe Pattianne could be someone's mother, with a son or a daughter who would maybe grow old enough to marry and receive such a ring. They went back downstairs, and there was Michael, standing by the window, watching her, nodding at her. She kept her hand tucked in the folds of her pale green, almost-white dress. Her ears were ringing, and there were sharp flashes of sunlight on the shining wood of the dining room table, the beveled glass of the hanging lamp, the small silver spoon in the pot of raspberry jam. Her head pounded gently.

II. ST. CLOUD

4: MY ANGEL

HIS DAD HAD SAID, "Young couples need to get away on their own for a start." His face was still puffy. He was sometimes out of breath. It was the end of summer and he hadn't gone back to work.

"He's kept up his volunteer work though," Michael's mom told him. "And he gets out. He's improving."

Father McGivens said, "Go. I'll stay in close touch."

It felt just plain wrong.

Claire had said, "It's only a three-hour flight if you need to get back quick." That was almost enough to make him turn down the St. Cloud School for Boys. He could keep his part-time job in Patterson and just keep picking up substitute-teaching shifts.

But Pattianne had been all for it. "Minnesota? That's amazing—that's like another country. They even talk different there. And we can have a house. Even a yard."

SECONDHAND SHOPS WERE A good chance for a break, to stretch his legs, change drivers. All the way across Pennsylvania, Ohio, Indiana, Illinois, Wisconsin, and up into Minnesota.

Pattianne would say, "I'm going to hunt us up some coffee. Meet you back at the car."

"Roger that," he'd say.

They were the away team. She'd bring back weak coffee in paper cups.

"Look," he might say. A piece of cranberry-colored depression glass. A Stangl pottery plate with a quail on it. A plate with a blurry blue design. There was something about mismatched dishes.

He'd set his coffee in the cupholder between the seats and set his cell phone right next to it. Then they'd hit the road again.

He liked secondhand shops. There had been a lot of them around her neighborhood in Montclair. The first time he ever went into one was on a rainy morning, right after they were married.

He'd hated leaving her in the mornings, in her little apartment over the dry cleaner's. It was almost as if it all hadn't really happened, the wedding. They'd talked about getting another apartment, but there had been his dad in the hospital, and then at home getting better. Spring had turned into summer. The St. Cloud job was still only a possibility then.

He went into the secondhand shop because of a red-and-orange-plaid golf bag. He saw it through the window. His friend Rory was the world's worst golfer, and his birthday was coming up. The place didn't have an Open sign, but he could see a guy sitting in there. The door wasn't locked.

It smelled like a basement. There was a rack of dresses and suit jackets, and a milk crate full of albums, and a set of TV trays with kittens on them, and a shelf of mugs. The tiny turquoise vase sat on top of a stack of *Encyclopaedia Britannica*, between the golf bag and a wedding dress. He didn't know why he'd picked it up.

The golf bag was stained yellow around the bottom with what looked like dog pee. The thin, white netting of the wedding dress hung down to the painted cement floor. The bottom of it was tangled up on a pink tricycle. There was a small football helmet underneath it. He wondered if the little girl had gone from the trike to a two-wheeler. If the little boy had ever caught a long pass. He took the vase to the counter. An old guy sat there in a red padded kitchen chair.

Michael wondered what had happened to the bride.

The old guy took the vase. He turned it over in his thick fingers. Michael wanted it back.

"McCoy," the guy said. "Real McCoy. Ha, ha!" He pointed to the name there. "Chip in the rim, damn shame. Dollar."

Michael had learned about McCoy, and Roseville, and Sebring, the names on the bottom, the light colors, like they'd faded. The candy-colored Fiestaware.

Secondhand shops made him feel sad, though. He'd wander, looking over things that seemed to be about someone else's leftover life. He didn't know why he would want to feel sad on purpose.

Late at night they pulled into a Comfortel outside of Fort Wayne. He plugged in his charger first thing, right next to the bed. He'd wake up in the dark and check it to make sure it was charging.

THE SCHOOL OFFERED FACULTY housing, 1325 South Fifth, on a dead-end street that might have been called a cul-de-sac in a different kind of neighborhood that had been built in a different decade, maybe the forties. Pattianne thought it looked cottage-like. There were wide yards and trees, chokecherries and sugar maples, old and overgrown, which she had identified from *Flora and Fauna of the Upper Midwest*. The backyards wandered into each other, changing shape and size at dusk, no fences, no border beds, just the lights of other houses shining through the trees, through the thickets of sumac and berry vines and drying bracken fern. Lightning bugs, and the winding wheeze of cicadas. Small, heavy things dropped from the trees in the dark, and there were sounds that only come into a house in the summer. Because the windows are all open, because it is too hot to do anything except notice every little thing, how those sounds become summer sounds—a car driving slowly along the gravel at night, a kid yelling on the next street, a screen door banging shut.

After the sun went down, the air grew closer and hotter. Corn sweat. The crops in the miles around the town released their moisture as the earth cooled at night, and just when it seemed like the day's heat was gone, the very air became a hot, wet blanket. Heat like that made her think she might panic. It made her wonder what was she going to do, like there was anything she could do about it, that heat, on the nights before school started, when Michael was out being the new English faculty member, the new baseball coach, at the St. Cloud School for Boys, which was not named after St. Cloud, and was not even actually in St. Cloud, Minnesota. It was in St. Joseph, which was part of St. Cloud, and Cloud was just French for Claude. It was a school for boys with behavioral problems.

She didn't mind the empty evenings with nothing to do except take long, cool baths with Avon Skin-So-Soft bath beads. Miss Mimi wrote that they also keep mosquitoes away. She'd sent a basket full of kitchen and bath stuff, bath beads and bath powder. Cocktail napkins with scenes from famous Impressionist paintings. A scented candle. And *Flora and Fauna of the Upper Midwest*.

Pattianne sat in the cool bath water and looked at the colored pictures. Chokecherry. Sugar maple. Sumac. Bracken fern. When it got too dark to see by the light of the candle, she got out and put on Michael's high-school basketball jersey. Number 12. It hung long over her thighs, and the thin-washed nylon barely touched her wet skin.

She went through the house in the dark, the narrow hallway, the paneled door of the linen closet, to the kitchen, a room like an after-thought, with a slanting ceiling and a row of windows. The linoleum was cool and gritty. She got ice cubes from the freezer without looking inside, trying not to let any of the light from the refrigerator get on her. Heat making her crazy. The sound of ice cubes in the glass, the sound of vodka splashing. It was all part of the coldness of ice cubes, all part of the craziness of that heat.

They drank a lot of screwdrivers. Jen told her that all the orange juice potassium in screwdrivers would help them adjust to the humidity.

The sky over the black shapes of the trees was dark pink, and she stood watching it through the kitchen door. A moth banged softly against the screen. Sweat gathered on the outside of the glass in her hand, and she leaned against the doorframe, the smells of dusty screen and cooling woods and Skin-So-Soft. She touched the icy glass to one breast and then the other, running it across her nipples, under the basketball jersey on the cool damp skin of her stomach. And then, "Excuse me, Mrs. Bryn?" and there was Frankie, only she didn't know it was Frankie, hadn't even met Frankie yet, didn't even think that there might be someone out there, on the overgrown walkway outside the kitchen door. A weird squawk came out of her, and the glass smashed on the floor. "Shit," he said out there in the dark. "I'm sorry."

She backed away from the door, glass on the floor, and a guy out there in a white T-shirt.

"Who are you? Never mind, what do you want? Never mind, who are you?"

He said, "It's okay," and he stepped back away from the door.

It was just some kid. Her nerves jingled in her elbows, her knees. Her nipples.

He said, "I'm Frankie, from the school."

"So who the hell is Frankie from the school?"

Frankie-from-the-school stayed down on the walkway out there, a skinny white T-shirt in the dark.

"Sorry," he said. "I'm pretty late. I'm just dropping off the lawn mower and the tree saw."

"What lawn mower?" She slapped around on the wall for the light switch. "What tree saw?"

"I do the yards, but tomorrow I won't have the truck."

"What truck?" A piece of glass sliced open her foot. "Shit." It didn't hurt, but there was that sick slithering in her stomach. "Goddamn it." There was blood, red even in the dark of the kitchen, and she hopped to the counter, and black red drops dripped after her.

"What happened? Oh man, you stepped on that glass." And Frankie the-guy-from-the-school opened the door, and he was in the kitchen, in work boots with glass crunching under them.

He said, "Where's the light?"

Her head going no, no, no, and she got a dishtowel and held it to her foot.

"No, no," she said. "It's okay, come back tomorrow and Michael will be here."

Frankie grabbed the string hanging from the fluorescent ceiling light and gave it a tug.

"Please, you can go," she said. "Michael will be home any minute." Trying to cover up in the sudden blue-white light.

He said, "I'll clean the glass up."

"No, that's okay."

She tried to look at the cut, and the blood welled up, and her stomach slithered, and the strap of Michael's basketball jersey slipped down off her shoulder. She stood there saying no, no, no, that's okay, and the shirt slid down, too, and she stood there, one breast bare.

She yanked the strap up.

"Oopsie," he said. "Go twelve."

That's how she met Frankie.

CLASSES STARTED JUST AFTER Labor Day, still hot, still summer, and Michael was up and out early, running four miles, back in the shower, half-dressed by six o'clock, aiming for the seven o'clock church service that started off the school days. He came into the bedroom, unbuttoned khaki pants hanging on his narrow hips, his hair wet. Her husband.

He said, "Get up, wench," and he stood in front of the mirror and ran his fingers through his hair. "Fix me some breakfast. I'm off to the world of the employed."

He might break into "Roll on, Columbia" any moment. She pulled the sheet over her head.

Actually, this sounded more like he was leading up to his Paul-Bunyan-in-the-north-woods schtick. She pulled the pillow under the sheet with her and said, "Just push the button on the coffee pot, it's all loaded up, ready to go."

"Hey," he said. "I'll make French toast."

He left the room, through the hall, and a pan landed on top of the stove.

The bedroom window faced north, into the backyard, a tangle of hazelnut tree and vines keeping the window dark and dirty. The walls were white, all the walls, in the whole house. She thought about painting the bedroom dark green and pulled her bathrobe out of the blankets on the floor.

The living room was full of sunlight. She stayed out of there in the mornings. The kitchen was still in shadow. Michael broke eggs into a bowl at the counter, his back to her.

He said, "Are you going to check out that Cathedral High job today?"

The coffee dripped in the glass pot.

"This afternoon," she said.

She sat down and watched it, drip by drip.

Michael set a glass of tomato juice in front of her and said, "We're out of orange juice." He laid a piece of toast into the bowl of egg. He always toasted the bread for French toast. He claimed it was the way to make perfect French toast.

"A high-school library job would be great," he said. "And I talked to the woman who has the scoop, she knows you're applying. And there's John the Twenty-Third Middle School kind of attached."

The wings of his shoulder blades made her heart hurt.

"Yeah."

"Yeah, what?"

There were dimples down low on either side of his backbone, wide, downy dimples.

"Yeah," she said. "I know we're out of orange juice."

She got up and stood behind him, pressed up against his smooth back, laid her hands on his shoulders. He flipped the French toast with a flourish of the spatula.

"Perfect." He didn't actually flip the spatula itself this time. "Always toast the bread first, and you get perfect French toast every time."

Every time, her angel-winged boy. Husband.

He set a plate of French toast in front of her and said, "You know Simon—he's a counselor at school? Well, his wife has a little bookstore here. He said she might be needing someone part-time, but I don't know why you'd want to work part-time in a bookstore when you could get a great gig like head librarian in a high school. I mean, he said he'd mention it to his wife—her name's Elizabeth—and I didn't want to say don't bother."

She slid the plate across the table to him.

"I'll just have some coffee for now."

After he left, she sat there. The sun from the living room edged into the kitchen, the morning slipping away, far-off sounds outside somewhere, and the coffee got cold. When she was ten years old, she went to six-thirty Mass every morning all through Lent, walking through the dark to Saint Thomas Aquinas. It was the nuns' Mass. Nuns in short black veils filed in and sat in the front row. There was no sermon, no music, just the scuffling of feet, the creaking of the kneelers, the priest's low chanting. There were small, empty sounds in the big, dark church. Closer to Easter, as the sun came up earlier, the stained-glass windows lit up during Mass.

There were moments here, now, when the air held everything still. They seemed to be about this faraway place, those moments. St. Cloud, a lazy little street. She felt her life all around her. Mostly they were mornings.

The truck door slammed out front, and Frankie called out, "Hello, House," the way he did at all the faculty houses, although apparently only during the daytime. His face showed up at the kitchen screen door, and she pulled the bathrobe close and stayed sitting.

"Hello, Frankie."

He said, "I smell coffee."

It was a short, cotton robe, not very sexy, or revealing.

She said, "I'll bring you out some."

"I'm working on that mess of Virginia creeper in the back."

She said, "I'll make another pot." He disappeared, and in another second, there was the clanking and squeaking of the truck's tailgate. She started another pot of coffee and went and got her cutoffs and T-shirt from the bedroom floor, and thought about putting up a curtain on the bedroom window, and went in the bathroom to get dressed. She pulled her hair back in an elastic. When she went outside with the coffee, he was standing by the house around back. There was an old red wheelbarrow, a rake, clippers, gloves. Bright orange flowers grew along the back of the house. He pulled on the gloves and said, "Touch me not."

She stopped. She held out the coffee.

"Thanks," and he took the mug in his gloved hands. At the end of his thin arms like that, they looked like Mickey Mouse's hands. He reached out and ran a fat, gloved finger along the orange flowers, and there was a soft, popping noise, and tiny black seeds sprayed out. "Jewelweed," he said. "We used to call them touch-me-nots."

"Oh."

He gulped down some coffee and set the cup down in his wheelbarrow. "It grows everywhere," he said. Inside the red wheelbarrow were the words *So Much*, painted in neat black letters. He took one of the gloves off again, pulling it with his teeth, and he took a spiral notebook out of his back pocket. He had a crooked front tooth. "Listen to this," he said, with the glove hanging in his mouth. He took the glove out of his mouth. "The seeds shoot up to eight feet," he read. "They grow everywhere from the southeast up into Canada. At eight feet at a time, it would take a plant 650 years to go one mile."

He stopped and looked at her. "Cool, huh?"

He put the notebook back in his pocket and the glove back on his hand and said, "Okay now." And he reached into the vines all tangled around the hazelnut tree and started yanking. "I'm supposed to take this hazelnut out," he said. "Too close to the house."

"How come there are no nuts?"

"Birds," he said. "And squirrels. I'll clear it all out and you'll get some light into the back bedroom."

Sunlight was slanting around the back corner of the house now, dust sparkling the air.

She said, "I like it dark in there."

"Red squirrels," he said. "And thirteen-stripe squirrels."

The sparkling dust was settling in his coffee. He backed away, pulling on the long vines, scattering red and brown leaves, and she got out of the way. His face was freckled and tanned. His arms were freckled and tanned. A bright red leaf was caught in the top of his hair. Cute. Maybe twenty-one, twenty-two. Maybe more. How you couldn't tell with some guys.

"Well," she said. "I'll be inside if you need anything."

"Red foxes, too," he said. "Course you don't see them too much. They stay away from the houses usually, except this time of year. They like hazelnuts. They steal from the squirrel stashes." He stopped and frowned at the Virginia creeper, or maybe he was frowning at the hazelnut branches. He had thick reddish eyebrows, like his hair. He looked at her, frowning.

"Thirteen-stripe?" he said. "Thirteen-line?"

He went back to yanking the Virginia creeper. He was out there all morning, and she was trapped out of the bedroom, him working right there at the window. She did the crossword at the kitchen table, and after a while she went into the living room, sunlight reaching into every corner now. Bare walls and bare wood floors, bookcase, chair, couch. For weeks, there had been just the blue glass bowl on the shelf of the bookcase, a fragile, handmade, round bowl that she was afraid to touch, a wedding gift. Then she had put her terra-cotta rabbit up there, too, and the McCoy vase, and Michael put a clay duck up there too.

He said, "They make them out of plastic now."

She said, "Old." It had faded painted eyes.

"Antique," he said. "When things cost that much, they aren't old, they're antique. We needed to rescue it." He rescued things. Like the bike, a silver Raleigh with no brakes.

Her carved wooden elephant went up there next, with the rabbit and the duck, all facing the same direction, a small wildlife parade. And then Grandma Anthony, a hand-tinted studio photograph, her cheeks young and faintly pink. She was posed leaning to the side and looking away a little bit, wearing pearls, gazing off in the direction of the parade. Since then Pattianne hadn't set out much else, just the green deer lamp that Michael had rescued from a yard sale. She hadn't really unpacked it, just moved it from the bedroom. The eyes caught the light at night and kind of gave her the creeps.

She wandered into the front bedroom, Michael's office. Boxes were stacked against the wall, all the stuff he'd had FedExed.

"Not a verb," she'd said. Michael loved verbed nouns. He Xeroxed things instead of copying them, and he Windexed the windows of the O-Bug.

Their wedding picture was in the top of the first box, a frame of openwork silver, Michael in a dark suit, white shirt, white tie standing above her, her sitting in a wing chair, the skirt of her dress sweeping down to her ankles, those strappy little shoes. The black-and-white photograph made her silvery-green wedding dress look white, bias-cut damask, short cap sleeves, a low, scooped neckline, neat and elegant, kind of Jackie O. She went in the kitchen to look for the hammer, looked in the pantry, looked out on the back step. Then she went in the bedroom and there it was, the hammer, on the dresser. Frankie banged on the window and yelled in, "Hey, got any more coffee?"

"It's cold."

In a moment, he was at the kitchen door. She took the hammer and went out there, the picture under one arm.

"Come on in. I'll heat it up on the stove."

He came in. "That's okay, I like it cold."

She waved the hammer at the pot. "Help yourself."

He tilted his head sideways, looking at the picture. "That you guys?"

"Yeah. Wedding picture."

"Fancy," he said. "You hanging it up?"

"Yeah," she said. "But I haven't decided where."

He came and stood next to her, looked at her, looked at the picture, looked at her.

He said, "You look the same."

"Well, it was only last winter."

"Big fancy wedding?"

"Nope. Small wedding."

"Did you, like, walk down the aisle and all that?"

"Nope."

Frankie went back out back, yanking on the mess of vines around the hazelnut tree, and she went back to pulling more crumpled pieces of newspaper from boxes in Michael's office. The small black speakers of the stereo were in a box by themselves, the CD player in a box marked *CD player* under the desk. She had thought about setting it up, but she didn't. There was the quiet of this place. Wind in trees. Birds far off. She hadn't come across her stash of Mozart yet. Maybe then she would set up the stereo.

She found the tiny painting tied with string in a bow, the tissue paper folded in careful corners around it. Smaller than the wedding picture. She got the hammer and the wedding picture from the kitchen counter and took everything into the bedroom. Frankie was spraying the bedroom window now, sheets of water falling without any sound down the windowpane. She hung them, the painting above, the wedding picture below, on the narrow space of wall between the dresser and the door. Frankie wiped the glass with a white cloth, the window squeaking and coming clean, and then he looked in.

He yelled, "Those look nice, those pictures like that."

She stood back and looked, and they did look nice, and what else she saw was the dark wooden crucifix, hung above the bedroom door, and all she thought was how that was why the hammer had been in the bedroom in the first place. She didn't like that crucifix being there, though.

HOT DOGS MAYBE, OR sour milk, some old cafeteria food smell, hit her in the face first thing. She went to the main office as directed by the signs with big red letters on every one of the four main doors—"Visitors Must Report to Main Office"—and stood at a long counter while people behind the counter talked on the phone, to each other. One guy was even talking to himself, but then she noticed his headset.

Finally, she said, "Hello?"

They all jumped to attention and stared, and then a gray-haired woman with long square-cut bangs bounced up to the counter.

"Hi there, how can we help you?"

"I'm supposed to meet with the librarian?"

It was like a reset button. They all turned to each other and started chattering away again, except the one at the counter, who said, "Welcome!" Her voice had jumped several octaves. "I'll take you right down there, it's down the hall. What's your name?" She held out a clipboard. The top page said *Visitors Please Sign In,* and there was a pen attached on a wire.

By the time Pattianne heard the question, she had already taken the clipboard and begun the awkward writing of her name, twisting the wire out of the way, and she said, "Anthony. Pattianne Anthony. Bryn." She scribbled out Anthony and wrote Bryn. She handed the clipboard back to Rosemary. "It's Bryn."

The woman looked at the clipboard and set it on the counter, pushed her bangs out of her eyes, and headed for the door. "Right this way, you just follow me."

They walked fast down a wide hall with shining linoleum tiles of blue and green, past classroom doors and display cases. One was full of bowling trophies.

The library was air-conditioned, but there didn't seem to be any books. There were rows of computers with kids piled in front of most of them and piles of backpacks on the floor around each kid. Pattianne turned around and looked at the door behind her as it clicked shut. There was a crucifix above it. Kind of a big one, in color, the blood red, Jesus's eyes blue.

"Here you go." The woman touched her elbow and steered her to a desk under a huge framed photograph of Pope Benedict. The man who sat there had a Roman collar and a black shirt and a jean jacket. A woman came out and sat at the desk, and Pattianne realized the woman was no longer at her elbow. Was in fact, gone. The priest at the desk didn't look up. Instead, he picked up the phone there and started punching in numbers. When he finally noticed her standing there not five feet away, he hung up, hadn't even started talking, and got to his feet.

"I'm sorry, did you need something from me?"

"I don't think so."

He sat back down. "Oh. Well, can I help you?"

"I guess I need to see the librarian?"

He sat back, smiled all big and easy. "Ah," he said. "The library position." He was pretty young, and when he crossed one leg over the other, she saw jeans, and big red-and-silver Nikes.

Then he said, "She isn't here. Why don't you just wander around and I'll send her over when she gets here."

Pattianne looked around and was going to ask when he thought the librarian might arrive, but he was back on the phone. So she moved off a little way, and there, around a corner, were shelves of books. That was a relief. She headed over that way. The first bookcase seemed to be a display of books on sea mammals. Then came a shelf of books about space. Below that was ocean, then desert on the bottom. Each shelf had books spine-out about halfway along and then the rest of the shelf was empty.

A bell rang, and her heart felt like it dropped, an old panic, late for class. It was 10:05. The kids at the computers just ignored the bell, but a new bunch of kids started banging through the door. They swarmed in and moved past her, looking at her as if she wasn't there at all.

She left. Out the door, down the hallway, out the big main doors and into the O-bug, almost without even taking a breath. She drove home and sat in the car outside their house, counting her breaths. When she got to one hundred, she got out and walked.

JOSH AND BRUCE SAT next to each other in the back. So far, two weeks into class, Michael still wasn't sure if they should stay that way. Bruce had huge, watery blue eyes. Michael was pretty sure he could sleep with them wide open. He'd been busted twice with marijuana, ending up here. Josh had a habit of getting on buses and ending up in other states. They didn't participate in class. They didn't even move, really. No squirming or dropping pencils, no wide, insolent, in-your-face yawns. Bruce blinked sometimes. One thing Michael knew about seventh graders was that he had to pick his battles. He was waiting to see if this was a battle. No pre-emptive strikes. You couldn't win with seventh graders that way. You had to resist them. He'd already learned not to stand by the windows, which was an invitation to the boys to stare outside. Now he stood near the door, across from the windows. He stood straight, his feet planted slightly apart. He didn't lean or put his hands in his pockets. He would let his face be warm, his voice be friendly, but his stance was firm and authoritative. His heels were stinging in his new brown leather shoes. He'd had plantar fasciitis a couple years ago, miserable. He'd had to have injections of cortisone. Now he hoped it was just these shoes.

He stood there in his teacher clothes. New khakis with a sharp crease. A light blue shirt with dry-cleaner folds. A tie, which he loved, and which felt weird. He kept catching sight of it there on his shirtfront. It was some other guy's chest. His dad's.

Theodore, who had decent handwriting, was at the whiteboard. Theodore drew comics everywhere, usually faces with stupid expressions, often closely resembling the other boys, which might have been why no one gave him a hard time about being named Theodore. Bathroom walls, desktops. He even drew on his arms, usually with black Sharpies. He had just last week discovered fine-point Sharpies and had tried to draw on his roommate's capped front tooth.

Today's lesson was about clichés. The boys were so unaware of their own language that they usually didn't realize they were repeating things they'd heard on TV, or in a video. And they were totally mediated, inundated with language. Using clichés made them feel clever. He knew. *Sorry, boys,* he wanted to say. He knew how nice it was to feel clever at the age of thirteen.

He started it himself, saying, "Don't have a cow." Theodore wrote it on the board. A few boys snickered. Josh blinked. Michael said, "May the Force be with you." Theodore wrote. One of the three boys named Aaron in the front row said, "Wackity wack," and the snickers rolled around the room again. Bruce was definitely awake.

"Sorry," Michael said, before Theodore could start writing. "No *South Park.*"

He made a list of clichés on the whiteboard. *Raining cats and dogs. Make my day. Day of rest. Sour grapes.* Then he asked them to write the same things in their own words. At this point Teddy Keller, who was overweight and red-faced and sat in the front row and so far had raised his hand to answer every question, jumped up, knocking his chair over behind him, and he yelled, "You want us to make up our own clichés?" The whole class broke into laughter. The sullenness vanished. Michael was charmed. Teddy Keller had been arrested for shoplifting from a liquor store. He had scored off the chart on every IQ test he'd ever taken.

The assignment was to pair off and write a dialogue using as many clichés as possible. The room got noisy. In the back row, Josh and Bruce hunched over a single piece of blank notebook paper. He didn't expect them to turn in anything.

But as the class filed out of the room at the end of the period, depositing papers into the wire basket on the corner of his desk, Josh did the same. The paper was wrinkled, and full of pen holes. The writing was scrawled. There were two lines.

I have a bone to pick with you.

You piece of shit.

Michael loved seventh graders.

At lunch in the faculty dining room, he sat across from Rick Smith. Reverend Rick, the school chaplain. Rick was warm and talkative, but not chatty. He usually seemed to talk about something important. Now, over a tray of shepherd's pie and green beans, Michael pulled the wrinkled piece of notebook paper out of his folder. He smoothed it on the Formica tabletop. His eyes filled with tears and his throat choked up. He was horrified and started to get up, fake a quick trip to the coffee urn, or grab some more paper napkins. Rick reached out and put a hand on his arm. Michael sat back down. He took a breath. Rick took his hand away. Rick looked at the paper. "All that anger."

His first thought was that he wasn't angry. But Rick was talking about the boys, of course.

Rick slid the paper back to Michael and said, "They get to me, too," and then, his voice quieter, "Cup of coffee after classes today?"

There was a deep flush of embarrassment, and Michael said, "No." He groped about for why not. "Debate," he finally said. "I think I meet with the debate team, the debate wannabes," and Rick laughed and said, "That's a risk, arming them with the techniques of conversational logic."

The shepherd's pie was crusty and dry and the green beans swampish.

• • •

FROM FAR DOWN THE block, Pattianne saw the genie, reading a book on a cloud of turquoise smoke over his magic lamp, between the JCPenney's store and the Ace Hardware Store. The genie's turban was purple and covered with gold stars. The blue neon square around the sign lit up thinly in the hot sunlight. Lamplighter Books.

The smell of incense was the first thing she noticed when she opened the door. And bells. And dark, air-conditioned air that touched every part of her. A woman in long blue robes stood back by a desk.

Pattianne said, "I'm looking for Elizabeth?"

The woman said, "And you have found her," in a rough low voice that didn't sound like her. It sounded like the voice of a tall person. This person was short. She stepped toward the door, into the light. Shorter than Pattianne.

"I'm Pattianne. Pattianne Bryn." The name felt strange in her mouth. Not easy, like a lie. Just strange.

Elizabeth glittered, long earrings of rhinestones dangling from a halo of red hair, and she said, "That's what I thought." She stepped forward with her hand held out, a bracelet of silver appearing and disappearing in and out of the wings of her blue robe. Silver rings on every finger. Bare feet, bells at her feet, her saying, "Simon said you'd be by."

Her face was very small. Her hands were, too, and cool. Pattianne's hands were sweaty.

"Would you like some tea?" A round, gold symbol hung from her neck. "Jasmine?"

She had a million freckles.

"Sure," Pattianne said, and the small woman said, "Come on in, sit, wander," and went through a beaded curtain into a room in the back, small. The robes were really a long tunic kind of top and gauzy, wide-legged pants. Some people know just how they want to be when they're out in the world.

Pattianne never did, never was sure how she looked from one mirror to the next, always had to check, and was never sure what it meant, however it was she ever looked, which today was a blue skirt that went just below the knees, but bias cut, a little swish, and a white shirt and brown, flat, slip-on, slingback shoes, kind of cute, and no stockings. She thought she probably looked like a librarian from New Jersey.

Shelves of books lined one long wall, with small lavender cards labeling every shelf. Taoism, Buddhism, Hinduism. Astrology, Graphology, Numerology. Ufology. Future History. Rumi. In the empty spaces between the books there were incense burners, rune stones, rainbow-colored candles carved to show the inside of the rainbow. A round table was stacked with books, and so was a square table, and there was a small pile of books on a wing chair, with shiny striped upholstery in dark jewel colors, in front of a low table of small wax creatures arrayed on a silky magenta cloth. There were blue stars in the carpeting.

Elizabeth came back out through the beads. She held two white mugs, and she said, "It's all kind of in its own order."

She bent, set the mugs on the magenta-covered table.

"The prices are penciled in on the first white page of each book."

The gold symbol from her neck swung and circled, hanging over the table and the mugs of tea.

"Also whether it's new or used. We have both."

The silver bracelet catching light.

She said, "That's all you need to know to start."

She stood up and raised her hands, palms up, "That's all," and leaned back against the desk and said, "Please, have a seat."

"That's all?"

The waxy creatures on the magenta-covered table were candles in the shapes of Indian gods, or maybe goddesses. Pattianne picked up a book about dreams from the beautiful chair and sat down, set the book on the table. One of the small lavender cards said *Light of the World*. She picked up a candle.

"You get a ten-percent discount," Elizabeth said. "But you can just borrow anything you want to read."

The candle had a fierce face.

"Twenty hours a week," she said. "That's Kali."

Pattianne set Kali back down.

"Simon said you used to be a librarian?" She had put on wire-rimmed glasses that made her eyes look big.

"Yeah," Pattianne said. "But I always wanted to work in a bookstore," which had never occurred to her before but seemed like the truth.

"Great." The wire-rimmed glasses magnified the wrinkles around Elizabeth's eyes. When she sipped at her jasmine tea, the glasses steamed up a little bit. "Do you like working with people?"

Just like that, it turned into a job interview.

"Well, I never really have." Instead of saying no. "Worked with the public."

"I think . . ." Elizabeth stretched out her bare toes and looked at them. "In this kind of place," she said, wiggling her toes, "it's important to let people find their own way." Each toenail was painted with pale rosy polish.

"Customers are the best teachers," she said. When she wiggled her toes, the bells around her one ankle made a small jingle.

Twenty hours a week. Open boxes of books that were delivered. Ring up sales. The desk had an actual cash register, and a leather-covered appointment book for tarot readings by Elizabeth. "By appointment only," she said.

The lavender card on the table of candles was propped on a small copper-wire stand. The letters were black and Celticish, curves and serifs. *The Light of The World Candle Coalition, 624 Elm Street, St. Cloud, Minnesota, the Earth, the Universe.*

They'd left out the United States of America, which she could understand, and the Milky Way Galaxy, which she could not.

"I can start next week."

When she stepped back outside, there was the white cement sidewalk next to the red brick wall of the hardware store, the hardware store window with the sun full on it, slick yellow paint lining the curb, and air shimmering above the black asphalt of the street. Everything was dazzling and hot and dreamy. Michael working. Now she had a job. They could get up every day, have breakfast, go to work. The downtown streets ended after two blocks, and she was back under the trees, out of the sun. It wasn't any cooler. Houses sat back in green lawns, empty and still—no birds, no lawnmowers, no kids. Michael's family wanted them to come back for Thanksgiving, and she already didn't want to go. Maybe they could come here—she'd cook a turkey, Claire could sleep on the couch, they could go to Mass with Michael at Sacred Heart on the Sunday after Thanksgiving, and she would stay home and make cinnamon rolls for breakfast, and then she and Michael would drive them back to Minneapolis to the airport.

The thick air moved past her. Sweat dripped down her ribs.

The house was cool inside, and dark. She took off her clothes and put on Michael's basketball jersey, and sat down in the middle of the living room floor and wiggled her sweaty toes. She could paint her toenails. She could wear a bell. She could read all the books in the bookstore, and Elizabeth could tell her future with tarot cards. The air around her, the house around her, the town around her, all quiet and easy and in a good mood, like the earth had stopped turning for just a moment, and the Milky Way was saying, "Hey, what about me?"

At four o'clock, she thought of orange juice. She thought of dinner. She had to get up off the floor, move, put on clothes, go back outside, into the turning world. She went out the kitchen door, through the shade. The car was in the sun, though, heat waves coming up off the hood, and the car seat was so hot she couldn't sit. She slid newspapers under her butt. The steering wheel was too hot to touch. She drove with two fingers, three blocks, only one busy street, to the little market, and went in, to air-conditioning, and she just stood there for a few seconds, dazed. She got orange juice out of the freezer and even colder air clouded out, onto the hot skin of her face, her neck, her arms. She stood with the cans of orange juice and thought of potato salad, sliced salami. She picked up a beautiful, overripe tomato.

An enormously fat woman at the counter said, "Hot enough for ya?" and she said, "Yes," and worried that the heat was a lot worse for someone like a fat person.

Back in front of the house, three boys on bikes were skidding back and forth in the gravel, raising a cloud of dust and then skidding through it. She drove through the dust and got out, and then Michael rode up on his new-old bike. The boys circled and watched him lean his bike against the side of the house.

He said, "Hey, guys," and waved, and they waved back, and he said, "Hey, girl," and he kissed her. He was dripping sweat, and his face was evenly, brightly pink.

She took out a can of orange juice and handed it to him.

He touched it to his forehead, went, "Ah," and held it to the back of his neck, and said, "Sweet Jesus. So, how'd it go? At the library?"

"Well, it kind of didn't. She wasn't there. And I didn't stay."

"She wasn't there?"

"It was creepy in there," she said. "It stinks, for one thing. Junk food."

"Oh," was all he said.

"Well, I stopped by that bookstore. I think I like it. I think I'd rather work there."

"Are you going to make another appointment at the high school?"

"How about a nice screwdriver?"

He changed into cutoffs and a white T-shirt and bare feet, and came back into the kitchen where she sat at the table, chopping at the frozen clumps of orange juice in the pitcher.

"You'd really rather work in a bookstore?"

"It's a really cute little shop," she said. "And Simon's wife is very nice." She sounded like her mother.

He poured vodka over the ice cubes in the two glasses she had lined up, ready, waiting. She sipped at one of the vodkas.

"Man, I have a headache," he said. "They just yesterday finished varnishing the floors on our wing. It stinks, whatever they put on there. Here, let me." He took over chopping at the orange juice lumps and looked down into the pitcher.

She said, "I love that smell."

"The smell?"

"Varnish," she said, and added more vodka to the ice to bring the glasses up to matching levels. "You want a Tylenol?"

The only cool part of her was her fingertips touching the glass. She didn't want to move, except to unstick the back of her legs from the kitchen chair.

"No," he said. "That's okay." He didn't usually take Tylenol and stuff like that. "Here," he said. "This is mixed up enough," and he poured orange juice into the vodka. A frozen lump splashed onto the table. She picked it up and dropped it into her glass and sucked her fingers.

Michael sniffed at her. "Are you wearing perfume?"

The smell of incense was still in her hair.

"No." She picked up one glass. "Not really."

He picked up the other, and he sat down across from her. He touched his glass to his forehead, said, "They've had all summer to work on those floors," and drank his screwdriver halfway down.

"There's potato salad."

"Maybe later," he said.

"Cheese and crackers? Summer sausage?"

"That sounds good," he said. "Maybe after a while."

"Do you know what ufology is?"

"What what is?"

"Ufology."

"Ufology?"

"Never mind," she said. "Here," and added more orange juice to his screwdriver. "Potassium."

He added vodka. "Varnish," he said. "Potassium chaser."

After the orange juice was gone and the potato salad eaten, after the house and the outside had grown dark, had grown hotter, she went into the bedroom and hit the light switch, and there was that clean, shining black window. No more vines. No hazelnut tree. She switched the light off again, turned back through the door, and bumped into Michael on his way in.

She said, "I need to hang something over that window."

"Why?" He put his hands on her shoulders, pushing her back into the room.

"You can see right in. That kid Frankie cut back those vines and stuff back there."

Onto the bed.

He said, "Nobody's out there."

His hands were sticky with orange juice.

He said, "Just leave the light off."

His mouth was orange-juice sticky. His skin was shining white, sweat slick in the dark room's closed-in heat, his fingers vodka clumsy with her shirt, pulling it up. He didn't even have his cutoffs all the way off and he was hard, and he fucked her hard, drunk hard, and it seemed like fun, get drunk and fuck your husband, until he said, "Maybe we just made a baby."

And when his breath fell into sleep, she whispered, "Michael?"

Stars were thick in the sky out the window. The sheet was damp and twisted under her, and Michael's skin was too hot to be near, and she was fucked sober and wide awake.

She whispered, "Let's not talk about babies yet."

There was no moon that night.

MICHAEL WOKE UP EARLY, too early, even for him, and he went into the shower for a long time. She stayed in bed, the morning light finally coming into the room through the shiny, empty window. Mist from the shower started to gather on the glass, no more air in the room, and she got her feet on the floor and got the hammer from the dresser and tapped at the edges of the window frame, where it was painted shut with years of white paint.

Michael came in from the shower, a red towel wrapped around his waist, and he said, "Stop," kind of loud. He said, "Is there any Alka-Seltzer?" much more softly.

"There's no air in here," she said.

"Hangover," he said. "I have a hangover."

"I'll get you some Alka-Seltzer." She set the hammer on the window-sill. "It was probably the varnish."

The bathroom cabinet was a shoebox-size space behind the mirror, but on a shelf in the hall linen closet was the extra toilet paper and Epsom salts and Rid-X and Alka-Seltzer. A box of tampons. At the bottom of the box of tampons, beneath the neat rows of paper tubes, was her last flat, round, blue plastic dispenser of birth control pills. She used to keep them in her underwear drawer, until she found out that Michael liked to run his hand around in there, in the silk and nylon, when he was in a sexy mood, when the drawer was open.

She didn't know what he thought on those nights like last night when they didn't use a condom. That it was just not the right time, or maybe he was hoping. She took the Alka-Seltzer out and closed the linen closet door and went into the kitchen, no sun in there yet, and filled a glass with water and dropped in the tablet and watched it fizz.

When she went back in the bedroom, he was at the mirror, humming a tune, a pretty, old tune, and when she handed him the glass of Alka-Seltzer, he took the glass, and took her hand, and he stopped humming and kissed her wrist.

"My angel," he said.

He drank the Alka-Seltzer down, and she sat on the edge of the bed and watched his throat, his Adam's apple, his long, narrow waist. He handed her back the glass and picked up two ties.

"What do you think?" he said. "Blue stripes or blue diamonds?"

"Wear the Donald Duck tie."

"Too soon," he said. "I have to establish control. I wear that tie too soon, I won't get no respect."

She didn't like either one of those ties. "Blue diamonds."

He turned back to the mirror and smoothed his fingers through his hair. His back was long and tan and there was fine black hair down low, where his hips curved, where the red towel covered him. Water drops on his skin.

"Are you looking at my butt?"

He took the towel from his waist and wiggled his butt at her. Then he turned, and he smelled like soap and shaving cream, and he tasted like toothpaste, and it was a slow, easy kind of fucking, and he watched her face and said, "I love you, I love you, I love you," each time he slid deep into her, into where she could still feel him from last night, into where she was still wet from last night.

She pulled him down, onto her, held him deep so he couldn't move in or out, or look in her face, and then she could make him come, and then she could come when he came, because she could never do that looking into Michael's beautiful face, could never come when he came.

5: A GENEROUS SOUL

NEAT KHAKI SHORTS. NEAT black cotton slacks. A neat blue sleeveless dress. She took everything out of her closet and tried it all on. She looked like a middle-aged librarian from New Jersey. She finally left the neat blue dress on and went out the kitchen door.

The road was lined with triangle-shaped trees. When there was a gap in the trees, she crossed to the other side of the road to stay in the shade, zigzagging back and forth, aiming for shade, until she got to a row of storefronts and windows, the genie on his turquoise cloud still two blocks away. Her feet were sweaty and slick in her shoes, and the armhole of the neat blue dress rubbed her armpit. She pulled her hair up on top of her head and wished for an elastic.

When she pushed the door open, she wished for a sweater.

Elizabeth was jingling around at the desk, and she stood up straight, looking across the tables of books, pressed her hands together in front of herself, and made a very slight bow and said, "Hot as hell, huh?"

Today she was dressed all in pale green, loose pants gathered at her ankles, and a long, green top with draped folds, sleeves like wings. The round gold symbol slipped in and out of the folds.

Above the door was a mobile of cranes, moving like small, real birds in the draft. The ceiling over the door was painted light blue. To stand in that doorway and look in—to be allowed to be there, under the cranes, in the cool, scented air—was to pause. And Elizabeth paused too and waited for her to pass through the portal into her bookstore.

"Sit down here," she said.

Pattianne sat on the tall stool by the desk.

"I'm doing returns," she said. "These are books I've had here for a year, and I'm returning them to the publisher for credit." She held up a small book, about four inches square. A book on Jewish mysticism.

"Not a hot seller," she said. She held it in her palm. "Beautiful book, though. And only six dollars. I like these little ones. Pocket classics. It seems like someone should be willing to take a chance on it. It's so small."

Pattianne wanted it. It was so small.

"So," Elizabeth said. "Want to just get to know some stock? You can just wander around and look. Pick up books, look at them, read the covers. Touch them." She put the small book in a big box. "Do you want some tea, or some water?" She reached out and touched her cheek. "I can feel the heat coming off you," When she took her fingers away, the coolness stayed, for a moment.

"Well," Pattianne said, and got down off the stool.

Elizabeth picked up another tiny book, *The Meditations of Marcus Aurelius*, and put it in the box. There was a whole stack of tiny books—a short, narrow stack of many tiny books.

"Are they all going back?"

"With my fond farewell," Elizabeth said, and picked up another one. "Away the little darlings go." She touched the book to her forehead. "Go find someone to love you." And she put it in the box.

Other books, on a table next to the desk, were arranged around a black porcelain tea set with six handle-less cups. Books about Japanese tea ceremonies. Six books on white wire stands in a row, one book next to each cup. A long black feather lay on the table in front of the row of books and cups, lay there like it had always been meant to end up on that table in Elizabeth's bookstore.

IT WAS A SOIRÉE at the home of the principal. Joseph Garrison stood next to a wildly blooming scarlet trumpet vine. She remembered him from the first faculty get-together. He'd teased her about looking sleepy, and she'd tried to blame the heat. She wandered over to him.

"So," he said, "everyone is here."

It was cool in the grass, down by her feet.

He said, "So how's the New Age business?"

He was the third person to call Lamplighter Books a New Age bookstore.

"What does that mean, really?" she said. "New Age of what, the Age of Aquarius? It's all pretty ancient."

"Ha."

Joseph had been eating the crudités with the roasted garlic spread.

He said, "Very funny, Age of Aquarius. I haven't even heard those words for at least twenty-five years—and quick too."

"It's my feet. They're cool."

This was a no-kids party. There was a keg of beer called Goose Island, and there was white wine in huge, round wine glasses. No vodka, though, and no orange juice.

"Seriously," she said.

He said, "Don't 'seriously' me about Elizabeth's bookstore. Not with her over there doing the Priestess of Delphi number on your husband."

Elizabeth was standing across the garden, wearing a long, straight dress, a string of coral beads around her neck and sandals on her feet, no bells. She did look a little Greek, with her long dress, but not with that cloud of red hair. She and Michael stood next to each other, and a couple other people. Elizabeth's two small hands held one of the round wine glasses. Michael had beer. He was telling a story. They all watched him.

"Okay," Pattianne said. "Let's talk about the weather."

The cloudless sky was stained a clear red. The sun was down. The humidity was closing in.

"Fabulous," Joseph said, and looked straight up. Red sky reflected in his glasses for a moment.

"Too hot. When does it start to cool down around here?"

"Don't ask me," he said. "I just teach it."

A mosquito whined around her arm and she slapped at it, and white wine sloshed onto her dress.

Joseph said, "Nice move."

The wine didn't show, lost among green leaf designs in the material, besides it being white wine.

"Don't you teach biology?"

"And one class of poetry."

"Biology and poetry?"

"The language arts teacher is afraid of poetry."

He touched her elbow.

"Wander aimlessly," he said, and he steered her out into the middle of things. "Mr. Smith," he said. "Coming our way. Don't look."

A teenager in a black apron with a tray of empty glasses headed toward them.

"I said don't look," he said.

The grass was smooth, like walking on carpet.

"Earth sciences, second term," he said. His fingers on her elbow were a light touch. "First term, I get their attention by teaching them about sex. Second term, I poison their minds by teaching them evolution."

They moved together around and through people who seemed to be saying hello without stopping their conversations.

"Who's Mr. Smith?"

A girl in a black apron filled their glasses with white wine from a carafe and then turned away, working her way through all the people, leading with her carafe. She wore a long-sleeved white shirt, a black bow tie, and black slacks. The carafe sweated. It made Pattianne hot just looking at her.

She said, "This is really sweet wine."

"Riesling," Joseph said. "A nice little breakfast wine. I must say, it goes well with your dress."

The buffet table was draped in white, laid with white china platters, little food things, silver tongs, forks.

"Carrot coins," Joseph said. "That usually means we're in the vicinity of artichoke-heart dip. Mr. Smith is the one back there talking to the woman in the red dress. He's probably lecturing her on the evil of red dresses."

Pattianne picked her hair up off the back of her neck, wanted an elastic, a hair clip, short hair. There were three women in red dresses and one that was a kind of a rose color.

"Which one's Mr. Smith?"

"School chaplain," Joseph said. "Aha."

He picked up a small bowl of green dip and said, "Grab those carrot coins."

She dropped her hair back down onto her neck and picked up the dish of carrot coins.

"Right this way," he said, and they were moving again, this time toward Michael and Elizabeth.

"So. You don't get along with the school chaplain because why?"

"I happen to like red dresses."

He held his wine glass with the stem hanging through his fingertips, the bowl of artichoke heart dip in the palm of the same hand. He took a carrot coin from the dish and dipped a glob of the dip. All this as they moved through the grass, as he said hello, nodded hello, laughed hello. He never faltered. Never sloshed. She was in the presence of a master.

"Do you dance?" she said.

He held up the carrot coin. "Not only do I dance," he said. "I dip."

"And this big kid," Michael was saying, "in third hour, suddenly leaps from his chair, the chair goes over behind him, slam, and he yells out, 'You've got to make up your own clichés!'" And everyone around Michael laughed. To get back to Michael, from all the way across a party, always seemed like a matter of perfect timing.

Elizabeth stretched up to her toes and kissed the air next to Joseph's cheek. He sniffed her hair.

"Sandalwood," he said. "Very nice." And to Pattianne, "I told her, Patchouli is illegal east of the Rocky Mountains except for in Ann Arbor, Michigan."

"Pattianne," Michael said. "This is Rachel, this is Martin, this is Harold. My wife, Pattianne."

My wife.

Martin and Harold said hello, and Rachel smiled, and they all looked the same, laughter left on their faces from Michael's story.

Elizabeth said, "Is that artichoke-heart dip?" She stuck her finger into the bowl of dip. Michael's eyes followed the finger to Elizabeth's mouth, and to the bowl of carrot coins. Joseph looked down into the bowl of dip, and at Elizabeth sucking her finger.

"What's this?" Joseph said. "A momentary lapse of social grace?"

"Sorry," Elizabeth said. "I'll never do it again."

"If you do," Joseph said. "You shall be forced to sip Riesling at soirées for a social season to be determined by a jury of my peers. Where's Simon?"

She waved her fingers out into the crowd, and they all looked, although Pattianne wasn't sure whom she was looking for. There was no place to set down the bowl of carrot coins. The sky had darkened, and there was a star. The party was enclosed by a wide circle of tall evergreen hedge and, standing close to the hedge, there was coolness, just a breath of it, down in the grass. Also mosquitoes.

Harold, or Martin, she wasn't sure who was who, touched Rachel's elbow and said, "Time to rescue the babysitter." They moved off into the center of things.

Whoever was left, Harold or Martin, said, "Talk to you soon about that." Something Pattianne could tell that she didn't care about. Then he said, "Nice to meet you, Patty."

"Anne," she said, and he went off in another direction.

Elizabeth handed Joseph her wine glass.

"May I?" she said to Pattianne, and she took the bowl of carrot coins. She dunked one in the dip.

"So," she said, "is this party going to get rolling, you think?"

She bit the carrot coin in half, one tiny bite, and chewed. Pattianne wrapped her fingers around Michael's elbow, felt for his pulse, in there where his skin was smooth and sweaty.

"You mean," Joseph said, "are we going to end up driving out to the Dew Drop Dead to go dancing?" He sipped her wine. His own glass was trapped in the hand with the artichoke-heart dip. "Definitely not. They have a cowboy band this weekend."

"We could start an argument about the new highway off-ramp," she said.

"Oh, please do," he said. "That would be a good excuse to leave."

"Exactly."

A young man in a white shirt and black bow tie passed with a tray of glasses, and Michael took Pattianne's empty wine glass and set it on the tray. The young man kept moving, and she couldn't get one of the full glasses from his tray, except then she saw that he was just collecting empties, and the girl with the carafe of Riesling was nowhere around.

Joseph said, "Of course there is that."

And them laughing, and other laughing breaking out nearby—other people, other laughing.

Elizabeth said, "Which isn't really."

And Joseph said, "It never occurred to me."

"And," she said, "if it was, it would be blue."

And he said, "No doubt about it."

The laugh of their voices was a duet, him and her, and then just as suddenly they were back, at the party. Some odd swoop had just happened between them, and Pattianne laughed at them, them laughing too, laughing at a party, drinking too much white wine and laughing at a party.

Michael's hands, on her back between her shoulders, nudged her around until she was facing out at the party again, and he said, "I have to introduce Pattianne to Rick," and she was once again being steered through the groups of people. Someone said, "Hey," and Michael said, "Hey." White shirts in the dusky dark, wine glasses shimmering in the light of citronella lanterns hanging from a wire strung overhead, and the ground, different after laughing, especially at a party.

"Who's Rick?"

"Rick Smith," Michael said. "School chaplain."

She looked around once to Joseph's face—how funny that she was about to meet Mr. Smith—but Joseph and Elizabeth were yakking it up, their faces close together. The sky had gone navy blue, and the citronella candles sent up curls of inky smoke.

"This Rick Smith is great," Michael said. "He's from up around Bemidji, and his family raises horses."

Small night birds darted in the air above the circle of grass, above the evergreen hedges, and for an instant, the air was cool.

"Horses?"

She told Michael once that she'd always wanted to learn to ride a horse. It had never been true until that moment, wandering around in the spring sunshine, one of those what-do-you-want-from-life conversations. She tried to remember what it was he had always wanted, maybe to see the pyramids.

"Rick, this is Pattianne."

Rick Smith didn't look like a minister. He was friendly looking and small. She would have thought him cute if she hadn't known he was a minister.

"My wife," Michael said, and his arm was on her shoulders, his skin on her skin. She stepped in close, put her arm around Michael's waist, his body hot under his shirt. Reverend Rick offered his hand.

"Pattianne," he said, and then something about finally meeting her, and she held out her hand and touched his fingers.

A man right behind them said, "No, it goes like this," and he started singing a song in another language. It sounded like German. A woman said, "They're not swifts, they're bats."

Pattianne looked up, into the circle of night sky. She was slightly high, in that woozy white-wine way. "That sounds great," Reverend Rick was saying. "I was just going to round up Lily and get going."

That flat Midwest talk, like every vowel is a short *E*, and every word is clipped off at the end, kind of like Swedish.

"Have Lily call Pattianne," Michael said, and goodbye.

After that, the party got thick-feeling, and they went around saying goodbye, nice to meet you, see you Monday, good night, good night.

Once they were in the O-Bug, driving, Michael said, "So that's Simon's wife?"

She leaned her head by the open car window, looking at the sky, and at the dusty leaves in the headlights along the side of the road. The air smelled bitter and grassy, and, driving slowly along in the dark, there was coolness, a definite coolness in the air.

In the morning, Michael got up early, nine-o'clock Mass. There was a kiss on the cheek, some words, his, some words, hers. She slept long after he left. The wine had settled into her bones, and she just couldn't get out of bed. It settled in her eyelids, and she just kept falling back asleep because she couldn't open her eyes.

When she got up, the sun was high and the rooms were all in shadow. She poured the last of the orange juice into a glass and sat at the kitchen table, and the glass slowly sweated. Michael had said football, soccer, something. She went into the living room and sat down on the cool, bare floor. There was a long, rose-colored rug in the window of the JCPenney's store. The rug could go longways across the living room, or the other way, kind of leading from the front door to the kitchen. She could go look at curtains. Except she hated curtains. The phone rang six or seven times. It was probably her mother, or maybe Mrs. Bryn—it was never Mr. Bryn—and she was sorry but she couldn't talk on the phone to anyone, just wanted to be quiet.

Thank God for Sunday. She couldn't bear the thought of being near a single person. There was not a smile or a hello left in her. All she wanted was to stay home alone and let her face be still. Laughing, white wine, the grassy coolness around her ankles in the perfumed night. Now there were mosquito bites there, and she scratched and then just sat still. There was the quiet around her, her house, her yard, the dusty road, the weekend. No birdsong. She went back to sleep in the afternoon.

She started out dusting the books on the Dreams shelf, and then moved on to the Light of the World table, and there was this book, on the beautiful chair. One guy had a purple face, like dark wine, and a happy smile. Four arms. The next guy was blue, two arms. The blue one seemed to be having sex with a white one, two arms. The names were mysterious, *K*s and *V*s and odd vowels that didn't give any real clue how to say them out loud. There was always a book—today it was this book—to fall open. She hung the feather duster on its hook at the side of the glass case and laid the big book open on the desk. The binding creaked and cracked. The end papers were brilliant violet, the pages thick and slick.

Books were starting to sprout at home like strange fungi, poetry books stacking up next to the bed, small, thin paperbacks that slid away underneath, maybe three or four poetry books under the bed. Maybe five or six. *Tribal Rites of the Lake People,* a photo-biography of eastern Apache elders, Ojibwa Indian myths, all sitting on the chair that stayed tucked against the wall behind the kitchen table.

The bells on the door rang in a very small way, and a girl stepped into the bookstore and stood under the blue arch. Long black dress, bare shoulders, pale face, black boots, gliding, moving, stopping at the glass case. The cranes hung still.

She said, "May I look at the tarot cards?"

Red lips.

The glass case had glass doors that slid sideways across the back. Opening it was a sharp glass-against-glass sound.

"All of them?"

Her black hair fell over her round shoulders.

"That one," she said, long thin finger bones under the white skin on the back of her hand. "And that one. And the one on the end."

Pattianne's hand was fluorescent lavender inside the case. She laid the boxes, one at a time, on top of the case, in a row.

"Thank you." The girl's red lips made her teeth look yellow.

Pattianne went back to the desk.

The girl held her hand flat, palm down, above the boxes of cards, moved her hand over the boxes, and then her red mouth smiled quick—"Thank you"—and she moved across the store in her black boots, out the door. The cranes hung still.

Pattianne sat back down at the desk, and the front of the store, the blue arch, and the cranes disappeared. The pages of *Deities of India* were glossy. Eight arms. Two arms. Four arms. Ten arms. The desk chair rocked a little bit, two arms, smooth green leather.

Elizabeth's message pad had *Joseph, 5:00* written on it in green ink. If they were having an affair, they weren't being very sneaky. They should go away, to a city, St. Paul or Minneapolis, a big, four-star hotel, or maybe one of the little cabins that happen in clusters along the edges of the ten thousand lakes.

It would be easy to disappear here, the whole Midwest spread out so far. All a person would have to do is walk away, along one of these roads, just straight and away, over a little rise, though wood lots and between fields, and disappear, under this flat, open sky. The trees on either side of the two-lane roads were heavy pine trees, the woods blue in the distance, and if she were to walk in under those trees, she would disappear into blue Canada. At the front of the store, two girls stood in the sun by the astrology books, high-school girls, leaning into each other, looking at a big book. The cranes moved in a slow circle.

The girls were dressed alike, blue jeans hanging low on their skinny hips, and brown, dusty sandals, the way girls that age dress alike. Pattianne was not there to them, and wouldn't be until they wanted to buy the book, or ask a question. Kids did that now, didn't see her, like some invisible change had made her invisible.

She could hide from Michael, stand very still and watch him, the happy air around him that drew all eyes to him, and sometimes he couldn't see out through that air. Sometimes he looked for her and his eyes moved right past the place where she stood. In Montclair, she could take three or four or six steps away from him, and then no one would see her.

Michael never hid. There was always the glittering self of him.

The girls were making little animal noises together.

Whenever Simon called, Elizabeth held the phone in both hands, turned away, talked in a low voice. Like lovers. When Joseph called, she would say, "You're late," or "Where's my copy of William Blake?" or "Busy, darling, call me later." Nobody said darling and meant it.

The girls were gone after a while.

Pattianne could hear her own heart. The motes were making the most noise of all. Her hands were not attached to her arms, there was a gap of body. No arms, feet, brown shoes with one broken shoelace tied in a knot. Being here. No deity, not even one with only two arms, would have shoes with a broken shoelace.

When she was five, she learned how to tie her shoes. They were red sneakers, and she was wearing red plaid pants, and she was having a fight with her mother about the red plaid pants. It was a loud, static-filled remembering, and Pattianne hated it, all that remembering that was her being a child, nobody talking, her just hiding out in her bedroom and wondering what was going on, and nothing was ever going on.

Elizabeth came in, jingling the bells, sending the cranes swirling, jingling and swirling herself, all in pale blue-green and bracelets and beads. Bright as a mote. She tapped a button and flute music started out slow, stayed slow.

"You know," she said, "you can play those CDs in the case. They're for sale, but you can play them."

She lifted the red hair off the back of her neck.

"Have I been gone long?"

All those bracelets, no watch.

The bead curtain did not chatter to Elizabeth when she went into the back room. But it might. It might chatter, *We Love You, Elizabeth. You Are the Queen of the Bookstore.* Pattianne had figured out that she didn't like jasmine tea but hadn't figured out how to say that to Elizabeth.

"A girl came in and looked at the tarot cards."

"What deck did she get?"

"She didn't buy any."

Elizabeth stood at the hotplate watching the kettle. She had taken off her sandals. Her toenails were polished copper. "Did she wave her hand over the boxes?"

"Yeah. So how does that work?" Pattianne waited, ready to laugh or not laugh.

"She can sense them," Elizabeth said, and she touched her forehead. "She can sense if it's a deck she can work with."

Not laugh.

"She's pretty good," Elizabeth said. "I want her to give classes here, but I haven't really talked to her. Quiet. Doesn't like to talk."

If Pattianne took off her shoes, her toes would look bare and white.

"I dusted Dreams."

"Always an important task."

Laugh. "And some girls came in. High-school kids it looked like."

"Oh yeah?" Sweaty lines of dirt crisscrossed Elizabeth's feet now, instead of her sandal straps. "Two of them? Look alike? Long hair?"

"Sounds like them. They didn't stay long."

Pattianne worked off one shoe with the toe of the other shoe. Her toes didn't look too white, not against the blue stars in the carpeting.

Elizabeth said, "What did they steal today?"

"Steal?"

"What were they looking at? Bet you anything it's gone."

"Astrology."

Elizabeth passed through the beads, and Pattianne followed, the beads chattering *Bad Bad Bad*, up front to the astrology shelf, to an empty spot on the shelf.

"The ephemeris," she said. "The purple Bantam ephemeris. They're getting bold."

They were so quiet, there and then not there. The bells didn't even ring when they left. Or when they came in.

Pattianne said, "Oh, no." But it wasn't enough to say, and she didn't say it very loud, didn't even know how to say it so that it sounded like she meant it.

"Oh, no." She should pay for the book. "Was it expensive?"

Elizabeth moved the other books together into the gap. "Not as expensive as this one." She put her finger on another purple book. "Not as good, either. Kind of illustrated. This one is just tables."

Pattianne didn't even know what an ephemeris was.

"I'm really sorry." *Bad Bad Bad.*

The row of books was neat and straight now. No wide empty spot now. Elizabeth would fire her now.

"Oh, they're good," she said.

"They've done it before?"

"Yep." She raised her arms, letting her sleeves fall back, pulled her curls off the back of her neck. "God, is it hot out," she said. "Do you think you could come in the morning on Thursday and Friday?"

"You know who they are?"

"Not by name," she said, and went back to the desk. "They've been in a few times before. Once they stole a candle. Imagine burning a stolen candle. Good way to start a fire." She took a catalog out of the drawer, opened it on the desk. "$29.95," she said. "That's a lot of karma."

The middle of Pattianne's stomach was a wide, empty spot.

"I should have warned you about them." Elizabeth put the catalog back in the drawer. "Now you know. You have to watch them."

Pattianne didn't know what to say.

"I don't know what to say. I'm so sorry. It didn't occur to me."

"Don't be sorry," she said. "Come here."

Twelve long steps. Six steps each, bare foot, shoe, bare foot, shoe.

Elizabeth reached her hands out, put a warm palm on each cheek.

"Don't be sorry," she said. "They'll be sorry. It's their karma."

Her red hair, her thick pale eyelashes, and Pattianne looked at one eye and then the other, not knowing where else to look, or what the proper way to stand actually was, being touched on the cheeks, or where her own hands were.

"Besides," Elizabeth said. There was fine gold hair along her upper lip. "Maybe they'll cast somebody's horoscope with that ephemeris and something wonderful will happen."

Her hands left Pattianne's face, left tears pressing behind her face.

"Are you okay?" Elizabeth shook her hair. "Breathe."

Pattianne did, and said, "I'm fine." Now if only she could look away.

"Can you come in the morning on Thursday and Friday?"

She breathed again, said yes.

"Good." Elizabeth stepped back another step, and another, and Pattianne breathed in and out.

"You know"—and now Elizabeth was frowning—"you only have one shoe on."

The kettle trilled in the back room.

"Hot tea before you go out in the heat is good for you," she said. The beads clicked gently as she passed through, and the kettle stopped whistling, and she said, "Stealing is really a crime against the self, you know."

The cranes hung still. The sun shone on the shelf where the ephemeris had been, where the two girls had been. Pattianne stood still, next to the desk, hating them.

Elizabeth said, "It seems like a crime against others, but it's not. Loss is a part of life. But to live with the crime of theft creates a dissonance in the spirit."

She came back through the clicking beads with two white cups of tea. *Our Queen Has Forgiven You. Put Your Brown Shoe Back On.*

"They'll live with the dissonance," she said. "Unless, of course, they return it, which I doubt, and then they'll have to apologize to you, directly."

"Why me?"

"Because you're the one they stole from. When you do something wrong, you need to make it right with the person you wronged. That's why murder is such a karmic fuck-up. You can never apologize to the person you killed. You have to carry it in your heart and then deal with it in your next life or whatever."

She held out a cup of bitter perfumed tea.

"Thank you," Pattianne said. She put her shoe back on.

ON SATURDAY MORNING, FRANKIE was outside, doing a lot of banging, and Michael was at Sacred Heart for Reconciliation. She took her coffee and opened the front door. The air had a dry, weedy smell. A row of storm windows leaned against the front of the house, strung with black webs of dust, and Frankie, backing out from under the porch, dragging yet another storm window, was all strung with black dust too, the butt of his jeans, the shoulders of his T-shirt, his hair.

Pattianne said, "Do you do this for everybody?"

"Eleven houses," he said, and he leaned the window up next to the others and went back under the porch. In just the last week, the sun had become a welcome thing, warming her cheeks and shoulders. The sugar maple had red leaves along one side, and another tree, a tall, skinny tree with small, round leaves, was starting to turn yellow. The yellow leaves moved in the air, even with no wind.

Frankie backed out again, pulling another window. A big blue-gray bird hopped down near the walk and screeched.

"Sure, now you're Mr. Nice Guy," Frankie said to the bird.

He leaned the window against the house with the others. The bird screeched again, and another bird, same kind, hopped onto the grass near the first bird. Frankie went around the side of the house. When he came back, dragging the hose, both birds screeched.

"What's with those birds?"

"Gray jays," he said.

He turned the hose nozzle and the birds flew off, not very far, into a pine tree, where there was yet another one. Frankie squirted the windows.

"They seem to have something in mind."

"I am of three minds," he said. "Like a tree that holds three gray jays."

"What?"

He squirted one window, into each corner, one corner at time.

"That's a poem, but it's about blackbirds," he said. "Not jays. Jays are usually pretty secretive. It's probably a food thing. Fall and all."

A flock of tiny birds, no bigger than specks, swooped between the trees, making a flutter in the air. They disappeared into the top of the sugar maple, and the sugar maple became full of squeaks and peeps.

Today was Rick and Lily Smith Day. Horse Day. Lutheran Minister Day.

It was supposed to be last Saturday. Michael had come home from going to Confession or whatever, and she stood in the bedroom brushing her hair and told him she had cramps.

"Cramps?" he said.

She didn't have cramps, she hardly ever got cramps, especially since she started taking birth control pills and her periods got so perfectly regular. But she didn't want to go to Rick and Lily Smith's house and ride horses and be sociable.

"My period," she'd said.

He took the brush, put it on the dresser, and laid his hand flat on her stomach. She laid her hands over his and turned her face away from the mirror, to the dark hallway, away from the lie of it. It wasn't even his sin. It was hers, and she didn't consider it a sin. Except the not telling him part. She would tell him somehow. When she was ready to quit taking them. Or she could tell him they were just to make her periods regular, some women did that.

Horse Day got moved to this week.

The Sears store was at the edge of St. Cloud. It was a sharp edge, a straight street. Along one side was a sidewalk and shiny new houses in a row, a ranch-style house with a garage that took up the whole front, then a Cape Cod with shutters, then a ranch, then a Cape Cod, all along the street across from the Sears store parking lot. Farther along the straight road was the Kmart.

Rick and Lily Smith lived a ways out in the countryside—that's how they said it here, *a ways.* The long road ran straight for a mile, crossed another straight road, another mile, another road. The car windows were all open, blowing Michael's hair. It was almost too windy to talk.

"My mom was into horses," he said.

Mrs. Bryn in jodhpurs and a short red jacket. Her long legs in tight-fitting black boots.

He said, "I think what she really wanted was to be the queen of the rodeo."

Pattianne rolled the window partway up.

"The queen of the rodeo?"

"I'm joking," he said. "But she lived out west for a while before she met dad. Montana."

Mrs. Bryn with a history. Pattianne rolled the window up the rest of the way. "So why did she come back?"

"What do you mean, why did she come back?" Michael said. "What was she going to do, stay there? In Montana?"

He turned on the radio, fiddled until the static cleared to a football game.

"Vikings, Detroit," he said.

She unbuckled her seat belt and turned so she could face him.

"It would be great if the Vikings went to the Super Bowl," he said.

"Since that we're here. You should keep your seat belt buckled. Now, what's the name of their road? We take a left somewhere—Coldwater Road?"

Michael's face from the side was a little boy's face. His nose went up a tiny bit, and his lips pouted out, and it was impossible to imagine him as an old man.

"I say Go Vikings," he said.

Red-winged blackbirds flew out from tall grass with purple flowers. Brown birds with yellow stripes dotted the telephone wires in twos and threes. Reverend Rick's map was squares and neat names written along the squares, one mile each, the way the roads were out here, long and straight, one mile each. Their house was marked with a small star, eight squares from St. Cloud. At Coldwater Road, Pattianne wanted to keep driving, but Reverend Rick's map was too perfect to miss the road, or pretend to miss the road.

She never wanted to get somewhere, always wanted to keep driving. She'd been hoping it would take longer to get to Reverend Rick's house. She was trying to remember wanting to ride horses.

Their driveway was long and straight, too, a wire fence along one side, up to a two-story house in a patch of green. There was a small white barn. The wire fence had thin flags of white cloth hanging still. They drove up the driveway and stopped, and when the O-Bug's engine quit, the air was quiet in a loud way for a bit. Then bird sound came in, and the horse smell. The gray front door was right in the middle. The windows had gray shutters. Pink cosmos still bloomed on either side of the front door. Even the cosmos were orderly.

Two horses stood along the fence close to the house. She liked the way horses stood with one back leg cocked, kind of casual. These horses looked bulky. One of them was gray and black. The other was just brown and dusty.

Michael put his hand on her knee.

She said, "What?"

"You feel okay?"

"Sure," she said. "Why?"

"You seem kind of quiet."

When Michael said that, he meant he was being kind of quiet, and she wondered how long she had known that.

Reverend Rick came out the front door.

"Welcome," he called out, waving his arm, walking out to the car.

Michael's face went into smile mode, like his most important job was to smile at Reverend Rick, and it was. Michael was the front man. Their marriage had its structure, which was slowly, in these small moments, becoming clear to her.

He got out of the car and stretched out his arms like he'd been driving for days. Rick slapped his hand into Michael's in a big business-guy handshake. His face split in a grin and there were neat, square, very white teeth and nice eye crinkles.

"Come on in," he said. "Pattianne, feeling better?"

Like she got to wear a sign now, Has Menstrual Cramps.

"Thanks," she said. "Yes."

Rick put one hand on Michael's back, one hand on her back, in between her shoulders—not as tall as Michael, not much taller than Pattianne—and they went up to the front door, and there was Lily, pushing open the screen door, a baby in one arm. She wore jeans and a sleeveless white blouse, and her arms were thick and tanned, and she was saying, "Come in, come in, come right on in. This is LeeAnn. Come on in."

A living room with gray and green furniture and gray carpeting and white draperies, and a decoupage plaque of Jesus, and some sheep over the couch, right in the middle.

"Gorgeous out here," Michael was saying.

"Any trouble finding the place?" Rick asked. Not joking.

"We're just finishing up," Lily said. That baby was as blond and round and pink as a baby could be. "Come on in."

They moved in a small group through the living room, through an archway, into a wide kitchen with three kids sitting on a bench at a long table, little kids, with crayons and paper. Thick, straight, blond hair on all three heads.

Lily said, "This is Mr. Bryn and Mrs. Bryn."

Michael stepped to the end of the table and put his hands in his pockets. The three kids stared at him.

"Hello," he said. "Now, what are your names? Tell me one at a time so I don't forget."

The kids looked at Lily. Rick stood back with his arms folded across his chest. No eye crinkles.

Lily said, "Lawrence?"

The biggest boy stood up and said, "Lawrence. I'm eight."

He had two huge front teeth.

He sat down quick, and the girl stood up, and she looked at Lily and said, "I'm Lisa, seven," and she sat back down.

The last one on the bench was a little boy. Lisa and Lawrence looked at him, looked at Rick, at Michael, at Pattianne. He had a red crayon in one hand and a blue crayon in the other, and he put the red crayon on the table and put the blue one in his mouth. Lily reached across the table, took the blue crayon out of his mouth, and set it on the table in front of him. He reached for it, and she covered it with her hand.

Rick said, "Lee we're waiting."

The little boy held his hand up in front of his face and looked at it, and with his other hand he pushed two fingers down and then held up his hand, two fingers and his thumb sticking up. "Three," he said.

"Very good, Lee," Lily said. "Now, can you tell Mr. Bryn your name?"

Luke waved his hand in the air and said, "Three."

It would probably be her turn next. *Pattianne, thirty-one.*

"Okay," Lily said. "Let's clean up."

And Rick said, "Come on outside."

The backyard was fenced in, and beyond the fence, a grassy field stretched away to trees a long way off. Rick, Michael, and then Pattianne walked along a cement walk that went right through the middle of the very green grass. In one corner, an empty garden patch with tomato cages stacked to the side. In the other corner was a swing set. If the swing set were set on top of the empty garden patch, the sizes would be a perfect match. They followed Reverend Rick, in his tight jeans and boots. There was something about boots that did something to a guy's butt, and Pattianne thought of saying, *Cute butt, Reverend Rick.* And what a bad thing that would be to do. He planted his legs apart and slid the barn door open sideways.

The barn was wide open on the other end, and sun slanted in, the air lit with motes. Rick took a hanging bundle of leather straps and, holding the straps behind him, went through the doorway, out to the field that sloped down to the road. Michael's butt wasn't as round. His legs were longer, straighter. Rick's legs went to the ground in a different way, like they were going right into it.

The brown horse was just outside the doorway in the sun. She stopped inside the doorway. The other horse was by the fence, watching. Rick kept the leather straps behind his back and let the brown horse eat out of his hand, the horse all snorty, big wet lips. Then Rick slipped the leather onto the horse's face, and it stepped sideways. Its front foot kicked at the dirt, and Rick was going "Hey, ho, hey," and then he turned and came toward Michael and Pattianne.

"This is a hackamore," he said. He was leading the horse by its face. "We won't bridle him up yet."

"Hackamore," she said.

Michael said, "Pattianne's always wanted to ride."

And Rick said, "This is Navarre."

Michael reached right up and touched Navarre along his long horse face, and Navarre shook his head like he hated that.

"Hey, ho," Rick said. "He's part Arabian. See how pretty his ears are?"

Navarre's ears were flicking forward, and then they'd lie down, back, like he was suspicious, and she was the one he was suspicious of.

"So," Rick said. "What do you think, Pattianne?"

She said, "Nice barn."

"Why, thank you," Rick said, but Michael laughed.

"Here, Michael," Rick said. "Hold right here," and Michael took some part of the hackamore and Rick came back, past Pattianne, into the nice barn, and Michael stood there petting Navarre's face, his hand right there by Navarre's mouth, Navarre's lips working like he was Mr. Ed. When Rick stepped back out into the sunlight, he had a loop of blue nylon cord with a heavy hook. He walked right up to Navarre and hooked the hook onto the hackamore, and then stepped backward, letting out cord from the loop. Michael kept petting Navarre's face like they were old pals.

Rick backed all the way to Pattianne. He held out the loops of cord and said, "Here."

Her hand reached for it, her fingers numb, and her elbows telling her hand *don't do it*.

He said, "You can handle this lunge line. Just hold it, there."

She took the loop of cord in both hands. "What will he do?"

"Nothing," Rick said. He had square short fingers, clean short fingernails. "Do you have a dog?"

"No."

Michael stepped away from Navarre and leaned against the fence, his hands in his pockets, like an old cowhand from the Rio Grande.

Rick said, "Did you ever have a dog?"

He took one of her hands off the loop of cord, turned her palm up, and laid the leading piece of cord across her palm. He closed his hand over hers.

"A dog?" she said. "Yeah."

Navarre just stood there, about ten feet away from her. Maybe closer.

"What was your dog's name?"

"Starla. She was a spaniel."

"Was Starla a good dog?"

Rick tugged at the line and Navarre's head moved.

"Yeah."

"Well," he said. "This will be just like taking Starla for a walk on a leash."

His hand held hers with the lunge line, his other hand on her back between her shoulders, pressing there. He tugged at the lunge line again, and this time Navarre stepped along, toward them, and Pattianne stepped in the direction of away, and Rick led them both out into the middle of the dirt.

Rick said, "He's a good boy," and he loosened his hold on her hand. There was no tension on the line, and Navarre just came along. She could feel the big footsteps through the dirt.

"Okay," Rick said, and then instead of taking the lunge line back, he let go of the line, of her hand.

"Go ahead," he said. "Give him some line."

She let a loop out.

"Little more," he said.

Navarre stopped coming toward her, but his mouth kept working, and his nostrils, and his tail. Black tail. Brown horse, black tail. Black mane. Black eyelashes, beautiful black eyelashes. Eyes.

"Okay," Rick said. He put his hands on her shoulders and started moving her around in a slow circle, and Navarre started going in a circle, too, around the dirt, around them, past Michael, his footsteps a steady, even, hollow sound on the dirt.

"Good," Rick said, and he took his hands off her shoulders. "Do that."

"Why? Where are you going?"

"Nowhere. I'm right here. Go ahead."

And she did. She made Navarre go around in a circle three times.

Then he said, "I'm going to get Fanny. You just lead Navarre around like that, get used to him at the end of the leash. Fanny's the gray."

Michael had hopped up to the wooden crosspiece of the fence. Pattianne turned partway. Navarre took a few steps. She stopped. He stopped.

"Make a slow circle," Rick said. "Don't get yourself dizzy."

They didn't actually get up on the horses, there weren't even any saddles, just another hackamore on the gray horse, and they took them for a walk out in the field to a path worn along the fence line. Navarre's ears kept twitching around, but Fanny just walked behind Michael, her face down low. Navarre stopped and stuck his face into some bushes, so Pattianne stopped too.

Rick said, "Don't let him tell you when to stop. Hey ho, come on boy," and he reached out and tugged at the line. Navarre ripped leaves off the bush and started following again, chewing leaves, a branch sticking out of his lips, and his teeth crunching the leaves like they were bones.

Rick said, "He's a good boy, Fanny's baby, born right here. Fanny was born on the next farm over." He waved his arm eastward, and Navarre's ears flickered. "They had her named Fantasy."

Fanny was like an old black-and-white negative of a photograph, her legs darkening to her black feet, her dark face streaked silver down the center of her nose, her ears black, her wide back silvery and shiny.

"Fantasy," Rick said. "Because she half disappears at night. Looks like a spirit horse, they said. Spirit horse."

The corner of the field was full of brush and breezy rustling and other reasons for Navarre's ears to flick back. He was close behind her, and she could smell stinky warm horse right near. He snorted and put his big wet horse lips right on her ear, and she kind of went whoop, the weirdest sound, and dropped the lunge line and jumped away sideways. Her ear was wet, and she had goose bumps all on one side,

Rick saying, "That's okay, Pattianne. That was a kiss. He's sneaky that way. He doesn't bite, ever."

She looked down at her shirt, a string of horse slobber strung on her shoulder, and one nipple pointed out hard.

Michael handed Fanny's line to Rick and wiped at the horse slobber. "Okay?" he said.

She could feel herself smiling like an idiot.

Michael touched her ear, pushed her hair back.

The goose bumps kept shivering up and down one side of her body. She'd never been kissed like that before.

She said, "Think you could learn that trick?"

Rick's face went a little straight, but Michael laughed, up at the blue sky, and Navarre just stood there and switched his tail.

Rick picked up Navarre's lunge line and said, "Well, let's head back for lunch."

He held the line out, and she took it. But she didn't turn her back on him again. That Navarre.

"That Rick," she said later, on the drive home. "He's an awful nice guy."

For a minister, which is what she didn't say.

And Michael smiled, easy, happy, saying, "I really like those folks."

IT WAS ON THE way home from Lamplighter Books that she saw the shop. There was no name on the door, no sign, and the door was open. There were racks of gauzy shirts and pants and dresses. Some were embroidered and dotted with tiny round mirrors, or tie-dye and batik, all bright, odd colors—mustard, rose, periwinkle, chartreuse.

A man with a beard sat behind a counter reading a book, and he said hello and didn't look up. He said, "Dressing room's back there, purple curtain."

They weren't the kind of clothes you had to try on, they were all loose and airy and long, lots of fringes and lots of elephant designs. Pattianne went around the shop, touching the colors. She pulled out a pair of wide black pants and held them up. A long, blue shirt, or maybe it was a short dress, dark blue that faded to purple at the edges of the loose sleeves. A small T-shirt of rosy, gauzy cotton. Everything was cotton. Everything smelled herbal. Everything was cheap.

The man looked up when she piled the stuff on the counter. He had gray in his long hair, and he wore silver hoops in both ears.

"Sale," he said.

He wrote the prices on a receipt pad and added them up, carrying his ones.

"That look right?" he said. He showed her the receipt. "My arithmetic isn't very good. I need one of those adding machine thingies."

"Twenty-two bucks?"

Cheap.

He took out a brown paper bag and a red ink pad and a stamp, and he stamped the bag carefully. It was a crescent moon shape lying flat like a shallow dish and, under that, the word SMOKE'S.

"That's an Indian moon," he said. "India Indian. And that's me. I'm Smoke."

He slid the pile of clothes into the bag.

"It means 'and,'" he said.

"And?"

He pointed at the moon. "And," he said.

He took her handful of bills and put them in the drawer without counting them.

"It's like at the beginning of a story," he said. "They say 'and' like we say 'once upon a time,' meaning all stories are connected. Only one story. Get it?"

"Cool," she said. He had clear, beautiful gray eyes, and she thought maybe that was why he was called Smoke.

THE FIRST TIME SHE wore the pink shirt and the wide black pants at home, Michael said, "Get some new pajamas?"

One thing about Michael was how he noticed girls. His eyes went to girls who were dressed like girls, and they didn't have to be sleek babes or curvy-gal types. He just liked girls in sexy clothes. When she wore tight jeans, he ran his hand across the back pockets without even seeming to think about it. He looked at women without even noticing it himself.

So she said, "Sort of."

"Pretty color."

"It's kind of a look," she said. "Big clothes."

She looked around in the kitchen drawer like she was looking for something in there, and when she looked back at him, he was reading the newspaper.

SHE WORE THE PINK shirt to Lamplighter Books with her jeans and left the big black pants in the closet.

Elizabeth said, "Somebody's been to Smoke's."

She stacked a small stack of books on her desk.

"That color," she said. "It's sacred. Hindu."

Pattianne looked down at her shirt. "Pink?"

Elizabeth wore peach today. "Rose," she said.

"The color of joy in a sorrowful season," Pattianne said.

"Rose?" Elizabeth put the small stack of books in her book bag. "What does that mean, sorrowful season?"

"In the Catholic Missal," she said. "The guide to the Mass? It explains the colors of the vestments the priest wears. That's what it says about rose." She didn't really know what it meant. "Purple for Advent and Lent, and I guess once in each of those times there's cause for joy, or maybe hope, and the priest wears rose-colored vestments instead of purple, purple being the color of sorrow."

Elizabeth poked around in the bottom of her book bag. "I can't find my scarf," she said. "Are you Catholic?"

"No. Was."

"Well, that whole priest thing, that's very weird. Total perversion of the Jesus message. He never said anything about anybody being the boss. It was just love, love, love. I like that about the colors, though. Where's my damn scarf?"

The bells at the door jingled, and Joseph Garrison came in. He grabbed the bells and jingled them again. Then he blew at the cranes and sent them spinning around.

"Consider me announced," he said.

Elizabeth said, "I'll be ready in a minute. I can't find my scarf."

Pattianne thought about lighting all the candles on the Hindu deities table after they left. Maybe turn on the heat. She would watch every person who came in like a hawk.

Joseph walked along the shelves, his hands still on his hips.

"So," he said. "Have the books introduced themselves to you? All you have to do is touch them, you know."

Elizabeth said, "Joseph." She was pulling open drawers in the desk.

"And don't cross your Tao with your tarot," he said. "You could end up with Darrow, and the animal spirit books are way up at that end of the wall with *The Secret Life of Plants*. Fairies right underneath the plants, which is where she says they like to hang out. What does she know? It is, however, her bookstore."

Elizabeth said, "That's right."

"It's all in its own order," Joseph said. "Although Elizabeth, honey, I'd like to point out that by putting Rumi right there by Sufism, you're bordering on the alphabetical."

She said, "That's okay."

"If someone from the metaphysicians' union came in," he said, "there could be repercussions. Or would that be reverberations?"

She said, "Joseph."

"That would be Local Number 9, I bet," he said. "We could look it up in numerology. Maybe we should just move Rumi down here by fairies."

He pulled Rumi off the shelf.

"Put Rumi back, Joseph."

He put Rumi back.

"Now here," he said, "we have a section in flux. *Mutant Message Down Under*? Fiction. Recently joined by Carlos Castaneda, who was banished from the company of Shirley MacLaine for telling fiction, the dog."

"Don't be a speciest," Elizabeth said, and she wrapped a huge orange scarf around her shoulders and head.

"Speciest," Joseph said. "You know, if this were the kind of bookstore with dictionaries in it, you probably wouldn't find that word in one. Well, maybe in one."

"Here," she said. "Carry my books."

And to Pattianne she said, "We'll be back in about an hour."

Joseph picked up the book bag and said, "What about lunch? I distinctly remember lunch being part of this deal."

She put her hands on his shoulders, turned him around, and pushed him toward the door, and said, "Maybe an hour and a half."

"If you need a task," Joseph said. "Just ask the store what it wants done."

He jingled the bells again, and then they were gone. The cranes circled. Lamplighter Books was empty. The cranes kept moving, so slowly she couldn't see them moving, but she looked up, and the red crane was where the white one had been. Another moment, the blue crane was there.

Michael called it Elizabeth's hippie bookstore. There had been kids at Cranbury High School who got into the hippie thing, and at least half the Ed School at Montclair was hippie, or a smearing of hippie and liberal, and a few people who just never wanted to leave kindergarten in the first place.

Jen was definitely not a hippie, but she used to go out behind the garage with the purple pipe after dinner before she settled down to spread out homework on the dining room table, chattering away, happily stoned.

"The angles of geometry are like playing pool in a mirror."

"Human biology is even better than wristwatches."

"My Lit exam on Theater of the Absurd? Aced it."

Michael only ever said, "It's illegal."

A man-size boy with no hair at all came in, the cranes swinging in a circle around his bald head, and he didn't even look at them, just walked in, stepping his legs out long. He had big feet in black boots, and he walked like he had just recently grown those feet, hadn't quite figured out how they worked. He big-footed it across the blue stars.

She said hello. Made it a singsong sound, like, *Hello, I'm your friendly New Age bookseller who has seen shaved heads before.*

He stopped by the Light of the World and put his hands together as if in prayer and nodded toward her like saying, *Hello. I knew you were there all along. I've seen these Hindu candles before, too, they're nothing new, nothing is new.* Two more steps, and he stopped at Tibetan Buddhism and turned his back to her, becoming a square of puffy blue nylon and a small shaved head, which wasn't exactly round in the back, sort of lumpy. She touched her own head, that ridge across the back, which felt lumpy, and which meant she probably shouldn't consider going with that particular look.

The boy took out two big books, brought them to the desk, and set them down, like an offering. *The Art of Ancient Tibet* and *Meditations of Color Photography*. His head was covered with fine blue dots where there had once been hair. He reached into his swishy jacket and took out a glittery card that said *Happy Birthday to a Dear Grandson*.

"Happy birthday," she said, careful not to sound too perky.

The card had money inside, Andrew Jackson showing through a hole in the card. The boy had long, dirty fingernails and, this close, he smelled like Jen's room used to smell when she was going through her gerbil-breeding phase. Pattianne opened each book to the first white page.

"Thirty-eight dollars," she said. "And nineteen cents."

A firm no-smile, no anything there on his face, nothing except pimples around his nose, chapped lips, dark surprising eyebrows, and red-rimmed eyes. He pulled several Andrew Jacksons out of the birthday card and said, "Could you by any chance spare a roll of quarters?"

He had a mouth full of lead-colored braces.

She said yes, and he said, "How about two rolls?"

He kept his face still, mostly by looking away from her, down at the blue stars, off to the side, not at the cranes or the Light of the World, just away.

"I'd be happy to give you two rolls of quarters."

Then he smiled, down, off to the side, away. The touch, the briefest connection, how you can make a stranger smile sometimes.

She liked vodka better than pot. She discovered vodka tonics in eighth grade and never looked back. No lime. Just vodka and tonic water and a couple of ice cubes. Her father drank scotch. He kept the vodka around for company. No one ever mentioned the vodka tasting watered down.

A young woman with a baby in a backpack looked at yoga books. Then her baby threw up, a thin dribbling curd of white baby puke, right into the center of the mandala on the front of a mandala calendar. The woman picked up the calendar with both hands and held it evenly in front of her, held it out, said she would now buy the calendar.

"That's okay," Pattianne said. "Accidents happen."

The calendar was one of the small ones, only five dollars and five cents with tax.

"Oh," she said. "I must."

She had long dark braids and long dangling earrings, a different one in each ear.

She said, "This mandala has been chosen by my son."

Pattianne offered her a small box of tissues.

"Your son," she said. "Has also chosen your braid."

A smile. One tooth in the front was bigger than the other, capped, bright white.

Vodka tonics were for drinking several of. Scotch was for sipping. When they went out to a restaurant and Pattianne ordered scotch, her father would say, "That's my girl."

And Jen would blink at her, a blink so blank it was full of a secret sneer. She always ordered bourbon and Coke, unless she was stoned. Then she ordered something like a sloe gin fizz or a daiquiri. And their father looked at Pattianne, a wink maybe, shook the ice in his scotch, that beautiful small sound. Their mother was there somewhere.

LATER, THAT DAY, AT home, in her house, the sun in the living room was warm and golden on the bare floor. She had a screwdriver, and there was wet lavender polish on three toes, pieces of tissue worked in between each toe, when the phone rang. She hated it when the phone rang and Michael wasn't there to answer it. She hopped across the living room with her toes not touching the floor. It was Lily, all *Hi, how are you, good, okay,* back and forth like that for a while. She said it was nice having them out to the house, the way people said that, *out to the house.* Pattianne balanced the phone between her shoulder and her ear and polished her thumbnail lavender.

"So," Lily said. "What's a good time for Sunday night?"

"Sunday night?"

She hated it when she got nail polish on her cuticle.

"Our sitter's a high-school girl, so early is better."

"Early is fine," Pattianne said, playing for time.

"Five thirty?"

"Fine," she said. "Let's say five thirty."

The *Seasons of Minnesota* calendar on the refrigerator had red trees and blue sky and nothing written in for Sunday.

"Can I bring anything?" Lily said. "How about dessert?"

Autumn blue, a certain shade of clear, dark blue.

"Pattianne?"

"Yes, great," she said. "That would be great."

Miss Mimi said to paint black first to get that color blue.

"Rick is allergic to shellfish," Lily was saying. "We went to Lander's house for dinner once, Tom Lander? Lower math? His wife, Mary? Really great cook, she went to cooking school in St. Paul or something, I don't know, but she fixed a spaghetti-and-scallops dish, really proud of it, and Rick couldn't eat a bite. I was so embarrassed."

"No shellfish. Got it."

"Okay," she said. "I'll fix dessert, maybe cranberry bars, fresh cranberries? Did you talk to Angela Park?"

Wife of Max Park, civics teacher.

"No, I haven't talked to her," Pattianne said. "Yet."

"If she offers to bring something to drink, talk her out of it." Lily's voice got lower. "She likes to make blender drinks. I don't know that it's such a good idea. Sometimes that doesn't work out, you know?"

"Right. I'll tell her to just bring herself."

"Well, I'm really looking forward to it. I think it's just a really exciting idea. See you then, bye."

By the time Michael came in the kitchen door, all ten toes were silvery lavender, two coats each. All ten toes and one thumb. She stuck both legs out straight.

"Like my toes?"

He dropped to his knees and grabbed her feet.

"Like your toes?" His fingers were too cold, tickle cold, shrieking cold. He held both feet and said, "I love your toes," and he kissed the ends of her toes on one foot and then the other foot, her trying not to kick him in the face while he was kissing her toes, but tickling her toes was a dangerous, dangerous thing. She finally got her feet back down on the floor and could breathe again, and he leaned back on his heels there at her feet and said, "So."

He looked at her and she looked at him, and it could still make the sidewalk fall away underneath her when Michael Bryn just looked his blue, blue eyes into hers, the sidewalk in this case being the chair she was sitting on.

He put his hands on her knees, which were not ticklish, and he leaned up and kissed her mouth. She held him by his hair, that thick mess of curls, and wrapped her legs around him and kissed his beautiful mouth open into her mouth and wouldn't let go of his hair or his mouth or his tongue or all of him squeezed tight in between her legs. They could fuck, right here, on their own kitchen floor, married, and alone in their own house.

He dug his fingers into her knees and stood up, letting out his breath, stood up right in front of her, her face right at the zipper of his khaki pants, him hard there, hard against her lips, and he made a deep, soft sound, her hands on his hips, the bones there, her fingers at his zipper. She hated zippers. She hated shirttails. His fingers dragged shivers across her shoulders, up and down her neck, her face in the cotton of his underwear, the smell of laundry soap. Michael always smelled like soap.

His hands around her arms, pulling her up, and he started to step away, pulling her with him, and she said, "No."

She said, "Right here."

She pushed down the waist of his pants and let go of him with her hands but not with her eyes and tugged down her jeans, and her underpants, slipped them down to her feet and kicked them away.

"Right here," she said, his arm around her holding her, his mouth somewhere near her ear, his breathing everywhere, and he was fast and hard and quick, crying out, everything hard and wet and lovely.

And then everything still. Beating like two heartbeats. Still and wet. Dripping and breathing. She wondered if he was thinking they just got pregnant, if he would say that, what she would say.

He whispered in her ear.

"Nice toes."

The way it tickled when he slid out of her all soft. The way Michael didn't always smell like soap.

She picked up her underpants with her lavender toes.

"Hey," she said.

He turned at the kitchen doorway.

She took her underpants in her fingers.

"Drop these in the laundry basket?"

She tossed them to him, damp, blue cotton, and he reached into the air and caught them and stuffed them in his shirt pocket, patted his pocket.

The sky went blue, silver, purple, almost black, and the house was cold. She put on spaghetti water, Michael singing in the shower, clouds of steam floating out into the hallway. "Splish-splash, I was taking a bath." His favorite soap was sharp smelling, sea smelling, Sea-Man, He-Man, Sloop-Soap or something. She dropped spaghetti into the water. Turned the thermostat up high. Went into the front bedroom and opened the box with the blue glass candlesticks from his Aunt Mary. This was her life. There was this perfect evening, her life before Michael nowhere to be found, it had happened to someone else. Back in the kitchen, the windows were steamed up, the spaghetti boiling madly.

The shower stopped, and she called out to him, "So, sweetie baby?"

"La la la la la Saturday night."

Her two fingers held a cigarette where there was no cigarette.

"Tell me, darling," she said. "My own true love."

She took a deep drag on her empty fingers, a deep drag that smelled like sex.

She said, "Why is Lily so excited about coming over on Sunday night?"

"Shit, I forgot to tell you."

He came out in his jeans, his shoulders still wet, his feet bare.

"It's kind of a planning get-together," he said. "What's for dinner?"

"Spaghetti. Planning for what?"

"An ecumenical men's prayer circle." He stirred the spaghetti. Drops of water clung to the curving small of his back. "When do we eat?"

"An ecumenical what?"

"It's Rick's idea. A group of men, different churches. There's this other guy from Sacred Heart who's been talking to Rick about it. He's a deacon."

He took a noodle out and threw it against the wall, and it slipped down behind the stove.

He said, "Does that means it's not done yet?"

"I think it means there's spaghetti behind the stove. So, Rick and Lily, and Max Park? And his wife Angela?"

She wanted to see her face in the window. She wanted to see his face in the window. She wanted him to be kidding about a prayer meeting, wanted him to say, *Ha ha, it's really just a poker game.*

"Just a little dinner, we're going to talk about some ideas, and I want them all to get to know you."

He was not kidding. The window was covered in steam. It was cold in the kitchen, and she was standing there in her sweatshirt and her lavender toes, and her thighs were sticky.

"Stir that," she said. "Will you?"

It felt like she was mad, but when she got to the bedroom, she just got her bathrobe off the floor and sat on the bed. The bathrobe was a silly long red thing with dramatic sleeves and black buttons. He'd rescued it from a garage sale, called it her Loretta Young robe. He was singing again in the kitchen, some Frank Sinatra spaghetti song, and she sat on the edge of the bed and looked at the crucifix above the door.

Damn.

Father McGivens had said, "Michael believes," but then she hadn't thought it mattered. She was afraid of how it mattered now, like God could step right into her kitchen and keep her from fucking her husband on the kitchen table. She decided to ignore it, practically hearing the words in her own head: *I am going to just ignore it.* She turned off the light and went back in the kitchen, to just ask him what that meant, an ecumenical men's prayer circle.

He threw another piece of spaghetti against the wall and it stuck there.

"So," she said. "What does that mean?"

"I think it means it's time to eat."

The phone rang, and she said, "Let me drain that," and he answered it hello like he was still singing.

"Angela," he said. "Hey, you and Max coming over Sunday, right?"

The beautiful copper colander had been a wedding present.

"Five thirty," she said.

"Pattianne says five thirty," he said, and then, to Pattianne he said, "Hey, sweet pea, she wants to know if you know what Lily is bringing?"

"Sweet pea?" she said. "Cranberry bars."

"Cranberry bars," he said. Angela said something that made him laugh. "Yes, we do. Okay, see you then."

He hung up the phone.

He said, "She asked do we have a blender."

"Did you call me sweet pea?"

"Sweet pea," he said. "Get it?"

Grandma Anthony used to call her that. Grandma Anthony, who

didn't even know her anymore, who was a Presbyterian, and thought it was silly that her mother didn't want her to take the girls to Roselle First Presbyterian Church with her on Sundays when they were little.

Father McGivens had said, "Do you believe you can uphold your husband's faith?" She wondered if this was what he'd had in mind.

She had never heard Michael say prayers, not before meals in the kitchen, not at night before bed. Sometimes he crossed himself, but it seemed more like something ironic, like when Mrs. Bryn told him on the phone that Claire had bought a brand-new SUV or when his debate team got paired up against the state champions from Minneapolis.

SHE COULDN'T FALL ASLEEP. Michael's breathing was deep and even, and she got up and walked across the cold bare floors to the living room window. The night sky looked so still. It wasn't. The stars were ancient explosions of huge brilliance and there were stars beyond stars, so many stars that it made her stop thinking.

She tried reciting the Lord's Prayer. It was so familiar and easy she could say it without using her brain at all.

MICHAEL WANTED TO RUN to the store for half-and-half.

"I'll be right back," he promised.

"No you won't. You'll end up talking to that lady."

Michael loved chatting to that store lady for some reason. And he wasn't back, and it wasn't even five thirty when there were three quiet knocks on the front door.

First was his nose.

She said, "Michael just ran up to the store."

It was a long, straight hatchet of a nose. The setting sun cast a sharp shadow onto the east side of his face.

"Please come in," she said, and Herman Walter ducked his head forward and stepped through the doorway and swiveled at his Adam's apple, leading with the nose, left, right, left.

"I'm Pattianne. I'm Michael's wife."

He wiped his hand on his pant leg and said, "I'm Herman Walter." Kind of a squeaky voice for such a tall guy.

"Please," she said. "Come in. Have a seat."

He took two long steps and then he bent at the knees and folded himself into the chair next to the green deer lamp. She switched on the lamp, and Herman Walter swiveled his head back and looked at the deer's leery, lit-up face.

"Can I fix you something to drink?"

A crooked smile, one side of his face spasming northward.

"No, thank you."

"Michael will be back in a minute." Damn it, Michael.

Herman Walter nodded once, twice, blinked once, twice. His eyes were palest watery gray.

"A cup of coffee?" she said.

His eyebrows reached toward each other in the center of his forehead.

"Coffee," he said, "makes me sneeze."

Then Angela came in, her husband Max right behind her, Michael right behind them. Angela wore a plaid dress that buttoned up the front with huge white buttons over her huge breasts. Angela and Max were the same height, same blond hair, him skinny, her curvy all around, how some couples end up like that, matching in spite of themselves. She handed him a round straw basket, reached her hands out to Pattianne and said, "Pattianne, I am so pleased to finally be meeting up with you," and gave her hands a squeeze.

"So," Angela said. "You and my Max have met, am I right on that? And Herman, how are you doing?"

Herman Walter never looked at Angela Park. His nose was pointed in any direction except where Angela was. She perched her curvy self on the arm of the couch and took off one blue high-heeled shoe.

"So," she said. "How you liking Minnesota?"

She looked inside her shoe, turned it over, and shook it. She said, "I could of swore there was a rock in there." And she put it back on.

Max said hello to Pattianne and hello to Herman Walter, who said hello to the ceiling light fixture, and Angela stood back up and took the basket out of Max's hands.

"So," she said, "Lead me to your blender."

"Oh, you shouldn't have." Uh-oh. "You should have just brought yourself." Too late now. "Right in here," and Pattianne took the half-and-half from Michael, who stood by the door grinning, the happy host, and she and Angela went into the kitchen.

Angela set her basket on the counter, looked at the table. "How pretty, all those different blue dishes. That is so cute," and she took out a bottle of dark rum, a can of apricot nectar, and a jar of home-canned peaches. She took out a bottle of ginger ale, too, and winked.

Pattianne picked up the peaches and said, "Boy, I bet these are good in ice cream."

"You can use store bought," she said. "But these are special, for tonight. I call this drink a Kris-and-Rita. Got ice cubes?"

She poured rum into the blender, and then the apricot nectar, and then she dropped in the ice cubes.

There was knocking on the front door, Reverend Rick and Lily, hello hello in there, and then Lily came into the kitchen. She set two square Tupperware dishes on the counter next to the blender and looked right at Pattianne, and said, "Hello, Angela, what's that?"

Pattianne shrugged her shoulders.

Angela spooned peaches into the blender and said, "Hey, Lily."

Lily snapped the Tupperware lids off and said, "Well. I couldn't decide. These are cranberry bliss bars. These are apple dream bars. I hope no one's allergic to nuts."

"Me too," Pattianne said. "Hope no one's allergic, I mean. Herman is, but to coffee. Herman Walters." And she took out glasses, seven. Three matched exactly.

Angela hit the button on the blender, and Lily shouted over the racket of the ice cubes, "Just ginger ale for us," and Angela winked again.

Lily shouted, "I'll see what Herman's having."

Angela turned off the blender while Lily was still shouting, and Herman said, "Just water, please," from the living room.

Angela said, "You want to be turning the blender off after just a little bit. You smash up the ice cubes too much it waters down your Kris-and-Rita."

Lily was a little pink in the neck. She went in the living room and said, "Herman? Water? Rick? Max?"

Angela started pouring foamy pink Kris-and-Ritas into the glasses. "We used to listen to that Kris Kristofferson and Rita Coolidge album a lot," she said. "So romantic."

"Just water for Herman," Pattianne said.

Angela took a square of tin foil out of her basket. There was a tangle of thin curled orange slices and slices of green honeydew melon, all speared together with colored toothpicks. She balanced one on the top of each glass. Herman's water and the ginger ales too. Pattianne set the drinks on a round metal tray painted with a pink rose.

"How pretty," Angela said. "May I?" And she picked up the tray, balancing it easily on one hand, waitress work in her past somewhere, and she went into the living room.

Pattianne followed with the Famous Impressionist Paintings cocktail napkins.

Rick and Lily took their ginger ales off the tray, and Rick said, "This is so fancy, Angela. Ginger ale, right?"

And Angela said, "You bet, Reverend Rick."

When Angela handed Herman Walter his glass of water, all decorated up with orange curl and honeydew, he took the glass in his long fingers and said thank you to the deer lamp.

"Why, you are welcome, Herman," Angela said. "And here," and she took Manet's *Olympia* from Pattianne and handed it to him.

Herman's head swiveled. His Adam's apple bobbed in and out.

Angela sat herself on the arm of Max's chair. "So," she said. "Isn't this nice?" She raised her glass. "Here's to Pattianne and Michael. Welcome to St. Cloud."

Pattianne raised her glass back at her. Rick and Lily sat next to each other on the couch with their knees lined up straight, and Pattianne sat down next to them, sitting slowly so the couch cushions wouldn't sink all one way. Lily tucked her elbows in. Michael stood by the bookcase, leaning, and raised his glass, happy. What a happy-faced bunch. Except Herman. Except Lily.

Lily said something about the purple sweet gum trees, and Rick said something about Vikings defense, and Michael said how they're hoping his folks could come for Thanksgiving, and Lily said, "Fall rummage sale," and Rick said, "No defense last year," and Michael said how they might expect to see the northern lights this weekend, and that in the southern hemisphere they're called something else. The Kris-and-Rita started out being tart and ended up sliding down all sweet and rummy.

Rick said, "Aurora Australis."

Lily said, "Folding tables."

Michael said the lake perch in the stores here was so fresh it wiggled, and Angela wiggled on the arm of Max's chair and said, "Wiggled, aren't you clever."

Herman Walter watched the heating vent closely. He said, "There are twenty-four churches on our list."

Angela shook the ice chunks in her glass.

Rick said, "Does that include the Seventh-Day Adventists?"

"Yes," Herman Walter squeaked. "And the Western Baptists." He actually looked at Rick. "The Western Baptists," he said, "would probably not attend."

An amazing Adam's apple.

"The Western Baptists," he said, "would definitely have to be invited."

Michael's Kris-and-Rita had settled into layers of pink and yellow.

"You don't want to insult the Western Baptists," Herman Walter said. It was as if his voice were only just now starting to change.

Pattianne's glass was just foamy pink ice.

Angela sat still until she caught Pattianne's eye, another wink, and tilted her head toward the kitchen, a quick blond bounce.

"Excuse me," Pattianne said and stood up, carefully, not jostling the couch cushions. They were all reflected in the window glass. "I have to check the chicken."

Angela stood up and said, "Me too, let me help."

"The Ryersons are Western Baptists," Herman Walter said. "They own the St. Cloud Daily News."

Michael said, "Let me write down some notes."

The chicken bubbled all oily gold in the broth, and Pattianne ladled broth over each piece. Angela poured more rum into the blender.

"Angela, you and I are the only ones drinking Kris-and-Ritas."

"Don't I know it," she said. She poured in apricot nectar. "And I can tell you are the type of gal can keep up."

Pattianne felt a warm rush of pride and sprinkled brown sugar over the chicken.

"What's this?" she said. "Brown sugar? Now, I'm sorry, hon, I don't mean to snoop, just let me get at them peaches, I won't even watch."

"Snooping? Looking at my chicken?"

Angela hit the button on the blender. Lily would be sitting all straight and worried in there. When the blender was quiet again, Angela said, "A girl's recipes are a private matter. They're between her and her mother."

Pattianne slid the pan back into the oven and leaned against the warm door. Her mother didn't even use recipes. She just cooked, and they just ate, every night her father saying, *Very nice dinner, Mother,* and she and Jen would say, *Yes, Mom.* Unless Jen was stoned. Then she would wax prolific upon the glories of their mother's dinners, the chicken, the green vegetable, the starch.

Pattianne said, "I got this recipe out of the *New Jersey Junior League Book of Cookery.*"

There was *Joy of Cooking,* too, and she had taken both to the store, trying to figure out how much chicken to buy for seven instead of four, and there was way too much, she could see, which was probably okay. She didn't have to put it all out.

She said, "I added ginger."

"Well, it's not like I asked, but since you mentioned it, ginger?"

Pattianne turned off the burner under the potatoes. "Fresh ginger." A huge pot of potatoes. "Grated."

Angela dropped more ice cubes in the blender. Her fingernails were short and painted bright red.

"Well," she said. "Fresh ginger. Aren't you clever?"

Cuticles too, bright red. She laid a wet hand on Pattianne's shoulder.

"And generous too. A generous soul."

She took her hand away and leaned against the counter.

"I was married four years to my first husband," she said. "And that mother of his, may she rest in peace when she finally dies, she never once gave me a recipe."

She hit the button on the blender again. When she turned it off, the talk in the living room had stopped. She took the lid off the blender and looked inside.

"It's not like I would of showed up at a covered-dish supper with her precious apple pork chops," she said. "Or her chicken-liver custard, which she knew I admired." She picked up a dish towel, brand new, blue. She held it in both hands and looked at it. "Four years, and she never once gave me a recipe."

Both of them reflected in the kitchen window.

"I said that to the divorce judge, too." She wiped her hands dry. "That divorce judge asked what was my cause for requesting this divorce action? Like I needed a reason. I'm thinking this might be Missouri—that was when I was still living down in Missouri—but it is a free country, and I said to him, sir. Four years and she never once gave me a recipe." She sighed, and the white buttons strained across her breasts. "Kris-and-Ritas, coming up."

Lily came in and said, "Can I help?"

The way some women said that, *Can I help?* It wasn't really a question. Some women said it when what they meant was *Excuse me.* Or maybe it was some kind of code. Like in this case, for instance, it seemed to mean, Okay, enough blender drinks, let's get dinner on the table.

She said, "How lovely."

There were Aunt Alice's blue glass candlesticks, with white candles, in the middle of the table, which, with the leaves opened, took up half the kitchen, and with the three women in the kitchen, Angela's breasts were even larger. Lily was sturdy and thick, but small. The short sleeves of her white blouse fit snugly around her arms. Substantial. Pattianne couldn't see herself in the window. Just them.

Lily said, "I'll put on a pot of coffee."

"It's all made. Just switch that switch." Four brand new matching coffee cups were lined up on the counter by the pot. "The cups are right there."

Angela poured Kris-and-Ritas into the glasses. She had a tiny waist, belted with a thin navy blue patent-leather belt.

Lily watched coffee drip into the pot. "Angela," she said. "Why don't you let me pour you some coffee? Don't you take milk?"

"There's half-and-half," Pattianne said.

Angela laid a honeydew arrangement across each glass. She handed Pattianne hers and then leaned back against the counter, leaning back on her elbows, the plaid straining against the white buttons. Something pink and lacy underneath. "What a cute place," she said. "Lily, remember when Kraskis lived here? What was her name? Maria?"

Lily watched the coffee drip, her hands held in front of her, like she was praying for that coffee. "Mia," she said. "Her name was Mia, Angela, and his name was Kaspar."

"Mia," Angela said, fingering the button at the top of her dress and just smiling up into the air. "And Kaspar, how could I forget Kaspar? He taught upper math. I think she made potato liqueur." There was a red ribbon at the neck of her dress. "Mia Kraski?" she said. "Mia had this theory about babies." She pulled the ribbon out of its bow. "Mia's theory was about how the sex of the baby was determined by who works hardest during sex."

"Angela," Lily said.

"Really," Angela said. "I have all girls." She unbuttoned the top white button. "Is it warm in here?"

Lily picked up the purple glass sugar bowl. "Isn't this lovely." And she set it back down. "Coffee's done." And she poured a cup, and turned and held it out to Angela.

"For me?" Angela said. "Lily, you are sweet. Misguided, but sweet."

Lily picked up the potholders. "Pattianne, can I drain these potatoes?" The potholders were crusty with burn marks.

Angela set the coffee down on the counter. She leaned back on her hands and hopped her curvy plaid butt up next to it.

"What I mean is," she said. "You are working at cross purposes here." She crossed her legs. One blue high-heeled shoe slipped off her heel and dangled on her toe. "Now," she said. "Don't let me forget where I left off. I hate it when I forget where I left off—now *that's* drunk."

Her blue high heel dropped to the floor.

"So, Lily," she said. "This coffee business? Let me tell you what happens when you give coffee to a drunk person—not that I am a drunk person, two drinks does not add up to drunk, and besides which I really haven't had but one thus far anyways. But you give coffee to a drunk person and they don't get instantly undrunk. They get all alert. Wide awake. Then what you've got on your hands is a wide awake, alert drunk person, you see what I'm saying?"

Lily stood over the sink with the pot of potatoes in a cloud of steam.

"Now," Angela said. "Kaspar Kraski. How could I forget Kaspar Kraski? Mia had all them boys."

"Pattianne, would you like me to save this potato water?"

Angela kicked off her other shoe and leaned over behind Lily. She held her hands out over the back of Lily's head and made a circle with her fingers, Lily's halo. Pattianne got another wink and winked back.

"That's okay, Lily," Pattianne said.

They finally all got seated around the table. It was more of a squeeze than Pattianne had thought it would be—her at one end, Michael at the other, Angela and Max sat next to each other, Rick and Lily next to each other. Herman Walter right across from Angela. Herman offered to ask the blessing. They all held hands, Lily's hand on top of Pattianne's, her grip a little on the firm side for just grace. Herman Walter had a fine, deep praying voice.

"The Lord bless us and keep us, the Lord make his face to shine upon us, and be gracious unto us, the Lord lift up the light of his countenance upon us and grant us peace."

Amen. All of them in the window glass.

They let go of hands, and Pattianne waited for someone to say something in that weird moment after grace. She waited for Lily to say *How lovely*, but she picked up the dish of potatoes instead.

Angela picked up the platter of chicken, her countenance a little pink in the cheeks and definitely shining. "Herman Walter," she said. "What a nice blessing. Now, would you like a thigh, or a breast?"

Pattianne didn't laugh out loud, coughed discreetly into her napkin, gave Michael a quick smile, pleased with herself. One of his friends had a wife who could be her friend. How very married.

6: A STORY-LISTENING CHAKRA

EVERY MORNING EXCEPT MONDAY, Michael got up and went running around St. Cloud in his red Montclair State sweatshirt and his green sweatpants, a Christmas elf ahead of schedule, and determined to stay that way. It was cold in the mornings now, except under the blankets, where his body had been, where she stayed, her face in his warm pillow.

The last dreams slipped away, and through the day she would sense them coming back, those dreams. She could be standing at the sink or walking under a pine tree, and a memory slipped by that she couldn't quite catch, and that was remembering a dream. It never came all the way close, but being here, in Minnesota, out in the open, away from New Jersey, it seemed like she almost remembered, like that slipping-away feeling was sharper.

On Mondays, Michael put on school clothes instead of running clothes and went to Mass. Monday-morning Mass had started when two boys at school expressed an interest in going. It turned out the two boys were only interested in going once, and it ended up having something to do with a bet. Michael kept going. Usually.

But today was Monday, and today the Christmas elf went dashing off, and she got up. She put her feet on the cold bare floor.

She said, "Rug," and dragged her bathrobe out of the blankets.

The rooms were dark, bedroom, hallway, living room. She turned every light on, bright rooms and glassy reflections, Loretta Young slipping out of the corner of the living room.

"Curtains," she said. "Sears."

In the living room, Loretta Young made a detour across to the thermostat and pushed it up to seventy. The red light on the coffee pot glowed red, and the coffee dripped and gurgled. Michael pushed that button and left, back in half an hour to a pot of coffee, the smell, and the way that smell worked its way into the rooms of a sleepy house.

He'd say, "Call me Mr. Coffee."

He thought that was funny. She thought it was funny that he thought it was funny.

This church shit was not funny, and running today instead of going to church was a good sign. She turned on the radio—a loud, Midwest voice insisting that a new Ford would make her happy—and she turned the knob past blips and static and chatter until a long, smooth cello note floated out into the kitchen. Then a French horn, or maybe an oboe or something. She got out a stick of butter and put it on an orange plate that didn't match anything else.

"Fiesta," Michael had said, holding the plate in his hands at the garage sale, which she thought was funny and turned out not to be.

The heater vent in the kitchen rattled, the old oil furnace reaching for seventy. She got out eggs, milk, bread, syrup. She'd make French toast, a special, fabulous breakfast. He'd be so glad he'd gone running instead of going to seven-o'clock Mass. When he went to school, she'd do the crossword puzzle and then go shopping for housewares, maybe even curtains.

His cheeks were brilliant red when he came through the door.

"Mr. Coffee," she said.

HE HAD LEFT FOR school, and the morning had fallen still when she saw the black bird with the yellow head hopping around in the bare lower branches of the sugar maple, and then the phone rang right next to her head. She slopped coffee onto the table, onto the crossword puzzle, and grabbed the phone.

"Hi, it's me, Angela. Is it too early to call you?"

There was the sound of a TV and a kid yelling Mom, and Pattianne couldn't remember how many kids they had except that it was all girls, and she just said, "No, it's fine, I was up."

She soaked up the coffee with the bathrobe sleeve. "Michael's already off to school. I was just doing the puzzle."

"Puzzle?"

"Crossword puzzle."

Thirty-five across and the whole left corner floated in a coffee-blue-ink smear.

"Oh, my gosh," she said. "Well, I knew you'd be good to ask, I just knew it. You are not going to believe this, but can I find a dictionary in this house? I cannot. MayAnn, get down off that table. Do I know what ecumenical means? No, I do not. MayAnn, go get your sister's shoes from out the car, I think they're still in under the front seat."

"It means kind of all together," Pattianne said. "Like worldwide. General. In a church way, Christian churches."

"MayAnn, I am counting to three," Angela yelled like she didn't mean it, and she said, "Well, I kind of knew that, but how do you spell it is more what I don't know."

"Just a sec."

She set the phone down and went in the living room, pulled out the dictionary and looked it up.

"E-C-U-M-E-N-I-C-A-L," she said. "I thought there might be a T in it somewhere."

Silence.

"So, where's the T at?"

"Oh, there's no T."

"Well, thanks hon. I'm drawing up some fliers. I'll bring you by one to the bookstore."

"Wait, Angela. Do you know any of the birds around here?"

"You mean like pigeons and robins and crows?"

"Yeah."

"Well," she said. "Pigeons and robins and crows. Sparrows."

She hadn't ever heard of such a thing as a solid-black bird with a yellow head, like it just dipped its whole head in a bucket of yellow paint.

• • •

SEARS STORES ALL SMELLED the same. Pattianne walked in through ladies' shoes, kids' clothes, past the Ladies' Room, to an escalator in the middle of it all, drawing her right up to housewares, second floor. Drapes. A long row of hanging pastels, and more shades of beige than she could ever have imagined. Complicated and pleated drapes, with instructions for how to measure for them, how to order them, how to have them installed. The fabrics were brocade or woven, and stiff, and they were all arranged to look like peoples' windows up on the wall.

Miss Mimi had purple drapes once.

There was no purple here. No Fiesta orange. No blackbird yellow. She kept walking and came to towels, and past towels she got to small odds and ends like throw rugs. She started touching. The rugs were thick and nubby, and here there were colors like a neatly shelved rainbow.

A wide curving pathway of gray tiles in the white floor led through arrangements of bathrooms and bedrooms and kitchens. And then the path forked, one way to major appliances the other way to the escalator back down to the middle of menswear, at which point she kept going, straight out a door that put her on the opposite side of the building from the O-Bug, facing another parking lot that looked west, over fields and fields. The sky was hazy blue. Nothing blocked the view. Her heart pounded in her ears.

THERE WERE NOTES FROM Jen, sloppy little notes full of news. Nana Farley's new blood pressure medication made her cough, Aunt Maureen had a girl this time. The old elm tree in front of the house next door to Mom and Dad had to come down. Jen kept in touch with everyone, including her, now. When Michael and she had left, Pattianne had teared up, and Jen said, "Don't forget your allergy medication," and Pattianne said, "What allergies?" and Jen had rolled her own teary eyes.

Michael talked to his father on the phone every Saturday morning, and always came into the kitchen, the living room, wherever she was and reported to her. "He sounded good." He always said those same words. Mrs. Bryn sent funny cards every couple weeks, and Claire sent drawings from the kindergarten class where she was a student teacher. Her mother did not send notes. Pattianne sent her notes, little Hallmark cards with cheery hello messages signed "Love, Pattianne and Michael," and she called her, every couple weeks or so, usually after she got a note from Jen, so she could keep up her end of the conversation. Usually on Sunday.

She woke up knowing it was Call Mom Day. Michael slipped away early to run through the quiet streets. The furnace came on, rattling the grate in the bathroom. He was going to tighten the screws, but she said no, she liked that sound. There were cardinals outside the bedroom, their busy bell sound under the window, then farther away, then back under the window. Maybe they used to have a nest hidden in the vines. Maybe they wondered where the hazelnut tree went.

She didn't want to call, she just wanted her to be fine, both of them. The parents.

The kitchen door opened, closed, a cabinet door opened and closed. Michael was singing "Oh, What a Beautiful Morning," which is what he usually sang in the mornings, and after a bit there was the smell of coffee. He went in the bathroom, into the shower, singing louder. She pulled her bathrobe out of the blankets and pushed her arms through the sleeves, which were wide and dangerous in the kitchen, unless she was just waiting for coffee to drip. They fell back and showed her wrists, like she should have a jeweled bracelet there, and a cigarette in a jeweled holder. They usually ended up in the butter or the jelly.

The kitchen window was covered in starry frost. Frankie called it hoar frost, said it was rare except in drafty old houses. A hole was melting in the middle of each small pane, the world outside gray, with a flash of red.

Michael came in behind her, and she stood there between the smell of coffee and the smell of roses, his face by her ear.

"I had to use your shampoo," he said. "Do I smell like a girl?"

"I have to call my mother."

He leaned his chin on her shoulder.

"Darling," he whispered.

"What?"

"Tell her," he whispered. "Tell her 'yo, Mom, what is it?'"

Sometimes she laughed.

"Okay," he said when she didn't laugh, and he picked up the phone and dialed, and there was hello, yes, no, friendly-sounding back and forth, Michael chatting up the mother-in-law, and then he handed over the phone.

"Hi, Mom."

The phone was warm from his hand.

"Your father's not here," she said.

"How are you?"

She paced between the sink to the table.

"We're fine. He went to the hardware store to get a new air filter for the furnace."

"Is it getting cold there?"

"Yes."

If Pattianne didn't say anything, neither would she. They would both let the long empty wires hang between Minnesota and New Jersey.

"How's Nana Farley?"

"Fine. She got new blood pressure medication."

Michael wrote on the edge of the newspaper and held it out. "Tell her you got new glasses."

"I got new glasses."

"Are you still working in the bookstore?"

"Yes."

Michael left the kitchen and came right back with the glasses. He held them out, frames open.

"I only work part-time."

He pointed to the frames, then the lenses, opened them and closed them, held them in his palm in front of her face. She pushed his hand away and didn't laugh.

Her mother said, "Aren't there any library jobs?"

Michael set the glasses down on the counter and went into the living room.

"No," she said. "I like the bookstore, though."

"Have you put up drapes yet?"

"No," Pattianne said. "But we have rare frost. It's shaped like stars."

"Well."

He came back in with Jen's note.

"Jen wrote me about Aunt Maureen," she said. "So, number eight is finally another girl. Bernadette?"

"Actually," her mother said. "It's Bernadetta."

"Sounds Italian."

"Really, Pattianne."

Michael leaned on the counter. He whispered, "How's the new washer?"

"How's the new washer?"

She said, "It's a very good machine."

Michael whispered, "New dryer?"

"Of course," her mother went on. "It's from Sears."

"We have a Sears coffee maker," Pattianne said, and Michael jumped upright and tapped his finger against the front of the coffee maker, the German name there in bold black letters.

Pattianne said, "Isn't Braun a Sears brand?"

"I don't believe so," her mother said. "Sears doesn't have its own brand. There is KitchenAid, Mr. Coffee, and that German brand, Krupp. There isn't a Sears brand."

Have you ever seen a yellow-headed bird? Where have you hung our wedding picture? Is it in the dark upstairs hallway, by your own?

"Well," she said. "Tell Dad hi."

"Goodbye, dear."

Michael took the phone and hung it up. She put her hands into the big pockets. A knotted tissue, a circle of used Band-Aid, a book of matches. How long after you quit smoking do you stop having matches in all your pockets? Warm air blew across the kitchen floor from the vent.

She said, "Coffee?"

Michael said, "Cups!"

The hoar frost was all wet drips. There were two trees in the side yard, copper beeches, with old, thick trunks and masses of dark purple leaves. Between them, maybe in the neighbor's yard, a maple with bare, lofty branches.

He went to Mass, and she did the Sunday puzzle. He came back, and there was football, and it was so still and clear on their street that it felt like a painting on glass.

THE NEXT SATURDAY, MICHAEL headed off to the ecumenical men's group. He didn't really want to go, but he went. The map was open on the seat next to him. He liked sleeping late, curled up around her. She liked making love in the mornings. Then she'd go back to sleep. He'd get up, put on coffee, and go for a run on roads through the neighborhoods. When he got back, he'd make French toast.

Today might be the day. There might be a baby starting right this very second.

The heater in the O-Bug was cooking his ankles, but his nose and ears were cold. He tapped the button three or four times fast. Sometimes that made the heater kick on. The wheels crunched on the gravel along the side of the road, and he realized he was aiming for a small group of election signs on the corner of State Highway 21 and Old Grasse Road. He came to a slow stop, tapped at the button a few more times. Sometimes he had to pull the button off and poke at a wire in there with a pencil.

The election signs were leaning into each other along the weedy ditch. They were starting to pop up everywhere. He usually ignored them. He voted on tax issues that were about public education. He'd voted for Al Gore because he thought George Bush was unintelligent. Then he might have voted for Kerry, but his father had a Bush/Cheney bumper sticker on his car, and he'd never actually had a bumper sticker before. They didn't discuss politics at home. Michael had just moved to his apartment anyway, and hadn't re-registered.

The candidates seemed to be more about social issues in this election. Gay marriage made him uncomfortable, and he didn't know why. Same with immigration. His mother's housekeeper was an older German woman from Pennsylvania. He thought people who came to the country illegally should be sent home. Except for political refugees. Except for children. He knew he needed to be more informed. He didn't approve of uninformed voters. All the campaigns were a lot of hooey. It was advertising. Just because it was in red, white, and blue didn't make it true or important. He discounted them as sensationalism.

Until he saw the sign with jagged horizontal line. It was like the line on the heart monitor above his father's hospital bed, where, in neon green, it had steadily maintained its small, even peaks, and the quiet beep tone. He would find himself staring at it. He would find his mother staring at it too, as they waited, and his father slept. He found himself loving it.

And now here it was, in red, white, and blue.

Under it were the words *Abortion Stops a Beating Heart.*

The cardiologist had shown them diagrams of heart cells, explaining how certain cells were possibly being attacked by a virus. How different heart cells had different functions. The work of certain cells was to beat in unison with the other cells. If they were separated in a laboratory, they didn't beat in unison at first, but after a while they did. He remembered being emotionally overwhelmed at learning this. He'd excused himself, said he had to use the restroom, and left the office. He walked out into the hall and leaned against a window that looked out to the river. The office was on the tenth floor, looking down on the Raritan River, and it made him dizzy. He'd felt his own heart beating.

A pickup truck zoomed past him, laying on the horn.

"Sorry, sorry," he muttered. He checked his rearview mirror and headed on to St. Wendel.

Herman Walter lived in a yellow house on the edge of town. He opened the front door as Michael walked up.

"Good morning," Michael said, walking through the door.

Herman Walter said, "Glad you could join us," and laid a bony hand on his shoulder. The hand was warm. Michael felt the strange sting of tears in his eyes.

Two men sat on a couch. Rick Smith sat on a dining room chair next to the couch. Another man sat in an easy chair next to the fireplace. Herman Walter gestured to a dining room table. There was coffee, and cups, and a plate of cookies, and a stack of white paper napkins. There was a tablecloth, and the sun was shining on it all. Michael remembered the sun glinting off the Raritan River. He remembered that Herman Walter didn't drink coffee. He reached for one of the small cups and saw that his hand shook slightly. He took a cookie instead, and a napkin.

Herman Walter moved a dining room chair into the living room and positioned it next to Rick's, and Michael sat. He set the cookie on the edge of the coffee table on the napkin. There was some conversation going on, and he was startled when Rick turned to him and asked him something.

He said, "Fine. thanks," but he could tell from the way Rick stared at him that it had been the wrong response.

"Sorry," he said. "I think I'm coming down with a cold. Ears are plugged up."

But then Rick reached out and took his hand, and Michael realized they were all doing that, they were starting with prayer. He joined in, taking the hand of the man in the easy chair. The words of the twenty-third psalm rumbled gently around him. His heartbeat sounded in his head.

Then the man in the easy chair, who was from St. Mark Lutheran, spoke about the pioneer cemetery just outside town. He wanted to clean the grave markers.

"The families are gone," the man said. "Some of those names haven't been spoken aloud in fifty years." Maybe it was the man's low, quiet voice, but Michael found it unbearably sad.

Then they got around to the public prayer project.

There was a charter school in St. Joseph that had removed the words *under God* from the Pledge of Allegiance. Rick felt it would upset the children further if they were to show up and pray in front of the school. Herman Walter said they could pray there on a Sunday, and the men nodded and voices mumbled yes, good idea. Someone asked what other ideas anyone might have, and Michael heard the Lutheran man say, "Planned Parenthood."

Michael sat up straight in his chair. Praying on the sidewalk in downtown St. Cloud was overt and political. But it was just praying.

He said, "Are there legal issues?"

Herman Walter said, "Yes." Then he pulled a cell phone from his pocket. "I can check—it's a matter of distance."

Michael bit into the cookie. It was a gingersnap.

PATTIANNE LIKED KUAN-YIN. SHE was made of stone and stood about three feet tall, and she held a little metal lantern. The lantern was lit, and the lamp on the desk was lit too, and the Kali candle on the Light of the World table was lit—small points of light here and there in the bookstore. Outside it was dark midday, wind blowing grit against the window, and whenever the door opened, the cold shot into the bookstore. Snow was predicted before evening, although nobody in St. Cloud seemed to believe the weather predictions.

The door opened, and the cold came in along with a guy in an orange hard hat. He took off the hard hat and shut the door and held the hard hat in front of him, and when the white crane floated past his face, he raised a hand to it.

He said, "Oh," and he tucked the hard hat under one arm and said, "Ho, that's real pretty," and he bent low under the cranes and came in.

Pattianne turned the *The Compassion of Kuan-Yin* face down on the desk. She said, "Cold out there."

He looked in at her and nodded. An older guy. He came in a few steps and stopped, and he looked at the bookshelves along the wall and tucked his hard hat more firmly under his arm. He looked at the Light of the World and unzipped his coat partway. A sage bundle on the tea ceremony table was burnt and black and sat in a teacup. He looked at it and the mustache under his red nose wiggled a little.

"Sage," she said. "It cleanses the air. A Native custom of the American southwest."

He sniffed the air. The mustache was red too. Not as red as his nose.

"Sagebrush," he said. "Yeah, I know about sagebrush."

He unzipped his coat the rest of the way, a puffy nylon parka and a round belly. He shrugged around in his coat.

"Sagebrush and greasewood," he said. "Sagebrush and greasewood for miles. I worked a highway project in Arizona once. Sagebrush and greasewood for miles. Air was pretty clear, too, I got to say."

His boots were coated with white dust.

He said, "You got any books about Buddhists?"

"Lots."

He was a big guy, tall, bushy red eyebrows like the mustache. She walked in front of him, past him. He didn't follow her.

He said, "I probably only need one."

Buddhism was the biggest section in Lamplighter Books. Tibetan Buddhism, Zen Buddhism, yoga, mandala calendars. He switched the hard hat to the other arm and chewed on his mustache.

"Right here," she said.

He stepped around the Light of the World, looking at the table.

"They're Hindu," she said. "Those candles."

"That little gal you got lit there, she doesn't look too friendly now, does she?"

He stopped again a few steps in front of the Buddhism section, took his hard hat, and held it in both hands behind his back.

"I got a girl," he said, and he cleared his throat. "She's been in school in Madison."

He looked back at Kali.

"She's a good girl," he said. "She's back now."

He faced the Buddhism section and squared up his shoulders.

"She's a good girl," he said. "I never was much for church-going, but her mother pretty much raised her up Lutheran. Now she says she's Buddhist. My girl. Not her mom. Her mom says whatever, says she's a good girl, so for me to don't worry."

He stepped one step closer to the bookshelf, leaned his face toward it a little bit.

"Kind of dark in here," he said.

"You're right." She was being compassionate.

He looked up when she turned on the lights.

"So," he said. "I asked my girl"—looking around Lamplighter Books—"I asked my girl what this Buddhist stuff means. She said how I should come here and get a book. She used to come here and look at books before she went to school. College. In Madison."

He took a step closer to the shelf, and Pattianne could feel the cold coming off his nylon parka.

"I like to read books," he said. "You got any Tom Clancy? He writes books. Not about Buddhism, I don't think."

She reached past him and pulled a book from the shelf. "You need a basic book about Buddhism then?" More compassion.

The thin yellow book called *Buddhism Without Beliefs* was the only one she'd really looked at in the Buddhism section, a beautiful book, a narrow pleasing shape, a painting on the cover of a man in a boat. She held it out so he could see the cover, could maybe take it out of her hand.

He leaned back and looked at it. "Buddhism Without Beliefs," he said. "I was thinking maybe of a paperback."

"You can have a seat," she said. "Take a look at it. Read a little bit of it."

The beautiful chair was empty for once, no books stacked there for once, just Kali burning away right in front of it.

"Nope, nope," he said. "That's okay. So, how much is it?"

"$12.95. Plus tax."

He leaned closer to it.

"It's pretty basic," she said. "I don't know too much about Buddhism, but I liked it. It's pretty, well, basic."

"Well," he said, "okay."

He took a step back and looked at Pattianne instead of the book.

"I'll pay cash," he said. "You got a sack? It might get dirty. It's pretty dirty in my truck. That's my truck."

He waved his hard hat toward the front of the store, at white, dirty pickup truck parked out there.

"Picks up a fair amount of dust," he said.

He looked up at the cranes on his way back out the door, and shut the door and stood out there for a moment and put his hard hat back on. He waved at her through the window before he got in his truck, which had an orange-and-black sign. Follow Me.

The cranes were still swinging when Elizabeth came in.

"Quiet in here," she said.

She took off her gloves and rubbed her hands together.

"Cold out there," she said. "I don't think it's really going to snow, though."

"Shall I make tea?" Pattianne said. "Jasmine?"

Everything seemed so perfect.

WHEN SHE GOT HOME, Michael was on the phone talking to his father. He'd met with the prayer guys again, and she didn't really want to hear about them. Herman Walters was creepy. She went into the kitchen and got out *Joy of Cooking* and was leafing through it. She wanted to fill the house with the smell of something wonderful. That would be her prayer.

She did wonder if Michael actually prayed, though, besides with those guys. He'd been trying out soufflés since he found a soufflé pan at St. Vincent de Paul. Maybe he prayed for the soufflé to rise. There were times when he talked like he was talking to himself. Maybe he thought she didn't see, or maybe it was praying. Talking to God. His soufflés always rose.

Father McGivens had said, "God doesn't need our prayers. We need our prayers. To pray is to open our hearts to the divine mystery."

Which was actually pretty cool.

Michael came into the kitchen, and she said, "How's your dad sound?"

"Great." He looked over her shoulder at the cookbook. "Well, better. I think. His voice is stronger. Talking more."

"Hey," he said, wrapping his arms around her. "Have you ever made homemade gingersnaps?"

THE FIRST TIME SHE wore the new pants to work, the cold wind went up each leg. By the time she got to Lamplighter Books, she was freezing. She took off her coat and hung it up in back and waited for Elizabeth to notice her pants, but she was on the phone.

Then bells rang at the door, and there was Angela in a fuzzy, crocheted beret of neon blue.

"Hey," Pattianne said. "Hi."

The beret matched Angela's eyes. She held a flyer up. "Ecumenical Men's Prayer Circle" in thick, Gothic letters across the top, all spelled right. There was a dove in each corner. The participating churches were all listed in three rows, and behind the names was a gray cross like a shadow.

Pattianne said, "You drew all that by hand?"

"I took a lettering class at the junior college," Angela said, and she winked. "Calligraphy."

"Maybe Elizabeth'll want to put it up in the window." Pattianne took the flyer by the corner. "It's really nice."

"Thank you. You are so sweet," she said. "I always was a doodler."

She stepped back and looked at Pattianne up and down.

"And look at you, all dressed up like the caliph of Hans Christian Anderson," she said. "We been reading Hans Christian Anderson, me and the girls."

"Thanks," she said, and then didn't know what else to say so she said, "I love your beret. Did you make it?"

"Gosh, no," she said. "Well, I got to run around and put some of these up places. Safeway has a bulletin board, and so does the community center, and of course the co-op."

And *jingle, jingle,* she was out the door. She got into a red station wagon with three little blond heads in the back seat, and she drove off with a loud pop and a puff of exhaust.

"So, hello, sorry, I was stuck on the phone," Elizabeth said. "Hey. I love those pants. Especially with that top."

And she shook her hair.

The long, blue-faded-to-purple top that was maybe a dress made Pattianne feel like she had a cardboard face and was trying not to smile.

"Here," Elizabeth said, "wear these," and she dangled a long string of purple and black beads from her fingers. "Maybe someone will see them on you and want to buy some."

Customers never even looked at those beads. Pattianne set the flier on the desk and bowed her head, and Elizabeth slipped the beads around her neck and then stepped back and looked, with her head a little sideways, her lips doing this kiss sound, like she was calling a kitten.

She said, "Cute."

Thanks seemed like the right thing to say, but Pattianne's head went into a spiral. She didn't want Elizabeth to think she was thanking her for the beads, since she didn't think she was giving them to her, just letting her wear them. And she wasn't sure if maybe she wasn't trying to get her to buy them, since nobody ever even looked at them. And she wasn't thinking of buying them, except now maybe she guessed she was, since here she was thinking about it, except she never wore beads. And she never wanted to be cute before, and didn't want to be cute now, but it was different when another short person said cute.

Elizabeth said, "What the fuck is this?" She pointed to Angela's flyer, not touching it. Her nose did something wrinkly on one side.

"Oh, yeah, Angela."

The beads were smooth, odd-shaped pieces of glass.

"Angela?" Pattianne said. "Angela Park? Wacky wife of Max?"

She ran the beads through the circle of her thumb and forefinger, and they clicked cutely, and she guessed she was thinking about buying them, except she never wore purple. Elizabeth was wearing purple today. Maybe Elizabeth thought she wanted to be like her.

"Sacred Heart, Valley Presbyterian, First Church of the Nazarene, Green River United Methodists." Elizabeth read every name.

Pattianne thought maybe she just wanted to dress like Elizabeth. She said, "Are you going to put it up in the window?'

"I am not," she said. "Sit."

Pattianne sat on the stool. Crossed her legs, let the blue-purple top flow down the sides of the stool, her outfit chakra tingling and balanced. Elizabeth sat in the chair, and her own purple outfit draped itself down to the floor. She opened the drawer and took out the big scissors. They made her hands look like a child's hands. She held the flyer up in the air and cut it in half in one loud slash.

Pattianne had never heard her say fuck before. But she had seen her make birds before. She made them out of overdue notices and mailed them back to publishers with her check. She made birds out of the Sunday funnies and dropped them in the street like litter. She made birds out of dollar bills and gave them to the little kids who came into Lamplighter Books with their hippie moms. Now she folded the first square into a triangle and then opened part of the triangle back on itself. After that the folds got smaller and smaller, and Pattianne got lost, like she always got lost, watching those small fingers instead of the paper, until one bird and then another sat on the desk. Then Elizabeth stood up and went in back.

Pattianne picked up one of the birds, all sharp folded points.

Elizabeth came back out shaking a silver can of Liquid Technology for the Hair.

"Highly flammable," she said.

She held one bird up, the shadow of the cross on its wings, and she sprayed it. The hair spray in the air tasted like strawberries. She took matches out of the drawer, took the bird over to Kuan-Yin, and took the candle out of Kuan-Yin's lantern.

"Goddess of mercy," Elizabeth said. "Lord, have mercy on us all when Jesus's white boys start getting together in a bid for heavenly power."

She touched a match to the bird.

Pattianne said, "I thought you liked Jesus."

The match caught, a quick blue flame up each wing.

"Hey," Elizabeth said. "Look who's here."

And there was Michael, looking in the window, his hair its own little whirlwind, his head tipped to one side.

Pattianne said, "Shit."

Elizabeth said, "What?" And then she said shit, too, and she tucked the burning bird into Kuan-Yin's lantern and stuck her finger in her mouth.

Michael came in, and the cranes bounced around his head as if they were laughing. He had a roll of the fliers in his hand. What showed was the shadow of the cross.

"Michael," Pattianne said, in somebody else's voice. Somebody who was not there. She held up the other bird. "Look what Elizabeth made."

He looked down at the really big pants, and he said, "Hi, Elizabeth," and there was a sudden smile in his voice, like he was trying to make something okay that wasn't okay. He stepped close, tucked the fliers under his arm, and took the origami bird from Pattianne, and he whispered, "Why are you wearing pajamas?"

Elizabeth said, "Hey, Michael, long time no see," like she was singing a song. "We're having a ceremony."

Michael turned the origami bird over, looked at it, the way you do with origami birds.

"It's beautiful," he said. "You're burning it?"

The burning bird had actually gone out, its one blackened wing smoking. The hair spray no longer smelled like berries. More like gasoline.

Pattianne said, "Why aren't you in school?"

He said, "It's made out of the flyer."

Pattianne realized that when Michael was confused it came out sounding like wonder.

"Kuan-Yin," Elizabeth said. "Is the Buddhist goddess of mercy."

She looked at Pattianne, a sideways kind of a look that said, *Watch me handle this.*

Michael looked at her too, the pants and the top and the purple beads and then down at the pants again. Wide as a skirt.

"Now, then," Elizabeth said. "Would you like some ginger tea?"

Now then. Pattianne wondered why people said that, what it could possibly mean.

"No, thank you," Michael said. "Really, I just wanted to show you these. The flyers."

"Angela brought some," Pattianne said.

She wanted him to look at her face, so she could smile at him, so she could make something all right.

"Well," he said. "I'm on my way to South St. Cloud High. Student Congress planning meeting." He looked at the shelf right there. Dreams. Astrology. He picked up a book with the large red title *Wicca: A Personal Journey.*

Elizabeth leaned against the desk and said, "There's construction on Front Avenue. You should go back to the highway and go around."

"Oh," he said. He put the book back with great care. "Okay. Thanks."

There was the tiny crease between his eyebrows. He touched Pattianne's hand, their hands down low, between them, just a touch. Then he left. The cranes pecked at the window, watched him go out the door.

Elizabeth said, "That was not good, was it?"

"Well, it was weird. I know that."

She said, "What's the deal?"

Pattianne pointed to the flier. "That's the deal."

"I figured that much," she said. "It's his deal?"

"Yes."

"Is it your deal too?"

And Pattianne said no, but it felt like lying, like she had thumb-tacked that crease between Michael's eyebrows with her own thumb.

"The prayer circle," Pattianne said. "That's something he and Reverend Rick put together."

"Fucking Reverend Rick," Elizabeth said. "What was that about pajamas?"

Pattianne felt creeping, crawling disapproval all over.

"The birds were beautiful," she said.

"Well," Elizabeth said. Her voice had softened. "Religion makes everything weird."

Pattianne said, "I know."

Thinking, *I don't know anything.*

OUTSIDE THE BOOKSTORE, MICHAEL felt rattled. He turned right instead of left, away from the car. But if he turned back, he'd have to walk past the window of the bookstore. The wind hit at his face. He tucked the roll of flyers into his coat pocket. It was supposed to snow. He didn't like Elizabeth and he didn't know why. Didn't even want to think about why. He kept walking. There was a display of blue snow shovels at the hardware store. He could hear himself saying, "I live in a place where they make a display of snow shovels. Ha ha." He would call his dad this afternoon. His dad had a snow blower now.

He went into the hardware store. It smelled like wood. And right there in front of him was a display of kid-sized snow shovels, four of them leaning upright against a piece of picket fence, next to a stack of bags of de-icer. He picked up one of the shovels. It was light, with a plastic handle. He wanted it. He wanted them all. He could get them for the daycare program at church. It was perfect. He could see the little boys there. It was about instilling a love of service. That's what he would tell his dad. He took all four miniature snow shovels by the little blue handles and went to the counter. They clattered and one slipped to the floor. Michael picked it up.

The guy there looked at the four snow shovels.

Michael said, "I want all of them."

"All those too?"

There were more, sticking up out of a silver trash can. And Michael felt a little embarrassed and said, "Well. I guess just these four."

"Got a little work crew going, eh?"

Michael fished in his pants pocket for his wallet. "I'm going to get them for the daycare kids at Sacred Heart." The roll of flyers fell to the floor and unrolled. He got out his wallet and then picked up the flyers and set them on the counter and got out some money.

The guy said, "Donation, eh?"

"Yeah. I guess."

"How about I give you our ten percent?"

"Great!"

The guy was smaller than Michael, older, had a red Ace Hardware jacket. Michael wanted to shake the guy's hand, but he was putting the money in the drawer, so he just smiled. The guy wasn't looking at him. Then when the guy gave him his change, Michael said, "Hey, would you want to put one of these up in your window?" He turned the flyers around to the guy.

The guy glanced at them. "Nope. Don't believe so."

"Oh." Michael kept smiling. He said, "Well, thanks very much."

He rolled the flyers back up and stuffed them into his pocket. He shouldered the snow shovels.

"Thanks."

The guy nodded. "Very welcome, come again."

Once outside he kept going, around the block, instead of back past the bookstore. The sun had come out. There might be more places to put up the flyers. A yoga studio. Probably not. The wind blew in his face and smacked at the snow shovels. A law office. No windows really, just the door with the names. A used record store with posters for concerts. Probably not.

He really needed to get going anyway. His hand was deep into his pocket, around the roll of flyers. He wanted to think of Pattianne working in a warm, friendly school library instead of that dark little shop. Burning the flyer. A ceremony. He turned the corner back toward his car. The wind hit at him hard, and he pulled up his hood. The flyers went flying, and he dropped the snow shovels on the sidewalk and went after the flyers, grabbing at them before they blew away. When he got the last one, he stood up. The sun was shining in his eyes. Elizabeth was standing in the window of the bookstore. She was just watching.

PATTIANNE WALKED HOME FACING right into the west wind, the wild west wind that blew in off the prairie. Invisible bits blew into her face until she was walking with her eyes almost shut. Her legs were as good as bare in the big black pants. She turned up every side street she could to get out of the wind, up Third Street for a block, past the used CDs-records-tapes store, up Fourth Street, past the Memorial Library and the International Eatery, up Fifth Street, past Smoke's. A long, gauzy dress like a nightgown hung in the window. There was a row of posters and flyers along the bottom of the window. The prayer circle flyer was there, too, neatly taped at the end of the row, upside down.

She never for a moment thought Jesus was a magical god come to earth.

Now she was someone in Minnesota with a husband who went to Mass.

A husband who prayed in a circle with a bunch of guys.

Jesus was looming.

Her nose dripped with the cold, and her ears tingled, and by the time she got home, she couldn't even feel her knees. The wind blew hard against the kitchen door and yanked it out against its hinges. The house was cold, and she pushed the thermostat up to seventy-five. The wind blew against the wide, blank front window, and when she turned on the lights, the outside went dark, and there she was, in front of the bookshelves, Grandma Anthony and the wildlife parade, all of them posing in the living room. She turned the light off.

It was Thursday. He'd be home right after school, no debate practice, no anything else she could think of. The *Seasons of Minnesota* calendar showed a blank October day.

If she changed her clothes, he might not even mention she was wearing pajamas at work, which they weren't, and which is what she should have said when she brought them home from Smoke's and Michael had first called them pajamas. Now it was too late, now she was already sneaky, now anything she did would be about burning the prayer circle bird. Now she didn't know what she wanted to do, besides wear long, beautiful clothes and know how tarot cards worked and what an ephemeris was. And she didn't want Michael to make hippie jokes, and Elizabeth wasn't really a hippie anyway. And besides, his hippie jokes were boring, and it made her sad when Michael was boring.

It was funny though, that upside-down flyer. Jen would appreciate it. Her mother would point out that it was upside down, and Jen would appreciate that too.

The bedroom heat vent rattled, and it was warm and dark in there, and she just sat there, on the bed where she slept with her Catholic boy. Where she made love to her young Catholic boy husband under his dark wood crucifix. Where he prayed to a Jesus who was a magical god come to earth. There were rules about their marriage, about how they could fuck and why. Some pope made the rules, and some other pope amended the first pope's rules, and more popes made more rules, and they all handed down the rule-making rule, one to the other, until they all forgot that Jesus didn't care about rules. Jesus hung out with whores and losers. Jesus was a political upstart with a beautiful sad face who inspired too much poetry for his own good.

The piece of brocade hanging over the bedroom window fit as neatly as a curtain. She had made the bed this morning. There was chicken to cook for dinner. She could bake it in onions and olive oil and garlic. The whole house would smell like dinner. There were small, sane moments to be had for the asking.

She didn't even notice the banging on the kitchen door at first, and then she noticed it, and noticed she had been hearing it for a while, and went out there. And it was Frankie, looking in the window of the kitchen door, wearing a big puffy maroon jacket. She pushed open the screen door, and the wind blew it back against its hinges.

Frankie caught it, and he said, "Mr. Bryn's not home yet, is he?"

"No." The air was twilight blue, winter blue, cold blue. "Come in here. It's too cold."

His jacket wasn't even zipped, open to his white T-shirt.

He said, "No, that's okay, I just wanted to ask him to steady the ladder for me. I got to go up on the roof. That old aerial is just hanging there. I was supposed to get it down by now, and I don't want the wind to carry it off into someone's window or something. I got the ladder in the truck."

"I'll help you."

Sometimes she got lucky in little ways.

"Just let me change my clothes."

He looked worried at her, kind of sucking on that crooked tooth, and she left him standing there. In the bedroom she pulled off the big black pants and dropped them on the closet floor and pulled on jeans. Dropped the blue-faded-to-purple top on top of the pants, and put on Michael's sweatshirt, and went back out in the kitchen, out the door. The wind was lying in wait for the screen door again, but this time she was ready for it.

Frankie was out behind his truck, pulling the ladder out of the back. He tipped the ladder up, and the wind tipped it back down, and he let it fall to the ground and then dragged it to the side of the house. He leaned it up against the house, steadied it, looked up at the aerial. The aerial was swinging in the wind, dangling over the eave.

"Is that safe?" she said. "Are you going to be able to get it down?"

He put his hands on either side of the ladder. "Probably."

He flexed the sides of the ladder and started up, and she stepped close to the ladder, leaning into it, holding on to the sides. The cold aluminum burned into her palms, and the ladder bumped and jerked, but it was Frankie, not the wind. What the wind did was blow right up the back of Michael's sweatshirt, up against her bare skin, against her neck. Her hands hurt, and it was so cold she had to pee, and it felt good to hurt like this, how sometimes it felt good to feel bad.

Frankie yelled down, "You doing okay?"

She yelled up, "I'm fine."

The ladder felt like it was cutting her hands, and she was afraid to let go to look and see if she was really bleeding, which she didn't think she was, but it felt like she was. She wouldn't care. She would bleed.

Part of the aerial came loose, and Frankie yelled, "Watch out," and it went blowing across the yard toward the house next door, flashing through the bare trees. Frankie yelled out, and the ladder jerked, and another big piece dropped and whipped her on the shoulder like the willow branch when they were kids and it was her turn to be Silver and Jen's turn to be the Lone Ranger.

Frankie yelled, "Are you okay?"

It hurt. "I'm fine."

He yelled, "Mrs. Bryn?"

She looked up at him, at his boots, and his face looking down, and the rest of the aerial whipping in the wind, and the black clouds moving fast through the dark twilight cold blue.

"You can call me Pattianne."

He yelled, "What?"

The last piece of aerial went flying end-over-end, off into the dark, into what used to be a bigleaf maple. Except now there were no leaves. She wasn't sure. And two warm arms wrapped around her, and Michael's quiet voice in her ear said, "Okay, babe, I got it."

Her hands were stuck to the cold aluminum, and Michael yelled up, "Frankie, come down from there," and he said, all warm breath in her ear, "Okay, let go," and she did. Her hands weren't bleeding. She ducked under his arms and tucked her hands into her armpits.

Frankie came down, and when Michael let go of the ladder Frankie jumped off the last rungs, and the ladder came down sideways with a quiet aluminum crash and bounce.

Frankie said, "I got to go round that stuff up," and he ran off under the trees.

Michael took the ladder by the end and hauled it to the truck and slid it into the back. She stood still, watched him, rubbed her hands together, and they burned with the blood running back into them. Her shoulder stung, and her hair whipped into her eyes, and she shivered from all the way inside.

Michael came back to her, clapping his hands together.

"Good idea," he said. "Climbing a ladder on a night like this."

She put her palms on his cheeks.

"Cold," she said.

He took her hands away from his face and pulled her toward the kitchen door, and she yelled, "Frankie, come on in when you're done."

He yelled, "What?" somewhere out there in the wind, somewhere out in the next-door neighbor's yard.

Michael opened the screen door, and the wind did its thing against the hinges, and he said, "Goddamn it."

He came in behind her. Gave the light string a yank, and filled the room with light.

He said, "What was that about?"

"The aerial." Even her voice shivered. "That whole thing was about the aerial."

She would make hot chocolate. There was peppermint schnapps.

She said, "Frankie was afraid it would blow away."

She got a pan out and set it on the stove.

Michael said, "Great. Instead, he almost got blown away."

She got the milk out of the refrigerator and stood there with the door open, and she couldn't tell if she was colder than the refrigerator or not. "Want hot chocolate? There's schnapps."

The screen door blew open again and Frankie came in.

"I'm going to have to replace those hinges in about a minute," he said. "Thanks, Mrs. Bryn. Did you get bonked?"

"You want some hot chocolate? With schnapps?"

"I can't. Gotta get going. I have a friend with me. Sort of."

Michael and Pattianne both said, "Where?"

Frankie's face was one big happy face, his smile all about that crooked front tooth, and he said, "You got to meet him."

He went back out. He didn't let the wind get the door.

Pattianne dumped powdered cocoa into the pan of milk, her fingers tingling, spilling cocoa onto the stove, and there were sparks where the cocoa was caught by the gas flames.

Michael came up behind her and put his hands on her shoulders and said, "I don't think Frankie is old enough to drink."

His hands were warm. His hands were always warm. She pushed

up the sleeves of the sweatshirt and stirred the cocoa into lumps, smaller and smaller lumps.

He kissed the back of her neck. Even his lips were warm, and he said, "What's this?"

He pulled the purple beads out of the back of the sweatshirt and they tickled across her nipples. The hinges screeched, the door blew open, the beads dropped back down inside her sweatshirt. The flame under the hot chocolate flared.

And Frankie said, "Meet Bullfrog."

A small white hound-dog type of dog with long brown ears and short legs. Pattianne dropped to her knees.

"Bullfrog?" she said. "Are you Bullfrog?"

He said yes. His eyes were hound-dog eyes, sad and droopy, and his long, oddly bushy tail thumped a couple times on the floor.

She said, "Is he yours?"

Bullfrog licked her hand and sniffed at her wrist, sniffed on up toward her elbow, his fat pinkish nose tickling the skin on her arm. She got goose bumps, and a funny cooing sound came out of her.

"He's gorgeous," she said, and she took his long ears in her hands. "His ears are cold—he was cold out there."

Unbelievably soft ears.

The hot chocolate in the pan foamed over, hissing into the flames, and the flames shot up blue.

She said, "Where'd you get him?"

"He was wandering around at Lewiston's place," Frankie said. "The old French teacher, from last year? He was going to call the pound. They kill dogs there, you know."

Michael took the pan off the stove. Bullfrog's nose bounced in the air in the direction of the hot chocolate.

She said, "He's hungry."

Frankie said, "He's always hungry. That's his deal. Eat. Sleep. Chase cats. He usually seems kind of disappointed when they run away, though. Or else he loses them. I don't think he can see too well."

After Frankie and Bullfrog left, she put pasta water on to boil, and she said, "What would cocoa have in it that would make sparks like that?" And, "Did you guys ever have a dog?" And she told him about

Starla, who was a spaniel, who piddled when she got excited, who lived until she was old.

"We had a retriever once," he said. "Or a lab. I can never remember which is which."

She cut sharp white cheese into triangles and laid them on a Flow Blue plate, only a buck at a junk shop in Popple Creek, no chips. She asked him when the next debate tournament was, and where.

"Tuesday," he said. "Mizpah."

And she said how Minnesota has some weird place names, and here's some white wine, and what's this blue plate called again.

"Flow Blue," he said.

"It looks like a mistake," she said. A windmill, all blurry around the edges.

"They were a mistake," he said.

He sat in the living room and opened the newspaper, and ten minutes later his head was leaned back against the back of the couch, reading through his nostrils, he liked to say, and then there was a soft snore.

She tucked the purple beads into the pocket of her coat, and then she touched his shoulder with one finger, two fingers, whispering, "Wake up. Let's have dinner. I love you. I love you."

EAST OF ST. CLOUD, the Mississippi made its claim, made everything about business, warehouses, shipping plants, industry. And the towns got denser, and it felt like New Jersey. West of St. Cloud, the land seemed to open up, and on Tuesdays sometimes, or on Thursdays sometimes, she drove the O-Bug over the roads as if she were going somewhere, somewhere west. There were trees, far back along the property lines, or in the dips in the fields where there were creeks maybe, flares of red and yellow.

"Crimson, scarlet, vermillion, gold, caramel, purple," she said — what she would write to Miss Mimi.

"Dassel, Kandiyohi, Manannah, Kerkhoven," reading the signs at the intersection in Eden Valley. A kid in a pickup truck watched her from across the intersection, a four-way stop, her turn to go. If there were a dog in the passenger seat of the O-Bug, she could be talking to the dog instead of riding along talking to herself.

A huge, lopsided pumpkin sat at the front of a hardware store. Really huge, as big as a wheelbarrow. Another one, not quite as huge but more lopsided, was posed outside the Good Days Food and Drug. Shop windows had orange and black crepe-paper streamers, and witches and skeletons hung from the lamp poles. There seemed to be a lot of hay bales here and there, and a lot of the really huge pumpkins.

When she stopped for gas at the Eden Valley Gas 'n' Go, there were bags of Fun-Size Snickers by the register.

Michael loved Snickers.

"Milky Way is better," she always said.

"Snickers have peanuts," he said.

"Milky Way," she would insist.

"Snickers has a better name."

She asked the Gas 'n' Go girl where she could get one of those big pumpkins. The girl looked up through thick black bangs.

"Got to grow one," she said. "For the competition. You grow them, you don't buy them. Ten eighty-five."

"And a bag of Fun-Size Snickers, please."

Just driving around.

MICHAEL AND RICK STOPPED inside the sagging gate. The cemetery was old. The grave markers were dark with black moss. Some were tilted. The boys bunched up behind them, quiet. Rick had the pickle buckets.

"Kinda cold," one of the boys said.

Another one went, "Shh."

Rick said, "The water's over here," and he led the way toward a short spigot that stuck up from the ground. Michael stepped aside, and the boys moved past him. No joking around. They fell into single file. Rick had that effect on them. Michael knew they weren't afraid of Rick. He thought it was respect.

There were five pickle buckets. A little dish soap in each one. Sponges. Rick knelt at the spigot and worked at it until the handle turned a quarter turn and rusty water dribbled out.

"Don't scrub too hard," Rick said. "The markers are fragile."

"Even after being out in, like, snow and all?"

"What's fragile?"

"Delicate," Michael said. "Flimsy. From the Latin *fragilis*. Liable to break. Same root as fracture."

One of the boys said, "You know, Latin is a dead language."

And another, it was Charles, said, "That's rude, dude."

And the first one said, "I'm just saying, like, we're in a cemetery and all." And Michael heard the rustle of a shove.

"I think cemeteries are kinda weird." That was Sammy.

When each pickle bucket was half full of soapy water, one set in front of each boy, Rick said, "Who remembers the prayer?"

The boys looked at each other, and at the ground. Michael could tell Gerard and Sammy were trying not to laugh or something. He could tell they were all a little nervous. And he loved them for that.

Rick said, "It goes like this: May the souls of the faithful departed, through the mercy of God, rest in peace. Amen."

Sammy automatically said, "Amen," and then he said, "Sorry."

Rick laughed, a small forgiving chuckle, and Sammy's face got red.

"It's okay," he told them. "You don't have to say the prayer out loud, but think it."

He handed out the pickle buckets, one to each boy, and they headed off in different directions, lugging the buckets as if they were too heavy. Michael felt a big feeling in his chest. An ache.

"But say the names you see on the markers," Rick said. "Out loud."

"Okay." That was John. John the Agreeable, they called him in staff meetings. He was too agreeable for his own good. Always getting led into trouble. Usually the one who got caught. He was small, his coat too big. The ache in Michael's chest got bigger.

He and Rick walked through the cemetery, listening to the mumbled prayers. Some graves showed whole families, their markers with dates going back a hundred years. It was late afternoon. The sun was low and the sky was clear. He could hear the freeway far off. Like everything else around here. The landscape made him homesick. It made him nervous. The cemetery was on a small rise. There was one tree, right in the middle.

"Some of these names haven't been spoken aloud in generations," Rick said.

Michael cleared his throat. He didn't know what to say. It seemed terribly important, and he just nodded. He heard the words of the prayer for the dead in his head. He wanted to say it out loud and was afraid to say anything out loud. His throat felt full of tears.

Rick touched his arm. "You okay?"

"I guess."

His parents went to the cemeteries of their families, but they never took him or Claire. He would change that. He longed for that sense of the generations, stretching out before him, after him. Seven months wasn't really that long to be waiting to get pregnant.

"Are you thinking about your father?"

"I guess."

He didn't want to talk to Rick about his father. Or about the empty flat space around here. He clapped Rick's shoulder and moved away, toward a crooked thin marker. There were flat markers in the brown grass around it, three on one side, two on the other. He brushed his hand over the crusty moss on the face of it, off the single letter R. He leaned against it, and then pressed it to see if it would straighten. There was a crunch, and he jumped back, and the tall marker fell over at his feet with a quiet thump.

"Oh my God."

"Michael, are you okay?"

"Oh my God."

It lay across one of the flat name markers. Amanda.

"Dude."

"Wow."

"Man, that thing was *fragilis*."

"Fractured, man."

"It's okay, boys," Rick said. "Let's keep working. It can be set back up. Accidents happen. Just don't lean on the gravestones."

Michael couldn't catch his breath.

"Jesus," he whispered. It had just collapsed. It was that old. It had stood that long.

"It's okay, Michael," Rick said, his voice low. "It's okay, boys," his voice louder. "Just be careful. They're old, and some of them are crumbly."

"Rick, what should I do?" Michael stared at the broken marker.

"It's okay. I'll call the sexton." Rick's hand closed around Michael's elbow. "Michael?"

He was shocked at the damage. He was shocked at the whiteness of the crumbled concrete around the base of the broken marker. He couldn't look at the boys.

One of them mumbled, "Sexton," and Michael heard giggles. Rick rolled his eyes, and just like that, Michael knew what to do.

"Sexton," he said loudly. "From the same Latin word as sacred. One who tends sacred objects. Back to work on your sacred objects, boys."

It was quiet and windy. It got cold. Nobody went near the broken marker.

He had Rick drop him off at home, and he took the pickle buckets in with him. The O-Bug was gone, the house empty. He was in the kitchen, getting ready to rinse the pickle buckets, when she came in. Her hair was blown all over. Her nose was red.

"Pickle buckets," she said.

They were stacked up on the counter, and the damp grocery bag was on the table.

"So, hey," she said. She looked inside the grocery bag, at the sponges and dish detergent. "What's up?"

He turned back to the pickle buckets. "Rick and I took some of the boys out to the St. Wendel Cemetery."

He felt the shake in his voice and hoped she didn't hear it.

"St. Wendel?"

"It's a pioneer cemetery," he said. "We cleaned the markers."

He worked one bucket up out of the stack and knew he wouldn't tell Pattianne about breaking the marker. About the lonely cemetery. The bucket was too big for the sink. He set it back.

About the prayer circles.

About how much he hated Minnesota.

"I was just rinsing these out," he said. "No one ever goes out there anymore." He didn't know what else to say.

He stood with his back to her. His hands rested on the stack of buckets. "No one is left to take care of the graves. Whole families died out, gone." He set the buckets on the floor. "Some of those names haven't been said out loud in fifty years." He turned and leaned back on the counter. Slid his hands deep into his pockets. There was white concrete dust on his shoes. He felt a little sick, picturing that white gash in the dark old place.

"So," she said. "Who's St. Wendel?"

She shook the bag of Fun-Size Snickers sat him, and it was like he came back into the kitchen.

"Hey. Snickers." Back to her.

"Milky Way is better," she said.

"Snickers have peanuts," he said. And he wondered what had been so sad. And what was suddenly easy.

THE BUDDHISM-BOOK GUY CAME in and set all the small cranes swooping in circles.

He said, "I have to tell you, I was thinking about you the other day, Tuesday—no, Wednesday, well, maybe Thursday last week." He sucked on one side of his mustache. "What day was it raining?"

Thursday, four in the morning, rain fell straight down onto their house. Then around five in the morning the wind came up from the west, slapping the last yellow heart-shaped leaves onto the window, and the last starry red maple leaves, and then the rain washed them all away.

"Thursday," she said. "It rained Thursday."

"Yep, well, then, it must have been Friday," he said, and he smoothed his red mustache in a single gesture of forefinger and thumb.

She hooked her heels on the rung of the stool, folded her hands together in her lap, settled on her backbone.

He reached one finger out to a blue crane.

"This one here," he said. "This bluish one here is the same as these cranes out by where I'm working at." The blue crane swung toward him, all the cranes swung toward him, and he pulled his finger back. "I asked one of the young fellas out there, out there along the meadow, it not being a meadow now, all that rain, turned it right back into a swamp, out there where the old highway goes up to the caves?" His eyebrows had worked themselves into a question.

"Never been there."

"Cranes," he said. "Kind of gray and blue colored, just like this one here. You can't hardly see them, same color of the grass clumps, about that tall, that tall swamp grass? You can hear them, though. The cranes, not the swamp grass. They make all sorts of noises, you can hear them even when you can't see any sign of them, way up in the air they start up, sounds kind of like a horn, coming down out of the sky." He didn't have his hard hat, and his boots didn't leave dusty footprints on the carpet. He got close to the shelf of herb books and said, "You got any books about birds?"

"No," she said. Angels. UFOs. Fairies. "No bird books, sorry."

"This young fella, he said, 'You ought to see these sand cranes,' that's what he called them, sand cranes, when it's their time, 'courtship ritual' he called it. I thought that was a nice way of saying it, courtship ritual."

From behind, he was a big puffy square of nylon and two legs in gray slacks and a head of bristly reddish-gray hair.

"We don't have any nature books, really. It's pretty much all philosophy and religion. New Age."

Facing her again, he sucked on his mustache and looked all around. "Well," he said. "I thought it would be nice to read up on them, seems they're real characters, dancing around and what all. That would be during the courtship ritual."

"So." Her feet unhooked from the rung, and her butt looked for the center of gravity. "How is that book on Buddhism working for you?"

His head set to nodding up and down. "I been reading it," he said. "I'm working that stretch of the old highway. Not much traffic. I'll read a little bit and then put it down and think on it. Funny how that works, thinking on something new like that. I start out thinking on it, and then pretty soon I'm not thinking on it, I'm thinking on something else, and I never even noticed, I never thought well, here, I'll stop thinking on such and such and start in on thinking about such and such instead—you ever notice how thinking works that way?"

Suddenly it was a question.

"Course it gets pretty quiet out there," he said. "That old highway never sees much traffic most days. Folks avoid it. It floods over pretty easy, that's why they're draining that swamp, widen that road." He planted his legs wide and crossed his arms and looked up at the ceiling.

"You know," he said. "Those gals they got flagging now, they're pretty sharp."

The neat collar of his pinstripe shirt poked at the thick red skin of his neck.

"Course," he said, "they had to redo all the signs. Used to be the signs said 'flag man ahead.' But that's okay. Gals got to work. A sign isn't any big deal. They say 'flagger' now, 'flagger ahead.' Every once in a while, I see an old sign, never got redone. Ho."

He looked at her, and she said, "Well, I have to admit, I've noticed those new signs."

He said, "I wouldn't want my girl working flagging. Dangerous. Now, working in a bookstore seems like a good job for a girl right out of college."

"She's looking for a job?"

"Nope," he said. "Got one. She works out at the clinic, and sometimes at the Planned Parenthood. I'm just trying to run her life, that's what the wife says, run her life. I got to go pick her up soon, the wife. She's at the hair salon, then we got to go out to see her dad, he's in the Castle Home. Nice place, not like you'd think of an old folks' home being. I got the Buick."

Instead of her center of gravity, she thought of looking for her soul chakra. It was down there somewhere too. Maybe there was a story-listening chakra.

"The wife, she doesn't like me driving her around in the truck. She says seems like folks will start following us, leastwise looking at us." He edged around the Light of the World. Kali wasn't lit today.

Pattianne gave him a laugh to let him know she was listening.

"Ho," he said, "That's not so dang far-fetched of a notion. I'm out there, the flagger gal waves me on out, and out I go in the pilot car, or in this case, pilot truck of course, and I got five or six in line. Right behind me, I got a hippie fella in an old GMC. Little gal in a Rambler station wagon behind him. Older couple in a newer-model Ford. Nice looking cars, those new Fords."

None of the Hindu Gods were lit today, only the red votive on the Japanese tea ceremony table.

"I get to the south end of the project, two lanes again, all the way to town, and the other flagger gal, she's got no cars lined up down on that end. I'm in the left lane, and I pull off to the shoulder, right there by the old Tanner Place?"

"Never been there."

"It's a wide gravel turnout," he said. "Mack Tanner drove an eighteen-wheeler."

He sat down in the beautiful chair. He laid his thick hands along the thin arms of the chair. His knees were big, shiny squares in his gray slacks.

"Well, he sold it. Went to work in the hardware store when the kids started coming along, so as not to be gone all the time." He ran a finger along one purple stripe. "Five of them eventually, five Tanner kids. So, I pull in there, into Tanner's turnout, and does that hippie fella cross the lane and head on south into town? He does not. He follows me right into the turnout, and then so does the little gal in the Rambler, and the folks in the Ford, well, they're stopped in the middle of the road—it's a wide turnout but still can only me and that hippie fella and that Rambler wagon fit in there. This Ford looked to be from down near the Cities. Well. Everybody just stops."

He shook his head.

Her story chakra was balanced and happy on the stool. "Ho," she said.

"I couldn't even get my own self out of that turnout without I would have had to go up on the Tanners' walkway up to their house," he said. "And that flagger gal, she's just looking. There's a beat-to-heck Corvair, you don't see too many of them, finally pulls out from the end of the line and goes on down the road like he ought. The couple in the Ford pull out after him. They don't ever look at anybody, that's how I'm thinking they're from the Cities, how city folks just look straight ahead? Then the Rambler pulls out. That little gal waves at me going by, see, that's what folks from around here will do, give you a little wave."

His fingers wiggled on the arm of the chair.

"And that hippie fella? He's just laughing and laughing. Kind of banging his head on the steering wheel."

End of story.

"Ho," he said.

His eyes were unfocused on something above the Light of the World. His eyes were blue, his head nodding.

"That's a good story," she said.

He stopped nodding, and his eyes came back to the here and now. "That was no story"—his eyebrows busy again—"that really happened. Happened just like I said."

One eyebrow went down. The other didn't. He said, "You think that hippie fella was high on drugs?"

"Could have been. But maybe not. You never know."

He laid both hands flat on his knees and said, "That's right, you never know." His fingers were short. There was a gold ring. "I noticed," he said, "There's some hippies got a fairly odd sense of humor. My girl has some hippie friends used to come out to the house. They'd laugh at stuff wasn't even funny. And they couldn't of been high on drugs, it would be at oh, say, six in the morning sometimes. They used to show up for breakfast. They liked to come over real early, her hippie friends. Liked to make cinnamon rolls out of those tubes? You whop the tube on the edge of the stove, and the rolls pop out, and you just bake them on the cookie sheet. Smell up the whole house. I'd call them whopping biscuits, that'd make them just laugh and laugh. They'd eat every one while they watched the sun come up out back over the Tuckfields' bean field."

Nodding. Him nodding. Her nodding. Then he stood up quick, how quick and easy-footed some large men were, and he said, "Got to go pick up the missus."

Pattianne nodding. The cranes all circling after him out the door.

How those cranes moved. They circled slowly, slower and slower, and she never noticed when they stopped, only that they were hanging suddenly still, like they had only just that second stopped moving. Like they were still moving, and if she watched, she would see one more small movement.

7: THAT KIND OF CATHOLIC

THE NOVEMBER SKY OVER Newark Airport—glimpses of it out long windows over the tarmac, over rows of blue runway lights, red lights on towers, yellow lights on trucks—was solid and low and flat and mean. Pattianne and Michael walked down the long, tiled concourses, and then went underground, finally, down a long, narrow escalator. Wars escalated. Tensions escalated. She thought down escalators should have a different name. Michael waited for her at the bottom, off to the side. One of his pet peeves was people who get off an elevator and just stand there in the way, and it surely applied to escalators as well. She didn't know how he kept getting ahead of her.

The turkey was home in the freezer, and when they got to the Bryns' she had to remember to call Lily Smith and cancel herself and her spice cake for the faculty wives' Thanksgiving brunch. Michael hadn't brought any clean shirts. He loved clean starched shirts. He said it was embarrassingly true. But he'd only brought dirty shirts. She would take them to a twenty-four-hour cleaner's in Edison. That would help.

She had asked for a red rental car. Red cars were safe. The woman on the phone said they didn't list them by color, and she offered a brand-new Mustang convertible.

"It's November," Pattianne said.

The woman said, "It might be red, though."

The car they got was a Mercury, dark blue outside and gray velour inside. It looked like a dad car. Michael opened the door and she got in, and in the time it took for him to get around to the driver's side, she knew that it smelled like a dad car, too, and that she loved dad-car smell. He got in. Started the car. Closed his eyes and laid his forehead on the steering wheel.

She said, "Want me to drive?"

He raised his face to the two yellow arrows pointing the way out of the underground garage. His eyes were glassy. Maybe from no sleep, maybe from the fluorescent lights. He shifted into drive. The car was so smooth she thought it had stalled.

The gray sky outside the car was any time of day except really early or really late. The hours had worked themselves into a hopeless tangle. Michael had picked up the telephone when it rang, sometime after he got home from school yesterday. That's when the hours started to get tangled. Mrs. Bryn was on the telephone. Mr. Bryn was in the hospital. Michael was on the floor, sitting against the wall under the telephone, and for a long time after that, he stayed sitting there. Pattianne booked the first flight she found. She called Reverend Rick, told him that Michael's father was in the hospital, and Michael would call from New Jersey.

Rick would tell Lily, and Lily would know she wouldn't be at the faculty wives' Thanksgiving brunch with spice cake.

He needed a new heart. He was going to have a heart transplant. They were going to take out Mr. Bryn's heart. She was back in New Jersey.

All those words were in her head. It was raining.

She and Jen used to believe that a hobo lived under the bridge where you turned off the turnpike into Newark Airport. Cranbury was a long way from Newark Airport, but all the neighborhood kids knew about the hobo. Their father was the one who first told her, just him and Pattianne in the car, as they passed under the bridge one time. It was dark and she couldn't see anybody. She had asked him if she could tell Jen about the hobo, and that made him laugh.

Michael drove, and the car was so quiet it was more like he just steered. There were three bridges, and she had no idea which one was the bridge with the hobo. She had no idea if Michael had heard of the hobo, him being from Edison. She had no idea if Michael would want her to ask him about the hobo now.

Her parents didn't know she was here. There hadn't been time. She hadn't wanted to. She'd had to get Michael up from the floor under the telephone. She would call from the Bryns'. She would ask her dad about the hobo. For one moment she was glad it wasn't her dad in the hospital. For a moment she thought, *What if it was?* What if it was her mother?

"Michael," she said.

Sour watery spit filled in the back of her throat. She needed to swallow, get different air inside her, say something.

"Michael," she said. "Have you ever heard of the hobo under the bridge?"

His face opened into a laugh, and then he held his breath, slowing, steering the car over to the paved shoulder lane, and he stopped and set the brake. He turned his whole body and put his arm around her, pulled her face into the wool of his sweater, so tight she could feel his breath, held in and then let out in one small cry that broke off short.

Outside the car was the whole world of New Jersey, the wet highway, trucks that went by and made the car shake. They were sealed inside of it, just Michael and her for a few more miles, a few more minutes. She could do things, go to the cleaners, make coffee in Mrs. Bryn's big silver coffee pot in her blue-and-white-tiled kitchen. She could figure out how to be helpful. It was weird how you stopped sometimes, stopped being yourself and started just moving around within your skin, used your fingers to make phone calls, heard your voice stay even, felt your heart beating inside your chest. Not pounding or racing or breaking or loving. Hearts beat, and then they stopped beating. That's all they did.

Michael sat up and drew his arms back into himself. He faced the highway.

"Of course I've heard of the hobo under the bridge." And then, "I just don't want to cry in front of Claire."

"Good," she said, with that sinking feeling that what she was about to say is the absolute wrong thing. "Because you sound like a wounded seal, and you would scare the shit out of her."

Not the wrong thing.

"Okay," he said—a small word that was a reach for breath and had a smile in it. Just a small one to get to the next moment, one moment after another. He looked in the rearview mirror and moved his foot to the gas. The engine revved.

"You're supposed to put this kind of car in gear," she said. "Then you drive."

Wrong thing. His shoulders dropped then, and he said, "Goddamn it."

"Maybe not just yet," she said, and her hand twitched on her leg, wanting to touch him.

When she cried, her eyes got red and bleary, and tear trails streaked her face, and her nose turned red. Michael's eyes got bright, with tears that dripped down his cheeks like rain down clear glass.

"It's going to be okay," she said. "This kind of surgery is pretty advanced. He's young, really."

He said, "I know," put the car in gear, and drove.

PUMPKINS DECORATED THE BASE of the gas lamp in the front yard— ordinary-sized, round pumpkins, next to the flagstone walk leading up to the Bryns' front door. Michael opened the door, set down their two bags on the flagstone floor of the entryway, and she followed him in. Inside were six stairs up and six stairs down, and as you stood there, under the huge carriage lamp hanging in the tall space, you had to decide, right away, up or down. Every time you came in the front door was a decision.

A note lay on the table there. Michael read it, put it in the pocket of his jacket, and said, "Will you stay here and wait for Claire? Mom's at the hospital. And there's a vigil."

Then he left.

She went up the six stairs to the wide hallway, to another decision, the living room through a wide archway on one side, or the dining room through a small archway on the other, the kitchen past that. There was rain, the world was muffled. She went through the dining room. Another, smaller carriage lamp hung over the table where she'd once sat across from her mother, next to Michael's great-aunt Alice, and her father on the other side, all of them together in that room of gray carpet and dark, shining wood. Great-Aunt Alice talked to her father about Pittsburgh Steel, and she gave Pattianne her recipe for hot milk cake. Once, on a February morning with surprising sun coming through the leaded-glass window, Mrs. Bryn stood there folding dishtowels and pillowcases on the table.

The kitchen table was small, round, tiled like Italian crockery, like the dishes. An unfinished crossword puzzle, a coffee cup half-full of black coffee, and the phone waited there. She tapped in Jen's number. Her answering machine said, "When you hear the beep, you know the drill." She hung up and stared at the phone, and it stared back at her, and she tried to think of who else to call.

Lamplighter Books would be closed. Elizabeth would be home with Simon, or out with Joseph. The road worker would be watching cranes or reading his Buddhism book. Her small St. Cloud life. It would be nice to talk to that guy.

Talking on the phone was too hard, though, the sound of any voice so small and disembodied, the real world around her too distracting. She always had to close her eyes to hear. For years, she hadn't even had a phone. When she finally got a cell phone, she used to leave it in her car. She doesn't even know what happened to that first cell phone.

Her mother answered on the fourth or fifth ring, just when she was about to hang up.

"Hi, Mom. It's me."

"Yes, dear?"

"I'm at the Bryns'."

There was the sound of the TV in the background, a game show, or a talk show.

She said, "Well. This is a surprise," like it wasn't a surprise, like she hadn't been surprised by anything in years.

"Mr. Bryn is in the hospital."

She said, "Is he all right?"

Yes, Mom, he's fine, they just put him in there for the hell of it.

"We just got in. It's his heart. There's going to be a transplant. Michael went right over there."

"Oh my God."

Pattianne had never heard her mother's voice jump like that.

"I'll call when there's any news."

She said, "Okay, dear, call when you have some news."

Pattianne waited for her to ask something else. Anything. She didn't want to hang up. But they were done. She wanted to ask her how she was. How is your heart, Mom? How is Dad's heart?

She could put away their clothes in the closet of the yellow guest room at the top of the next set of stairs. She could look in the refrigerator and think up something to make for dinner. She could snoop around. She remembered a photo album in the bottom of the bookcase in the living room. She'd like to look in Mrs. Bryn's top drawer. She could make more coffee. The coffee maker sat on the clean, tiled counter. It looked like a miniature spaceship, and had a panel with little diagrams instead of words like Off, On, or maybe Brew.

She could just wait for Michael to come back. Or Claire, who would be getting in from Slippery Rock sometime, maybe any second.

French doors led to the deck out back, where the gas grill was covered with a neat black cover, and the flower boxes were empty, and rain bounced on everything. Mr. Bryn had built the deck himself, and the flower boxes, and the picture frames that held the photographs lined up above the French doors—Claire in a yellow wading pool, Mrs. Bryn pregnant and laughing, Michael and a black Labrador retriever and a ball, one of their black labs. Michael said they always had black labs when they were kids.

Last summer, on an early evening, the air not even close to cooling off, Michael and Mr. Bryn had been outside there, the flower boxes full of nasturtiums. On the kitchen counter, salmon steaks were dressed with dill—pink salmon, lacy green dill, blue platter, a dish of lemon wedges. She and Michael'd had two vodka tonics before they came over. She'd worn a short, flowered dress with little straps. They had been late. They had made love in the shower. It was okay, just a picnic on the back deck, her in-laws, summer. She'd picked up the platter of salmon steaks and Mrs. Bryn had touched her arm and said, "Wait."

Michael and Mr. Bryn stood one on each side of the gas grill. Mr. Bryn's hands were in the pockets of his khaki shorts.

Mrs. Bryn said, "Let me show you how I make that salad dressing."

It was just balsamic vinegar and rice wine vinegar and olive oil. It was just pressed garlic and a little ginger. Pepper and salt.

"See?" she said. "I press the ginger through the garlic press. It's better than grating it."

She said, "You have to mix the oil in slowly. I use this little whisk."

She said, "Why don't you open that pinot blanc?"

When Pattianne looked out again, Michael and his father were standing at the railing of the deck, looking out over the backyard, and they each had their arms crossed. They looked the same from the back, same shoulders, same neck, same light blue shirts. Her head was swimming a little, vodka tonics in the heat, garlic and ginger in the air.

They sat down to eat at the table out there, and Mr. Bryn said grace. He said, "Bless us as we struggle with our decisions," and then they ate the beautiful pink salmon, and the green salad with radishes and carrots and ginger and garlic. They drank pale gold pinot blanc. The air was thick with humidity, and she thought that was all, the gentle Atlantic humidity that pressed down on your head and made white wine more dangerous than vodka tonics.

On the way home, she asked Michael what they'd been talking about.

He said it was nothing. Then he said it was okay. Then he said, "Dad wants what's best for me."

Mr. Bryn wanted Michael to take the job in Minnesota. Said it was good to take a year off, get out in the world a little bit. Said his health was fine, not to worry. When they got home, he called his father and they talked for a long time. She fell asleep on the cool living room floor.

Now the doorbell chimed, a soft, three-toned ring that scared the shit out of her, sitting there at the bistro table, and both her elbows knocked on the tiled edge. She went down the stairs without even wondering if she should open the door, who it could be. She didn't live here. She opened the door, and a small, old woman with bushy white eyebrows stood there in the porch light. It had gotten dark. She came right in. She wasn't any taller than a kid. Pattianne stood there rubbing her elbows.

"You're Pattianne," she said. "I know you are. Well, I saw your wedding picture, but I bet I would know you anyway—well, I knew you would be here, too, Dory told me, but I would know anyway. How are you doing, dear? I am so glad to meet you. We are so glad you came."

She took off her coat and gave it a shake, black drops on the slate floor.

"I can't stand in the rain. I had the pneumonia last year. Well, I'm seventy-six trombones this year." And she opened the door of the coat closet and hung up her coat.

"You have to be careful sometimes, and I can't stand in the rain, but

I can still make coffee with the best of them," she said, six stairs up.

She stopped on the third step.

"Oh, well, I'm Sister Anne Stephen. I bet you didn't know that, did you? Ha, ha!"

She took a deep breath and sucked on her teeth.

"I know that coffee machine Dory has is a ten-cupper," she said, and she was going up the stairs in her blue Keds, not like seventy-six trombones. "But I know where the big dealie is. Did she say to make it in the big dealie? An urn, it's a great big coffee urn," and she went through the kitchen to a pantry that Pattianne didn't even know was there and stood there pointing up.

"Up there," she said.

Pattianne said, "I'll get a chair," and she dragged in one of Mrs. Bryn's kitchen chairs, set it next to the shelves, and Sister Anne Stephen hopped right up. Didn't groan, didn't even lean on the back of the chair. Didn't even come anywhere close to reaching the urn. She got back down a little slower.

She said, "The knees aren't what they used to be."

Pattianne got up there and got down the big silver dealie, set it on the pantry counter, dragged the chair back to the table. Sister Anne Stephen brought the silver dealie from the pantry and set it next to the sink. It was as tall as she was. She pulled out the spray nozzle from the sink and aimed it into the top of the dealie.

Pattianne took the nozzle. "Let me."

Sister Anne Stephen said, "Why don't I go back down there and unlock that door? There's to be folks coming by, and they'll just come on in if the door's unlocked, so I'll just be unlocking it."

Within her vowels was music, and within each word, a secret R somewhere. Whatever she said ended up like an invitation. Irish maybe, or South Boston.

"The coffee is in that thing there," she said when she came back up the stairs. "That canister. Isn't it cute now, a cow, coffee in a cow? Makes me think of how the cow ran away with the spoon and all. Here, it's a twenty-six cupper, I got to count, hold on." Counting scoops of coffee into the filter. Her hand shook in the few inches between the coffee cow and the filter, but she didn't spill a single grain of coffee. Twenty-six and then one more.

"One for the urn now," she said, and then she put the filter into the top of the urn and plugged it in and said, "There," and she sat down. Her face was evenly bright red, and she fanned herself with a dishtowel.

"Got to sit," she said. "Here, sit by me. I got to sit for a bit. I got the pressure."

Pattianne sat.

"So," she said. "Dory says there's pound cake in the fridge, and we got cookies, and we'll set out a couple bowls for whatever folks might bring. Tell me about yourself. You and Michael got in this afternoon? It's so good of you to come," and she leaned forward across the table. "Have you seen Michael Senior?"

"Michael went over to the hospital as soon as we got in."

"I think he'll be okay, you know, I just bet." Her pointy chin was pointing, her eyes milky dark brown, long white eyebrow hairs curling right into her eyelashes. Her face wasn't as red as it had been a moment ago.

"So you're Michael's bride," she said. She swung her blue Keds, her feet not touching the floor. "I've known that boy since first grade, a good boy, just like his father, a lot like his father, you know."

Sitting at a table with a tiny nun in Mrs. Bryn's kitchen.

"And come back to do his father's work at the clinic," the tiny nun said. "That will help a lot. The praying at the clinic is Michael Senior's most important work, you know."

Praying at the clinic.

Sister Anne Stephen said, "What are you looking at?"

"I'm sorry?" Pattianne said. She was too tired. She couldn't figure out what she was hearing.

"Chin up, Bridey," the tiny nun said. "I learned that early, being shorter than most, you know—had to be looking up, chin up. Even if you're afraid, it will make you feel better. Don't look down."

Pattianne lifted her chin. That meant looking slightly down her nose at Sister Anne Stephen, who chattered on. "We got to make this little gathering a little upbeat. It could get depressing, as they say. That's not what the Lord has in mind for us, not in my opinion. What with Michael Senior being sick, and praying out in the rain, that can be a sad thing."

Looking down her nose made Pattianne feel cross-eyed. And this nun had said praying in the rain and praying at the clinic, and Michael coming back to do his father's work, and two tight fists were forming and unforming in Pattianne's stomach. The smell of coffee was starting up.

The nun said, "They still got the folk Mass where you kids are?"

Pattianne's head ached behind her eyes. "I don't think so."

"Now, folk Mass, that was a good thing, they don't do it as much as once upon a time, but it made folks smile, tap their toes a little bit. I think snapping fingers is a good idea. Sister Francine, she cantors at Christ the King, she tends to disagree—well, on most things, but especially folk Mass, and especially finger snapping. But then, she was once upon a time Sisters of the Holy Names, them with their ways of thinking about music, plus she's even older than me. Never was too happy out of the holy habit. Good Pope John wasn't quite to her liking, God bless him and keep him. I say you got to go hunting around for joy, it sure isn't going to come hunting for you on this good earth."

She leaned forward again.

The coffee started to steam. The coffee cow sat silently. The stack of paper filters was left out on the counter.

Sister Anne Stephen's feet quit swinging.

"Now, for joy," she said, "there's babies. That's their work in the world. And that's all I'm going to say. It isn't polite to be asking young folks about when they're thinking the babies might be coming along, but there you have it. You want to make joy, babies bring joy right into the world with them, and as long as I'm saying something—only once and then I'll be shushing up about it—it would sure be the thing to bring Michael Senior around, I just bet."

She blinked, and her whole face got caught up in a wrinkly smile, and she sat back in her chair and kicked her feet out.

"So," she said, "Tell me what Minnesota looks like that's different from hereabouts."

And, "Share a piece of that pound cake?"

And, "How old are you?"

When the phone rang, it was Michael calling to say they were on their way home, he and his mother. Pattianne said, "Sister Anne Stephen is here."

Sister Anne Stephen nodded and waved at the phone, and then slipped out to the dining room.

Pattianne said, "So, tell me about this, where are you and all? How's your dad?"

He said, "He's tired. Is Claire there yet?"

"No, just me and Sister Anne Stephen, and twenty-six cups of coffee."

"What?"

"How's your mom doing?"

He said, "We'll be there soon."

Claire got there right after that, with three wet kids—an older boy, maybe ten, and two smaller ones, little kids. She herded them all in the door ahead of her, a big to-do taking off coats, then up the stairs, into the living room, and then into the kitchen. She hugged Pattianne. There was a faint smell that wasn't right, a smell Pattianne knew, cigarettes, in her hair.

"This is Joel," Claire said. "This is Theresa. And this is their cousin, Paul Junior. You guys, this is Uncle Michael's wife, Aunt Pattianne."

Uncle Michael. Aunt Pattianne. The kids had red noses and red cheeks. They had all been out in the rain praying—Claire, Paul Junior, and two little kids whose names were already lost. Paul Junior was the big kid.

He said, "I'm supposed to bring out the sugar thing."

Claire said, "Take."

Paul Junior stopped, like a game of statues, then put his hands deep into the pockets of his big, baggy pants. He had to bend down to get his hands into his pockets, his pants hanging low like that.

Claire said, "Take to, bring back."

He shrugged. "Yeah, that's what Sister Anne Stephen said, take that sugar thing and put it on the table." And he picked up the sugar bowl and went sliding along in big sneakers, back out to the dining room. More people arrived, and Sister Anne Stephen's voice was all hello hello hello.

The two little kids had dark, damp hair hanging in their eyes, which were big, and staring at Pattianne from down around Claire's blue jeans.

The boy said, "We can go sit under the piano now."

The girl said, "On the red rug."

The boy said, "It has dragons."

"One dragon," the girl said. "It's only one dragon really, but it's all over the rug."

They were talking to Pattianne.

"Um" was what she said back.

Claire turned them around by their heads and said, "Go ask Sister for some pound cake. You can take it under the piano." And they went.

Pattianne said, "How are you?" and Claire's eyes flowed over, just like that, before Pattianne could say, *How is your mom holding up?* Before she could say, *Where's Michael?* Before she could say, *What's this about praying at the clinic?* Pattianne put her arms around Claire's thin shoulders and Claire squeezed and pulled back.

"Okay," she said, blinking and breathing in deeply, once, and then again. "Okay. We're so glad you're here. Michael can tell you all about it. You guys are in the guest room, right? Michael's old room is the computer room now."

"So, how was the, at the clinic?" Pattianne wasn't even sure what she was asking, but it was the right thing because she smiled, beautiful Claire, and said, "There were forty-five of us, not counting the kids. Two hours. I wish you could have been there, but thank you so much for waiting here with Sister Anne Stephen and all."

Why wouldn't you count the kids?

Michael came in then, wet, and Mrs. Bryn, wet, and she came to Pattianne and hugged her, kissed her cheek, and said, "Is everything okay?"

Sure, Pattianne thought. *My husband isn't the one getting a heart transplant. I'm not the one who's been standing in the rain at an abortion clinic.* She said, "Want a cup of coffee?"

"Thank you, dear, that would be great. Father?"

And there he was, right behind her, Father McGivens.

"Hello, Pattianne."

He got called back out into the other room somewhere, and Mrs. Bryn followed him, and Michael kissed her and whispered, "Thank you," and then he went out too.

She was alone in the kitchen for a second, before she followed them all out to the dining room. The people there looked at her. Two women said, "Michael Junior's little wife," and "Hello, dear."

Pattianne poured Mrs. Bryn a cup of coffee from the big silver dealie, and said hello back, and went through the big archway to the living room.

A large, pale gray room with dark wood and all the empty space accounted for, with small, upholstered chairs at neat angles, and two couches facing each other, and the piano on its red dragon rug. Mrs. Bryn sat on the piano bench, her long legs in gray slacks, the two kids sitting still and tidy beneath the piano, eating pound cake. And there were others, a lot of others. Maybe a dozen of them. Not counting the kids.

She gave Mrs. Bryn her coffee, and she said, "Oh thank you, perfect. Pattianne, this is Lynn. She was Michael's second-grade teacher at Christ the King."

Pattianne said hello to a woman who didn't look old enough to be that old, a tall, dark-haired woman with freckles, who said, "We're so sorry you couldn't join us tonight. Maybe tomorrow?"

"Did you want some cream or sugar?" Pattianne asked Michael's mother, who always took her coffee black.

"No, thanks, this is perfect."

There was a burst of laughter from across the room—Michael, standing there with three guys, making them all laugh. He looked around the room, found her, and opened his arm toward her, her husband, so she went to him. His hair was damp and curly, his cheeks red, his hands cold.

"This is Rory, and Jerry, and this is Pattianne." And they all said hi and hello, and she wasn't she sure who was who. It didn't matter. Michael kept talking.

"Fishing for teachers," he said, and they all laughed.

"There was this rule. No playing with sticks on the playground," Michael said. "But I was using a stick to show how I learned to cast." He held his hands out, like he was casting a fishing pole. "The first time I did it, I have a long stick, I'm casting, and here comes some teacher."

"Mr. Blewitt."

"Old Mr. Blewitt," one guy said. "The playground cop. 'Put the stick down, boys,' he says."

"After that, it worked every time," Michael said. His hands fishing. "I'd pick up a stick, start fishing, and here comes a teacher."

"Fishing for teachers," another guy said.

"Caught one every time," Michael said.

Saving up their laughter like applause.

Claire sat next to her mother at the piano, and then she turned and played "Twinkle, Twinkle, Little Star," slowly, softly. The two kids came out from under the piano with their cake plates and stood next to her to sing, but they didn't know the words. They looked at each other, and the little girl put her finger in her mouth.

Pattianne knew the words, even to the second verse, and the third verse, but she was tired all the way to shaky, and the gray carpet was too thick and soft, she couldn't feel her feet, and she couldn't sing either, couldn't even carry a tune. She went up to the yellow guest bedroom while they were working on "The Moon Sees You."

What is this business about prayer vigils? Or maybe just, *You didn't tell me there was going to be a prayer vigil.* Or maybe, *We should talk about these prayer vigils.* Or maybe just, *Michael, my darling, I had an abortion, it might have been your baby, and I sneak a birth control pill into my mouth every morning of every day.*

She couldn't think of what to say to him.

Late at night she woke up, that quiet waking, no-dream slipping away, eyes just open. She slid away from Michael's sleep-warm body, his even breathing, out into room, to the window. The numbers on the clock were red cuts in the dark, 1:15. The heater vent under the window blew warm air on her ankles, and the café curtains on their little rings were a metallic moment of sound. Down on the back deck, in black and white, Claire was having a smoke, in her bathrobe. The moon was full and lopsided in the sky. When Pattianne closed her eyes, the lopsided moon was still there.

She hated digital clocks. She liked friendly clocks with faces and hands, clocks that were about the past and the future, clocks she could ignore in the dark.

Rain at 2:43.

A motorcycle at 4:18.

A train at 5:10.

Piano notes dropped into the middle of a dream of starlings.

Michael hit the button on the radio alarm and got up out of the bed in the cute yellow guest room of this house in River View Estates, or Metuchen Meadows, or whatever it was, the river long since disappeared under a highway through a drainage pipe. The meadows plowed under fifty years ago. Her mother-in-law's house in Edison, New Jersey. Her father-in-law in the hospital. 6:15.

Michael came around and sat on the edge of the bed, and she curled around him where he sat, her face on his thigh, a taste of yesterday's shower still there. He whispered, "Mass."

She kissed his thigh, kissed again, slid her hands like a prayer between her legs, the warmest place on her body, warmest place in the bed, warmest place in this house. Mrs. Bryn's house.

"Okay," she whispered back. "See you in a little bit," and she turned the pillow over to the cool side, turned onto her stomach. The pillowcase didn't feel anything like her pillowcase at home. It was ironed, crisp. The dream had starlings in it, and a big backyard, and piano music.

Maybe not piano music.

Michael said, "Father McGivens says seven o'clock Mass," and he stood up, the bed letting him go, the bedsprings making a small sound. The bathroom light clicked, and after a while, he was standing there in his blue underwear, or maybe the gray ones, sexy low-cut under-pants that she had bought him that he really didn't like wearing, maybe because the package said *Bikini Briefs* in swirly letters, and a really cute guy modeling them. The bathroom light behind him was shining on the curve of his chest into his waist. A waist like a girl. She closed her eyes. Her pillowcase at home was soft and far away.

The bed sank down at the edge again, and he leaned over her, kissed the side of her face, a smooch of a kiss that was all about not being sexy. It was all about cinnamon toothpaste.

He said, "Sweetheart."

The very idea of cinnamon toothpaste grossed her out. "Why did you bring that toothpaste?"

He said, "Come on."

A sharp edge of headache lurked behind her eyes. Not enough sleep, still on Minnesota time, and her brain got stuck trying to think of which way the time went.

He said, "You come with us." He stood back up, pulled on slacks, and his bikini butt disappeared. He put on the same pale striped shirt he'd worn yesterday, left it unbuttoned, and went out the door, his feet bare, his chest bare, the shirt opening behind him like wings.

There was Mr. Bryn, in the hospital, and she was afraid to be mad at Michael for wanting her to go to Mass. For Mr. Bryn, she could go sit in a beautiful big building that would be freezing cold and have about

ten people in it. Father McGivens would wear robes and talk about
something that probably didn't really happen two thousand years ago.
For Mr. Bryn, she would listen to Father McGivens chant in a language
that was not made for chanting, American English with Gregorian
rhythms, stupid and unbeautiful. He would genuflect and raise his arms
and perform antique, liturgical playacting, and they would all kneel,
rise, sit, kneel, rise, sit.

Just for Mr. Bryn, they should all skip church and go find some hobo
and take him to brunch. Just for Mr. Bryn, they should invite a hobo
under the bridge to stay here. He could sleep in the yellow guest room
with its glass case of dolls from around the world, and she and Michael
will sleep on the red dragon, where they will have sex at night after
people leave, "Twinkle, Twinkle, Little Star" echoing around the big
empty living room. Who knew what really worked?

Michael came back in with a cup of coffee. He set the coffee on the
dresser and stood, looking at it. All she could smell was coffee. It smelled
strong, like gasoline.

He said, "When we go to Communion? You can go too."

The muscles of his stomach in the mirror caught the bathroom light.
Those muscles flexed just a touch.

He said, "Cross your arms like this," and he crossed his arms over
his chest, a hand on each shoulder, in the mirror. "When you get to
Father, just bow your head and he'll give you his blessing, instead of
offering you the host. If that will make it easier for you. If you don't
want to receive Communion."

She had one sock on and one sock in her hand, not wanting Michael
to look at her in the mirror, and he didn't. He buttoned his shirt. She
hated it when Michael buttoned his shirts, his chest going away from
her for the day. The sapphire ring on her hand flashed. Her head ached.

MRS. BRYN SAT IN the back seat of the rental car with Claire. One of
them had perfume, or hair spray, or something that tasted like rusty
metal. Michael steered them under the brick arches of Raritan Valley
Acres, out to the curving streets of Edison, orderly and empty, and
then the straight, short blocks of Edison where people waited at bus
stops and cars waited at stop lights, all the dark way to Christ the King,
and the cement steps where they had all stood, Easter Sunday, meet

the meerkats, Claire wearing lavender shoes. Now she wore short black boots that zipped partway up the side and disappeared under dark, slim pants. The sky had a sodium orange color on one horizon that Pattianne didn't think was east.

Michael pulled open the tall wooden doors, all carved with figures, and surely there would be a unicorn in there if she ever had a chance to look, which would not be right now. He held the door for the three of them, Michael Bryn's three women, and he followed them into the vestibule. The smell was a taste and a memory, all memories, of all churches. Once her parents took them to a brand-new church in Jamesburg, the first Mass. It was a low, modern building of pale brick. The stained-glass windows were geometric patterns of red and pink. The smell was this same old church smell, like it had secretly always been a church, waiting for the building to go up around it.

Michael took his mother's elbow and went in, then Claire, each of them blessing themselves at the holy water. She dipped her finger into the cold water, and touched her forehead, and her finger was icy cold. She thought, *I have lost my mind.* She touched the middle button on her coat like she was just touching the middle button on her coat, like she had not lost her mind. Like there was not this burning icy cold spot on her forehead now.

Christ the King was mostly empty, single figures here and there, kneeling, praying, no one looking up at the sound of Claire's footsteps in her little black boots. A row of old women sat in the very front. There was organ music, somewhere between a roller-skating-rink tune and a Vincent Price movie. The main aisle seemed like it was moving for a second, stretching forward, and she was dizzy for a second, and then she just followed the Bryns up toward the huge crucifix.

Michael pulled the kneeler down perfectly silently, and they all knelt. She was between Michael and Claire, and Claire's hair was damp, and the smell of rusty metal came closer, like it would burn the skin on her cheek. She shut her eyes, and the sharp edge of the headache was there again, so she opened them.

She didn't even know any of the words anymore.

She could remember how to say a rosary. Like saying a rosary would help Mr. Bryn. God like a Saturday-night radio DJ, taking requests and dedications. *Hey all you folks out there in church-land, this one's from Pattianne, and it's going out to you, Mr. Bryn.*

There was an aching hollow inside her chest, and she wanted to hold that empty space inside her and send that to him, through the air, setting it on his chest as he lay in bed with his new heart.

What if everyone who knew him sent him invisible boxes full of the space from inside their hearts? Except there is no space inside hearts. Hearts are full of blood and muscle tissue, all that space where hope is supposed to be.

Tears burned at her eyes, and points of light from all around the church broke into prisms and scattered, and the music got louder. A girl and a boy in the robes of acolytes came down the aisle with tall candles, and then Father McGivens in brilliant green vestments that flowed behind him. They all stood. His hands held the big red book of the Mass, held it up in front of his heart, small plump hands, hands that were to bless her by just touching her.

Her father's hands were thin and knuckled. He wore a signet ring with a black stone.

Her mother's hands were clenched in small fists, thumbs tucked in.

Jen's hands were usually in her pockets. Nana Farley was always making her take her hands out of her pockets, especially when Jen actually spoke to her. Nana Farley said it was rude to address an adult with your hands in your pockets.

To think of Michael's hands was to be touched, flash points around her body in odd places, behind her knees, her ears.

Even-Steven had beautiful, white skin and burn scars and cuts and yellow mustard under his fingernails.

That road worker had red, rough-skinned hands. The thin yellow book on Buddhism had looked small when he held it. He'd reached out one thick finger to touch one crane.

Father Koberstein had been their priest when she was small, at St. Francis. He used to gently shake his scotch and ice when he came over for dinner. She thought he looked like Fletcher Christian in *Mutiny on the Bounty*. He could have blessed her by touching her forehead, but all he ever did was lay a dry host on her tongue.

How love could flow through skin.

At one side of the main altar, the Prince of Peace glittered in his royal scarlet robes. On the other side was a small altar with its own communion rail, and a tall white statue of Mary, Queen of Heaven, and an arched door beyond that.

A man in a baby-blue cardigan got up from the front pew, went to the pulpit, and read from the Old Testament, and people started calling out names—Mrs. Somebody whose daughter is sick, Mrs. Somebody Else who is sick. She didn't remember being allowed to yell out names in church. And then Michael, "Lord, bless our father, Michael Bryn," his voice so suddenly big and loud beside her that she jumped.

Another short reading, Father McGivens's rich voice echoing in the church, and then Mrs. Bryn and Michael and Claire all leaning across, hugging each other, hugging her, the sharp metal smell a close taste, saying, "Peace be with you," the old women in the front row moving around in their pews.

Suddenly it was quiet again.

The shrill bells of the consecration rang three times.

The kneelers thumped and echoed when the row of old women got up and went to receive communion, and then Michael raised their kneeler, perfectly, silently.

She could do it. Michael was behind her, Claire in front of her. Father McGivens was laying hosts in everybody's hands. It used to be only the priest could touch the host. When a priest was ordained, his fingers had to be bound in holy oil for two weeks. The host was made out of a wafer that wouldn't splinter when the priest broke it apart, so none of the consecrated shards would fall to the altar cloth. The sisters at First Communion said, *Don't even let the host touch your tooth.* Now Pattianne did just like Michael said: crossed her arms over her heart, rested her fingertips on her shoulders.

Father McGivens's hands held the big, bright, gold chalice with its black engraving, curves and lines and letters. He didn't touch her forehead, and she looked up at his face, and when he reached out then, the green silk fell back with a sound like water rushing. He touched her forehead, the spot where the cold holy water still burned, and his hand stayed there, and his eyes stayed still and open and hard like pieces of rock. He took his fingers away.

Claire moved along the communion rail, where an old woman held out a crystal glass of pale wine. Claire took the glass and sipped and handed it back to the old woman, who wiped the rim with a stiff white cloth. Michael's hands on Pattianne's shoulders moved her toward the old woman, the crystal glass starting to brighten, the tiny cuts of crystal sparkling. She didn't drink from the glass. Michael was somewhere behind her.

Back in the pew, kneeling, she shut her eyes, and where it was usually black behind her eyes, colors jerked, the shape of the chalice, and the sharp edge of pain made its own red line through all the other shapes.

Her eyes opened, and the red line stopped. Sparks off the candles shot in perfect arcs of white that broke in prisms and kept reaching toward her, perfect arcing colors. She didn't understand. She couldn't look, and went back to the line of red pain behind her eyes.

The old women stood, everyone stood, left the pews, Pattianne behind Claire and in front of Michael. The organ music roared out and then got quieter. They moved to the back of the church, past the holy water, through the doors, past Sister Anne Stephen in the vestibule. Pattianne's heart was at the very bottom of her throat beating light and fast, and it tickled. She couldn't speak around it. She smiled, and her face made that shattering sound, all the edges around her sparkling red. Michael held her, his arm around her waist, out to the car.

She said, "I have a headache."

After that, she said, "Headache," again. And after that, she didn't say anything, not even in her head, no words, only bright red lines. Back home, up the stairs, she got on the bed, the pillow over her face, and red light seeped around the edges of the pillow. When the heat came on and the vent rattled, the red flared. When Michael opened the door to come in, the red flared. When he sat on the edge of the bed, all her bones shattered, and she cried.

She woke up in the dark, lying as still as she could, and the red lines were gone. She woke up again, and then she woke up again, and finally she woke up and Michael was there beside her, sleeping. There was the dresser, with Michael's slacks hanging from the top drawer. The case of dolls had a curved glass door, and light from somewhere on the surface of glass. Just light. No headache.

There had never been pain like that.

It didn't even seem like pain now that it was gone.

In the morning, he said, "What happened? What was that all about?"

She said she didn't know. That it was a headache. That they didn't have to talk about it, so they didn't. They didn't talk about prayer vigils either. Michael and Mrs. Bryn went to Mass, and Pattianne stayed in the yellow bedroom listening to the house, listening to the rain, listening to Claire in the kitchen. Everything seemed normal, except that the muscles in her temples were tender when she touched her fingers there. She went down the stairs to the kitchen slowly. Claire was just hanging up the phone. She had dark circles under her eyes, and when Pattianne hugged her, she smelled like shampoo or maybe soap, not rusty metal, and not a cigarette.

"Are you feeling better?"

"Yeah, thanks."

"There's orange juice."

"I don't know what happened, it was just this weird intense headache."

The phone rang again, and Pattianne took her orange juice into the dining room, into the living room, back into the kitchen, and Claire said, "I love you too," and she hung up the phone.

"So," Pattianne said, setting the orange juice glass on the counter. "What's going on?"

Claire said, "Was it a migraine?"

"I mean, about the prayer vigil?"

"Daddy." Claire took a deep breath and let it out. "Project Life." She stopped and took another breath, and then tears spilled over and down her cheek. "I'm just so fucking glad you're here." A big gulping sob. "I'm sorry," she said, and Pattianne knew two things—that Claire had just said "fucking," and that she herself did not want to fucking be there. And thank God, Claire turned away and tore a tissue from the box on the tiled bistro table. Her shoulders squared a tiny bit, and Pattianne stared at her back, just stared, just stood there watching her get her breath and stop crying. Project Fucking Life.

"I have to go to the hospital." Claire's voice was contained and full of held breath. "It's only immediate family, but do you want to go with me?"

No, she didn't want to go. No, she didn't want to say no. The phone rang again, and she put the orange juice glass in the sink and went back upstairs, quick this time, and put on jeans and a sweater and socks and sat there on the bed. The big sapphire flashed on her finger. Claire came up the stairs and stood at the open door.

"I should stay here," Pattianne said. "I have to call my mother and make some calls back to St. Cloud. Should I make some lunch? When do you think you'll be back?"

Claire came in and sat next to her on the bed, and Pattianne wished she had at least straightened the blankets.

Claire took her hand. "Will you pray with me?"

Pattianne closed her eyes as if she had said yes. What did she know about praying, maybe not saying no means yes, and she couldn't pull her hand away, it would have been like slapping her. Claire started in on the Our Father, and she said the words with her, mumbling them, at least she knew the words. But by the time they were finished, amen, Claire was crying again and she put both arms around Pattianne, and Pattianne put her hands somewhere, sitting side by side, kind of patted Claire's elbow.

Claire said, "Thank you so much for being here. I'll call from the hospital," and she left, the tapping of the little black boots on the slate in the entryway, out the door.

Pattianne counted. She counted by twos, two four six eight, and kept counting by fours for a while. Then she said, "Fuck." Said it as loud as she could. It didn't say half of it.

"Fuck. Fuck. Fuck," down the stairs, into the kitchen, picked up the phone and dialed Jen. Some new smart-ass message, and she said, "Goddamn it, Jen, answer the phone."

"Jesus, Pattianne, take it easy."

"Why do you have to screen your calls? Haven't you ever heard of caller ID?"

Pattianne closed her eyes and talked in the swirling eyelid-dark. "Michael's dad is in the hospital."

"So I heard."

"It's his heart," Pattianne said, breathing evenly. "He's getting a new heart."

"Damn."

"I had the headache of my life yesterday."

"I bet."

"No, I mean really." How much to try and say about that? "There were colors and weird smells."

"Colors?" Jen said. "Smells?"

"There was a prayer vigil."

"For a headache?"

"Goddamn it, Jen."

"What?"

Pattianne opened her eyes, to the rain on the deck, the picture of Michael and the black lab. "They all went and prayed at an abortion clinic."

"Oh, right, Project Life. Your father-in-law was on the news, like, just a couple weeks, month ago. Big crusaders."

"I don't know what the fuck to do, this house is filled with priests and nuns, and just now I sat holding hands with Claire and said the Our Father."

"You?"

"What was I supposed to say? No, Claire, I don't want to pray with you?"

"Well, did you?"

"Want to pray? With Claire? With anybody? What do you think?"

"Well," she said, "we never really ever talked about that, did we? I kind of assume you're kind of like me. But then, I probably wouldn't marry into a family of religious fanatics." And she snorted a bit of a giggle.

"Are you stoned?"

"It's eight in the morning."

"Even Michael has been praying with them. He's been going to church more and more at home, and now there's this. It's like he's turning Super-Catholic."

"Do you go with him?"

"To church? No."

"Does he want you to?"

"He did yesterday, and I got the headache, this really weird headache. But not usually."

"Well, it sounds okay."

"No, there's more. He hangs out with this other prayer group."

"Serious? Does he act different? Like, does he pray around the house?"

"Well, no."

"Look," she said. "I have to get ready for work. What are you doing today? Just waiting at the hospital?"

"I'm here at the house. I'll call you later, or you call me."

"Pattianne," she said. "Don't be a feeb."

In Mrs. Bryn's room, there was a crucifix on the wall and a dark wooden Madonna on the dresser centered in front of the mirror. Rosary beads on the nightstand. Claire's old bedroom was pink, posters of horses on the wall, and a small pink crucifix with a delicate golden Jesus hanging above the door. A girl's crucifix. In the yellow guest room there was a small brass crucifix above the door.

Pattianne straightened the blanket, and then pulled it off the bed completely, and then the sheet too, and made the bed from scratch. Claire might have left her cigarettes in her bathrobe pocket, she could step out back, have a quiet smoke. She got Michael's shirts and took them downstairs and sat at the kitchen table and wondered how to find a dry cleaner's nearby, and she thought she'd get a cell phone. She wondered what the name of the black lab was, in the picture with Michael over the kitchen door. She wondered if she could figure out the space-age coffee maker. She wondered why Jen thought she was a feeb. She was dialing her number again when the doorbell chimed its three pretty chimes.

Sister Anne Stephen stood there with a brown paper bag and a big manila envelope in one arm and an umbrella held open over her fuzzy gray head. A nun, but at least a fun one, a distraction.

"I talked to Dory on the phone from the hospital. Michael Senior seems to be doing okay so far, bless the day. And she said you were here. I bet you like bagels—all you young people like bagels nowadays," and she was in, handing over the grocery bag and stamping her blue Keds on the gray stones of the entryway. She closed the umbrella, closed the door, and looked at Pattianne, her glasses fogging up.

"I do," Pattianne said, sounding for all the world like she was up for some fun. "Bagels, love 'em."

"And Dory's got raspberry jam because I made it last summer and gave it to her." She headed up to the kitchen. "Now me," she says, "raspberry jam is the dickens with these pretty teeth of mine—the seeds, you know."

The manila envelope landed on the dining room table on the way through, Pattianne following the nun into the kitchen, where she stopped and gave her a look from under those bushy eyebrows.

"You weren't doing so good yesterday morning now, were you?"

"I had a headache."

A small gold pin hung crooked on the collar of her blue striped blouse. There seemed to be a spot of egg there too. The pin was round, with a cross and initials were worked in there, official somehow. Her official I-am-a-nun pin.

She said, "There's a reheat button on this coffee pot. Just a headache? A little stomach upset maybe?"

Pattianne said, "Just a headache. I have to wash my face, I'll be right back." She ran up the stairs, and splashed cold water on her face again and again. Everything in this house felt sticky, and outside was New Jersey. God knew how long she and Michael would be here. She was married to a stranger. She married a stranger.

She thought, *I fucked up.*

Her wet face in the mirror was just her own: Pattianne Anthony, nobody's wife, nobody's daughter-in-law, just the same old someone who could be invisible in the corner of a bar and live happily ever after. Not a stranger.

Nobody's mother. The last thing she wanted to be was somebody's mother.

The smell of toasted bagels came up on the air, and coffee. She went back down.

Sister Anne Stephen said, "There, I'll grab this stuff and my coffee, and we'll just make ourselves useful. And there, you grab those bagels." And off she went out the kitchen doorway, picked up the manila envelope on her way through the dining room, and went down the stairs, all the way down, to the room that was Michael's old bedroom, long since turned into an office.

The walls were blue, the carpet tan, the desk stacked with mail. A big old Mac stared out blank on the desk, and sliding glass doors stared out into the rainy backyard, which stared back. There was a Nerf ball hoop on a metal wastebasket and a library table in one corner.

Sister Anne Stephen set down the manila envelope and her coffee cup. Pattianne set the bagels down and took one. The cream cheese was melting into the butter. She hadn't eaten anything but pound cake in a long time.

There was a small crucifix of pale wood over the door.

Sister Anne Stephen went to one bookshelf and stood there for a minute, then went to another, stood there.

"Aha." And she knelt, and groaned, "Here we go, we're off to the races," and she pulled a leather-covered scrapbook from the bottom shelf. She put the scrapbook on the table next to the manila envelope and her coffee. She lined up a pair of scissors from the desk drawer, and a roll of Scotch tape, and four or maybe five pens.

"So," she said, "sit yourself down, Bridey. We get to stay home on a rainy day and play with scissors." They both sat themselves down.

Pattianne tried to picture Michael sleeping here, living here. Bunk beds on the back wall, maybe. Now there was a bookcase there, mostly videos and DVDs, Star Wars, old games, Super Mario. They moved him down here when he was fifteen, a boy's room. It felt like it had always been the computer room. Sister Anne Stephen pulled a clump of newspaper clippings out of the envelope.

"So," she said. "First we need to sort through and arrange these by date. Most of them got the date there, either written in or cut out so the date is there. See here," and she opened one article up onto the table and smoothed the fold, smoothed it open on the table, running her bent, wrinkled fingers over and over the piece of newspaper.

Project Life Lawyer Found in Contempt of Court.

"This one, see, headline, still has the date. Let's see, I need to clean off these specs. Hold on." And she took off her glasses and pulled out a shirttail.

Two men in suits on the steps of a building, one looking at the camera. It was Mr. Bryn.

"There we go," Sister Anne Stephen said, putting her glasses back on. "That one is pretty recent. There's others in here I know are older. Here we go. You might want to snip the edges, make them nice and tidy, like all of what's in here." And she opened the scrapbook. It was fat with clippings.

Prayer vigils were the least of it. In one photo, police were dragging a girl away. Another showed the broken windows of a building, police standing in front of them. A crowd shot, protest signs held high.

Sister Anne Stephen said, "Bless them."

Outside, rain. Inside, Pattianne sat, hating Sister Anne Stephen, hating the people in the picture. She had always hated them, an irrational, spinning rage that went away after driving past a clinic, or after turning the page of a newspaper, or when a different news story came on the news. Christians and Right-to-Lifers, always lumped together and dismissed.

"These aren't the best pens. This one's out of ink," Sister Anne Stephen said, and she tossed a pen into a wastebasket, the loud ping of it ringing on Pattianne's skin. "I'm the kind of person that throws away a pen when it quits on me," she said. Then her voice got lower, softer. "Now look here, look here." And she held out a clipping, a color picture of a building blackened by fire, fenced off with yellow police tape. In the foreground is Mr. Bryn, on his knees, his eyes closed, his hands clasped in prayer.

"Looks like Michael Junior in that picture, wouldn't you say?" Sister Anne Stephen leaned close, her finger pointing, barely touching the picture. "Look at those beautiful curls, and such a sweet face, all closed in his praying."

You married into a family of religious fanatics.

Don't be a feeb.

"Bridey," Sister Anne Stephen said. "Don't let that butter get on the papers, girl. Here's a paper towel."

He did. He looked just like Michael. His face was calm and sweet. The words in her head were *I hate them all.* The words in her head were *I have to get Michael out of here.*

They snipped and taped, and Sister Anne Stephen talked about God knows what.

After she left, Pattianne washed out the big urn. She figured out the little coffee maker on the counter. She accidentally dropped a pretty Italian pottery plate, and it smashed into a hundred pieces.

She fixed tuna-salad sandwiches, and they all came home late in the afternoon and crowded around the bistro table, and she waited for them to bow their heads and hold hands and say grace first. She waited for a chance to say, No, I can't do that, I'm not like you. But they all just sat down and ate—Michael, and Claire, and Mrs. Bryn.

They all stayed up late, talking in the kitchen, drinking coffee.

Claire's coursework at Slippery Rock. St. Cloud and the St. Cloud School
for Boys. Pattianne would get up and pour coffee, put cookies on a
plate. She cut up some cheese and pale green Granny Smith apples. The
phone would ring, and every time it did, they would all stare at it for
a moment, and then Michael answered it, slowly—a cousin, a friend—
and he would take the phone into the dining room and say the same
words: *He's stable, on a waiting list, coronary care, thank you thank you.*

Father McGivens came, and she went to bed. She fell asleep hearing
their low voices downstairs. She woke up when Michael came to bed
and didn't hear him say his prayers. He didn't get on his knees. She
didn't want to talk about how wrong it was for her to be here. He curled
around her and held her, and his body was hot and sticky. She worked
herself out of his arms. She cried without making a sound.

In the morning, they all got up to go to early Mass and then straight
to the hospital. Michael kissed her cheek and said, "I love you. Stay
sleeping." He went down the stairs—six footsteps, and then six more.
She got up, after the house fell quiet, and went to the kitchen in her
bathrobe, sat around and tried to hear something in the rain, maybe a
pattern. She did the crossword puzzle.

She called Jen, who had to leave for work.

She called Miss Mimi, who had her breakfast book group over. She
said, "Last month we read a book about an Islamic girl in the sixteenth
century, a novel. I get to choose the Jewish novel for next month. We
call ourselves the People of the Book Club. Know any good Catholic
novels?"

"*The Power and the Glory?*"

"Oh, good one. I have a book on hummingbirds of the Midwest for
you. Beautiful pictures. I'll mail it to you. I'd love to see you, dear, but I
know how it must be. So call me back, let me know how Michael's father
is. What hospital did you say? Got to go, my gals are here."

She called her mother, who said, "It's good that you're there, to
stay at the house and answer the phone and fix them a few meals." She
sounded worried. Pattianne thought of her being Grandma Anthony's
daughter-in-law—Grandma Anthony, who was so stern with everyone
except Pattianne herself—and she said, "Thanks, Mom." Her head
throbbed.

She took Michael's clean shirts out to the car, and she drove around.

It was still raining, soft and steady straight-down rain, and that was the only thing that seemed right. She drove down to Montclair, past their old apartment, and she tried to remember what she'd been thinking when she'd said that she would marry Michael Bryn. She drove down the street where she had the abortion and tried to remember which building it was. She tried to remember ever talking with Michael about babies.

Mr. Bryn was stable, no visitors, only immediate family. He was at the top of a waiting list.

The third morning, Mrs. Bryn and Claire left for the hospital, and Michael was up in the yellow bedroom, and she was in the kitchen staring at the telephone. She wanted to call someone, but she didn't want to talk to anyone. The door chimes rang, and she went down there and opened the door to Father McGivens, who reached out to touch her shoulder, it seemed. But she backed up and held the door open wide for him. She didn't want to feel the warm smile that landed on her.

He said, "Feeling better?"

"I'm fine."

Michael came down the stairs, and the two of them moved together into a big, wide-shouldered embrace, and then they headed down to the computer room.

Michael said, "I'll be down here if Mom calls."

They were there for a long time.

She vacuumed the gray carpeting in the living room. She washed the Italian pottery cups and saucers. She made cheese sandwiches, and cut them in triangles, and arranged them on a plate that matched the table and the cups and everything else.

She called Jen. "What do you mean, I'm a feeb?"

"You don't pay attention to the obvious," she said. "You pay attention to what's not obvious."

"What was I paying attention to?"

"Why did you go to Mass with him if you weren't going to go Catholic?"

It felt right, the music, the idea of Communion.

"I don't know."

"Yeah, well, they're Catholics, missy. You need a better answer than that. Why did you marry him?"

"Love."

"Oh, please," Jen snorted. "That's a terrible reason."

"Sex?"

"Only marginally better."

"I think he wants babies."

She said, "Duh."

"I don't. Well, not right now."

And Jen said, "Me either."

"Ever?"

"No," she said. "But I'll probably change my mind. That's the kind of person I am. I'm not the kind of person who would ever marry a Catholic, though."

"I didn't think he was that kind of Catholic."

"There's only one kind of Catholic."

"Yeah."

"Time to deal with it."

"It's just this thing with his dad. It's just the stress or something."

"Doesn't sound like stress to me," she said. "Sounds like wanting a baby. I think that's how wanting a baby works."

"I can't breathe in this house."

"Go home," she said. "Go live in Minnesota."

AND FINALLY, THEY DID. They left Michael's father in stable condition, in coronary intensive care, waiting for a heart, and they drove the rental car back to the airport, did not see a hobo under the bridge, and did not talk about antiabortion protests or having babies or anything. She told herself Michael needed space.

They waited in the airport, at a snack bar with coffee that tasted like the paper cup it came in, with a *New York Times* crossword that she just stared at.

Why she married a Catholic was she thought it didn't matter.

She'd asked him once, *What about the pope?*

And Michael told her, *We don't all agree with the pope. You can be Catholic and not necessarily agree with the pope. Popes are human.*

She said, *I don't want to be a Catholic.*

And he said, *You just be you.*

She never said, *What about you being a Catholic and me not liking it?*

Minneapolis was a shock of cold in clear sunny air that burned her lungs and made her eyes water. She dozed in the O-Bug all the way home, rising to the surface of sleep, and fighting her way back down.

St. Cloud felt like home. Their house was quiet and contained— walls, windows, yard, bare trees, the edge of town, the edge of all the wide fields. She could think, about being the kind of person who would marry a Catholic, about being the kind of person who didn't want babies. About Mr. Bryn.

The windows of their house were wide and bare, like eyes, and it was warm inside, and she turned on the deer lamp. The bare floors were straight, shiny old wood, and there were her footsteps, and there were Michael's.

He said, "Why don't we have curtains?"

She didn't know why they didn't have curtains.

He said, "We'll go back for Christmas."

She didn't say, *You go back for Christmas. I don't want to go back for Christmas.*

8: NEVER DRINK CHAMPAGNE IN THE AFTERNOON

THERE WAS A SMALL cemetery on the highway out of St. Cloud, the next rise after the clinic, out toward the Sears store.

"Please," Michael had said at six thirty, getting up for Mass. "Go with me."

"I can't," she said.

But maybe she could do curtains.

The cemetery was surrounded by fields and didn't have a name. She had noticed it before, and now she pulled in and stopped. Three crypts stood in a row along the back, under a bare black tree, a road winding around in a circle. The sky was low and gray, and everything was black and white. She sat there with the window down and the heater on high, probably running down the battery, and not even warm. Chickadees beeped. She heard them, and then she saw them.

Rows of gravestones, a different number of gravestones in each row, as if people planned on dying but not in any particular order, and a round cap of snow on top of each one. Her mother's relatives were buried in a huge cemetery in Long Island, rolling hills of graves that go on and on. There was a map. She went there once, when her great-aunt Grace died. Pattianne never even knew her aunt Grace. She went with Grandma Anthony to her son's grave once, Uncle Stanley. She was about eight, and didn't remember it except that it was a cemetery on a sunny day, and how odd that he was Uncle Stanley, an uncle who didn't live long enough to be an uncle. Her grandfather's grave must have been right there too.

She started up again, and the O-Bug slipped around in the snow, and she prayed not to get stuck, not exactly praying, just saying *please, please* as the car slipped on the packed snow, fish-tailing back out onto the highway. Thank God, she wouldn't have to explain why she was there, in a cemetery, running down the battery, since she didn't even know.

The parking lot of the Sears store was full, and she had to park pretty far back. The air was so cold it snapped at her face as she walked through eleven rows of cars. And then, right by the door of the store, the road worker sat in a big blue station wagon. The Sunday funnies were spread open across the steering wheel, and music and cigarette smoke drifted out the open window. Today was Friday. Sunday funnies on Friday.

"Hey, hi," she said.

He didn't jump or even look surprised to see her standing there all of a sudden. He turned the music down, some toe-tapping showtune, from *Oklahoma!* maybe. She was glad he'd turned it down quick before it could get stuck in her head.

"Hello there," he said. "How you doing, young lady? Out hitting the big sale? Ho." The cigarette smoke was pipe smoke. He set the pipe in a beanbag ashtray on the dashboard next to a box of apple-cranberry juice with the straw sticking out.

"Big sale?"

"White sale," he said. "I'm waiting on the Mrs. in there, buying up some white folks, ho. That's a race joke." His short hair was that pale pink color that red hair gets when it goes gray. He had hat hair. Maybe from his hard hat. "Probably not very funny," he said. "Race jokes aren't ever funny, but it seems like they should be, as long as they're about white folks. My girl says not so, though—no such thing as a funny race joke."

Pattianne pictured hordes of happy consumers within. "Maybe I should wait until after the sale," she said. The ring of cash registers, the thrill of the hunt.

"Sale runs all weekend," he said.

"You have the Sunday funnies already?"

"Last Sunday," he said. "Science tidbits, I always save out the science tidbits. I was reading up on fireflies. They flash more when it's really hot, it seems, and these fellows don't seem know why they flash at all. Listen here." He rattled the paper. His fingernails were trim and neat, even though the skin on his knuckles was red. All his skin was red. He was sort of a red-skinned white person. Small hands. "Heatless light called bioluminescence," he said. "They might be flashing secret messages to other fireflies. Ho."

"We used to catch them in jars," she said. "My sister and I. In New Jersey."

"They don't even have fireflies out west," he said. "But I hear they have silver water in the ocean out there instead." He stared out past her up into the gray sky, and his eyes were that same color gray. "The Pacific Ocean. The great weather-maker. I read that."

"The boys used to smash them on their arms," she said. "It made kind of a smeary glow."

She'd thought his eyes were blue, before.

"I hope to see that for myself someday," he said, looking at her, and yes, blue eyes. "Silver water," he said. "They got that out west, in the Pacific Ocean. Not smashed fireflies. I was always just as glad we had a girl, I have to tell you."

Pattianne didn't ask him about Buddhism. It seemed like privileged information somehow, like she could only ask about books if they met in the bookstore, like the privacy of the confessional. Instead, she looked at the tall white brick walls of the Sears store.

"Well," she said. "I guess maybe I'll come back when there isn't a sale."

THE LETTER FROM MISS Mimi was a stiff square of creamy paper, her messy handwriting that used to be only a little neater. She had spoken with Pattianne's mother, sent her best wishes to Michael, and she was moving out of her house, to Valley Village, maybe in the spring, and Pattianne should give her a call.

Valley Village was a retirement community landscaped out of the rolling farmlands around Cranbury. Tiny apartments, housekeeping, medical care, a dining room, planned activities.

"My friend Iris lives there," she said when Pattianne called her. "Last week, I went with her on their bus trip to Chadds Ford to see the Andrew Wyeth paintings. Iris moved into Valley Village after her Herbie died, three years ago."

At first, after someone died, people said *passed on*, or *passed away*. Eventually they said *died*.

"You're selling your house?"

"Sooner or later," she said. "It will take some doing." She coughed delicately. "Excuse me, dear."

Pattianne heard her turn away and cough again. She would be taking a sip of water. There was always her water glass nearby, a small glass with violets painted on it. It was part of a set of juice glasses. There was a set with cherries too, and a set with ivy leaves. Pattianne always chose her glass with a certain amount of care when she visited Miss Mimi.

Miss Mimi laughed her wet laugh. "I've been here thirty years," she said. "The roots are deep, and the closets are full."

The small gray house, with white trim and black shutters. Pattianne could never live there, just down the street from her mother and father, just down the street from her childhood, from the beige living room, the den with the television turned on. She had always wanted to just get away from there, fields all planted and fenced, private drives that went into business parks and world headquarters and places like Valley Village.

Here, the prairie started up and went for a thousand miles west.

Miss Mimi said, "Are you coming home for the holidays?"

And she meant when, not if, because your husband's father is gravely ill, and of course you are coming home.

She said, "Are you keeping your feeders filled with sunflower seeds for the songbirds?"

Yes.

THE LIVING ROOM GOT dark, and Pattianne lit a Miss Mimi candle, a thick blue one, and set it in the window in an orange Fiestaware saucer. For Michael, to bring him home. She opened red wine, and chopped up sweet red peppers, and mixed olive oil and anchovy paste. She didn't know how things were between them when he was gone. She kept looking into the living room as it got dark, as the candle glow got bright and filled the bare, clean window.

When he came home, the house smelled like dinner, and she kissed his cheek and said, "We have to make plane reservations for Christmas."

He kissed her back, came into the warm house, said, "I already did." He reached past her and turned on the deer lamp, and the candlelight dimmed. She folded the blanket on the couch, and he hung up his big jacket.

She held out Miss Mimi's letter. "She's going to move out of her house. She sends her best."

"I have to call Mom," he said. "I have to talk to Claire too." He went into his office.

She brought him wine in a glass with a blue stem, hand blown. There were three of them, a dollar each.

"Sangiovese," she said.

"Thank you, darling." He laughed and spoke into the phone. "No, I was talking to my lovely wife." And then he talked to her again. "Father McGivens sends love."

She didn't know how things were between them when he was here either.

SATURDAY MORNING, HE WAS gone early. Maybe he'd said debate tournament in Bemidji, or maybe she'd dreamed that, like maybe she was dreaming all of this. She got up a long time later and reheated the coffee. The floors were icy, and she pushed the thermostat up moderately high, and then higher. A light dusting of new snow blew in gusts and swirls around the yard. She went into his office and looked through a box of paperbacks until she found an Elmore Leonard book she couldn't remember. She could get curtains for in here too. By the time the heat vent in the kitchen was rattling happily away, she was back in the bedroom, where the dark brocade over the window kept the day in here with her, not out there with icy bits of wind, and she was asleep before the plot got familiar.

SUNDAY MORNING, SHE MADE cinnamon rolls from tubes when he went to Mass, whopped them against the edge of the stove, popped them out, and baked them on the cookie sheet. The house smelled sweet and yeasty when he came home from Mass.

He said, "Great minds run the same channel," holding up a whole bag of cinnamon rolls from the bakeshop next to Sacred Heart.

And she said, "Fools think alike."

They ate them all, he read the sports page, she did most of the cross-word, saying, "More coffee, my darling fool," and "Pass the cream, oh Great Mind."

He didn't remember that particular Elmore Leonard book either. The Golden Gophers were playing U of M on TV. While he brought the TV out of his office and set it up in the living room, she put his big jacket on over the Loretta Young robe and went out and scattered the last of the bird seed around the front yard, the world all black and white and shades of gray.

Sunday. Easy. Eventually Michael snored a quiet, buzzing snore, and she curled up next to him and lay Elmore Leonard open in her lap. The snow kept blowing. The window was full of white winter daylight. She prayed the phone wouldn't ring, and it didn't.

On Monday, she headed back out the highway, thinking plain white tab-top curtains on black iron rods. Two windows, eight screws. A brand-new bag of sunflower seeds rested on the seat next to her. She drove into the cemetery and turned off the O-Bug. The sunflower seeds spilled down between the seats when she ripped open the bag with her teeth. She got out into the cold gray day and dug her hand deep into the bag. The seeds were sharp and slippery. She tossed them, one handful, two, and they clicked and slid on the icy snow. Then she got back in the car and waited until the chickadees came, landing and hopping around all the seeds, black and white and gray, pecking and beeping and then flitting away so quick she couldn't see their tiny wings. They were different from New Jersey chickadees. They had brown caps instead of black. If ashes were mixed in with the seeds, maybe the chickadees would eat the ashes too, and then fly away, up into the bare tree, beeping that long *beep, beep*, over and over. Beautiful. Like early mornings at Grandma Anthony's house in the summer, chickadees in the ginkgo tree. And Grandma would come to her bed in the screened-in side porch and say, *Wake up, Pattianne chickadee.*

Pattianne wanted her ashes mixed with birdseed. They could feed her to the chickadees. She didn't know if that would make her a chick-adee or not. She would have to ask Elizabeth. Maybe you couldn't circumvent reincarnation that easily. Or else that was reincarnation, which made sense. She wasn't too worried about God. There seemed to be plenty of room for God in that idea. Jesus was just Jesus. There were chickadees and candles.

She went back home instead of to Sears for curtains.

PLANNED PARENTHOOD WAS ON Belmont Street, about five blocks away from Lamplighter Books. Everything in St. Cloud was about five blocks away. Their house five blocks from the library, the little grocery store about five blocks another direction. She went past Lamplighter Books, past a thrift shop and a tap-dancing studio, her own heels tap-dancing on the sidewalk, a small-town morning. She hated pelvic exams, and now she was proud of herself for making the appointment, getting it over with.

The reception area was done in the quiet colors of all Planned Parenthood offices everywhere, and there was the usual dusty ficus by the window, and magazines on a blond wood table. Glossy, colored brochures in a plexiglass holder said *Birth Control & You* in flowing lavender script. The woman at the desk didn't look like the road worker at all.

The exam room had colored diagrams of the female reproductive system on the wall, colored photographs of Minnesota on the ceiling.

The doctor was a woman, and she said, "Call me Maureen."

"THIS MAY PINCH," DR. Maureen said. "This may be uncomfortable for a second."

They always said that. Like it sometimes didn't. Like it sometimes wasn't. The world was full of lies.

After she got poked and pinched and was sitting in a chair next to the examining table, instead of lying face up on it looking at a picture of fall maple trees that were way too red for a doctor's office, Dr. Maureen asked her more questions. Did she want to continue oral contraceptives? Yes. Has she thought about a patch? Yes.

Dr. Maureen stopped putting check marks on the clipboard and waited.

"No patch," Pattianne said.

"Okay." The doctor clicked her pen shut and put it in her lab coat pocket. "Any questions?"

"It said something about headaches on the form."

Dr. Maureen had the kind of mouth that pursed to show she was listening.

Pattianne said, "Just ordinary everyday headaches?"

"There is no such thing as normal everyday headaches," Dr. Maureen said. She pulled her pen back out. "Do you get headaches every day?"

"Oh, no," Pattianne said. "I just meant, you know, headaches that you sometimes get, what kind of headaches that might mean, on the form."

She clicked her pen. "What kind of headaches do you get?"

The kind where light stabbed eyes. The kind where sound cracked her face bones. "Just from reading too much. I probably need new glasses."

"This is really in reference to severe or chronic headaches," clicking her pen and putting it back in her pocket.

The kind where your heart beats like a fast tickle in the throat.

"So," Pattianne said. "Exactly what is a migraine?"

"Oh," she said. "Don't worry. You'd know if you had a migraine. They tend to be quite disabling. They're quite serious, especially when it comes to taking any kind of drug. They're not just a bad headache, so don't worry."

Back at the reception desk, Pattianne filled out a long, yellow form that ended with a space for a signature. She signed *PT Anthony* as messily as she could, essentially unreadable, and paid in twenty-dollar bills. The receptionist handed her six small squares of plastic with the yellow and white pills lined up in their clear pockets. She put them in her pocket, and they made a small noise that she tried to quiet with her hand wrapped around them.

She started for the door, and the receptionist said, "Wait a sec."

"I don't need a receipt."

The receptionist said, "Katie or Marianne can walk you out if you want."

Two young women stood up, and the smaller of the two stood up on her tiptoes to look over the shade on the window. The sun came in over the top of the shade and lit up her short spiky hair, shades of purple and magenta.

"They're just praying," she said. "It looks pretty quiet."

Pattianne moved like she was in a dream, across gray-blue carpet with pink crisscrosses in a pattern that made her dizzy, next to the short woman, that purple hair at the edge of what she was seeing. What she was seeing was people at the end of the narrow walkway out to the street. What she was seeing was people on their knees praying.

"They won't bother you," someone said.

"We just have to walk through their circle," someone said. "They move apart when they see you coming."

"Sometimes they just sing," someone said.

"They have those kids out there again," someone said.

The three L children. And Lily Smith. Other people.

"There's another way out," the punky girl said. "You have to go through the bar next door. Where did you park?"

"I walked. I guess I'd rather go through the bar?"

The punky girl said, "I'll show her."

She wore overalls, and she headed down another hallway and through a steel door into a smoky little bar. A guy sat in the sun by the window. He poured tomato juice into a glass of beer and looked up when they walked past him.

The girl said, "Hey, Jackson," and he raised his red beer to her, a Harley-Davidson T-shirt over thin arms, a cigarette smoking in the ashtray.

Pattianne wanted to stay, bum a smoke, have a red beer with Jackson. She followed the overalls. "Are they there every day?"

"We're not open every day," the punky girl said. "But every day we're open, yeah."

They went down a narrow hallway, past a bathroom, past a messy office.

"The same people, every day?"

She said, "I'm only here part time." She opened a back door. Two dumpsters and an alley full of sun. She said, "Where are you going?"

"Work."

"They don't cause too much of a fuss. They know we only do referrals here." She touched the very tip of Pattianne's elbow. "Are you all right?"

How such small kindness can bring such big, quick sadness.

"I just have a headache." And Pattianne turned her sad-filled face away, and the wind blew grit into her eyes.

They thought they were saving lives. If she was trying to save someone's life, she'd do more than kneel in the sun and sing. If those praying people thought murder was happening, how could praying and singing be enough? How could they think it's okay to murder for Middle East oil, or for someone else's national boundaries, but not for freedom in your own body? How all this sounded like a letter to the editor in the Sunday *New York Times.*

She didn't believe she was a murderer. Michael would think she was. If he knew. If he knew anything. Right now, she didn't like him. There had been love growing, and she couldn't find it now. She didn't like his father or his mother or his sister or Sister Anne What's-Her-Name. She hated Father McGivens.

Bells rang from high up in the windy, sunny sky. Late for work. She turned toward Lamplighter Books. Brown shoes, gray cement, heels hard, the cadence of prayer, the cadence of footsteps in empty space where she did not love him completely anymore, empty space where she did not feel like tap-dancing up the street.

THE SMALL BELLS RANG their small sound, and the cranes spun in a circle, except the white one, which seemed not to move at all, how they did that sometimes, those cranes. One would hang perfectly still as the others bobbed and bounced. Elizabeth stood up from the bottom of Dreams, her bracelets chiming, long blue sleeves fluttering, beads of amethyst around her neck. "Oh, good, you're here." And she shook her hair.

She was glad Pattianne was here. Pattianne was glad too. Glad was easy.

"Sorry I'm late."

"Not to worry, I couldn't remember what time you were supposed to be here anyway. How you doing? Isn't it gorgeous out? Want some tea? With chicory and vanilla and stevia leaf—you'll love it." Moving near, away, moving around the store, her purple cape thrown over the beautiful chair, a dancing god with four red arms and a burning face.

"There were people praying on the sidewalk. Over on Belmont Street."

"Yeah," she said. She went through the beads. "Project Life. Planned Parenthood is there. They do abortion referrals."

Water, the teakettle, Elizabeth's bracelets, the small sounds of the bookstore. A new feather, long and thick and white, lay neatly alongside the black feather on the tea ceremony table.

Pattianne took off her coat and shivered in the warm air. "There were kids there."

"I know. Isn't that sick? Maybe it will keep them from turning into thieves, though."

Pattianne followed her back through the beads.

"Art of the Houses," Elizabeth said. "Volume One. Gone."

Pattianne's teeth bit down hard together, and she stood there so full of hate she wanted to stop breathing.

The phone rang and Elizabeth said, "Give that about three minutes to steep," and went back out front.

Michael could be at Planned Parenthood right now, on his knees in the sun, with his hair blowing in the wind, the cold wind on the back of his neck. She wanted to ask him what the difference was between the condoms they used to use and the birth control pills she used now. What was he thinking then? That murder is okay if you're single and don't want to get pregnant? What if you're married and don't want to get pregnant?

Elizabeth's laughter came through to the back, and she said "Bye-bye," on the phone. It had been three minutes, or maybe five. There was a clock out front. This was all about Michael's father. She could call up Planned Parenthood and ask if they were still there. She could say, *Please go tell the one named Michael to go home. Tell him I'll meet him there. Tell him I love him.*

Elizabeth said, "Can you smell it?" and Pattianne jumped, the jolt going all the way down her arms to her fingertips.

"Hey," Elizabeth said.

All the way to her forehead.

"I just have a headache," she said. "Those people praying, that weirded me out."

Elizabeth took the top off the teapot and sniffed the steam.

"I know," she said. She poured the tea. "It got truly theatrical out at the clinic on Highway 42 during the elections. Signs with colored pictures." The steam catching in her curls, her bracelets chiming. "Praying through megaphones. They had those plastic fetuses that they laid out in the road. Planned Parenthood is low-key compared to that. They do actual abortions out there." She held the mug of tea in front of her face, the mug in her small hands, a smile on her small face, everything that was beautiful, that was Elizabeth.

She said, "Smell."

Vanilla. Tea.

"I try to hate them," Elizabeth said. "It doesn't work." And she went back out through the beads. "But enough. Here, look at our new feather. A swan feather. Joseph was up by Timber Bay yesterday. The swans are migrating. I had to beg and plead for it. He had a whole bundle of them." She swirled the purple cape off the back of the beautiful chair and around her shoulders. "I'm off to the bank, and then I have to go try on a pair of boots I saw in the window of Winkelman's. Blue boots. Suede."

It wouldn't work for Pattianne to hate them either. She wanted to be married to him. Their little house on the prairie, their warm nights in a heap under the blankets, note cards to her mother every other week, and she could make dinner and make the bed and make love and just be married, and they would have this little life. They didn't need babies.

Even-Steven had just been a way to be alone and still have someone to sleep with. It was perfect. There was an Italian pre-med student named Vincent, and before that a depressed potter named David, just places to be for a while before she went back to being by herself. Working in the library, talking in whispers, pointing to books, looking things up in this database or that file, just sharing time and space and silent language with strangers.

Now they had their own small crowd. Joseph. Elizabeth. Frankie and Bullfrog. They should get a dog. She hadn't had a dog since Starla died. There was Reverend Rick and Lily. It was important to have people you don't like in your life. She was someone to all of them. She had to let Michael have his praying, his father would get a new heart and be okay, and Michael would get up off his knees and come back to their life, tell funny stories, drink too much when it wasn't a school night, play Scrabble, go hunting for garage sales on Saturdays. A small, good life with people around the edges and a calm space in the middle. She imagined a conversation with Jen: I love this place. I think we might stay here longer.

She bought a bottle of Tullamore D.E.W. on the way home.

A small yellow station wagon sat in the driveway, and Frankie was there, putting the coiled garden hose into the back. And Bullfrog was there. He bounced over to her, jumped up with his front paws, and bounced off her. He seemed like a very bouncy dog for being so low to the ground.

"Hi, Frankie. Hi, Bullfrog," she said, and she chirped, "Bullfrog, Bullfrog," and Bullfrog wagged his bushy tail and stuck his nose between her legs.

Frankie said, "Hey. Bullfrog, down. Out of there." Frankie's face went pink in the cheeks. "Sorry. Come here, Bullfrog. Sorry."

She pushed Bullfrog out of her crotch and rubbed his head. His long ears were cold, and as soft as silk velvet.

"He always does that," Frankie said. "Not just to girls. Women. Well, and girls. And guys." His cheeks getting pinker by the minute.

"New car?"

"New to me," he said. "Four hundred dollars."

The driver's door hung open on the Fiat station wagon. The seats were covered with striped wool blankets. A big bunch of white feathers was tied in a bundle laid on the dashboard.

"Hey, are those swan feathers? Can I see?"

They were much bigger than the one on the tea ceremony table. They were tied up in a white shoelace, as white as the feathers. They were pure white, even the quills, which were thick as pencils. The feathers were stiff at the edges, and down toward the bottom of the quill they were soft like fur. A tag of brown paper hung from the shoelace, words in careful black ink: "Hope is the Thing with Feathers." All of it inside a heart.

"The mutes are gathering up by Timber Bay," Frankie said. He took the feathers out of her hand. He pulled off the piece of paper and put it into his back pocket. "Friend of mine goes up there."

"The mutes?"

"Mute swans," he said. The bundle of feathers became something awkward in his hands. "That's what kind of swans they were. Their tail feathers are a little longer than the tundra's, or the trumpeter's."

"Are they mute?"

"No, they make all kinds of noises. I don't know why they're called mutes. They're as noisy as any of them. Noisier even. Their wings make noise. Most swans are quiet when they fly."

The world is full of lies.

She said, "Can I have one?"

He held out the bundle and she tugged out one huge feather, and he tossed the feathers onto the car seat, onto the striped blanket.

"Thanks. It's so big."

"Okay, lowrider," he said. "In you go." And he clapped and pointed, and Bullfrog got his four fat legs going up and into the front seat next the feathers, over the feathers, over the gearshift into the other seat.

"He's smart," she said.

"Yep," Frankie said. "Okay, see ya." And he got in, too, shut the door, which bounced open, and he shut it again. After two tries, the Fiat started up, jerked into reverse, and they drove away.

There was a message from Michael about debate practice, about coming home late, and another message from someone named Father Chuck, about reading at Mass tomorrow morning, please call back. She played it back and listened, the Midwest slant of vowels, the clipped-off endings. She didn't delete it. Not even by accident.

He got up in the mornings and went to Mass. He prayed in a circle on a sidewalk somewhere. She didn't think Catholics did that. The rooms of her house were empty and neat, the couch and the chairs set straight, away from the walls, and the wooden floor was shiny and clean all the way into the corners. There was nothing on the walls in the living room, nothing on the walls in the bedroom except the small dark stormscape and the wedding picture on the narrow wall next to the door. And the crucifix above the door.

She tossed her jacket on the bed and laid the feather on the dresser. The dark sunset light filled the room. It turned the white feather pink. The world is full of lies. Some of them were beautiful.

The crucifix had to come down. She wanted it gone. There was no reason it couldn't be in his office. The hammer in the kitchen drawer was a cute, lightweight hammer, a girl's hammer, he said when he found it at a yard sale. She dragged in the chair from his office.

The crucifix wasn't heavy at all. The face of Jesus was shiny, as if it had been touched again and again over the years. The rest of him was dark tarnished bronze. There may be a right way to hold a crucifix. She wrapped her fingers around the face and went after the nail with the claw end of the hammer. She tossed the crucifix on the bed, watched it bounce on the gray wool blanket. How Michael bounced her when he fucked her really hard sometimes and made her laugh, bouncing her. They hadn't fucked like that in a long time. There was nothing more irreverent she could think of, a hollow in her chest where she didn't believe in Jesus but where it felt like a terrible sin anyway.

There was a nail hole in the white paint, and the phone rang. She went out there, listened when the answering machine picked it up, and it was Michael.

"I'll be home around seven. Let's cook steaks. Pop some bakers in the oven, why don't you? I love you."

The packets of birth control pills rattled in her jacket pocket and looked like tiny blue pills of pure headache. She stuck them down into the bottom of the box of tampons and made a pot of coffee and thought of another headache, of colors and sounds that hurt. She was afraid of getting pregnant. She poured the coffee and a big dose of Irish whiskey in on top. She was afraid to tell Michael that she didn't want a baby. When did she start being so afraid?

But she wasn't afraid to say it to herself. That was a surprise. It was easy. She popped some bakers in the oven. The house was getting dark around her, and she made another Irish coffee, this one with a teaspoon of brown sugar. She lit one of the thick blue candles and set it in a saucer. She poured the whipping cream in a bowl and beat it with the whisk by candlelight. To call Miss Mimi and ask her why she never had children, what it meant, was not something she could do. It seemed almost taboo. A sorrowful thing. It didn't feel sorrowful in that moment. This was more like understanding something she had always known. It felt like the third Irish coffee, going down easy and warm.

The O-Bug's headlights filled up the dark living room, and she ran around and turned on the kitchen light, the living room light, the porch light, kissed Michael, who was all cold air and red lips, who kissed her back, who said, "Were you sitting in here in the dark?"

"Candlelight, tired cowboy," kissing his cold cheeks. "And Irish coffee."

He dropped his coat on the couch and tossed the steaks in white butcher paper onto the counter and sat down into the chair as if, finally, there was a chair, a kitchen, the end of a day.

She kissed the cold smooth skin of his forehead.

"Tullamore D-E-W," she said. "It's the guy's initals, Not, like, dew. Maybe it's just the name, but I think it's the best Irish whiskey. And the key to making Irish coffees is brown sugar."

It was there, between them, but she didn't want to go there yet, and how can you say something like that, or did you have to? She didn't know how people went about not having kids, how they made that decision without wrecking something, wrecking a whole marriage. She would think longer, and talk about anything else.

"Hey." She unwrapped the steaks. "Nice-looking steaks, where did you buy them? Rib eyes. I love rib eyes. New Yorks just don't have the flavor."

She put the mug with Tullamore D.E.W. and coffee and whipped cream in front of him and he wrapped his fingers around the mug and just held it.

He said, "You know what they had at the store? Pheasant. Well, you had to order it, actually. Have you ever had pheasant?"

"Oh my God, those beautiful ring-tail ones like at the side of the road? That's awful—they eat those?"

"Ring-necked," he said. "The kids hunt them with their dads or uncles. Bird season around here is a big thing."

"A ghastly ritual of death," she said. "I would love to have one of those tail feathers though. Hey."

She went in to the bedroom. The swan feather lay on the dresser, white in the dark of the bedroom, and she took it back out to him. "See what I got?"

He took it, held it, and he said, "I had to be an angel in this third-grade play." He stared off into space. "My mom was supposed to make my costume. She found these wings from an opera. They were made of feathers like this, huge white feathers."

"Did you get to keep them? The wings?"

"They were my worst nightmare. I threw a fit. I hated those wings. They were really more like wings for a little cherub, you could tell, and man, I almost punched Bobby Martin for making remarks. That kid was a smart son of a bitch, knew Latin in third grade. And I don't mean Pig Latin."

She had no idea whether Michael had ever been in a fight. It seemed like something you should know about someone. It seemed like something that would bring Michael back to the here and now.

"Blink, darling," she said. "Have you ever been in a fight?"

"Nope. I could weasel out of most things. There were a couple older brothers I had to seriously avoid."

He twisted the swan feather in his fingertips. "So, what's with this?"

"From Frankie. Joseph went up to some place where they're migrating, and Frankie had a whole bundle of them, tied up in a shoestring. It was so pretty, with an Emily Dickinson poem attached to it, that one about hope is a thing with feathers."

Frankie had a bundle of swan feathers with an Emily Dickinson poem tied on by a white shoestring. Elizabeth had one, and she had to talk him into giving it to her. Frankie called Joseph his friend.

"Hey," she said. "Is Joseph gay? Cause I think him and Frankie might be, you know, maybe sweethearts?"

Michael set the feather down and said, "What?"

"He gave him a bunch of feathers, they're swan feathers. I just thought of it. That white shoelace, the poetry thing—I tell you, I'm a regular Agatha Christie sometimes."

Michael sat up straighter in the chair and took a drink that left a sweet blob of whipped cream on his upper lip. He said, "You shouldn't just go around calling someone gay."

"I'm not. It's just a guess."

"Well, don't go repeating that."

"What am I?" She set the steaks on the broiler pan on the counter. "Some old gossip?"

The science tidbits Frankie was always coming out with, the poetry. It all added up.

"It's not against the law," she said. She got out a dish of butter. "Oh, sure, there's the Bible stuff. Just like mixing dairy and meat is against God's law. And shellfish. And don't forget about clothes buttons and servile labor on Sunday."

Just like birth control pills.

"Here's one way to look at it," she said. "You think that, if there is a God, he would care who fucked who, or how?"

Michael sat there with his mouth open, and she went to him and quick licked the whipped cream off his lip, and he jerked away from her and he said, "*If* there is a God?"

She got her Irish coffee from the counter and sat down.

"Well, look at it this way," she said. "With the whole universe, and whatever is beyond it, I think a God would have more to do than make deals with earthlings."

He reached across the table and took her wrist, hard, knocked over her Irish coffee, and it spilled over the table.

"Listen to you." His voice squeaked. "Is this the kind of bullshit you learn at that hippie bookstore?"

The instant of rage that flared up into her face felt ugly, and what she didn't say was *Your priests are bullshit. Your Pope is bullshit*. She didn't say it because he said, "Oh, fuck, I'm sorry." He let go of her wrist, and he looked straight up, at the light overhead, at the ceiling. Or maybe his eyes were closed, maybe they were full of tears. It sounded like it when he said, "What is going on?" He rubbed his eyes hard. He kept his hands over his face.

She could feel his fingers around her wrist. The only thing she wanted to say was *I'm sorry*. Was *I love you*. She was afraid if she said anything, anything at all, it would be *I don't want to have a baby*.

Who knew how long they sat there quiet. A while. She listened, for the wind against the side of the house, for a car along the gravel road, for the small pieces of their life falling back into place. The phone rang, and they looked at each other until Michael picked it up on the fourth ring.

A heart was ready, they were going to take out Mr. Bryn's sick heart and put in a new one. They were going right into surgery.

He said, "We'll be on the next flight out."

He hung up the phone and leaned his forehead against the wall, breathing. Then he called the school secretary at her house. Pattianne sopped the Irish coffee with a pile of paper napkins and wadded them up in the middle of the table. He hung up. Then he called Father McGivens.

It was a cigarette moment.

Michael said, "We'll meet you at the hospital. Claire is on her way there." He was leaning his back against the wall and looking at her. His hair was sticking straight up in front. "Thank you, Father. Thank you. And we can be there for prayers at the clinic on Friday night." He hung up, and his eyes stayed right on her.

He went into his office and logged on to the airlines. She leaned on the table, listening to the tapping.

He called out, "There's a flight from St. Paul to Newark at one-twelve in the morning."

The swan feather was soaked with brown.

He came back into the kitchen, stood in the doorway.

"Michael, you go."

He put his hands in his pockets, and she could see them curl into fists and then uncurl. This boy who had never been in a fight. He said, "You need to come with me."

"I can't."

"What do you mean, you can't?"

She knew the words to say. *I don't want to watch you pray the rosary in the hospital. I don't want to watch you pray on your knees outside an abortion clinic. I don't want to be back in New Jersey.* It would be easier to hope for Mr. Bryn from here, from their house, from St. Cloud. Elizabeth would light a candle, she would light a candle, and she'd stare at the tiny life in the flame and hope for him.

"I mean I don't want to," she said. It felt like a terrible mistake, to not go. "You go."

The whipped cream in his Irish coffee was floating in oily yellow clumps. She slurped up the biggest clump. The coffee was still hot, and she choked the big swallow down, her eyes tearing up with the heat of the coffee. She wished it wasn't her sitting and him standing over her like that.

"You can't even drive," he said. "Can you?"

Then he called Reverend Rick.

He went into the bedroom and she listened. The light switch. The closet door. A dresser drawer. She could clean up this mess or she could go in there. She could at least put the steaks away. Mr. Bryn was going to be all right. Let Michael go do his prayer vigil. Let him be the loving son. When he came back, there would be time to talk. Their house, their quiet life, her, it would all still be here. The edge of the swan feather was spiky and sticky, and she didn't know what those edges were called, the silky hairs along the shaft. Quill.

Michael stood in the kitchen doorway. He held his crucifix.

"I was going to rehang some stuff, that little painting," she said. "You just go be with your family, they need you."

She wiped the edge of the swan feather along her sleeve.

"Call me as soon as you see him," she said.

The Irish coffee on the table was drying into a sticky mess.

"THANKS, REALLY," MICHAEL SAID, and stopped. "Sorry."

Rick said, "Really. It's fine."

His head was a wreck. He needed to explain but he couldn't. Because he didn't know what to explain. That she wouldn't come. That she was drunk. That she didn't believe in God. He didn't know what to be mad about.

Rick said, "Do you want to talk?"

"No."

Then he was embarrassed. "I'm sorry."

"It's okay."

The light, slushy snow wasn't sticking. The windshield wipers swiped silently. He took out his phone and checked his messages.

"I need to call my mom," he said.

She didn't pick up.

"I get in at at 3:20," he said to the voice mail.

He tried to remember the flight.

"I'll get a cab."

She was probably at the hospital. Of course she was at the hospital.

"I love you." He didn't want to say that with Rick right there.

He checked his flight number and called Claire, but she didn't pick up either.

"Delta, flight 652. I'll catch a cab. I love you."

They pulled onto the highway.

They never said that, I love you, the way some families did. Saying it now was awful in a way. It was how serious this all was, that now they had to say that. He checked his messages again. Then he settled back in the seat holding the phone. Staring straight into the snow in the beam of the headlights made him dizzy, and his head ached. He shut his eyes.

His grandmother used to take out her rosary every time she got in a car in snow. He wanted his rosary beads now. He wanted that small clicking in his fingers, and the rote prayers that could be in his head without any room for any other thoughts. He used to say his rosary in secret. He wasn't even sure where his rosary was. The beads were faceted onyx. It was his father's father's rosary. He'd gotten it when he was confirmed. He was pretty sure it was in his desk drawer, in the dark red leather pouch. He wished he knew for sure. He tried to remember the last time he'd seen it.

It was an hour to the airport, and it was quiet in the car. There were towns off in the dark and exit ramps with gas stations sitting in the middle of nothing.

He said, "Let me ask you something. What's the school's policy on gay teachers?"

It was just something to talk about besides the fact that his wife didn't believe in God. And that his father was having a heart transplant. And that he hated this big empty place.

HERE'S WHAT SHE LEARNED that night: that the little house was just the right size for one person. The wood floors got warm if you turned the heat up to seventy-eight, but then the bare windows got foggy and dripped. You could clean a swan feather with a toothbrush dipped in dish detergent. Irish coffee would keep you awake and drunk all through the night. She didn't even know what a human heart looked like.

She woke up on the couch, the Loretta Young bathrobe twisted around her legs, and she was all sticky and sweaty. The yard was in dark blue shadow, and everything was frosted thick and white. She drank Alka-Seltzer and went back to sleep on the couch until almost noon, when the banging in her brain turned into someone knocking on the front door.

Angela Park stood there in the bright middle of the day, wearing a fuzzy pink beret that seemed to buzz. She had on pink lipstick too, same shade of pink, her jacket too, and she was standing there on the front porch.

"Honey," she said with those pink lips, "I just heard about Michael's daddy, and you know we're all just rooting for him. How you doing?

You get any sleep? You heard anything?" Her pink, blue-eyed face was ringed in clouds of breath.

Pattianne's feet were bare, and she backed away from the cold that came in the door. "Jesus." An icy draft on the back of her sweaty neck. "Come on in."

"Boy, you got that heat jacked up or what?"

"I was just going to make some coffee."

The wad of napkins was still on the table, the steaks were still out on the broiler pan.

"Look here, hon," Angela said. "I stopped by the bookstore and Elizabeth said how you weren't working today."

The Tullamore D.E.W. bottle was down to less than half. Sadly less than half.

"I was at the school this morning and Max told me. A new heart, can you believe that? Max is taking care of the debate team. They got a debate over in Tyre this week. Michael called him this morning."

Michael had called Max, but he hadn't called her. Angela set her shoulder bag on the counter next to the steaks. She looked over at the table. She looked at Pattianne.

"Hon," she said. "You look like shit."

Instantly hilarious, laughing that almost took her breath away, but only for an instant.

"I think I have a headache." She was either laughing or crying, or both. "My brain feels like those steaks look."

Angela took off her big pink jacket and hung it on the chair, and pushed up the sleeves of her red sweater. Its tiny pearl buttons strained over her breasts.

"Why don't you go jump in the tub? I'll make a pot of coffee."

"I have to call Michael."

Angela stepped back and checked out the Loretta Young robe, the number 12 basketball jersey, the bare feet. She said, "Not as much as you need a tub and a cup of coffee."

If anything had gone wrong, he would have called.

"Go on," she said, "I'll get the phone if it rings."

The shower was as hot as she could stand, and then she switched it to cold, then hot again, and got out, dried off, like she couldn't move fast enough, and got into jeans and the number 12 basketball jersey, the nylon of it sticking on her wet back, some hangover panic making her hurry. Her hands shook. She tied her wet hair back in an elastic. Someone would have called.

The kitchen sink was clean and empty, and the counters were wiped and the table scrubbed clean, and Angela sat there, one black stretch pant leg crossed over the other, her red sneaker thumping against the table leg. She was writing things down on a list with a pencil.

"Hey, there. I was just working on my grocery list. You look like you might just feel a whole lot better, maybe ready for a cup of coffee?"

The steaks were gone. The ice cube tray was out on the clean counter. The kitchen window was filled with daylight, wiped clear of drips.

"Thank you. I do. I am. I have to call Michael."

"Just milk, right? Here you go, ma'am. Now, I have to go run up to the corner, that grocery store, so you talk to Michael, and I'll be right back. I'll just let myself in. Have you got a hammer?"

"Do I have a hammer?" Oh God, the hammer. The crucifix. She would hang it back up above the bedroom door. "Yeah, I do. Hey, could you pick me up a toothbrush?"

The number for the hospital was on Michael's desk, small round numbers on the clean sheet of notebook paper in the middle of his neat desk next to a stack of school comp notebooks, a manila envelope, a schedule of debate practices that said *Debate Practice Schedule* across the top in neat round letters. His collection of dashboard Madonnas was along the windowsill. The yard was full of sun.

She asked the woman who answered for Michael Bryn. "Mr. Bryn's son," she said.

Blue frost shadows under the trees.

Claire came to the phone.

"He's in post op," she said. Her voice was rough. Pattianne heard cigarettes smoked outside the hospital doors in the cold.

"You sound pretty beat."

"The surgery took seven hours," Claire said. "Michael is with my mom and Father McGivens. They're saying a rosary."

Angela was cracking ice cubes loose in the kitchen. Maybe Claire could hear it. Maybe she would assume they were rosarying it up here too. Maybe Pattianne would tell her that.

"Tell them I called," she said instead. "I'll be here waiting."

Which would be the greater sin, lying about saying the rosary or not believing in the rosary in the first place?

"God bless you, Pattianne," Claire said, her voice not flat now, not far away, but rich with some sound—love, hope, some crazy emotion caught there in her throat, and maybe she did hear the rosary. "I wish you were here." And that was a whisper.

All Pattianne wanted was a cigarette. The worst time to have one, hungover, her stomach threatening dire consequences for anything. Then there was the unmistakable pop of a champagne cork in the kitchen.

"I wish I was too," she said, and bye, and love to your mom, and she hung up quick.

Angela had wine glasses out, and they were filled with cracked ice. Dark purple liquid pooled at the bottom of each glass.

"Got to have your Vitamin C," she said. "Now watch this."

The orange juice was in a bowl, and she had beaten it to froth. "Some egg white makes it foam up all nice like that," she said, and she poured the frothy foamy orange juice carefully over the ice, about halfway up the glass. The purple at the bottom stayed purple. The orange stayed orange. "The trick is you pour real slow," she said. Then came the champagne, and a twist of orange peel that glittered. "Dipped in egg white and sugar," she said. "Here you go, this is my own invention. It's called a Mimi-mosa. Now that purple stuff is this purple-flavor liquor." She tapped her pink fingernail on the gold cap of a small liqueur bottle. Parfait d'Amour. Then she picked up her glass. "Here's to Michael's daddy. Tell me how he's doing. You okay?"

"He's not back awake yet. I just talked to Claire. Michael was with his mother. They can't go see him yet." One sip of orange juice and fizzy cold champagne made the whole kitchen brighten. "Wow. This is great."

Angela unbuttoned her sweater a few buttons. "So his sister is there?" she said. "You know, it is really warm in here."

"She goes to school in Pennsylvania, Slippery Rock State College, and she was there, she answered the phone at the hospital."

"Now this is not my undies, it's a summer top—I don't want you to think I'm going out of the house in my underwear." Angela took off her sweater. A pearl button popped off and rolled under the table. "Oops," she said. She was wearing a candy-striped tank top. "I know I'm too fat to wear this."

"You're not fat, Angela." Angela was sexy and beautiful. She said, "You're beautiful."

"You are so sweet. Now, did you say Slippery Rock?"

"That's the name of the college."

"Why, my first husband, Hal, he used to watch Slippery Rock play football on the TV or something, I remember that name from him watching football—he loved his football. Well, that's good that she lives so close. So Michael is just going to stay till his daddy comes home from the hospital?"

"Maybe longer, make sure things are going okay."

"They have good insurance?"

"Oh yeah, they're pretty well off."

"I bet Michael wishes you were there right now. I think it's just a shame that you couldn't go with him. A new heart. Imagine."

No, she couldn't imagine. It didn't make sense. How did they hook it up? What did they do with the old heart? What did anyone ever do with an old heart? The sweet orange juice foam, the bite of champagne, now that made sense.

"Angela, what are you doing here?"

"Oh, holy buckets, I almost forgot my errand. There's a vanilla envelope of flyers, one of those big yellow kind? I told Rick I'd pick it up for him. He was out front of the school when I dropped Max off, and I got to go out there this afternoon so I said how I'd bring it. You want more Mimi-mosa? I think it's putting some color back in your cheeks."

"More flyers?"

"These aren't more of the pretty ones, these are for the prayer vigil Michael and Rick got going Friday. It's got the rules, like about how close we can get and all."

"Planned Parenthood?"

"No, the other place out on the highway." She stirred her Mimi-mosa with her finger and stuck her finger in her mouth. She sucked on her finger, staring down into her Mimi-mosa. "They actually kill babies out there."

"Oh, Angela, not you too? Just tell me what exactly it is you're doing? Trying to save the babies?"

Angela filled their glasses back up with Mimi-mosa. Her spiky black mascaraed eyelashes were like the eyelashes of a baby doll Pattianne got for Christmas one year. Pattianne sucked the foam through her teeth, foam, orange, then sweet thick purple. She'd hated that doll. She'd been hoping for figure skates.

Pattianne crunched the ice, pain shooting through her back teeth, and she said, "Trying to save the mothers from committing the sin of murder?"

"Well, my word," Angela said. "There's that too, there's those poor girls besides the babies, which, God will take care of the babies, but those poor girls." She slurped up a piece of ice. "Those poor girls."

The swan feather was white again, but it was stiff and separated along its feathered edge that Pattianne didn't know the word for. She smoothed it out. Her hands weren't shaking now. Mimi-mosas. "I have a friend named Mimi. Miss Mimi."

"That's a pretty name," Angela said. "Oh, and here." She held out a brand-new toothbrush in its shiny toothbrush package.

"My friend Miss Mimi is an older woman. She was the Avon lady."

"I get Avon. One of the boys at school? His mom is the Avon lady. She sends out catalogs. I got some new Avon right here. Not this color I got on, I believe this is Maybelline."

"I miss her."

"Your friend Mimi?"

"She never had kids."

Angela added a touch of Parfait d'Amour. "That's a sad thing, I think, no kids, growing old with no family. Does she have family? I have my nieces which I adore, and my sister's got a new baby boy, so there's a nephew too." She filled her glass up with champagne.

"Mimi doesn't seem sad. She has a beautiful house, and she's beautiful too. She has to be at least eighty."

"You can adopt now, even if you aren't married. Some folks are single parents. If they got a home for a child, they're allowed. There's so many kids need homes, they ought to be allowed to have at least one parent, at least as long as it's a mom."

Pattianne added champagne to her Parfait d'Amour and tried to imagine kids running around Miss Mimi's house, running around her life.

"Miss Mimi loves purple."

Angela picked up one of the glittery orange twists. She stuck it in her mouth, chewed it. Took it out.

"There was one time," she said. "Summer before last, that field behind that place caught fire, and I was hoping it would just keep burning right up to the clinic and just burn it down."

"Right," Pattianne said. "That would solve the problem."

"I tell you what." Angela set her glass down carefully. "Wasn't any killing done that day. Everything on the whole road was stopped up with that field burning. I couldn't even get out to Sears. I remember I was going out there to return this pair of the cutest pink boots that were too small for even my little one. Sears is always good about taking returns."

The window light made Angela's eyes opaque, bright, glassy.

"I just want to stop the killing. It breaks my heart, I tell you. It does. We could help find homes for all those babies their mamas don't want."

Pattianne just wanted her husband back. Maybe not her husband. Maybe her boyfriend.

Angela bit tiny bits off the orange peel. "Those girls killing their babies," she said. "I don't know, I guess folks' business with God is their own business."

"If you really think it's murder, is praying and holding up signs really enough?" Pattianne said. "If it were Michael in there being murdered, I think I'd do a lot more than just pray."

There was a flash of yellow out the kitchen window, and she knocked the table getting up too fast. "There it is," she said, and "Oh, shit," when the wine glass broke, purple, and she went to the window and leaned over the sink. The yellow-headed blackbird was under the birch tree on the frosted blue ground. "It's that bird I was asking you about."

Angela came to her side and looked out. "Why, I have seen those, I think, now that I see him here. He is a pretty boy, isn't he now?" Her face was all joy and smiling again.

Pattianne said, "You look so pretty in lipstick. Most women look dumb in lipstick."

Angela's cheeks blushed. "Oh, you are so sweet. But I think any woman looks good with a touch of color. Here, come here and try this new color out, this is the Avon."

She set her purse on the table and groped around in it, looking sadly at the table. "We broke your pretty wine glass, Pattianne."

The white swan feather was now lavender. Pattianne wiped it off on the leg of her jeans and stuck it into the elastic in her hair.

"I never wear lipstick," she said. "It just doesn't feel right on me."

Angela held up a gold tube and twisted off the cap.

She said, "I guess it's kinda red," and they both laughed. They were back to laughing, God left behind in the conversation.

"Just try it," she said. "Here." And she handed Pattianne a small round mirror in a red plastic daisy.

Pattianne put on the lipstick. "I look like Bozo the Clown," she said.

Angela said, "Now don't make me laugh," and she put on red lipstick too. Pattianne didn't make her laugh, and Angela's hand was steady until a single loud knock at the door made Angela's hand jump. Red lipstick across the top of her lip like a red Halloween mustache.

Reverend Rick's car was in the driveway. "Oh, shit," Angela said. "I promised I'd get those flyers to him by the end of second lunch."

Pattianne gave her a napkin and said, "Here," and tried to not laugh. "You get the door, I'll get the flyers." She went through the living room in a steady line, into Michael's office, grabbed the manila envelope and scattered everything else, fuck it, and walked steadily and carefully back out to Rick and Angela, who had not done a very good job of cleaning the lipstick off her face.

"Thank you again so much for driving Michael last night. I just talked to him. I mean, to his sister." She had to put her sentences together very carefully, which is why she should never drink champagne in the afternoon, and which was maybe why there were no nice eye wrinkles in his face. She said, "Come on in," and he looked past her, past the pillows on the floor, and the blanket in a tangle, and balls of Kleenex stuffed into the back of the couch, into the kitchen, at the broken wine glass, purple Parfait d'Amour in a puddle on the table, the half-empty champagne bottle. Him, Pattianne, and Angela all standing there in a silly triangle.

"Well," Angela said. "Maybe I should get myself going here." She got her red sweater off the back of the chair. "The kids are at the center after school." She slipped the sweater over her bare, white arms and started buttoning it up over her candy-striped breasts. For an insane moment, Pattianne thought of offering Rick a Mimi-mosa.

Angela got down on her hands and knees and looked under the table. "Now where's that button?" Her black stretch pants stretched across her butt.

"Angela," Rick said, no nice eye wrinkles in his voice. He looked Pattianne's way now, not at Angela's round black butt sticking out from under the kitchen table. "I'll drive you home," Rick said. "Max can pick up your car after debate practice."

Pattianne was glad she was not Angela. She was not sure she was glad she was Pattianne.

THE PEARL BUTTON WAS in the corner of the kitchen. She put the broken wine glass in the trash, and the champagne in the refrigerator, and she wiped up the sticky purple Parfait d'Amour until the table was clean and empty. She put the sticky swan feather on the edge of the sink. The pillows back on the bed. The house back in order. She sat back down at the table. Mr. Bryn's chest would be sewn back together. It must be huge, the incision, long and red. Black stitches. Think of it. She dared herself. They say the human heart is about the size of a fist.

She would brush her teeth with her new toothbrush. Michael would call. He would come home. She would get up and go outside, under the birch tree, and look for a yellow feather, which she didn't believe she would find.

9: WHAT HEARTS DO
INSTEAD OF BEING IN LOVE

THE ROAD OUT TO the Sears store went right past the clinic, where there were no picketers, or protesters, or people praying, nothing going on, just a low building set back in the smooth snow. The cedar siding caught the low light of the sun. It looked like your average dentist's office, or real estate office, or abortion clinic. Then there was a feed store, and a row of self-storage units, and the cemetery, everything spaced out along the road until the intersection with gas stations on each corner, and then the Sears store.

Christmas lights were her favorite part of Christmas, especially on the roof lines of houses at night, especially blue lights. There was a small peak over the front porch of their house, and she wanted to put blue lights up there, and maybe around the big front window. She would ask Frankie to help. She would surprise Michael when he came back.

Pattianne was never at her best in a Sears store, but she found the Christmas-tree-lights section with no problem, up the escalator and next to housewares, and there were blue lights, strings and strings of them, tiny blue twinkle lights, big blue bulbs, and small zippy lights that looked like they were running around a track. She got the big ones. They seemed old-fashioned.

"I have an aversion to those running lights," she told the woman with the Sears badge that said *Rosette*.

"Me too," Rosette said. She was a gray-haired woman who didn't seem old enough for gray hair, and she had two pencils behind one ear. "Now, I like those all-red ones too. They look like those red candies for decorating on top of Christmas cookies. Cash or on your Sears card?"

Pattianne was surprised to think she must look like the type of woman with a Sears card.

"Cash." She stacked the four boxes of blue lights on the counter. "And I think I need an extension cord too."

"How about some of these too?" Rosette pointed to a display of boxes of small plastic clips right there on the counter. "You just hang these up over the edge of the gutter and then kind of clip the string of lights into these little doohickeys and there you go."

"Great, thanks, yeah." She was Pattianne's accomplice. "I'm going to surprise my husband."

Rosette put everything in a glossy white shopping bag with a poinsettia printed on it like a stencil. There were other shopping bags with holly stencils. The familiarity of Christmas, the words to the songs, the easy, pretty lights and glitter and wrapping paper. She would show Michael that she was not completely non-Christian. That she could be open-minded, that Christmas mattered to her.

She called the school secretary when she got home. "I need to get ahold of Frankie."

The secretary's name was Katrinka, and she said, "Can I have someone call you back, Mrs. Bryn?"

"It's not an emergency. I wanted to ask him to do a special job for me."

"How are you doing all alone?" Katrinka said. She had kind of a chirping voice, like someone named Katrinka might have.

"Okay," she said. "Thanks." She had never actually met Katrinka in person. "Michael should be back pretty soon."

"That's what he said when he called," Katrinka said. "So, are you going to be home for a while?"

"Yeah. I just need some help putting up my new Christmas lights outside."

"Oh, well," Katrinka said. "My boy, Scottie? His Boy Scout pack is having a Christmas-tree sale in the parking lot of the Kiwanis Club, and they're doing stuff like that to earn money."

Katrinka didn't sound old enough to have a boy who could put Christmas lights up on a porch roof.

"He'd need a ladder and all," Pattianne said.

"That's what they do," she chirped. "They're earning money to rebuild the fence around the playground at the St. Joe City Park."

"Well, Frankie knows where the plug-ins are and everything," Pattianne said. "Why don't you just have him call me? But maybe I'll get my tree from the Boy Scouts." Suddenly she was going to get a tree. "Where's the Kiwanis Club?"

"To be honest," Katrinka's voice got lower and quieter. "Frankie isn't really working today."

She stopped and didn't say anything next. The phone line sounded empty.

Pattianne said, "Hello?"

"I better have someone call you back."

"Okay," Pattianne said. "Anytime. I'm here, or I'll be right back."

"But, hey," Katrinka's voice chirped back up. "The Kiwanis Club is out on the highway going out to the lake? It's Fourth Street in town and changes to Highway 3. You can't miss it, there's a red barn."

Pattianne knew about stringing lights. Her father was a model of efficiency when it came to Christmas. The strings of lights measured out and tested. She and Jen were allowed to hand him the ornaments for the tree one at a time, and he would position them on the perfect blue spruce, one ornament by each light. They never had all-blue lights. They never had outside lights either. "Italians," her mother said, although the O'Learys had outside lights, and the Schmidts had outside lights, and the Kowalskis had outside lights. Jen smirked privately when their mother said things like that. Pattianne tried not to laugh. Jen's smirk was a gold-star smirk. It could almost always get her, especially when it was about their mother.

She laid the new blue lights out across the living room floor, one string at a time, and plugged them in. All working. Beautiful. She checked the extra bulbs that came in a box of four. All working. She checked to see what would happen if she took one bulb out of the string.

All the rest working. Beautiful. She laid the lights across the back of the couch, up over the top of the bookcase and on to the top of the kitchen doorway, then around to the top of the front door, lots of lights, plenty of lights, more lights than her mother could ever imagine.

Now there was nothing to do until Frankie called. She stepped across the strings of lights and went into the kitchen and poured a touch of schnapps over a single ice cube.

A tree would require more lights, and she would need ornaments, and a Christmas tree stand. It was starting to seem like a lot of stuff, but the window in the living room had been so bare for so long, and now she understood why: it was waiting for a Christmas tree, a perfect blue spruce with blue lights that she would light up for Michael when he arrived. Maybe she could suggest a flight that would get him here at night. Apple cider and rum with cinnamon sticks. Gingerbread. She would make gingerbread so their house would be filled with the smell, and maybe she'd even get him an early Christmas present, and wrap it, have it waiting under the tree and make him open it, one of those weird Christmas ties maybe. It sounded like another trip to the Sears store. It sounded like a trip to the red barn.

Back out the door, back into the O-Bug, and off to the far edge of town, north of the Sears store. She turned on the radio, mostly static, but she fiddled and fiddled, hoping for some Christmas tunes. What she found was "I'll Be Home for Christmas," which is what she considered a fake Christmas song. Even "Santa Claus Is Coming to Town" was better than those weird Bing Crosby / Pat Boone songs about Christmas in the fifties or whatever. She turned the radio off. Turned the turn signal on. Turned into the big red barn that said Kiwanis Club and Pack 254.

The smell of fresh-cut Christmas trees was an instant hit of home in a way that never meant home, sweet and sad and far away, so far it was gone somehow. She would fill their house with that smell. Trees were leaned against makeshift fences strung around the lot, and the whole place was all about that smell. A short, skinny kid in a hat came up to her and said, "Merry Christmas, ma'am." Smart-ass, calling her ma'am. Or probably not. This was, after all, a short skinny kid in a hat, a Boy Scout hat, and he had on a cute tie to boot. She could call him dearie. He just stood there.

"Hey kiddo," she said. "Merry Christmas yourself. Got any Christmas trees?"

"Yes, ma'am." There was weird dark fuzz on his upper lip. He held out his arm, waved across the lot. "They're all right here."

There were bushy emerald green trees and dark green trees that were a little less bushy. The kid trailed around after her, sounding asthmatic. At the back of the lot were the blue spruces, one short row of them, and they cost twice as much as the others.

"Do you guys sell rope, too?"

"No, ma'am."

"I need some to tie a tree to my car."

He waved toward the trailer at the front of the lot. "We're selling bungee cords," he said. "Donated by Ace Hardware."

"What a scam," she said. "I'll take two."

"Two trees?"

"Nice try, dearie," she said. He grinned at her and turned red, and she was filled with joy. "One tree, two bungee cords."

ORIGAMI BIRDS. THAT'S WHAT she wanted on her tree. Origami birds and blue lights. White birds. Doves of peace, or cranes. On the way back into town from the Kiwanis Club, the snow flurries started, icy bits ticking against the windshield, teasing her. There hadn't been any big snowstorm predicted, but there was hope in the dark, fat clouds piled up over the direction of the lake, toward Canada. A northeast storm. Sounded ominous. She turned into town and stopped at Lamplighter Books, parking up ahead of the store, a ways up the block where she hoped Elizabeth wouldn't see the Christmas tree.

She went in, under the cranes, and there was Elizabeth, her arms crossed, looking at her, looking out the window, the white day shining on her face. She said, "Celebrating the season in the traditional pagan style, I see."

It turned out that the Druids loved their trees, pointing to heaven. She had Elizabeth's blessing.

"I need to borrow your origami book," she said. "And I need some origami paper. Where can I get origami paper? I want all white cranes on my tree."

"You can make your own paper," she said. "You just have to cut the paper perfectly square."

Joseph came out of the back room. She started to say hello, but he turned and went back through the beads without a word.

Elizabeth said, "You can borrow my paper cutter if you want."

She went back there and came out with the paper cutter.

"There you go," she said. "Be careful of that blade, it's sharp as hell."

She set the paper cutter on the desk and folded her arms into her sleeves. She was all dark green today, and a red stone hanging around her neck on a black silk cord, and surely, surely, she wasn't wearing red and green on purpose. Joseph stayed in the back room. Elizabeth did not shake her hair. She did not jingle her bracelets. She looked out the front window and said, "Happy season of Mithras."

"Oh?"

"That's where the old Romans got the idea of Christmas. They co-opted Mithras celebrations, the invincible Roman sun god. And that wasn't until the fourth century, when Mithraism was the official state religion."

"So Jesus wasn't a Capricorn?"

Pattianne thought she would like that. She thought it would make her smile. But she curled one side of her lip up.

"Capricorn. Ha. For one thing, if the shepherds were watching their flocks the night he was born, it was probably in the spring, not winter." She took the origami book from the shelf behind the desk. "That's the only time the shepherds stayed out all night, lambing season. But who knows. There's no record of any great census that might have gotten Mary and Joseph to Bethlehem, anyway." She tossed the origami book on the desk, and her bracelets jingled. "There you go. Birds for your Mithras tree."

Joseph came back out, and this time he gave her kind of a hello look, but his lips were weird, all straight and tight. He held his turquoise down coat by the sleeves, dragging it across the carpet, the turquoise swirls in the carpet like threads from the coat.

Pattianne said, "I'm putting up lights around my porch." It sounded like the wrong thing to say.

Joseph sat down in the beautiful chair so that he was facing away from them. Elizabeth slipped her arms up inside her sleeves.

"Blue lights."

Then Elizabeth looked at her and shook her hair. It was like they were in a play.

"I was actually trying to find Frankie to help me with the ladder and all," which suddenly felt like it was not the next line.

"At one point it was declared a sin to observe the birth of Jesus," Elizabeth said. That didn't feel like the right next line either. "Being born was too ordinary, him being divine and all."

"Making up sins to suit their politics," Joseph said. The right line.

The shop was quiet except for Joseph's breathing, which was slow and measured, and Pattianne was noticing it.

"So," she said. "I guess I'll go home and wait for Frankie to call." She picked up the paper cutter and the origami book. "So, I'll see you Thursday?"

One of Elizabeth's hands came out of one sleeve and waved at her, like a small bird of fingers, like she was being dismissed.

Then Pattianne got brave. "What's going on?"

Joseph stood up and faced Elizabeth, who stood still as a statue. Her hands had disappeared again. He put on his coat. The nylon swish of it was loud in the total quiet of Lamplighter Books.

He said, "I'll tell Frankie to call you," and he went to the door, opened it so gently the bells never made a sound, and he closed it just as quietly. The cranes swung wildly, though, and he went past the window, up the street past the O-Bug with the Mithras tree sticking out of the trunk, and the cranes kept swinging in wild circles, and Elizabeth sat on the tall stool and watched him. The window light washed all the color out of her eyes. The white crane was the only one still bobbing when she said, "Joseph is on administrative leave."

The white crane slowed to the point where Pattianne knew that as soon as she looked away, it would stop. She looked away, at Elizabeth, who said, "And Frankie quit."

Still, she said, "Frankie quit?"

Elizabeth sank down into the beautiful chair. She said, "I hate this town. I hate the St. Cloud School for Boys. I hate Rick Smith. And I hate hating." And every time she said the word, her voice got lower, and not sounding like hate, sounding colder than that, like something quiet and still down around her heart.

"What happened?"

Elizabeth stretched her legs out in front of her and looked at her blue suede boots.

"Are those your new boots?"

She pulled up the long, dark green wool of her skirt and showed off the new boots. High as her knees. She wore bright orange tights.

"Orange tights? With a green skirt and top? Is that legal here in St. Cloud?"

"Probably not," Elizabeth said. She dropped her skirt back down. "Frankie and Joseph have been together since Frankie was eighteen. Before that he was a residential student at the school and Joseph was his advisor. Joseph switched him to one of the other advisors, and they've been waiting until Frankie turned twenty-one."

Secret lovers. Pedophile and victim. Frankie as Lolita.

"Waiting for what?"

Elizabeth leaned her head back and looked at the ceiling. Her eyes were red-rimmed, and she closed them and shook her head. Her hair looked so perfect against the purple and gold and turquoise stripes of the beautiful chair, and yet her tights clashed.

"Waiting to come out I guess," she said.

"No one knew?"

"People kind of knew about Joseph. They didn't know about him and Frankie. Rick Smith didn't know about him and Frankie." She opened her eyes. "I guess it was only a matter of time until he figured it out."

Or until someone outed them.

"What will they do?"

She stood up and shook out her skirts, and the white crane bobbed at her.

"I don't know." She shook her hair. "I think they should elope."

The bells rang, and a woman with a kid came in, both all bundled up in swishy nylon coats, the cold chasing in after them.

The woman said, "UFOs?"

OUTSIDE, THE ICY BITS blew harder. It felt like they were cutting into her cheeks. It felt like she deserved it. She had told Michael, Michael must have told Reverend Rick, and it had caused a big mess. She stopped at the Hallmark Gold Crown store and went in to buy paper to cut up for birds. She didn't even know what administrative leave meant. There were laws. This wasn't the eighties, or even the nineties. But St. Cloud School was a private school run by Christians, and this was the Midwest, and she had a big mouth. It was about the swan feather, and Emily Dickinson. It was about Tullamore D.E.W.

The only white paper was wedding paper with silvery swirls and bells and doves and roses, all white-on-white, and none of it seemed right until she saw that the designs would be cut up and folded into hiding and that wedding paper would be perfect. That put her in a slightly better mood, distracted by some pretty thing, and she drove home, "Rudolph the Red-Nosed Reindeer" playing on the radio.

The Mithras tree could stay in the O-Bug in the driveway for now.

It was warm in the house, the windows just slightly fogged over, and she went into the kitchen and got out milk, dark powder, sugar, schnapps.

Real hot chocolate.

She even got out Michael's double boiler, thirty-five cents at a yard sale on the road out past Reverend Rick's, the road that led to Birch Lake and beyond to the blue trees of Canada, the caves of the cranes, everything. She made hot chocolate for schnapps and spread the paper cutter, the wedding paper, and the origami book all out on the living room floor. She turned the heat up and took off her shoes and socks.

Michael and Rick, a pair of old gossips, riding in the car to the airport, Michael upset and scared about his father and unloading on Rick, Rick goading him for information. She tried to picture it, that hour-long car ride in the dark, the two of them confiding in each other, but what she saw was herself, drunk, giddy over a swan feather, blabbering on about whatever popped into her head. And isn't that how marriage is supposed to work? You're supposed to be able to blabber. And didn't Michael specifically say she shouldn't repeat that to anyone else? And then he goes and does just that.

It was all about the survival of the tribes out there in the desert back then. They had to spend all their time breeding in Biblical times.

But this was all about his father. This was about a new heart, and she should be there with him, except that he was on his knees saying the rosary in a hospital room, or on his knees outside an abortion clinic. She was on her knees on the living room floor, a mess of scraps and a flock

of Mithras cranes all over the floor, which made sense. Cranes everywhere, her fingers making them, easy, not thinking of cranes, thinking
of Michael. It felt sacred. It felt right. They were together somehow.

The window was slightly fogged over, and suddenly it filled with
light, and the whole room filled with light. She got up off her knees and
opened the door to Bullfrog, of all people, out in the yard, and Frankie
getting out of the Fiat, and a swirl of thick snowflakes that were only
just starting to cover the grass. Bullfrog was bouncing, and her heart
bounced too, all the white, in the air, on the brown grass, on the branches
of the small trees in the yard, on Frankie's dark red hair.

"It's snowing," she yelled, and he slammed the door of the Fiat, and
the door bounced back open and he slammed it again. Bullfrog was up
the steps by now.

Frankie's face split into that grin that was all about that crooked
front tooth, and he said, "One must have a mind of winter / to regard the
frost and the boughs / of the pine-trees crusted with snow."

"Huh?"

"Wallace Stevens maybe? I hear you need some help with your
lights."

"Blue lights," she said. "Want some hot chocolate with schnapps?"

Bullfrog bounced on in the door, and Frankie came up the steps, and
it was suddenly not about the beautiful snow and the blue lights.

"Listen," she said. "I'm sorry about what happened. What happened,
anyway? Come on in."

She didn't want to close the door on the snow.

"Boy, it's pretty hot in here," he said.

"I heard you lost your job."

"My apartment too," he said. "I don't care."

"How can they kick you out of your apartment?"

"The apartment comes with the job," he said. "Wow. Origami."

"For my Mithras tree," she said. "Here, here's one for you. It's a
crane. Is that legal, to get fired and all? What does administrative leave
mean, anyway?"

"No," he said. He fingered the crane, opened its wings, folded them
back flat. "Joseph could fight it. Should. I just want to leave."

Then it was suddenly about Frankie being gay, and she saw that she
had completely missed that, all this time. He took a cup of hot chocolate.

"It's not very hot," she said, and he held the cup out and she poured in schnapps. "You're pretty good at being a secret."

"Yeah, well it sucks." He slurped. "I remember this. You made this for me once before."

"The first night I met Bullfrog." Who was sniffing around the edges of the room, his tail wagging easy, like he belonged here. "He's a very cool-looking dog, you know."

Frankie's crooked tooth front disappeared, and his face went blank, and he said, "Yeah."

Bullfrog got to the braided rug in front of the sink and started going around in circles like he was going to curl up and have a snooze, and then he didn't. He just stood there, like instead maybe he got dizzy and forgot what he was doing.

"Okay," Frankie said. "Show me where you want these lights."

"We need a ladder."

Frankie drank down the rest of the hot chocolate and schnapps. "Got it," he said.

She took the schnapps bottle and they went back into the living room, where the blue lights were strung around the couch, the shelves, the floor. The white cranes were vaguely blue, and scattering in the cold wind coming in the open door. Frankie propped his crane on the windowsill.

The ladder stuck out the back of the Fiat, and he pulled it out from where it was worked in all the way to the front passenger seat. She kept trying to see gay in him, and he was just Frankie, but different now. He dropped the ladder onto the snowy grass.

"Extension cord?" he said.

"I'll get it." She couldn't tell if maybe part of her knew all along, how you find out someone is gay and part of your brain goes, Oh, of course, that's it. The new extension cord and the boxes of doohickeys were on the table. She took it all out to Frankie.

"Check these out," she said.

"Is that librarian lingo?" he said. He looked at one of the boxes of hooks, and then he looked at the roof of the porch, and then he said, "So, did you keep the receipt?"

The doohickeys wouldn't work. There were no gutters on the porch roof. He handed her back the box.

"I'll just bend a nail up kind of at an angle," he said, and took off his coat and dropped it on the ground. "Those down coats are a pain in the ass," he said, and he headed on up the ladder. The wind blew his T-shirt, and his long legs leaned into the ladder. He had seemed like he was just this side of being a kid, all skinny and goofy. Now he was someone's secret lover.

Bullfrog sat in the doorway watching. Pattianne plugged in the first string of lights and handed them up to Frankie.

"It's beautiful," she said, and sipped the schnapps. At the end of the first string, she handed him the schnapps bottle while she got the next string.

"I don't even like Christmas," he said, and he hiccupped.

"Season of Mithras."

The schnapps went down, and the blue lights went up, and the snow fell thicker. She put on more hot chocolate, and Bullfrog curled up in the doorway. She fed another string of lights up to Frankie on the ladder, and at the top of the peak, he climbed up onto the roof and straddled it, sitting there like he was on a horse. His white T-shirt glowed in the snowy dark and the blue lights.

He raised the hammer to his face like a microphone.

"The snow had begun in the gloaming, / and busily all the night / had been heaping field and highway / with a silence deep and white."

"I think you should get down from there."

A little red car pulled up in the driveway, lighting up the front of the house, and at first she thought, *Michael*. But Joseph got out and stood there looking up. Bullfrog ran out the door, bouncing like he does, and poked Joseph in the crotch.

Frankie waved the hammer in the air.

"This one goes out to all the pretty boys at St. Cloud School," he yelled out, and then he crooned, "Call me irrepressible."

Joseph pushed Bullfrog down. He put both hands on his hips and he said, "That's irresponsible."

Frankie stopped and said, "Why?"

"It just is," Joseph said. "Get down from there."

She held her breath, and Frankie swung his legs over the peak, quick, too quick for her to breathe, and he got back onto the top of the ladder.

"Almost done here, boss," he said, the hammer turned back into a hammer. Joseph and Bullfrog walked across the snow to the front door, Bullfrog bouncing and wagging like Joseph was a special friend of his.

"So," she said. "How are you doing?" And then she wanted to take it back, that casual question that doesn't mean what it seems to mean, and she was sorry she asked it so free and easy, like nothing was wrong.

Joseph watched Frankie steady himself on the ladder and said, "Pretty good, how about you? I like the blue."

"It's getting pretty slick to be up on a ladder," she said, chattering away like she wasn't socially inept. "So, are you here to help with the blue lights, or the white birds?"

"I'm here to apologize for being a jerk at the bookstore," he said.

"That's okay. I mean, you weren't being a jerk."

"I knew it would come to this sometime," he said. "Nobody gets away with anything in this town."

"Yeah," she said. "Well." And she went past him, out into the blue snow, out toward the road, all the way to the mailbox, and then turned and looked. The sharp peak of the porch roof was just as she imagined it would be.

Joseph said, "You guys must be freezing your tails off."

She said, "We're fueled by peppermint schnapps and hot chocolate." The hot chocolate. "Shit," she said, and ran up to the door and through a flock of paper cranes that scattered on the living room floor behind her. The hot chocolate was just about to boil over, and she grabbed the pan off the flame and only got the top part of the double boiler and dumped the boiling water in the bottom part right over her hand.

"Shit," she said to the empty kitchen, a big red welt was rising across her palm and fingers.

She held her right hand under cold running water and poured hot chocolate into a mug left-handed. Turned off the water and opened the schnapps with one hand. Poured in some and then some more and took it back out front.

She held it out to Joseph.

"Schnapps?" Joseph said. "Great. You guys are drinking and climbing around on the roof in the snow?"

The blue lights strung over the peak of the porch roof were at least three different shades of blue.

"Are these Sears lights?" Joseph said.

"No," she said. "These are real lights." Her line.

"Now," she said. "The tree."

She made footprints through the snow over to the O-Bug and managed to unhook the bungee cords with one hand but her burned hand really hurt if she so much as bent it, and she tugged at the tree one-handed and gave up. Joseph stood still in the middle of the yard, looking up at Frankie, his face lit with blue, and the fat snowflakes coming down into the blue light. Bullfrog sat at his feet, watching Frankie, too, or maybe he was watching the snow coming down, and then he yawned a big squeaky yawn and got up and headed for the porch. She followed him, leaving Joseph in his beautiful blue snowy moment.

She went in the bathroom and looked for something for her hand. The light was oddly yellow and bright, as if the only good lights in the world were blue lights, but she found the aloe vera ointment from last summer's sunburn and worked it onto her palm. It was an ugly red burn, and it hurt like the dickens. One of her favorite sayings. *Yes, Michael, I burned my hand and it hurts like the dickens. If you were here, you could do this for me.* She slathered on the ointment and then opened a roll of gauze, which she should have done before getting ointment all over, and which was easy compared to getting out the adhesive tape and the nail scissors and trying to lay snips of tape along the counter so she could tape the gauze once she had it in place.

They had the blue lights up around the window when she went back out to the living room. The window from inside was as perfect as it was from outside, since she had never fucked it up with curtains. Joseph and Frankie were out in the yard looking at the house. She stood in the blue window and waved at them.

"Come on in," she yelled, and she turned off the lights in the living room so the blue would shine, and shine it did. Joseph came in, and Frankie followed him with the two empty cups.

"More hot chocolate?"

"No, we should probably get going," Joseph said. But Frankie said, "Sure, I'll have another cup," and Bullfrog laid himself down with a groan. She took the two cups in one hand.

Frankie said, "What happened to your paw?"

She waved her bandaged hand at them. "Attacked by a double boiler."

They stood there in the center of the window, framed in blue lights like a movie marquis.

"But it's perfect," she said. "I'll get some more hot chocolate."

She went in the kitchen, and turned back to ask Joseph if he wanted schnapps in his or not. The window was clear, and the snowflakes outside were thinning. Frankie had put his arms around Joseph's neck. He was drunk, maybe just a little, vamping it up. They were the same height, and when they kissed, she thought of how cool that would be, to be the same height. She had never had a short boyfriend. Then the window behind them lit up like a movie screen, them in the middle with their arms around each other, two beautiful boys kissing, lit up for all the world to see.

Except it was not all the world. It was Michael and Reverend Rick, pulling up in the driveway.

WHAT HE SAID WAS, "What the hell are you thinking?"

That was after Rick drove away, and after Joseph and Frankie and Bullfrog left, Pattianne saying, "Thanks for the help," and "Don't forget your crane," and she stood in the kitchen wiping up hot chocolate with her unbandaged hand. The refrigerator stopped humming, suddenly, the way refrigerators do.

"We need you," Michael said. "We all need to be together."

She just said okay. She could tell by the way she said it that she was giving up. She just didn't know what.

"I'm home with my father, you're here drinking with Angela in the middle of the day with your faces painted up and feathers in your hair? Rick said she wasn't even dressed."

"Nothing, that wasn't anything. Our faces painted?"

He went into the living room. Extension cords trailing across the floor, boxes from Christmas tree lights, paper bags with poinsettia stencils. He kicked an empty box, and it went pretty far, more than you might think an empty cardboard box would go, and the paper cranes scattered. "That boy was drunk," he said, and he kicked at the roll of wedding paper. It unrolled across the floor, wedding bells and doves and hearts. "Wedding paper?"

"No," she said. "Well, yes, but it's for cranes, look." And there she was, on her knees, gathering up paper cranes, holding them up to Michael like a gift, like an offering, like a fool.

He said, "What happened to your hand?"

"Nothing. I burned it."

He took her bandaged hand in his and looked at it. The adhesive tape was coming loose and there was chocolate on the white gauze. He wound the adhesive tape back around her thumb. So gently.

"It hurts like the dickens," she said.

"We have to go home for Christmas," he said. So softly.

"Okay."

He hadn't shaved, and there was blue shadow on his face.

"We have to talk," he said.

"Okay."

His hair was longer than he liked it to be.

"I have to go to bed."

"Okay."

She didn't know why she kept saying that, because it wasn't okay. He was here instead of back there with his family, and she was afraid to ask why. She wiped the stove, rinsed the cups. She ate some crackers. When she heard him get in bed, she went in there, in the dark. She undressed, and he breathed and wasn't asleep, just breathing.

They made love without a word, and then they lay there wrapped up together until her arm was numb under his shoulder, and she could hear his eyes blinking in the dark, and it was almost light when she heard far off sirens, a train.

The morning was clear and fine. She got up when Michael went into the shower. She unwrapped the sticky gauze and poked at the blister that ran across her palm that hurt like the dickens when she grabbed empty blue light boxes and rolled up the wedding paper and shoved about a dozen white paper cranes into the bag with the poinsettias stenciled on it. She was dragging the sleeves of the Loretta Young robe through the butter by the time he came out into the kitchen ready for school.

He stood behind her for a moment. He kissed her hair. There was barely a breath of space between their bodies, and that breath of space was what it was all about, and she didn't know what to apologize for, but she said, "I'm sorry."

More space between them, and he said, "I want you to come with me."

"Now?"

"Oh, please, Pattianne." He took the coffee cup she had ready for him, a little too much cream, a touch of sugar, and he said, "Of course not now." He sat down at the table and sloshed coffee on his shirtsleeve and said, "Damn it," said it softly. He set the cup carefully on the table, and she handed him a dishtowel, and he blotted his sleeve.

"When?"

"When we go back," he said. He rubbed at the coffee spot on his sleeve. "I want you to come too. I want you to talk to Deacon McMann. I'm worried. This weird behavior is freaking me out."

"You haven't even talked about how your father is doing," she said, using a knife on him, knowing it, doing it anyway. "You come home without telling me, you don't call while you're gone. My weird behavior? What weird behavior?"

"Rick told me about coming over here and you and Angela were drunk, and your faces were painted and all. And last night, what was that? Joseph is about to be fired, the school may try to bring criminal charges, and you're getting Frankie drunk? Making them paper cranes out of wedding paper?" His voice went up a notch. "They were kissing." Another notch. "In the window." Shouting.

"Our faces weren't painted." It felt like a growl, like, *You don't get to sit across the table and shout, even if you are Michael Bryn.* "The cranes are for our tree. And why would I want to talk to a deacon? I'm not the Catholic around here, remember?"

He looked at his watch.

"Yes," he said. The shout gone from his voice. He was the exhausted husband who'd flown home late last night and had to be at school ten minutes ago. "I remember."

The fine clear day outside was so quiet it was as if they were alone in the world. Then the heat vent rattled, and she jumped, terrified, and said, "Don't go to school today." And she didn't even know why she said that.

He said, "He's a doctor." Looking right at her. "He's a deacon at Christ the King. He's a specialist. I want us to see him."

Her face seemed to move on its own then. It felt like a snarl. She clenched her burned palm into a fist, and both sleeves drooped into the butter. "You want me to see a specialist?"

Then it was different. Everything was.

"About why we can't get pregnant," he said. Quiet. In control. Somebody else's husband. Maybe somebody's father. "He's a fertility specialist. Jim McMann. You may have even met him, maybe at my parents' house, after the vigil."

A moment went by then. She saw it go by. She could have said something that was true. She sat there and stared at him, and instead she said, "You're late."

"I know. We have to talk. I'll be home right after school."

She said, "There's a Christmas tree in the car."

Nothing was going to happen. She was not going to New Jersey to see a doctor. She was not going to have a baby.

He said, "Okay," and he walked out the kitchen door.

She was not going to stay married to Michael Bryn.

And she sat there for a long, long time.

There were other thoughts, actual words, but they weren't thoughts so much as Pattianne Anthony Bryn listening to how it would sound to say it, what needed to be said, and then how it would feel to be the one speaking those words. Saying, *No thank you, Michael. I don't want to be the one after all*. She was sad all over sitting there. She opened her eyes, only then realizing that they had been shut. The sunlight shone into every window of their house, lighting up the blue lights around the window, a lone paper crane in the corner of the floor. The clean bare wood floor.

The phone rang and the answering machine clicked on. Nothing.

She would stay here, in this house, in this town that wasn't even really a town, just a place on the edge of things, not New Jersey, in this chair, staring at this linoleum floor, in this ridiculous robe. Just not in this marriage.

The newspaper thumped onto the porch out front.

She got dressed. She smoothed ointment onto the blister across her palm and then wiped the ointment off with a tissue. There was the fact of the tree, the car still sat in the driveway, and she had to take a birth control pill, and she didn't think she had to work at the bookstore until Thursday. And if she left the birth control pills out where they could be found, doors would blow open as if a small explosive had gone off in their little house. The wrong way to do it. There was no right way to do it. She didn't know how to tell the truth. She never had known how to tell the truth.

She stepped out into the brilliant morning, the air so cold it took away her breath, slapped at her face, made her eyes water, and she didn't know how it could be so cold and yet so bright. She yanked the Mithras tree from its bungee cords one-handed, its green Christmas scent so pretty, and she dragged it to the door and leaned it there. Then she got in the car. She didn't have any idea what to do next until she thought of the key, and went back inside and got it, got her purse, got her coat. Picked up the lonely crane on the floor. Shut the front door of the house.

Just get through Christmas. Just get through until Mr. Bryn is home again, or back at work. She tried to imagine telling Mr. Bryn she wasn't going to stay married to his son, and thought she couldn't do that, not ever, not possibly, and instead she imagined him, back at work, organizing protests at abortion clinics. Just get through until Mr. Bryn is better.

Her mother would say, "Oh, Pattianne."

Jen would say, "Don't be a feeb."

She wouldn't even tell her father, she'd let her mother tell him. Or maybe she would, and he would say, "That's my girl." But probably not.

The roads west of St. Cloud were shiny black ribbons with the sun behind her, mist collecting in the dips and the sun laying down shine and no warmth. It felt good to go fast. She slowed down past a grade school and then went fast again. She hated grade schools. It made her sick to remember being trapped in there on mornings like this, any morning. The whole trapped feeling of being a kid chased after her in the car, through fields sitting black and waiting, and past neat rows of houses with people like her parents sitting in breakfast nooks and dogs chained up in backyards. Small towns seemed about to begin and then just trickled down to subdivisions that jutted out into some field and, beyond the field, bare black trees, or the surprise of a stand of conifers on a bit of a rise, catching the sun and shining green. A crossroad every mile, with a gas station, a grocery store, and always something else, a nail salon or a day care center or an auto-body place or a dentist's office.

There were churches here and there, short stubby bell towers seemed to be the preference around here, churches without much presence, not like the tall, revolving A&W sign, or the red roof of Pizza Hut, or the big red K. The buildings and houses disappeared. She downshifted into misty dips and up over tickle-belly rises, and when she hit those rises the sun behind her might catch the beige plastic Virgin of the Dashboard, the road going straight one mile and then straight another mile. Or if you wanted, you could go left to Mizpah or right to St. Wendel, or another straight mile, then Kerkhoven to the south, and another mile and another mile, until there have been a couple intersections with no signs, only the gas station, the grocery store with the neon Espresso sign, and maybe a cluster of leftover election signs. The red, white, and blue one was the Republican candidate's sign. Michael had a button in his desk drawer—Pattianne not paying attention, just looking for stamps or maybe the scissors—a red, white, and blue button that said *Abortion Stops a Heartbeat*. And there was that line, like on a heart monitor, like Mr. Bryn. Not a flat line, but living, beating. What hearts did instead of being in love, or maybe breaking, or maybe turning cold.

The black ice was invisible, and inevitable, and driving west turned into a slow-motion stop jammed up sideways against a cement culvert abutment with the morning sun shining down now, onto the Virgin of the Dashboard. The windshield cracked slowly, all the way across, one long crack, and the rising sun caught there and made a prism. The car stalled and stopped. She rolled down the window. Stalled.

She laid her forehead on the steering wheel and wished she could cry, but she didn't even feel like crying. It had been so easy to decide to marry him, and now deciding to unmarry him was going to be hard and sticky and messy. Even thinking about it made her sick. She didn't understand why it had seemed so easy to decide to marry him. She wanted to call Jen. She wanted to go back and read old horoscopes for back then. She looked up.

A thick cloud of black smoke was rising into the ungodly blue eastern sky. Something worse than spinning out on black ice. It was the only thing in the sky, in the world, in the universe. Bad news, somebody fucking up, a big mess, rising round and boiling out of itself, the sky so blue, the cloud so black, the Virgin of the Dashboard so gently beige. Then there was a twinkle of red and silver in the sky, and another twinkle, white. Two tiny helicopters were up there.

The car was going nowhere. It was jammed up right, front-end tight, against the cement culvert abutment, and the engine started just fine, but then the whole car just laughed at her.

She could wait for someone to drive by and notice an orange Volkswagen that hadn't ended up in the creek. She could watch the bad black smoke drift over good beautiful farmland dotted with simple modest steeples. Throw the Virgin of the Dashboard out the window. Then go get her. Smell the burning stink in the fine morning air.

A county sheriff car came up from behind, brown car, yellow stripe, lights flashing. The siren let out a yelp and it screamed on by.

There were chickadees down in the creek bed, and something red flitted in the weedy saplings across the road. The frozen creek was still, with banks of snow along the creek sides that were blue-white in the shadows, with words in the icy cracks of the banks' undersides where it had begun to melt, maybe in the afternoon sun yesterday, or some other day, melted and then frozen again. Words in the wisping black cloud, too, and the long line across the windshield was a blank space where a dash had replaced an expletive above the Virgin's spot. It just took the inevitable to read it all. The sky was clear, the wind moving the black smoke to the east. The west was clear. It took the inevitable to understand signs where there were none. It took the inevitable to do the wrong thing for the right reason.

Just wait. Another car would come, one with a cell phone. Call AAA. Ask them for a tow. Anywhere.

IN THE END, IT was easy. The sheriff's car came back, and the apple-cheeked young sheriff asked if she was all right. He radioed AAA for her. They came and got her out. She drove home. Michael came home and she said, "I slid onto a cement thing. Dented the car a little bit." He said something back. They were both saying something, both not saying too much.

10: RED WINE ON BEIGE CARPET

SHE RECOGNIZED THE PICTURE. The road worker. Emerson Paul. The news story on page one went from the headline all the way down the page. There was a picture of him, standing next to his wife, Annabelle, who was in a wheelchair. The three news stations all started out their broadcasts with the fire at the clinic that did abortions and had been the target of protests and threats and, once, a concrete block smashed through the door. The TV ran footage of the fire, and footage of the wreckage after the fire, and more pictures of Emerson "Bud" Paul, who'd died of smoke inhalation at St. Cloud Mercy, and footage of his wife, Annabelle, who'd had a stroke at the birth of their second child twenty years before, and their daughter, Mission, who was a security guard at the clinic. Graveyard shift.

It was sunny, and five degrees.

"Michael, will you go to the funeral with me?"

Michael said, "Why are you going to this man's funeral?"

But she couldn't say, and he would have to miss school, and he didn't want to, didn't seem to want her to go.

She wrapped Aunt Shirley's soft crocheted scarf around her neck. It was purple and royal blue. It matched the lining of her coat. She would leave it in the car.

She prayed that it wouldn't be open casket.

Mizpahven Funeral Home, Family-Owned Since 1896. She sat in the car and thought of a hundred years, and wondered how that name was pronounced, and watched people moving slowly through the sunshine. The Virgin on the dashboard watched her until she took it in her hand and just held it. It was cold, and when she realized that the Virgin had grown warm, and that its sharp, plastic edges were digging into her burned palm, she put it in the glove box. There seemed to be a lot of people heading into the wide front doors. Kids. Two Asian men with long orange robes and shaved heads. A man with bagpipes and a kilt and cold knees, surely cold knees. Three people in white face paint with tall black hats and black-and-white striped shirts.

She looked at her face in the mirror. "Don't cry," she whispered.

She checked her purse for a tissue, found the white paper crane with a wrinkled wing. And one tissue. She waited in the car until it seemed like no more people were going in. And then she waited some more. And then she went in.

Soft organ music played. It was that song from *Breakfast at Tiffany's*.

She had never been to a funeral before that wasn't in a Catholic church, except one, and that was in an Episcopal Church.

Rows of white wooden folding chairs were full of people, and a room off the side was full of folding chairs and people too, and she slipped into a chair in the last row by a gray-haired woman who held a big, blue, polka-dotted canvas purse in her lap. The three mimes standing in a still row off to one corner in the back. Way up at the front there was a map of the United States on an easel and a box on a small table. It was small, smaller than a shoebox, and square, and she was afraid to look at it. There was also a row of blue Christmas-tree balls. In front of the box was a row of tiny blue glass vials, too small to count from here, and they glittered their blue in the light of tall white candles in the tall candle holders that were lined up all along the back of that space that would have been an altar except this wasn't a church.

Off to the side was a gathering of men in shirts and ties, each man standing as if at attention, each holding an orange hard hat in front of him, and that made sense, and the floor beneath her shifted.

She stared at the small box on the table.

There was a shuffle and a thumping, and the men with their orange hard hats went in a line up the aisle. When they got up to the front, they kind of jammed up a little bit, big men, small space, and a young guy with a long, black, braided ponytail stepped forward to the pulpit, which was probably called a podium here. He had big square shoulders that looked too big for his white shirt.

He said, "I sat at the tavern writing a poem, about Bud and sandhill cranes and roads."

He set his hard hat on the podium.

"He was always talking about Crane being Echo Maker, because of its sound." And the hard hat started to slide down the slanted surface of the podium. He stopped it.

"And how Bud might start a story first at lunch, and after the whistle blew at five, he'd start right up with it again, something like, So, if the door opened to the left instead of right, the first thing she'd see would be the catalpa tree."

The hard hat slid again, and he laid his hand on it again.

"He drove the pilot car after running the paver for years, did it diligent, like it was hard, was careful, kept count of cars and stories going from one road to the next. How Crane took Rabbit to the moon, Eagle couldn't fly that high, couldn't or wouldn't, and Crane was rewarded with that beautiful crown. Hard to come by, those red feathers."

He held his hand up. There was a small red feather in his fingertips.

"Bud ate half an apple every day after lunch, so the seeds would have half a chance. He said half an apple got the peanut butter out of his teeth, and he'd wing the rest off into the trees because of the look of a wild apple in spring, a few reachy branches of white flowers in the messy woods, and in fall, the thick way apples would hang to the branch. And catalpa trees, even winter bare, with those seed pods."

He lowered his hand with the red feather.

"He waved people on, as if that was just what they needed to get on down the road, to get on with their lives."

She was afraid to breathe.

"Crane is called Bird of Heaven." He shrugged. "I was just too sad to write a poem."

He turned around, and the men with their hard hats kind of shuffled some space clear for him to get at the table, and he set the red feather next to the wooden box.

Pattianne mopped her eyes with her sleeve. The woman next to her hiccupped. The hard hat on the podium started to slide again. People started to laugh. By the time the hard hat clattered to the floor, everyone was laughing, and the young guy picked it up, his shirttail coming untucked from his jeans, and then he and all the men looked at each other, and they all shouted out, "Ho!" and then they trooped back down the aisle. People clapped.

She was thinking that Michael should have come.

She was thinking what she could possibly say about the road worker.

She was glad Michael hadn't come.

The woman next to her held out a tissue. She had a whole box of them in that purse, and not one of those small boxes, either. It was a regular-size box.

A girl with reddish, bushy hair got up from the front row. Her face was red and her eyes were a mess, but she stood at the podium and took in a breath that lifted her narrow shoulders, and you could tell from that breath that she was done with crying for now. What a simple thing to do, look out at all of them, like she was looking at every single person there.

"My dad would love this," she said. "He always said the modern world amazed him, and he said part of that was how we've learned to celebrate. Like his last birthday. He wanted to take a road trip. He was always wanting to take a road trip, anywhere west."

He'd wanted to travel the great highways. He had loved highways since he was a small boy, and when the interstate system was completed, he marked all the interstates in red on his map of the US, which had hung in their dining room.

He'd written President Eisenhower a congratulations note about the interstate system and had gotten a handwritten note in reply, thanking him for his love of the great American road. It hung in a frame next to the map that had hung in their dining room.

The map from the dining room stood on the easel next to the table now.

Mission said, "This is my mission." A happy chuckle kind of rolled around the room, and when she smiled, tears overflowed from her eyes.

The old woman whispered, "I remember when she was Barbara. But she was always saying that. 'This is my mission.' And Bud started calling her Mission, and next thing we knew . . ."

"My mission," Mission said, "is to help Daddy get to all the places he wanted to go. You are his friends and fellow travelers in this life. If you can keep traveling with him, if you can take him on one last journey, if you happen to be heading for the California Redwoods, or the Alamo, or the Grand Canyon or the Pacific Ocean."

Shiny blue stars dotted the map. Those were the places he wanted to go, the places he hadn't made it to, every star so sad Pattianne couldn't count them. There were twelve blue vials. There were twelve blue glass balls.

Mission went to the picnic table and picked up one of the blue vials. "Please," she said. Then she didn't say anything else, and a huge sorrow filled the whole place. Maybe it had sneaked in when that chuckle rolled around the room, when no one was watching, when they were all just trying to breathe and make some sense of death and blue stars.

The mimes went up there. One mime up the left side of the room, one mime up the right side, the third mime straight up the center aisle. They stood there, not smiling, their faces hidden behind their faces, in that slightly malevolent way of mimes that makes you wait and wait and then start worrying about whether to laugh or flee.

Mission went back to her mother in the front row. The blue glass vials and the blue glass balls glittered on the table. An air vent rushed air into the room somewhere, and the stillness began to shimmer, and Pattianne began to panic, a flutter like a tickle at the bottom of her throat. She needed to touch the woman next to her, needed to remember something about the day outside, needed the mimes to speak.

One mime stepped sideways to the picnic table, and, one at a time, picked up all twelve blue glass balls, handing each one sideways to the next mime without looking, all three mimes staring straight out with their weird mime eyes, the second mime handing balls to the third mime.

And then the piper began.

"Moon River."

The piper walked up the side aisle in his green-and-white-plaid kilt and his wheezing bagpipes. When she looked back at the mimes, they had begun to juggle the blue glass balls.

Nothing as sad as pipes.

Nothing as weird as mimes.

THERE WAS A GATHERING to follow at the St. Joe Elks Lodge next to the Piggly Wiggly store.

Pattianne just followed a lot of other cars out of the parking lot and turned west with them instead of east toward her house, west toward the Piggly Wiggly and the Christmas-tree lot and the St. Joe Elks Lodge. She couldn't remember what day of the week it was. Debate practice, football practice, history club, Ecumenical Men's Prayer Circle. She was locked out of her brain. There were no thoughts in there, or if there were, she wasn't going to be allowed to know what they were. She was all in her body. Her heart ached, and her eyes let go thick wet tears. She wanted to love someone that much. She wished she had known his name. She wished she had a story about him. She wished Michael was with her, maybe driving her home and telling her he loved her, saying *There is someone next to you who will make sure you have a fine and funny funeral.*

She pulled into the gravel lot of the Elks Lodge, other cars doing the same, people getting out and slowly moving toward the stairs that went up to the small green door that was open. No mimes. No piper. There was Mission, helping her mother up the stairs. A big boy in a letterman's jacket hauled the wheelchair up the stairs after them. The woman with the polka-dot bag. A road worker with a white shirt and a tie and jeans and no coat. Everybody who went in the green door seemed like someone she knew now. She sat in the O-Bug and watched and cried and wouldn't let herself think of Mr. Bryn dying, ever.

Finally, she wiped her face with the big, soggy wad of tissue and got out. She thought maybe she could go in and say something nice to Mission, maybe tell her she was the one who gave him the book about Buddhism, say how she liked him, and then maybe just slip back out the door. The gravel parking lot was full of potholes, and the potholes were crusted around the edges with thin ice. She walked through a cloud of cigarette smoke. The road worker who talked about Bud and the cranes was standing, leaning on a shiny old blue pickup truck having a smoke.

"Hi."

"Hi."

"That was really nice, what you said," and she heard her voice crack, felt her face go all screwed up trying to not let out any tears, watched the cigarette go up to his mouth. He blew a long stream of smoke up into the sky. The sky was turning a dark pewter color. She got her face back under control.

"Thanks," he said. He shrugged. "How did you know Bud?"

That was how you do it at these things, you say how did you know the person, like at a wedding, are you a friend of the bride or the groom.

"I work at the bookstore."

A red-and-white pack of Marlboros showed through the pocket of his white shirt.

"Lamplighter?" he said. "Or the Borders out at the mall?"

"Lamplighter."

He nodded. "He liked that place." His long black braid was pulled around front over his shoulder. He was maybe Native American or maybe Hispanic. He didn't look Italian.

"So you worked on the highway crew with him?"

Nod. "I wish I could take him on one of his final journeys," he said. "I'd like to take him to the silver tide."

She wrapped her hands in Aunt Shirley's scarf. "Yeah, he said something about that." She was shivering cold deep, deep inside. "What's a silver tide?"

He dropped his cigarette to the gravel and ground it out. Then he pulled out the pack. "One more before I go in," he said, shaking one up out of the pack, and he held the pack out to her.

"Thanks." The hand that reached out and took a cigarette wasn't shaking. The cigarette slipped between her fingers like it had a mind of its own, like her fingers remembered just what to do. He lit his cigarette and held out the lighter. "Maybe I'll save it for later," she said, and he laughed a little.

"Funeral smoker," he said.

"Funeral smoker?"

"You got your tavern smokers, your wedding smokers, all kinds of situational smokers." He dragged and blew the smoke high. "I'm an off-work smoker, and a not-at-home-smoker."

She was a haven't-had-one-for-over-a-year-smoker.

"My girlfriend's pregnant," he said. "So I told her I wouldn't ever smoke around her or the baby."

Pattianne worked the pointy black toe of her shoe into a pothole, crunching the ice.

"I might call him Bud. She wants to name him after her dad, but I might just call him Bud. It's going to be a boy. She's due pretty soon, three weeks, and I guess that's maybe anytime." He waved at someone behind her, people going into the Elks Lodge.

She said, "There's not a mime behind me, is there?"

"What?"

"Never mind. So what's a silver tide?"

"Oh, mimes, no, I don't know where those guys went. I don't think they're here. Those monks in the orange robes are here, though. I think they're going to bless the ashes or something."

A flock of crows went shrieking across the sky. They were black against a tinge of pink.

"And the silver tide?"

"Vancouver Island," he said. "On the west coast of British Columbia. I went there once, and the tide turns silver, like light, and it's like there's writing everywhere you step, and in the water, where there are fish, they leave silver trails."

His cigarette smoke drifted over, smelling nice.

"Tofino," he said. A small, grateful laugh. "He wanted to go there."

He dropped his half-smoked cigarette and ground it out.

"Wanted to see the Pacific. Said it touched ancient China and mystic Russia. He read that to me from a book he had."

"He called it the great weather-maker," Pattianne said.

He nodded. Then he picked up both of his butts and tossed them into the back of his truck. "Some people don't think cigarette butts count as litter," he said. "What's your name?"

"Pattianne."

He held out his hand. "Ed." His hand was warm and calloused. "Nice to talk to you. Coming in?"

"Maybe in a minute."

The lights were on inside the Elks Lodge, tall windows lit up warm and yellow. She wanted to look up Vancouver Island. She wanted to smoke the Marlboro. She wanted to go home, wanted to be alone in her house on the edge of things.

She pulled everything out of the glove box, the Virgin too, looking for matches, and put it all back in. Then she searched through the bottom of her purse. Then she gave up and put the Marlboro in the inside breast pocket of her coat, careful, where it would probably break anyway, and that's where the matches were. The first drag was awful. So was the second. She put the cigarette out and tossed it into the back of Ed's truck. Her head was spinning from the crying, from the cold, from the cigarette. She had to drive away, just leave Bud there with all his friends.

The front bedroom window of Michael's office was lit with the steely light of the television, and he was in there, moving back and forth by the window. She waited out in the darkening day, in the O-Bug, and the Virgin of the Dashboard waited too, retrieved from the glove box, restored to the dashboard. The circle where it sat wasn't faded like the rest of the dashboard. She could replace it to its exact spot.

Sorrow was a huge round thing that took up all the air in the O-Bug. Her eyes ached with tears that slipped out, ached from holding on to the tears that didn't slip out. How sad and glorious it all seemed, how undeniably glorious. She was afraid of the fact of the funeral. Death was close, and she couldn't look, not even at some heaven or rebirth. The moon was rising, almost full, at the end of the road, misshapen and yellow, and she wondered where he was, the road worker, if he was actually anywhere.

A light went on in the house, the hall light, then the living room light, and Michael passed the big window. Then he came back to it and looked out. She waved her fingers at him from where they rested on the steering wheel. He walked away from the window.

Mr. Bryn was alive, breathing, sleeping and waking in his hospital bed, and death was close, right here, and of course Michael couldn't go to the funeral, and she was sorry for being unthinking, for not paying attention.

If her father died, she would be afraid of the grief that would build silently, secretly, over years, until she suddenly became aware of it in a moment, and was knocked to the ground with the loss of what she'd never had. If her mother died, she would be sad for her, maybe, more than for herself. Then she heard herself saying if and not when, and she had to go in, quick, had to get to Michael. She could tell him she was sorry.

He stood at the door of his office, his arms crossed over his chest. He watched her hang up her coat, and then she stood there. He turned and looked in at the muted television. The light of it made his face an ash color, and she crossed the room to him. She would tell him not to worry. His father was doing well. Everything will be fine. The news played footage from the fire, and a picture of Emerson "Bud" Paul. The phone rang, and Michael answered it, looking at her, saying, "Yes, she's home. No, I'll call you," and the silent news footage started over again with the fire. He hung up.

She put her hands on his shoulders and said, "I'm sorry."

But the picture was a bright-haired woman in a blue hat being led to a police car in handcuffs. The woman was Angela Park.

She said, "What is going on?"

The silent screen said *Arson Suspect.*

His eyes never blinked. His face spoke, only his mouth moving.

The words were, "Did you smoke a cigarette?"

When he said it, she could smell the stink of cigarette.

"I was just at the funeral," she said. "I thought about you." And it seemed like she should take him in her arms.

Then she said, "Angela Park?"

"She turned herself in," he said. "She said she set the fire."

That was too weird. That had to be all wrong. She wouldn't start a fire. It must be hard to start a fire that would burn down a whole building. She didn't think Angela could even figure out how to do it.

THINGS HAPPENED REALLY FAST after that, and all Pattianne knew for sure was they just kept getting worse. The Christmas tree leaned outside next to the front steps and got iced over. She set the doohickeys for hanging lights on the counter and poked through the trash until she found the receipt so she could return them to Sears.

Michael decided they would drive back to New Jersey, stay for the whole Christmas break. That they needed to be home.

Elizabeth was in a dark mood. She'd ended up with Bullfrog because Frankie said he was moving to New York, and she was pissed and sad because she thought Joseph might move there with him. She said, "That dog drools, and he smells. And sleeps. That's about it." She said she was a cat person. She said, "Joseph can talk me into anything."

Pattianne felt bad. It was her fault. She'd outed them, and she didn't know if Elizabeth knew, if Joseph or Frankie knew. The store was busy. She found herself waiting for the road worker. She felt closer to him than when he'd actually been there, in the store, just because now she knew his name.

She didn't smoke another cigarette.

Michael left the house early and came home late, after dinnertime, three days in a row. When he was in the house, he looked stiff and too handsome and unreal. Being home alone was the only thing that felt right, and that didn't feel good, it felt all broody and low. She would get there and turn on lights and turn up the heat. The first night she made chicken cacciatore. The next night she made shrimp stir-fry. The third night she opened a bottle of pinot noir and ate cold chicken cacciatore standing in front of the refrigerator. Halfway through the bottle of pinot noir, she started crying and just went to bed. Loving him felt like years ago.

In the morning she got up after he was gone, with a headache, a hangover, and puffy ugly eyes. She'd started her period. She ached. She had cramps. She changed the sheets and wandered around her house like it was bigger than it was. She never had cramps. The leftover shrimp smelled like a goldfish bowl Jen used to have on her dresser. Just a few tampons rattled in the box. They barely hid the packets of pills. She could run errands, buy a box of tampons, return the doohickeys to Sears. She got out the bag with the poinsettia on it and put them and the receipt in it, little boxes down there in the bottom of the big bag, and that made her cry too, the boxes looked sad and small down there. She hadn't even turned her blue lights on again.

The sky was solid and low and gray, and comforting. She read part of an Elmore Leonard until she remembered the plot, and then she went back to bed. The bedroom was dark, and she turned on the small lamp on the table, its light small and warm and yellow and no good for reading. Life felt separate, like it was all happening somewhere else and she was supposed to know where.

She left for the bookstore. Just walking out of the house felt good, but as soon as she was down the block where she couldn't look back and see it, she wanted to be back there.

The bookstore was empty. The lights on, the music playing. She went through the beads, and there was Elizabeth, brushing off her purple cape with a lint brush.

She looked up and sighed a dramatic sigh and tossed the lint brush to the table.

"That dog," she said.

I'm sorry was the first thought. Pattianne didn't say it.

She said, "Things are kind of a mess, huh?"

"I don't want that dog," Elizabeth said. "He's not even Frankie's dog, really. He's only had him a little while. He was just some stray. It's not like it would break his heart to take him to the pound and let someone adopt him." But she wasn't talking to Pattianne. She was talking to herself.

And Pattianne, talking to herself, said, "But he's old and stinky, and they kill dogs if they don't get adopted right away."

And then to Elizabeth she said, "I'll take him." Took a deep breath. This was crazy. But it was the first time she'd seen Elizabeth smile since everything went to shit.

"You mean take him adopt him, or just keep him for a while? I don't think they're coming back to St. Cloud once they leave."

"I mean take him take him. I'll adopt him."

Elizabeth said, "I'll go get him right now," and she picked up her purple cape, which wasn't all that hairy, and she said, "No, I'll call Frankie. He can bring him by."

Pattianne thought of calling Michael. She didn't want to. She thought she'd just surprise him. She knew it was crazy. But there were dreams to be dusted and a stack of books on the beautiful chair and The Light of the World to tend to.

She'd always had a dog. She'd had Starla since she was in grade school, and before that there was a beagle named Short Stop who slept with his nose at the crack under her bedroom door, wanting to get in. Her mother said, *No dogs in the bedrooms.* And then when they got Starla, she heard them one night after dinner, her mother saying, *No dogs in the bedrooms,* and her father saying, *Oh, what can it hurt?* That night, she learned something about her father. She was only little. And it was her bedroom, not Jen's.

She was just starting to realize that she really should call Michael, and maybe she should at least go buy some dog food and spend some time with Bullfrog before saying *Yeah, I'll take him to be my dog,* but then there they were. And she wanted him, as soon as she saw him, all down low and wagging, and not shedding all that much, really. He was mostly white, just a few brown spots, and soft brown ears. She got down by him.

"Well," Frankie said. "Really? You'll take him?" He got down too. "To keep?"

"Yes," Elizabeth said. "That's what she said. To keep."

Then Frankie got all teary, and Pattianne did, too, and he handed her a brand-new red leather leash with the price tag still on it. It matched Bullfrog's collar.

"I have a twenty-five-pound bag of dog chow in the car," he said. Teary.

"Okay."

"And a big box of Milk Bones."

"Okay."

"And his rabies papers and all are in here."

He handed her an envelope, and then he hugged her, and they were a circle with Bullfrog in between them, Elizabeth laughing, although she didn't sound very happy, but she was laughing. Michael would laugh too. Bullfrog was a funny guy.

SHE PUT A BLANKET on the floor in the bedroom, and Bullfrog stepped on it, circled around, and then hopped up on the bed. He landed on the Loretta Young robe and circled around there and pawed at it and worked it into a nested heap and then plopped himself down.

"Cool," she said to him. "We can share it."

She poured a glass of wine and took it back in the bedroom, and dragged the robe out from under Bullfrog and robed up. She went back out and turned up the heat, and came back in and opened the envelope with the dog's papers. They were folded inside a notecard, a watercolor of a wolf with St. Francis behind it. She could tell it was St. Francis by his knotted belt and the birds on his shoulders. A halo of blue glitter shimmered around them both.

Wolf Spirit Tales, it said.

"Cheers," she said to Bullfrog. He watched her.

St. Francis apparently rescued the town of Gubbio by convincing a marauding wolf to extend its paw in peace. *Come to me, Brother Wolf*, St. Francis said. *In the name of Christ.*

Michael showed up at dinnertime with Reverend Rick and someone else. Their voices out there in the dark house were low, and they went through the living room into the kitchen. The leftover chicken was sitting in the sink, or maybe on the counter.

He came into the bedroom and turned on the ceiling light, stood there in the doorway with his arms crossed over his chest.

"What's that dog doing here?"

"He's our new spirit guide," she said, funny, this sleepy old hound being anyone's spirit guide. "Meet St. Francis's Brother in Christ."

Michael said, "Why are you in bed?"

"I'm not. We're just hanging out. Who's out there with you?"

But she'd never seen a face like that on Michael.

"Michael, what is it?" It was like no face. His mouth was a straight line. His eyes were another straight line.

"Get dressed," he said. His voice was flat. "Come out here."

The floor was like ice. The sweater she pulled on over her T-shirt was instantly too hot, and she balled it up and stuffed it back in the drawer. She looked in the mirror. Her lips were wine-stained purple, and sometimes that got Michael all nibbling and sweet. This was not one of those times. She couldn't tell who was out there with him besides Reverend Rick. She combed her fingers through her hair, did what she could. A green blouse straight off a dry-cleaner's hanger, a hair clip, she even found some green socks. The blouse smelled like dry-cleaner fluid. She shut the bedroom door, shutting Bullfrog in there.

The living room was dark. She turned on the deer lamp, banged her elbow on the doorjamb of the kitchen, where they were gathered like the three witches, Michael, Reverend Rick, and Herman Walters. Michael held the bag of coffee. The chicken cacciatore was on the counter next to the Sears bag.

"Here," she said, and moved toward the sink, the coffee maker, the chicken. They all watched her. Herman Walters sat in a chair, his legs crossed, one bony knee poking up above the edge of the table. Next to him, Reverend Rick stood stiff and straight like a Boy Scout. The fluorescent light made sharp-edged shadows on the shiny walls. She put the pan in the sink. Reverend Rick put his hands on his hips. Asshole. She got a spoon from the drawer and took the bag of coffee from Michael. Measured coffee into the filter. Poured in water. Behind her nobody moved. Her hands shook ever so slightly. Her elbow throbbed. The coffee smelled like dry-cleaner fluid.

"May I speak?" It was Herman Walters.

"Sit down, Pattianne." That was Michael.

Reverend Rick just looked at the floor.

Then Michael said, "Please." His voice was choked, and the air inside her dropped through her to the gray linoleum. She was dizzy for a flash and then not, and when she looked at his face, he faced away. She couldn't think of what she even wanted from him.

Herman Walters slowly unfolded himself from the kitchen chair, and when he stopped unfolding himself, his arms hung down loose and his face did, too, the shadow of his head on the wall, his tall body and his great nose. Then his watery gray eyes went upward, and the threat of prayer filled the air. The dizzy feeling flashed again, but mad dizzy, she wanted to throw the spoon on the floor, and she didn't say *How dare you pray in my kitchen?*

It was Herman Walters's fine, deep voice. "The voice of thy brother's blood crieth unto me from the ground." Not his squeaky allergic-to-coffee voice. "A great tragedy has occurred in our midst, and we feel it redeems us all if you speak out."

He was talking about Angela, but what he said made no sense, and she waited for it to either become clear or else for him to say more. She tried not to look at his shadow on the wall. The light around his head was buzzing.

"Mrs. Park," he said, "has spoken at length to the attorney we provided for her, and she has implicated you deeply." Maybe the fluorescent light was going out. "Your moral culpability demands an explanation to your family and your community, and forgiveness from the Lord."

She set the spoon on the counter. She said, "What the fuck?"

That did it. Michael's hands landed on her shoulders from behind and spun her around. "Have you lost your mind?" His face was twisting, his eyes opening and squinting, and his mouth wasn't his mouth. "Pattianne, a man has died."

And with his hands on her shoulders and his face right at her face some voice that snapped out of her said, "I know that, Michael. I went to the funeral, remember?"

Michael pushed her into the chair and leaned over her and said, "What did you say to Angela?"

Her breath was fluttering, stuck at the bottom of her throat. "What did I say to Angela when?" It felt like he was still grabbing her shoulders.

He looked up to the ceiling. "I don't know when, whenever you told her she should burn down the clinic."

"The date was December sixth." Reverend Rick spoke very softly. "It was the middle of the day."

The *Seasons of Minnesota* calendar showed a snow-covered field, an old red barn at the field's crest, a brilliant blue sky, *December* in green Gothic letters. December sixth was a Wednesday.

Reverend Rick sat down and folded his neat, square hands on the table, speaking softly. "Angela has been under a doctor's care for years." He opened his hands toward her, as if he were showing her some small thing. "She shouldn't drink, but she does."

"So," Pattianne said, trying to work past the breath stuck in her throat, her turn to speak, her kitchen, *Seriously, you guys, what the fuck are you talking about?* "Angela really set the fire?"

Herman Walters's shadow on the wall nodded.

She said, "How?" Like that mattered.

"Pattianne." Reverend Rick's voice, *hey hey, easy now*, like he was talking to Navarre. "We need to know what you two talked about that day." His hands seemed so relaxed. Her hands worked the bottom button on her blouse. "I came over here," he said. "You and Angela were drinking. You had red lipstick and a feather in your hair. She had red on her face like war paint. You were both in your underclothing."

"It was nothing." She pushed her hair back, how it never stayed up in a hair clip. "We talked about makeup. She just dropped by and we talked about makeup."

He folded his hands back together. "You were both drunk," he said.

"She brought stuff to make some fancy drinks." Foamy purple champagne cocktails.

Herman Walters breathed deeply through his nose. Michael stood next to the refrigerator behind her, back there somewhere far away.

"She talked about a field catching on fire right there once," she said.

Herman Walters sank neatly back into his chair, his watery gray eyes level with hers.

"What do you mean?" she said. "She 'implicated' me. 'Deeply.'"

Herman Walters nodded. "Did you speak of saving women from the sin of murder?"

"We talked about abortion, I guess. She had some more of those leaflets for you, flyers about some protest you guys were doing. She stopped by to pick them up for you."

Reverend Rick sat back in his chair.

"We didn't talk much about it. More about lipstick. Then you came and picked her up. You drove her home. I don't know, what did she say to you?" The coffee was dripping into the pot. The heater vent rattled. "We were just trying on lipstick. There was no war paint."

Michael got out four cups and set them on the table.

"Coffee makes him sneeze," Pattianne said. They all jerked their heads up like their heads were on strings. "Coffee makes Herman sneeze," she said, turning to Michael. "I was just waiting for you to call. You went to New Jersey, and I was waiting for you to call. You never called."

Herman Walters cleared his throat. He said, "Did you tell her a fire would solve the problem?"

"No," she said. "I would never say that."

THE DISTRICT ATTORNEY'S OFFICE was in a low brick building that looked empty this time of night. Coming in from the cold, her eyes watered, and a young man with a very clean face met them in a shiny, wood-paneled lobby. A security guard was standing in a corner next to a fake ficus tree.

The young man with the clean face was the lawyer that Reverend Rick had arranged to meet them there. He shook her hand, his hand soft and plump, and he said, "Just tell the truth," and then they walked down a long, wide hallway that stretched out like it was moving. Fake ficus trees next to each door were strung with twinkly white lights that broke into prisms. There was a snowman thumbtacked to the door of Room 112. He had a row of thumbtack holes in his black top hat from Christmases past.

Angela was charged with arson and manslaughter.

Room 112 was a fluorescent white room with beige carpeting and a bare desk and two chairs, and Michael was in some other room with Reverend Rick and Herman Walters.

A woman in a cheery red blazer came in and said hello to the young man, and it sounded like she called him Davy. She told Pattianne what her name was and then opened a file folder and sat down. Davy stood back by the door. The woman asked how she was doing and said how this was a tragic situation and she wanted to talk about Pattianne's relationship with Mrs. Park and their work with Project Life. A huge rhinestone Christmas-tree pin hung on the woman's lapel, weighing it down and pulling the collar crooked and twinkling madly with jerking colors that ended up being red.

Pattianne said, "I hate Project Life."

The woman tapped her pencil.

"I don't know anything about Project Life. Except that Michael's father is in it."

She moved a piece of paper in the file. "That would be Michael Bryn?"

"Senior. His father. In New Jersey. Not my Michael."

Except maybe he's not her Michael anymore, and maybe she doesn't get to say that anymore.

The woman had dark hair with gray at the roots, and when she wasn't looking down at the folder, she looked straight at Pattianne. She tapped the eraser of her pencil on a yellow notepad each time she spoke.

"Can you tell me about your work with the Ecumenical Men's Prayer Circle?"

She pictured the door behind her, pictured getting up and just leaving. "I'm not even involved in this," she said. "Any of it."

The woman didn't tap.

"I believe in abortion," Pattianne said. "Not that. I mean, I don't believe in it."

The woman tapped. "You don't believe in it?"

Pattianne couldn't remember the woman's name. If she saw her somewhere else, she might think she was someone's aunt. She was that in-between age, older than her, not as old as her mother.

"No." She was starting to cry. "I don't believe in it. But it's private."

The woman opened a drawer and took out a box of tissues and set it on the bare desk, and it was too loud for a box of tissues.

"What do you remember about your conversation with Angela Parks on December sixth?"

Purple champagne and red lipstick, Angela's big blue eyes full of tears about saving babies.

Pattianne closed her eyes and tried to swallow, her heart beating sharp, right at the bottom of her throat. There was the smell of her blouse, sharp, like it was burning the skin of her throat.

"Angela came over to pick up some flyers with rules for a protest they were having."

She remembered Angela crying. She remembered her talking about finding homes for babies. She remembered her talking about a field that was on fire once right behind the clinic, how she hoped it would burn the clinic down.

"I said how that would solve the problem. I was just joking."

"Not very funny."

Pattianne got out of the chair and turned away from the cheery red blazer and the Christmas-tree pin. The clean young man said, "Mrs. Bryn?" He got out of her way and she fell against the door and opened it. Michael was at the far end of the long tilting hallway. The twinkling lights on all the fake ficus trees stabbed at her eyes. The door behind her shattered shut and she whispered, as far away as he was, "You have to help me," and she threw up, red wine on beige carpet.

Reverend Rick drove. The Urgent Care Center was in a strip mall, neon letters everywhere, and the doors rushed open. She kept her hands over her eyes, and Michael's arms around her guided her in where she knew the lights were too bright, red lines of light through her fingers.

A woman asked Michael questions while the small gray waiting room pulsed its sharp light through her closed eyes, pulsed like her head, each pulse not quite cracking everything into pieces.

Any allergies?

Michael said, "Strawberries."

History of blood-pressure problems?

He said, "I don't think so."

Family history of heart disease, stroke?

"Her grandmother had a stroke," he said.

"Do you smoke?"

Michael said not really. He said she used to. He said maybe occasionally.

"Any medications? Allergies, antidepressants, birth control?"

Michael said no.

Pattianne said yes.

THEY DIDN'T GET HOME until one in the morning. She went to bed and slept hard. He kept looking in at her. She was piled in the blankets, and that dog was there. It was lying on her bathrobe on the floor. It wagged its tail when he looked in.

She had been taking them since before the wedding. When they'd been using condoms. He'd kept a box in the table by her bed in her apartment. She would laugh at him when he shook it to see if there were some in there. Like a game.

He felt sick to his stomach. He'd eaten a meatball sandwich yesterday. He couldn't remember where, but he had never eaten a meatball sandwich before.

He packed clothes in the small gym bag. Folded his T-shirts carefully. Jeans and two blue sweaters. He hung a pair of dress slacks and two dress shirts in the hanging bag. His ties hung on the tie rack on the door of the closet. The blue one with the monogram of his initials. His father's initials.

He'd told her he wanted to name their first child after his father or his mother.

He couldn't remember what she'd said. If she'd said anything. If she'd laughed.

He pulled the silk tie off the rack, sliding it over his hand, and then anger rushed through him that left no air for breathing. It was the tie he'd worn when they got married. He hung it back up. His hand shook. He took the green-and-gold-striped tie and rolled it neatly. He zipped closed the hanging bag and took it out to the car.

He looked up the routes back to New Jersey. He made toast. He was being as quiet as he could. He wanted her to stay asleep. He lay on the couch and felt his heart beating hard. Too hard. He thought of his father's heart beating this hard, and now he had to tell him about this.

Everything was weird. Time was weird. He always stopped his students from saying weird. He would ask them, *What does that mean?*

When it finally got light, he left her sleeping. He'd get the oil changed. Get the tires checked. The day was weirdly sunny.

He drove toward the school, past the grocery store on the corner, where he'd sometimes stop to pick up something for lunch and visit with the obese woman who owned the place. That was it. "New on the deli menu," she'd told him. She'd handed him the foil-wrapped meatball sandwich, the size and shape of a football. "This will make you happy." She said things like that, never cracked a smile, or laughed.

He called Father McGivens from the small waiting room at the oil-change place. No one else was there. He told him about the fire and the birth control pills and that they were coming back early. That he would quit his job. That he wanted to bring her back home and stay there. Finally, he didn't know what else to say, and stopped. The sounds of the garage were loud. Guys were shouting at each other.

He said, "I don't really know what to do."

Father McGivens said, "Come here first. We'll talk before you see your folks."

He went to the school. The kids were already gone on break. The halls were empty. He went into the office, and the office manager, Sister Therese, was there, at the copy machine. She had on jeans and a Green Bay Packers sweatshirt instead of her usual clothes.

She said, "Hi, Michael. Got your grade book for me?" Not really looking up from her copying.

Other than that, everything was quiet. Weird.

He thought about telling her he wasn't coming back after break. He wanted to tell someone. He wanted to explain to someone.

He could just say, *My father is ill.*

Or, *I need to be with my family at this time.*

What if he said, *My wife has gone crazy, starting quite some time ago, actually, so you see, we really have to go back to New Jersey. Sort things out.*

What he said was, "Rick in yet?" His voice felt weak.

"Nobody but us church mice," Sister Therese said.

Relief. He took some mail from his box and went up the hall to his classroom.

The desks were in their rows. The whiteboard was clean. The stack of graded final papers was on his desk, all the edges squared. He sat down, and the rows of empty seats stretched away in front of him. He felt the crying well up in him, and he pulled out his grade book. He looked each paper over and entered each grade. When he came to Joshua's paper, inked all over with his own trademark bright green corrections, with C- at the top, he stopped. Reread it. It was pretty bad. He got the green pen from the drawer and changed the C- to B-. Entered it in the book and went on.

When he was finished, he sat still. The late winter sun across his desk showed the dust. They'd had a conversation in class that last day about graffiti. He had told them about Kilroy. World War II graffiti, he'd told them. No one knew for sure who Kilroy even was. They'd all agreed it was weird. And now here was Kilroy, drawn in the dust on his desk.

If not for this moment, with the sun across the desk, he would never have seen it.

He said, "Fuck," out loud, but not very loud. Then he left.

She was up when he got back. She was wearing that pink hippie shirt. The toast was still on the plate on the kitchen table. The dog was on the couch. Its tail wagged, and that flash of anger came and then was gone.

He said, "We can't take that dog home with us."

She stood perfectly still in the middle of the living room. He didn't want her to wear that shirt.

She said, "I'm not going."

The sky was turning red and purple out the window behind her.

He said, "What do you mean?"

The sunset clouds streaked all the way across the sky.

She said, "I think we're breaking up."

She'd been crying and her face was red. She looked awful.

He said, "What about my father?"

She held out the sapphire ring.

He said, "What about my mother?"

She just kept holding out the ring. So he took it. His hand was not shaking. He put the ring in his pocket. She just cried, without sound. She wouldn't look away. Her face looked like it was cracking apart.

He went into the office. His bag sat by the desk. He picked it up. It wasn't even heavy.

He went back out, and she hadn't moved. She was still crying.

"I'm sorry, Michael." Her voice was choked.

He said, "So you mean divorce?" It sounded like someone else's voice. Not his.

"I think so." Her nose was running, and she wiped it on the big pink sleeve.

He went out the front door and it clicked shut behind him. His running shoes were on the porch step, like he wasn't really leaving. But he was. He picked them up and went down the walk and looked back. She stood in the window. He got in the car and shut the door quietly. She didn't move. He started the car and she still didn't move. He had to drive away.

By the time he got to the highway, the sky was purple and black.

THE LIGHTS HURT HIS eyes, so he rubbed them a lot and was glad when it got dark, but then the headlights of cars across the interstate were worse. The rest of him didn't feel anything. He rolled the window down. He rolled the window up. Down and up.

His cell phone rang. Rick. He let it go to voice mail, and a moment later, it chimed.

Rick didn't like Pattianne. Rick had told him about her, with Angela, their faces painted and feathers in their hair. Drunk in the middle of the afternoon. In their underwear. He'd been shocked as Rick spoke. Confused.

Somewhere in the bright mess of Chicago, the handle came off in his hand. The window was half open, half closed.

Gary, Indiana, spread out, off to the north. There were grids of factory lights in colored patterns that didn't seem like they were on the ground. Just floating. Like the highway was just floating. Like he was. This was what it must be like to not believe in God. How could anyone not believe in God? What else was there to believe in? He lay on the horn. After a while, he realized he couldn't even hear it.

This was what it must be like to not believe in God.

He banged his hands on the steering wheel until they hurt.

The sky went from black to gray over Ohio. It was a shiny steel gray. It was going to be a clear, sunny day, and that made him cry. Actual tears. He wanted it to still be night, or maybe snowing. Maybe a blizzard. When the sun finally cracked the horizon, he pulled into a huge truck stop and drove around until he found a spot away from the loud idling semis, behind a tire warehouse. He pulled his coat around him and pulled his stocking cap down over his eyes and didn't think he would sleep. His eyes twitched. He heard a sound that he realized was him, grinding his own teeth.

Father McGivens had said to stop for rest and food. He had not said that everything would be okay.

He woke up with shooting pains in his neck. The sun was shining on the car, but it was freezing. He should call her. He held his phone and stared at it. The battery was dead. His eyes didn't focus. Both legs had pins and needles, and when he got out, he had to lean against the car and shake each leg.

He went into the truck stop store limping, and bought a large black coffee and dumped sugar in it instead of cream. He thought it would help keep him going. He bought a pair of plastic sunglasses. He stared at the big map. New Jersey was a long way away. Farther ahead than St. Cloud was behind him. He should turn around and drive back to her.

They were married. There was no just breaking up. No divorce. A sick feeling filled his stomach. He gulped the coffee, and it was too hot. It scalded his tongue and burned his throat. It hurt all the way down.

He put on the sunglasses and kept driving. He bought more black coffees and kept driving. He argued with her.

"How can you not believe in God?"

And what if she explained how?

"You've been lying to me every time we made love."

And what if she said she wasn't sorry?

"We're married. We're Catholic."

She wasn't.

"How can you do this to my parents?"

That would make her cry. He wanted her to cry.

He stopped and got a Big Mac and a vanilla shake. She teased him about vanilla being his favorite flavor. He had never understood why she thought that was funny. Now it seemed like he knew. Something about the ordinariness of vanilla. He was ordinary. He believed in God and rules. But they had used condoms, and they hadn't disentangled, and he had lied to his parents and Father, pretending they weren't living together. The Big Mac was too big, even though it wasn't as big as a meatball sandwich, and he took huge bites and forced it down. He had lied to them, but he hadn't lied to her. He hadn't tricked her. He drank the shake fast, and it gave him a headache.

He pulled onto the highway, and a semi roared past with its loud horn blasting, like it was blasting him right off the road, and he could have gotten killed right then, with sins of omission on his soul.

The roads and highways started to fill in the fields, and the green highway signs got filled with information, and the names became familiar. He drove faster. He got to the dense tangles of Pittsburg, Highway 27, Highway 38, the New Jersey Turnpike.

It was dark when he pulled into the small driveway behind Christ the King. Empty coffee cups rolled around on the floor. The sludge of all that sugar was all over the floor mat.

He didn't know how to do what he had to do now.

He got his bag, and got out, and locked the car, even though the window was half down. The back door opened before he knocked, and Father McGivens stepped aside for him to go into the kitchen. He set the bag on a chair and said something, and Father said something. His throat was sore. Father poured them both a drink, a shot of dark whiskey, which burned his throat when he swallowed it in the one gulp. He leaned his elbows on his knees, and stared at the floor, and felt the road in his body. He stretched back and wished something would crack in his neck or his spine. He got a Kleenex out of his pocket, and there was the sapphire ring. It was so heavy. It glittered in the kitchen light. For the bride of their first-born son. It had always looked big on her hand. Her bitten fingernails, her hangnails. Next to her thin, gold wedding ring.

Father said, "Are you angry?"

"No, I ate at a McDonald's."

There were probably a lot of places to get a meatball sandwich now that he was back in New Jersey. Back home.

"What she's done is a grave betrayal. Certainly grounds for annulment." Father's voice was low, almost a whisper. "But you can help her."

Help her. Change her. Fix her. Convince her to have a baby. Her red

Keds and wispy hair and that scared look, like someone was about to notice her.

He said, "She doesn't believe in God."

"You need to get some rest. Come on to the guest room. Take a hot shower. We'll call your folks."

Michael closed his hand around the ring. How could he face his father? Now he felt it. The sharp pain inside him. It felt like it was inside his chest, and in his stomach. Disgust, like nausea, like a meatball sandwich, rising.

DAY BY DAY, SHE went to work and she came home to the house, to Bullfrog wagging his tail and oddly happy. She sat on the couch, at the kitchen table, on the bed with Bullfrog, and she tried to imagine what she didn't really know. She tried to fill in bits and pieces from the news. She wondered if she'd heard the siren that day. The siren that was a man who rushed into a burning building early in the dark before dawn because he thought his daughter was in there, his daughter who sat in the clinic at night and read books about Buddhism, getting up every hour to walk through the building and make sure everything was all right. She looked out windows and doors and scanned the parking lot, which was lit with tall lights. There was never anyone there, and there was a cozy windowless room off the reception area of the clinic that once was a supply room. It had a soft leather couch, and a CD player with spacey meditation music, and a little windup alarm clock, and the daughter had catnaps there sometimes. The man took her breakfast at five a.m.—cinnamon rolls that he made himself from a tube that he whopped on the edge of the stove and called whopping biscuits. The tube popped apart, and the cinnamon rolls popped out, and he baked them for fifteen minutes on a cookie sheet while he shaved and dressed. The smell filled the house. He left one on a plate for his wife, next to the coffee pot full of coffee, and he wrapped two of them in a paper towel and put them in a bag along with two small boxes of juice. He loved those boxes of juice, with their little straws attached. The modern world amazed him. The morning of the fire, it was apple-cranberry juice. The morning of the fire, his daughter wasn't dozing in the cozy room, she was out in the back of the building, calling 9-1-1 from her cell phone.

Pattianne decided what to do, one thing to do, and she and looked up the number and called. The daughter answered.

"Hello, my name is Pattianne." She stopped because she didn't know her own last name, or what to say next, or why she was doing anything, or how anything could make sense.

Mission said, "From the bookstore?"

So he had told her. Pattianne hadn't even known that he'd known her name. When had that happened, that he'd learned her name and she hadn't learned his?

"Thank you," Mission said. "He liked talking to you. That book you gave him was perfect."

"I just wanted to call. I liked him."

"Well, thank you."

And she made the decision she hadn't known she would make.

"I'm going to Canada," she said. "I might be. I mean, to look for the silver tide."

Mission said, "Can we meet?"

So she came to Pattianne's house, knocked at the door, stood there for a minute in the cold wind, her hair wispy and red, and she seemed even smaller than she had at the Mizpahven Funeral Home. Pattianne held the door wide and she came in. The living room was empty, except for the couch, a table that used to have a deer lamp. Empty bookshelf. A box of books in the middle of the floor.

"I'm moving." Pattianne's voice seemed to echo.

"To Canada?"

"No. I'm looking for a place here. In St. Cloud. Would you like some tea?"

And she made jasmine tea for Mission, and said that she always wanted to go west, and that yes, that was her dog.

"The silver tide," she said. "I could go there, to that town. Tofino. I could take your father." Swallowing hard. "On that journey."

Mission's eyes were clear blue, and she closed them over the steam of her tea, sipped, opened, tears brightening and then slipping back.

Pattianne said, "I'm so sorry."

She said, "I can tell."

But forgiveness wasn't hers to grant, and Pattianne was on her own.

"Please," she said. "I would be so honored." Which sounded awkward and not even close. "Humbled, I guess."

Not that either. Mission sat there blinking those eyes, and Pattianne couldn't remember the color of the road worker's eyes, just his bushy twitching eyebrows.

"I just promise I would do it right," she said finally.

"All by yourself?"

Pattianne nudged Bullfrog with her toe, and he groaned in his sleep. "Me and him."

Mission smiled then, the tears slipped down her cheeks.

"When?"

Pattianne didn't know, except that it probably didn't matter. Maybe right after Christmas, before Michael came back. "Next week?"

Mission reached into the pocket of her shirt, and when she held out her hand, there was one of the blue glass vials, lying flat in the middle of her small palm.

Pattianne said, "Okay," and took the vial and closed her own fingers around it and held it.

AND AFTER THAT, IT all came down to boxes, what to put in which box, and then what to do with the boxes. They were everywhere. In the living room, in the kitchen, in the bedroom, in Michael's office. Open corrugated-cardboard boxes, the flaps making tricky geometric patterns in the sunlight on the floors, each box with just a few things in it. There wasn't enough of anything to fill up a whole box. The blue glass candlesticks in with the antique duck decoy. A small wildlife parade in a box with a picture of Grandma Anthony. A rose-colored shirt in with *Flora and Fauna of the Upper Midwest* and a blue scented candle. A silver-framed wedding picture that kept moving from box to box.

She put the dark wooden crucifix in with his college yearbook and his Donald Duck tie and the orange Fiestaware chip set with no chips. Purple beads and white origami cranes went in another box. Michael, her, Michael, her.

A deer lamp with eyes that glittered. Michael. Extra jeans, a blue flannel pajama shirt, the Scrabble game. Her. The tiny stormscape. Her. She broke down then. Hard, loud sobs all through the small house.

All the ways to stop what she'd started.

III. TOFINO

11: THE DRIFTING FOG GAVE IT A FACE

THE PINK DOLPHIN MOTEL was almost to Tofino. She and Bullfrog were driving, winding along the road, the road getting darker, the sky getting darker, the tall Douglas fir trees forming a tall, dark wall along the road. And there was the sign, up on one of the trees, a wooden sign, painted white, neat black letters, "Pink Dolphin Motel—Stay with Us," and a smiling blue dolphin. About a mile down the road beyond the sign was another sign, "PINK DOLPHIN MOTEL" and another smiling blue dolphin, and a driveway off into a grassy clearing. She caught a glimpse of a low building, white-painted cinderblocks, and then the wall of fir trees closed back in around the Fiat.

"Looks like a dog situation."

Bullfrog was curled into the other front seat. His tail wagged one wag.

"Dogs?"

Another wag.

"It's dogs!"

Then he got his fat basset legs under him, and he sat partway up. He yawned a yawn that ended in a certain yawn squeak that he had, and he shifted his butt around so he could stick his face out the window. His nose bobbed in the wind. A gray film of perpetual dog slobber now coated the windowsill. Bullfrog was half basset, half something else. His nose was all basset.

Pattianne cooed at him.

"Mr. B!"

If she cooed high and singing, Bullfrog could hear. He looked at her and shook his head, flapping his ears. That's how she knew when he heard her. And she liked it when he heard her. She would think, *I'm not alone.*

She slowed down, watching for a wide shoulder spot, slowing and listening. The dense green of the trees became black, and the sunset clouds turned copper in the long clear stretch of sky above the road. Bullfrog was curled back asleep before she found a gravel turnout to turn around to head back to the Pink Dolphin Motel. She stopped on the gravel. The air smelled rich and wet, and was full of sound, like night birds in the rain forest, or a murmuration of starlings, a covert of coots, a dule of doves. It was the same evening chirping that was in every forest everywhere, the New Jersey woods, the back yards of Minnesota, public television specials of Kalahari desert oases.

Bullfrog snorted in the seat.

"I suppose you wonder where we are."

The sky was dull silver, and the copper had gone to purple. Bullfrog bumped his nose against her elbow. A request for a dog break.

It was not quite dark, except for under the trees. She turned off the key, and Frankie's Fiat choked and jerked and quit.

She opened the door and planted her feet in the gravel and let her knees straighten slowly before she stood and went around to Bullfrog's side and opened his door. He got his long self out and standing on all four cute fat short legs, and he shook, flapping his ears and jingling his tags, and wrapping a long silver string of dog drool neatly around his nose twice. She took in a deep breath that eased the ache in her back, and she tasted the cold marine air deep. If she sniffed short little sniffs with the end of her nose, she caught sharp scents of pine and damp leaf.

Not too long a dog break. Bullfrog was old, and short breaks seemed okay with him, and there was only so much time before the bad feeling started in her chest. Not her heart, but right around there. Driving, it was just a lot of messy thoughts. Stop, and it turned to a nameless drifting bad feeling. She'd driven across Saskatchewan, only stopping for gas and to pee and to buy more coffee for the thermos. She'd stopped to sleep in Calgary, though, after she almost sideswiped a Winnebago with two old ladies in it. She didn't need more bad feelings in her heart. Except it wouldn't be in her heart. In her chest maybe, but she wouldn't say heart.

Bullfrog peed on two tires and then they got back in. And then the Fiat wouldn't start. Again. Every time, all the way from St. Cloud, she remembered Frankie saying something about the starter.

She took one of the long deep breaths and put the key in her pocket next to the blue glass vial. She got her wallet out of the glove box and put that in there too, and the pack of Marlboros, and she scooped a handful of dog kibble into her other pocket. She pulled the neat stuff sack of her sleeping bag from the back. She hooked Bullfrog's new leather leash to his collar.

"Walk?"

His tail wagged in wide, full circles.

It was all the way dark before they got back to the Pink Dolphin Motel, and the birds had quieted. There were seven white reflectors along the side of the road, and one blue one, and she had no idea how many actual steps it took, because she was going to stop counting things.

There were nine yellow lights above nine doors. The office was the door next to the Coke machine, and she looked in through the window. A very fat, beautiful woman with black hair sat in there on the couch, and Pattianne looked away because her stomach lurched like she might throw up, and then she looked back, because the woman seemed to have extra arms. She wore a long, bright dress, there was turquoise and magenta, and then two little girls climbed out from behind her, and the woman only had two arms.

The door opened to a low counter, and there stood Mr. Patel. She guessed this because a small wooden plaque that hung on the wall said YOUR HOSTS! THE PATELS!

"Hi," she said. "Um. How much are your rates?"

"Fifty-five dollars plus tax," he said. "No car?"

"It wouldn't start. Do you allow dogs?"

Mr. Patel looked past her, at the open office door, to Bullfrog, sniffing along the edge of the doorstep, about to sniff his way in.

"Oh, yes," Mr. Patel said. "Oh, yes, please sign your name here, et cetera, all the blanks. You have been walking along this road?"

Mr. Patel was small. There was the ease of a small person looking across a small distance instead of down from even a slight height. He had dark circles in the dark skin around his eyes.

"Just since I turned around to come back." She was too tired to explain that the Fiat would start again in a couple hours, or in the morning, that it was maybe a sign that they should stop here for the night.

"Oh, yes?" he said. He had a musical accent, and she wanted to listen, instead of having to understand, and respond, and know what he said, that beautiful sound, a surprise of syllables that jumped to odd registers. "Of course," he said. "Yes, please just fill this out. Mrs. Patel, number eight? Where is a daughter, Mrs. Patel?"

Mrs. Patel on the couch was watching a television that was turned up loud in another language. Pattianne could hear it, not see it. What she saw was the light of it lighting up Mrs. Patel and all the colors in the room. Mrs. Patel laughed with gold teeth and dangled a baby by its arms. The baby screamed, laughing too. There were more little girls now, four of them maybe, on the couch with Mrs. Patel. There was a lot of pink. And orange and purple and magenta and bright yellow.

Mr. Patel said, "Yes, I think number eight will do very well," and he held out a key on a metal ring. "There are nine doors. Number eight is the eighth one to your left."

"Thank you."

"Yes," he said. "A daughter will bring an extra blanket."

She started to tell him that it was okay, she had her sleeping bag, but he had turned back to the bright mass of people in the room behind him.

Squares of cement formed a walkway along the wall. Part of her didn't know how many squares, and part of her knew there were fourteen. She pushed open the door to number eight, and let the yellow light over the door shine into the room. Bullfrog headed on in, sniffed as far as the bedside table, went under it, curled up, laid down his head, and watched her. Her move. She turned on a light in the bathroom.

Toilet, sink, shower. Smell of soap, mildew, ammonia cleaner. No Bible in the drawer by the bed.

The daughter knocked one knock on the open door. She was thin and flat except for small new breasts under the word Princess in glitter across the front of her lavender T-shirt. She held out a pink blanket.

"Cool," she said.

"Yes," Pattianne said. "And damp."

"No," the girl said. "Like, your dog. Dogs are cool. We have a cat."

"Well. Cats are nice."

"What kind of dog is that?"

"He's a St. Francis Hound."

"Cool," the girl said. "If you want anything else? You can ask my dad. He stays up late."

That's okay, she wanted to say, *I have my sleeping bag,* but the girl was gone, ponytail bouncing.

Then came rain, falling down straight into the clearing, and Pattianne sat on the step with her eyes closed, and remembered, way back where remembering was safe. Early in spring, the year she was ten, her parents moved from a brick building in Newark to the small old house in Cranbury. Fruit trees lined the backyard, and beyond them the woods, and a creek, overgrown with someone's dark red roses tangled along the deep bank. Goldfinches lived down in the roses. Grandma Anthony taught her to listen for the dropping notes of their call in-flight.

IN THE MORNING, THERE was fog outside the Pink Dolphin, and a path that led away to the trees. Bullfrog headed along the path and she followed, to where the path stopped at the leaning stalks of last summer's foxgloves, and then the thick woods, tangled vine maples and salal crowding underneath fir trees and ragged alders and no more path except back through the fog to number eight and then on down the road to the Fiat.

Which was gone.

She had broken some rule. There were none of the neat little red and white signs that said NO PARKING AT ALL EVER. But still, the Fiat was gone. She could take a train back maybe, if they allowed dogs on trains. She knew they didn't allow them on buses. She tried to imagine hitchhiking. She and Bullfrog walked back through the fog to the Pink

Dolphin, trying not to get melodramatic. The Fiat was somewhere. She had money for a while.

The television set was on, and two little girls sat facing each other on the floor, clapping their hands together and singing a clapping song. Laughter came from back beyond the television, laughter in another language. At the desk, Mr. Patel had the telephone to his ear.

"My car is gone," she said.

On a shelf was a small radio playing a sitar version of "Moon River." A sign, but she didn't know of what.

"Yes, yes," he said, smiling whitely.

She waited and then he covered the phone with his hand and said, "Please, I will drive you in to town! Was it parked along the road? I believe it may have been towed to Ucluelet. That is just south of Tofino!"

"Tofino."

AND SO THEY ARRIVED, at the end. "Ruby's Roadhouse—at the End of the Road." That's what it said on the hanging wooden sign, and right under that, it said "No Dogs," and right past that, the Pacific Ocean took up all the rest of everything that wasn't sky. She wasn't ready for the end of the road. Days and days and miles and miles to get here, but she wasn't ready.

Bullfrog got his fat front feet under him, got up and sat next to her on the seat and sniffed. His nose bobbed in the air.

"Thanks," she said. "Very much."

"Please," Mr. Patel said. "You are so welcome. But what about your car? Ucluelet would be just south of here."

She opened the door and slid out, as if she hadn't heard him.

"Please," he said. "I would be happy."

She thanked him again, and Bullfrog wiggled out the door after her. She slammed the door. The windows were fogged up, and she could see Mr. Patel's hand waving goodbye as he pulled away, turned around down by the TERMINUS, and drove back past her. Still waving.

"Ocean," she said.

"End of the road," she said.

"No dogs," she said.

Bullfrog couldn't read. She didn't think he could read, anyway, but then she used to think he couldn't talk either. She thought, *I am not crazy. Not even a little weird really. Foolish. Guilty. Exhausted.* Her thoughts weren't connecting.

It felt like a long story. Driving across Canada, from Minnesota, starting at International Falls, it kept trying to gather in her head, all flying around in there, words, sentences, feelings, facts, memories, lies, all in a big leaf pile on a windy day. She counted miles, llamas, women truckers, yellow cars, vehicles bearing dogs, and license plates from Florida. She counted seventeen different things in four days and sixteen hours.

She was going to stop now. Stop counting. Stop driving. Stop looking for signs that the universe thought she was doing the right thing. Or not.

She would go into Ruby's Roadhouse and get a cup of coffee. She'd write a postcard to Jen, which would simply say, *Dear Jen — Love, Pattianne,* and it would make Jen laugh. She'd write another chirpy postcard to her parents, which they would hang on the refrigerator as proof that everything was fine, and that they shouldn't worry. Taking a little travel time is normal for a person getting a divorce, or breaking up, or whatever it was they thought she was doing. As if they would ever even wonder what she was really doing, as long as she didn't make too much of a fuss about anything. But now she was getting in a bitchfest in her head. She pushed it all away and sat on the wooden bench along the wide front porch, by a small table with a checkerboard painted on the tabletop.

"Or maybe chess," she said to Bullfrog.

The bench was wet. The buildings of the town were here and there on the hillside that sloped down to the beach. She started to count them, got to seven, and stopped because she thought she'd counted one twice. They weren't in straight rows, and she was going to stop counting things anyway. Grass-lined dirt tracks wound around on the hillside, and some of the buildings were houses, with curtains, and smoke came out of one rusty metal chimney pipe. A lot of the buildings seemed to be sheds, three for sure. One of the buildings was actually a large, gray rock.

She closed her eyes and could still see the grass-lined tracks, the sheds, the large gray rock, the chimney pipe, the dark smoke. There was an empty ache in her stomach, a calm spot right below her ribs, where there was a heart that beat, not calmly, and tried to claim some duty other than beating. But it was a muscle. It had no nature of its own. A dog may speak before a bloody muscle does.

There were seagulls and the low rhythm of breakers, the rhythm missing every few beats, and then a crack like far-off thunder. Bullfrog's tags jingled as he sniffed around on the porch, and the air was wet and kelpy. Inside Ruby's Roadhouse a phone rang and was answered: "Hello, Ruby's Roadhouse," a singsong, British-sounding voice.

Pattianne opened her eyes. It was not a dream. It was like everything else was a dream. St. Cloud, Minnesota, in the rearview mirror was a dream. Driving four days and sixteen hours was a dream. The intersections and horns and red lights and green lights of Vancouver, the ferry to Nanaimo that cost a fortune, the black water, the road up the Inside Passage, tall snags of Douglas fir with two bald eagles on each snag, eighteen bald eagles in twenty-three miles, all of it a dream. The Pink Dolphin. Now even the Fiat was a dream.

The door opened behind her and the musical British voice said, "Well, what's this then?"

It was a woman, with a white scarf twisted around her head and earrings of pink shells, and jeans that were folded high above her bare-boned ankles. She stood tall, holding a broom in one hand and a white piece of cloth in the other, the cloth very white, and her skin very black, almost blue.

"Can I help you, young lady?"

"Oh," Pattianne said, standing up too fast, a little dizzy, and she leaned against the bench. "Maybe just a cup of coffee for now."

Bullfrog sniffed at the woman's shoes, big, polished penny loafers with no pennies.

"Is this your dog?" she said, and Pattianne loved her voice, but it was not happy, and the woman pushed her broom at Bullfrog, saying, "No dogs at Ruby's Roadhouse. Says so there on the sign."

Bullfrog ignored the broom and sniffed on past her shoes to the welcome mat.

"Just on the porch? Can he just stay on the porch while I have some coffee?"

"Well." That's all she said, and she leaned the broom against the wall by the door, and went to the railing at the edge of the porch, her steps coming through the floorboards, through the wooden bench, through

Pattianne's bones. She ran the clean white cloth along the railing, her hand large-fingered and bony, the knuckles big. At the end of the railing, she snapped the cloth out over the bench at the far end of the porch. She stopped there and looked up.

"Go on now, why don't you?" she said. "Or is it out here you want it, cause there's a pot on the sideboard with take-away cups if that's it. There's a jar for quarters."

Pattianne wanted her to say more, but she didn't. "I'll just go on in then."

The woman was looking at Bullfrog, who had plopped down in the middle of the welcome mat, sniffing at himself, and Pattianne went in before he started licking himself, which was what he seemed to have in mind.

Inside was a wide room, floors of rough wood worn smooth, with blue braided rugs. There was a desk, with a rack of postcards. Empty shelves lined all the walls below the windows and either side of the open stone fireplace at one end of the long room, where a fire burned. It was a small, quiet fire.

She was in this big room all by herself with the Pacific Ocean right outside, and it was time out of time, how everything stopped and started as human beings came and went. She didn't seem to really be there when she was alone in a place, it seemed like no one was anywhere.

A wide archway near the desk opened to the tiny coffee shop, and the smell of coffee, and five small tables in a tight cluster. In a pastry case in the small counter, with quiches lined up, and seeded bagels, and pink frosted doughnuts. The windows all looked out at the gray ocean and the gray sky.

"Sit anywhere you like."

The waitress, a girl in a blue apron over overalls.

She said, "I'll be right with you, you want coffee?"

"Yes. Please."

Five tables, each set with two careful placemats and coffee cups and a spoon and napkin. On the placemats was a map of Vancouver Island, with a compass rose in the bottom corner. The only direction marked on the compass rose was West, like it was penned on by a scribe, serif, bold, and only West. It said to her, *You Are Here.* It said, *You Are Somewhere.*

The waitress brought the coffee, with cream, and a glass of water.

Pattianne said, "Thanks," and took out her pack of Marlboros and set it on the table.

The waitress said, "Sorry, really sorry, but it's all nonsmoking in here."

"That's okay," Pattianne told her. "I don't smoke."

The coffee at Ruby's Roadhouse was rich, and the cream was real cream, not milk, maybe half-and-half. It turned the coffee golden. Coffee with milk was thin and gray. Coffee with cream tasted like food, and she drank it, and let it count for lunch. The waitress came back with the pot.

"Thanks," Pattianne said. "Can I ask you a question?"

There was pink frosting on the girl's overalls.

"Do you know anything about the silver tide?"

"Nope," she said. "Heard of it, I guess."

She said thanks and the waitress left.

She was courting danger. Two cups of coffee, maybe three, maybe three and a half, but four cups would keep her awake, and she didn't even have anywhere to stay awake in. Although she would at least have the zip to hike eight miles down the road to Ucluelet and find the Fiat.

As Pattianne was going out, the tall woman in the scarf was coming into the dining room. She stepped back, behind the desk, and she said, "Right there on the doormat, sleeping, so that I had to step right over him, and him never opening an eye."

Pattianne gave her the thick coin with the Queen's picture.

She handed her back some change, which Pattianne dumped into her pocket without looking.

The woman said, "Is there something wrong with that dog?"

"Old," Pattianne said. "He's an old soul."

Bullfrog hopped up when she opened the door, and the door bonked him on the head, a small thunk that hurt to hear. But he wagged, and they headed down the road, past the sign that said End of the Road, to the crumbling end of the pavement, to the sign that said TERMINUS.

The firm sand squeaked in the still, cold air, and there was a fine misting rain. The beach was empty of people. Time out of time. Seagulls screeched. A huge crow made deep, gargly noises. Flocks of small surfbirds chasing the waves in and out on invisible bird legs were too far away to hear, or maybe not making any noise at all. Bullfrog trotted ahead, his tags a close, familiar sound. The sky to the west was black clouds, and the cold wind blew in, smelling of far out in the ocean. Not that she had ever been far out in the ocean.

"What do I know?"

She knew that this ocean smelled different from the green Atlantic at Sandy Hook. There was a big-sky smell about this ocean. It was not so close and salty. This ocean reached to mystic Russia and ancient China. It was the great weather-maker of the earth. It brought the night. The blue glass vial shifted in her pocket.

Behind Ruby's Roadhouse, another road, with a low, square building, and two more, three more houses, maybe more than that, led back toward the highway. The windows of the low, square building were empty, except for two, three, four with curtains hanging, one with the window open. There were places like this everywhere, all over New Jersey, all along the turnpike, even in St. Cloud, Minnesota, and all across Canada, sad little places where not just anyone can stay, only if you're sorry enough. Only if you are truly full of despair, and *forgive me, Father, I have committed the greatest sin. I have a smart mouth that gets other people in trouble.* And for your penance you can drink gray highway coffee that tastes like a paper cup and lie sleepless on a mattress that smells like someone else's cigarettes and count things that don't matter and wait for signs that do.

It was raining actual drops by the time they got back to Ruby's Roadhouse, and Bullfrog headed for the welcome mat.

The tall woman watched out the window.

"Bad idea." Pattianne nudged him with her foot, and he got up and went under one of the benches. He was smart that way. She went in. The woman stood there, arms crossed, looking out at Bullfrog. Except she couldn't see him now. He was under the bench.

She said, "Get yourself caught in the rain?" She shook her head, and the pink shells swung against her long neck, as though they should ring like bells. "An El Niño year," she said. "All rain. Warm."

Pattianne took a deep breath, down to where her chest ached. "I'm looking for a place to stay?"

"One that allows dogs?" the woman said, "There's the Pink Dolphin out on the highway."

"I need to stay here. At the beach. I'm waiting for a silver tide."

The woman straightened up and looked at her, at least Pattianne thought she was looking at her. Pattianne looked out at the town. She was at the woman's mercy. She was at the end of the road.

"Check at the post office. Mr. Bleakman there, he can tell you what's to let with dogs. There's the cabins."

A SMALL, SQUARE HOUSE like a shed leaned toward the ocean, leaning down the hill, the metal stovepipe leaning off the roof. Bullfrog peed at the scrubby bushes of bright leaves that crowded the step. The two windows were closed over with wooden shutters, and the door in the middle was locked with a padlock. Mr. Bleakman opened the padlock and yanked at the door, which was warped, wanting to stay shut. He yanked it open and handed her the padlock.

"There you go," he said. "Have a look. Don't usually rent this one. But with a dog, well. Lock it up when you leave. I got to get back."

He went back across the grass and turned downhill toward the post office, past a huge rock, and disappeared. Mr. Bleakman was the kind of person who, after he left, you couldn't recall his face. He didn't seem very friendly.

One room. The floor was long dark planks. When she stepped in, the planks were soft and giving. She walked into the middle of the one room, and the floor was not so soft and giving there. Bullfrog started right next to the door, sniffing along the wall. There was a sweet, musty smell like Grandma Anthony's basement where the window lit shelves of colored glass jars, a rusty toy fire engine with the ladder that worked, Grandma's gardening tools hanging in their places.

A black woodstove sat squarely on a curling piece of gray, flowered linoleum, and a stove and a deep sink and a short squatty refrigerator all gathered in the corner. A light bulb hung down into the middle of the room. She pulled on the string, and the light bulb popped a blue flash and went out.

A narrow door in the back wall opened to the bathroom, a toilet with a tank up above and a black chain hanging down, crowded in there with a water heater. A tap stuck out of the wall high up, above a drain hole in the floor. The floor was the same gray flowered linoleum as around the stove.

"Not much closet space," she said. "Good thing we don't have any clothes."

Bullfrog said, *No bed. Good thing we're not tired.*

Or maybe, *No bathtub. Good thing we're not dirty.*

Or maybe, *No anything. This won't do at all.*

BACK AT THE POST office, Mr. Bleakman stood behind the counter.

"It's perfect," she said.

He shrugged and didn't stop sorting a stack of yellow envelopes. His fingernails were long and ink stained.

"Electric is turned on already," he said.

"I need to find some stuff. A bed, maybe a table. Actually, I need to find my car."

He stopped sorting the yellow envelopes.

"Your car?"

"I think it got towed."

He looked at her over the top of his glasses, all fingerprint smudges, and his watery eyes looked like he was about to cry.

"Towed?"

"It wouldn't start. Out on the highway. When I went back to try to start it, it was gone."

"No parking along the road," he said. "It's too narrow. The tourists would just park there and go off hiking into the woods if it wasn't no-parking."

"It didn't say no parking."

He started sorting the yellow envelopes again, laying them into three separate stacks on the counter. It was an old wooden counter, golden, waxy wood like in an old schoolhouse. The smell in here was comfortable, and she liked Mr. Bleakman, how some people played this little game of being contentious, and you knew the rules, you could either be contentious back at them or be sweet-tempered and irritate them even more and still get what you want.

"So," she said sweetly. "Where do you think it got towed to?"

"Ucluelet. There's a yard there. They tow the illegally parked cars to the yard there."

He gathered the three stacks into one stack and put a big red rubber band around the one stack and dropped it into a mailbag.

"Down at the grocery store," he said. "She's got some stuff in the storeroom down there. Maybe a bed and such. One hundred eighty plus tax."

"For a bed?"

"The cabin. Payable by the week."

THE OLD LADY IN the grocery store called her dear. *The bed is in the storeroom, dear. The boy can haul it up there for you. Here are some old copies of the* West Island News, *dear. You can use it to start your fire. Are you sure one chair is all you need, dear? Come down in the morning, dear. I have fresh cinnamon rolls.*

It made her nervous, a strange old lady saying dear.

Finally, a long afternoon later, when there was a bed and a table and a chair in the house, Pattianne balled up sheets of the *West Island News* and piled them into the woodstove. She laid five sticks of kindling neatly across the newspaper, and two split logs on top of that. She touched a match to the bottom edges of *The West Island News*, here and there, holding her breath until the flames caught. Bullfrog settled beside her, she fed sticks to the flames, and cedar smoke and wet-dog smell blended in the damp air of the house. It was getting dark, and Nana's basement was all around her, damp smells that anchored her.

THE BEACH AT TOFINO was layered with fog the next morning, a dense fog that seemed to drift on the wet sand and catch in the trees on the edge of the beach, up into branches and snags. It hid everything down low. Even the ocean was only sound, and the beach felt big and creepy, like anything could show up out of the fog at any moment. And then something did, a small old woman who looked at her across the foggy distance. The woman was so small that Pattianne got a little dizzy and couldn't tell how close she was, like maybe the old woman was far away and not so small. The old woman kept walking, wide around her, toward the back of the beach, and then she was gone.

Coffee didn't really count for food.

Now she didn't see Bullfrog. She looked carefully at the smaller rocks along the back of the beach, looking for a particular brown-and-white rock, with a tail and a red collar. Walking back, the sand hard, she didn't even see her own footprints, much less any pawprints.

She called out, "Mr. B," long and loud, and a big, ragged crow gave a low croak from the top of a boulder. Along the bottom of the boulder, a sandy path led up though the rocks, and the crow croaked again and then lifted off into the fog. The path led up into the scrubby pines, tree roots forming steps into the woods, and then the quiet of the woods became louder than the washing of the waves. The path went in, around a big stump, and it was dark and nothing moved.

"Bullfrog, Bullfrog." Her voice sounded small and useless. She tried to think of the last time she noticed him beside her or behind her, and she ran out on to the beach and looked back. The fog seemed to be lifting, but she still couldn't see far, and she started to run and then stopped because she was running instead of looking at every small rock, at the big logs, out at the edge of the ocean where the waves washed in and out.

Look, look, look at every rock. They appeared out of the mist, and she went along the back of the beach to see behind them. The town came into view, and surely he couldn't have come this far back. She turned and went the other way. He was so small, and the beach was big and wide.

She found she was crying. Odd, quiet tears that were just wet on her face.

She said, "Please."

And she sat on the sand and looked one way and the other, tears just running out of her eyes, and it didn't even hurt to cry this way, even though she wanted so badly to see his tail, hear his tags, find him. She looked back to the trees.

There he was, tail high, nose low.

She just got up and walked over to him.

"Okay." She took his ears and rubbed them. "Come on."

He followed her, and she went back to where the path led into the woods, stepping silently onto the path, stirring up the sharp, rotting perfume of the damp duff. His tags jingled behind her. Her heart was beating in her ears. The tears had stopped. She touched her wet cheeks. Tasted the wetness on her fingertips. Wondered if these tears tasted different from those hard, ugly tears that she always fought. The scrubby pines gave way to vine maples tangled in the undergrowth.

"I'm going crazy," she said to him.

She wanted to sit in here. It felt better to be in here, out of the fog. Maybe this was a place to think.

She whispered, "I'm sorry," but she didn't believe it. It sounded silly and self-serving, far off the mark, not at all close to the truth of the feeling. It seemed she had to keep it to herself.

Tall pillars of fir trees in here, their branches starting high up the trunks, arched in the fog. She saw her then, the old woman from the beach, standing in the middle of the woods just ahead, and maybe this was her woods, maybe Pattianne was breaking another rule. The woman didn't move, and when a crow flew low under the cathedral branches and landed on the woman's head, she became, in truth, a small weathered snag alongside the path.

How heart muscles could race and bang.

As Pattianne got close to the snag, the shoulders became broken, the whole piece a jagged split stump, its parts lying around it, the inside pale and rotted. She touched it, dry dust a surprise on her fingers, and Bullfrog lifted his leg at the base, where moss grew, and thick, ruffled white fungus.

She walked on, the snag waiting behind her, and she kept looking back. The path twisted through the woods, and it was like the snag turned to watch, and the shadows of the high branches and the drifting fog gave it a face, an old woman, a hawk, and she kept looking back until the stump was no longer in sight.

They came out behind a burned-out building. The walls around the boarded windows were sooted black. Around front, grass and weeds grew into the gravel of the parking lot, and her feet made too much noise. Thorny vines massed around the broken wooden steps. There was a steeple, painted white, peeling gray. The roof was caved in over the front porch.

She was not looking for signs, and there was cold air around the muscle under her ribs. At the road was a sign, Church of the Holy Family, all the letters still there, but faded, and she wondered who'd set the fire, and if they would feel bad about it forever.

12: WALKING IN THE SAME RAIN

BULLFROG FOLLOWED HER BACK along the highway past the Church of the Holy Family, getting wet, looking sad. At the last curve in the road heading into Tofino, a farm market sat back in a muddy lot. The wooden screen door hung slightly open, and the light inside was warm and yellow. The apples were cheap—this was apple country—so she went in. Low wooden shelves ran along inside the screened-in front porch. Red apples, green ones, and beautiful yellow ones, a lot of apples everywhere, in boxes along the floor, in baskets on the shelves, and the smell of them in the air. She picked up a yellow one, then three more.

"Golden Delicious," said a man behind her. "Washington State." His red T-shirt was stretched across his chest, stretched over the muscles in his arms.

He said, "Is that your dog?"

Bullfrog was nosing his way in.

"Sorry," she said, and she had to walk close by the man, a young man, a teenager maybe, to open the door and scoot Bullfrog out with her foot.

"What kind of dog is that?"

"Just a mutt."

"Good-looking dog," he said. "Looks like he has some Brittany."

He reached past her to pull the door shut tight, and the black hair of his forearm was powdered with sawdust. She bought a bag of Golden Delicious apples, and when she went to leave, he said to come again, asked was she new in town, what's that dog's name, and she just said bye, thanks.

That night she couldn't remember the dream that woke her up, but it was still dark, and she was awake all over. Bullfrog snored under the bed, his snore interrupted, an acknowledgment, like it was him saying, *it's okay, it's just a dream, go back to sleep*. She didn't. She lay there awake, staring at the window, knowing it would get light soon. It didn't. The window stayed dark, and she knew she just wanted to be held. The bloody muscle inside her chest was behaving badly. She counted by twos, by fives—she had always loved counting by fives. She counted by tens, always too quick. By threes, too confusing. The gray finally came to the window.

SHE HUNTED DOWN THE Fiat in Ucluelet. It was easy. She asked a Chinese man in a convenience store. All she had to do was say, "I'm trying to find where my car might have gotten towed to," and he pointed down the road to a fenced-in lot. The Fiat was the only car there. It cost seventy-three dollars for the towing. The short kid in coveralls said, "Starter's shot."

"What should I do with it?"

"I can see about getting the parts. You can leave it here if you want."

There was a box in the back, extra jeans, a long-sleeved flannel shirt, some books. The kid gave her a ride back to Tofino with the box. Said about three words. Something about Fiats. He liked Fiats, she thought he said.

Back in Tofino, she wandered the fifty steps down the hill to the phone booth outside the store and took out a shiny new phone card.

Jen's voice mail said, "If it's you, leave a number. You know who you are."

"I don't have a number," Pattianne said, and Jen picked up and said, "Why don't you get a cell phone like the rest of the world?"

"The rest of the world doesn't have a cell phone."

"So did you find out when the silver tide happens?"

"No. I got a cabin and I'm waiting for it. I have to watch for it at night."

"A cabin? Like with an address?"

The wind picked up off the ocean, and she tucked into the phone booth.

"I'm in an actual phone booth."

The old lady inside the store was working on a crossword puzzle at the counter on the other side of the window.

"Wow. And the cabin?"

"It's a one-room place with no bathtub. There's kind of a shower. There's a woodstove. I can see the ocean."

"What, you're turning monk now that you've dumped the Catholic boy?"

"Not too monkish. I'm fifty steps from a little market that sells pinot noir and merlot for under ten dollars a bottle."

"So you what, just drink wine and drive around and wait for this silver tide?"

"Kind of. Except the Fiat's starter is shot."

The wind was wet and warm, and it smelled like something she couldn't remember, and she decided not to try to explain this.

"Sounds like you're screwed," Jen said. "If you didn't have that dog, you could get yourself back home. What are you going to do?"

"Nothing."

Jen snorted. "Good plan. Mom will love that."

"How they doing?"

"They wondered if you have a new address in St. Cloud," she said. "Do you? In St. Cloud? Or wherever you are?"

"They can write to me care of Lamplighter. I told her that. And the dog has a name."

"No, it doesn't. It has a label, and it's not even the right label."

"It's a he, not an it. He's Bullfrog. He's a very cool dog, if you ask me. Not that I want to use up my phone card telling you about Bullfrog."

"So why are you using up your phone card?"

Pattianne didn't know. "This place is wild," she said. "There are eagles, pairs of eagles even, and there are these huge crows that follow you on the beach and make the weirdest sounds, like someone's knocking on the door. And huge black rocks all over the beach, big as cars. It's wild."

The rain blew sideways in sheets, and she couldn't even see as far as the beach.

"Got it," Jen said. "Huge. Wild. So, are you going to get that car fixed?"

She didn't know, but she said yes because she could hear how she sounded, like some crazy woman who has returned to the wilderness or something. She said she'd call again soon, and Jen said, "Don't be a feeb."

"I'm not."

"I know," she said. "I'm just saying this is no time to start."

THE OLD LADY IN the grocery store had pure white hair. Pattianne liked that. It was pulled into a thin, wispy clutch at the back of her neck, held by a hairnet that had tiny colored beads here and there, and she liked that too. She was very small, smaller than Pattianne. Pattianne liked small people. She liked everything about the old lady except that she called her dear.

"So," she said. "How are you settling in, dear?"

"Fine. We're settling in fine."

Her apron was blue flowers on a pink background, white polka dots in the pink, and all trimmed in pink rickrack, and she was dusting cans of tuna fish with a dust cloth that was all yellow daisies, a former apron surely.

She said, "How is that mattress, a little damp?"

"No. Well, a little, but I like damp."

She turned from her cans of tuna fish and squinted through her glasses.

"Fine," Pattianne said. "Everything is fine."

"Got a cold?"

"No."

"Did Mr. Bleakman get that heater working?"

"It works okay."

The one electric heater along the wall warmed up the floor of the house after about an hour. Then the coils inside the heater started to glow, and when she turned it off, and the wall above the heater would be warm to the touch.

"It's supposed to have a thermostat. He fix the thermostat?"

"I don't know."

"You got to keep after Mr. Bleakman," she said. "He'd sooner not than do." She folded the yellow daisy dust rag. "Me, I like to keep moving. My secret to eternal youth: you got to keep moving." She wore blue running shoes. "Most folks think that means going on walks for your heart or doing some exercise class, but that's not what it means. It means you got to get up out of the chair." She crossed the aisle to an open box on the floor and started taking small bags of potato chips out, clipping each bag to a rack on the front of the shelf. Her fingers were swollen straight, and large purple spots spread across her wrists.

She said, "Maybe not eternal youth, but a good long old age, which is not a bad thing if you do it right, especially considering the options."

Pattianne chose a can of tuna fish and a loaf of bread, the loaves on the shelf all lined up, the twisted ends of the bags all in rows, and she got a small carton of milk. She paid in colored bills.

"There you go, dear," the old lady said. "Is that all you need?"

Good Lord, no.

"Yes ma'am."

She wondered what the old lady's name was. It seemed like she learned it when she'd gotten the furniture from her back room, but she didn't want to ask. The old lady would ask her name in return, and she didn't know what she would say.

She said, "Thank you."

Outside, in the sideways rain, she thought about mayonnaise to go with the tuna fish. She looked back into the store. She remembered the old lady's name was Mrs. Taskey.

At home, she opened the tuna fish, and Bullfrog wagged at the can opener sound and then sat patiently, focused and sure that good things would come to him, that the world was in good working order, his sad brown eyes gazing, his ears paying attention, not quite the agony of anticipation, just the peace of patience. She drained the oil onto kibble and gave it to him. So far, what she had observed was that he loved tuna-fish oil better than anything except cat food and M&M's. She sat on the bed and ate the tuna fish out of the can, watching him, and it eased her bloody beating muscle that he ate all his kibble and then pushed his chow bowl around the room, licking it. She gave him the tuna can to lick out, and she lay back on the damp smelling mattress. The curtains were open to sky and clouds. The tuna can scraped on the floor. She pulled the sleeping bag over her.

Miss Mimi used to paint in oils. She painted clouds mostly. Clouds above meadows. Her oil-painted clouds never looked real. They were as unreal as the real clouds of the real sunsets out over Pennsylvania, out over the meadows that edged the neighborhood on the other side of the woods. She would call their house, and Pattianne's mother would answer the phone in the kitchen.

"Have Pattianne look out the front window. Have her call me back."

"What colors did you see?" she would ask when Pattianne called her back.

Magenta.

Copper.

Lemon.

"And cerise," Miss Mimi might say. "And gold, pure gold, there at the end."

There was a town over there, to the west of their neighborhood, and at night, Pattianne saw the dim glow from the town's lights in the low sky. There were hills and fields and meadows and a state line between her and that town, but at night, she knew exactly where it was. On nights when the sky was cloudy, the clouds were part of that low light, dark lit purple under all the rest of the sky, Atlantic thunderheads gathering up that dark light.

"Paint that," she would say to Miss Mimi. "Start with all black on your canvas."

"Ah," Miss Mimi would say. "A lover of dark clouds."

Pattianne had never dreamed clouds could be so dark. She would write Miss Mimi a note about this place.

Bullfrog barked low friendly grunts in the doorway, his tail wagging across the wooden floor in low sweeps. The dusk outside the door was the dark dusk of inland, and if there was color in the sky behind her, out over the ocean, it didn't show in the face of the old woman standing in the yard, wrapped in her gray blanket.

Pattianne said, "Who are you?" and wondered at the rudeness.

The old woman said, "Don't sleep," and then she said, "If you sleep, only your sad story will be real."

The way they talked here, sounds clipped at the ends of words, more like Minnesota than Minnesota.

The woman smiled with her eyes, and turned away, down the hill, disappearing behind the huge rock.

Pattianne got back under the sleeping bag, and it was still warm under there, down by her feet.

In the morning, the door was still open, and it was raining, a soft, fine rain that stopped and started, falling straight down onto rocks and grass and straight down onto the roof of the cabin. Bullfrog never said whether it was a dream, or if it was, why. When the rain finally seemed to let up, when the sky seemed to get lighter, she went to shut the door and the Patel daughter stood there in the watery light, black hair, her black eyes too big for her face, her lips too big for her face, her face too real for the early morning, all right there at the bottom of the three steps.

Pattianne said, "Hello?"

Bullfrog sniffed past her out the door, sniffed down the step, past the Patel daughter. The girl held out her hand, and lying flat in her palm was the silver chain with the small silver cross set with its amethyst.

She said, "Is it yours?"

"It used to be mine."

"I found it." She held her hand still, the dark silver against the skin of her palm, her fingernails painted with a pearly lavender color, and bitten short. "It was in the grass, on the path."

Pattianne closed her hands together behind her back and decided this for sure was not a dream.

The girl said, "I drove here. Daddy's in Vancouver. We're out of milk, so I, like, drove? Plus to give you back this. What are you doing? Did you just wake up?"

"Yeah."

"Is that coffee?"

"Yeah."

"I'm allowed to have coffee."

The wet black rocks steamed in the sun, and so did the roofs of the buildings. High clouds layered the sky, vaguely pink, and the sun would soon slip back behind them.

Pattianne said, "What's your name?"

"Lakshmi."

Lakshmi poured the silver chain from one hand into the other. It made a thin silver sound, and she said, "It's so beautiful, so tiny and all."

"Why don't you keep it?"

The chain dangled from her fingers. "Don't you want it back? We're not Christian anyway. Hindu. From India. Well, Vancouver. But not Pakistan Hindu."

She held the cross up to her neck, and looked down at where it hung on the pink T-shirt, not down as far as her small breasts. There was pink glitter on her eyelids. "Won't Daddy be mad!" She slipped it back into her palm. "But I don't think I should, really."

Mr. Bleakman stepped out the back door of the post office and dumped trash into the can there. Lakshmi waved at him.

She said, "That guy is such a creep."

"You want some coffee, Lakshmi?"

She swung the cross around on her finger, and she said, "Yeah, I love coffee," and she leaned in the doorway while Pattianne poured hot water into the other cup, spooned in instant, stirred.

"Milk? Or sugar?"

"Yes, please." The giggle. "A lot, please. Of each."

So Pattianne put in a lot of each, and maybe this was not okay, but they would sit outside in full view of Mr. Bleakman and the rest of the world. She took the cup out and sat down on the top step, and Lakshmi sat down next to her, taking the coffee. The chain and cross dangled from her wrist and slid down to her elbow, and she slopped the coffee on the step.

"So you live at the motel, what is it, the Dolphin?"

"Pink Dolphin," she said, and a giggle slipped out like breath. "When it's holidays and we get off school and all that, we go to Vancouver. All the aunts and uncles and, like, cousins live there? They come here a lot. I might go to high school in Vancouver next year, instead of Port Alberni, but Daddy says there's, like, drugs and all. Where are you from?"

"New Jersey."

"Is that by New York?"

"Yes, right by New York."

"I have a friend named Leah from New York City, and she saw Woody Allen walking on the street. You know who that is, Woody

Allen? I never saw any Woody Allen movies, but Leah's, like, if you live in New York he's this movie star and all, plus she's Jewish, and he makes Jewish movies. She says stuff that he says all the time, and he's all, like, funny?"

"Yeah," Pattianne say. "I like Woody Allen."

She says, "Are you Jewish?"

"No."

"Just American?"

"Yeah."

She doubled the chain over her wrist like a bracelet.

She said, "Is Bullfrog a very old dog?"

"Yeah, pretty old."

She said, "Here, Sugarlips."

What's your cat's name, what do you do in school, how do you get that glitter off your eyelids. But the girl just chattered away at Bullfrog, filling the space on the step with herself.

When she left, Mr. Bleakman leaned against the back door of the post office, watching Lakshmi go down the path, bouncing in her big white sneakers, around the rock. She went to the store, and he went back inside the post office and Pattianne and Bullfrog sat on the step until the pale sun rose into the midday clouds, and there was more rain in the warm breeze.

IN THE MORNINGS, SHE looked out at the ocean first, because she could, it being right there. She didn't even wait for her eyes to open all the way. She didn't even wait to be all the way awake. Then came one morning when what she saw was the western sky out over the ocean colored like sunrise, as though everything had gotten turned around while she slept and the sun now came up in the west. This western sunrise didn't fool the seagulls, though, they were all sitting, maybe standing, lined up along the beach, spaced wide apart, each turned inland, each puffed up, white breasts tinged faintly pink, and so was the wash of sea foam behind them, and so was the light layer of clouds out over the ocean. When the sun was finally all the way up, behind the trees of the island to the east, her sense of direction settled calmly back into her body. It was slightly disappointing.

Days were stringing along behind her.

A card came from Michael's mother, in a peach-colored envelope, which she pulled open with excruciating care because she didn't want to open it at all. Personal stationery with her initials in gold, and a message: *We miss you. Come back home.* She tucked the card back in the envelope and laid it gently in the drawer between the stove and the sink.

The town happened around her. In the morning the children appeared, heading up the hill in pairs, or small groups, or sometimes a single child straggling, toward the school building out near the highway, set back in a wide, muddy lawn. The maroon station wagon from the Pink Dolphin Motel drove up and parked in front of Ruby's Roadhouse. The daughters got out and went into the store, and then on up the hill to the school, and Mr. Patel went into Ruby's Roadhouse. Even when she wasn't watching, even when she was hiding away from the window with the door shut, and didn't see the station wagon full of Patel daughters, she heard them. She heard their giddy, screaming laughter. If one of those children were hers, she was afraid she would insist that the child not ever scream like that. She would hide behind the door.

ONE QUIET MORNING, A big white feather was in front of the door in the grass. All her breath rushed away. She dropped to her knees, wet knees instantly, and she touched it before she picked it up. It was as long as her forearm. She was sure it was an eagle feather and she wanted it. She carried it in her two hands and walked with it, not believing it, it was so big and so white, the quill as thick as her finger. Then she wanted to hide it when she saw Mrs. Taskey and the pink-faced, dark-haired young man in the priest's collar walking down the sidewalk, him holding her arm. Bullfrog got it into his head to be Mr. Sociable, and he wagged right up to them, running ahead of her.

Mrs. Taskey called out, "Hello, dear."

The priest tucked his hands into the pockets of his canvas jacket, and he looked happily at the feather.

He said, "Lovely." His voice was soft and high.

Mrs. Taskey held onto his elbow with both hands, and she said, "This is Father Lucke." And, to him, "This is Pattianne Anthony Bryn."

The sound of her name surprised her, disappointed her. She was thinking that maybe no one knew it, except Mr. Bleakman.

Father Lucke's dark hair stuck up in wavy cowlicks all over his head, especially in front.

She said, "Lucky?"

"L-U-C-K-E," he spelled. "Here from Nova Scotia. Same side of the continent as yourself, eh? All the way from New Jersey, Mrs. Taskey tells me."

Mrs. Taskey said, "Will you come for tea after Mass, Pattianne?"

Apparently it was Sunday.

She said, "I can't." And then it seemed like she had to say why not, and she couldn't think of why not, and Bullfrog just stood there wagging, no help at all.

"So what are your plans here in Tofino?" Father Lucke said. "Any interest in the choir?"

"No. Can't sing a lick."

"We have Mass in Ruby's now," Mrs. Taskey said.

Since the church burned down.

"Lovely acoustics," she said. "And Father Lucke is a fine tenor."

She said it more to him, how old ladies do, flirt with priests.

"Fair tenor," he said. "Good cantor."

Pattianne said, "Well," and they both said, "Well," and he said he hoped to see her again soon, and have a nice Sunday, and he reached down to pat Bullfrog, who sniffed his fingers, and it was all goodbye, thank you, and they didn't say anything else about the feather. She put it into her pocket, careful not to break it or crush it or hurt it. There was a cluster of people, a church cluster, on the porch of Ruby's Roadhouse.

Pattianne went down to the beach angry. Being this close to church, to a priest, made her angry, and it wouldn't go away. She didn't even know it was close again, this God thing chasing her across Canada. She thought it was fire, or maybe guilt, or maybe Michael Bryn, and here was God, taunting her. *Look at all those people on the porch. You can hear them singing if you listen. Here, upon the wind I will bring to you songs of My glory. Try and ignore Me.*

Bullfrog trotted alongside her, head down.

"Yes," she said. "It's your fault. Did I want to go meet a priest? No. You did."

He said, *Hey, I'm sorry, but he smelled like bacon.*

She said, "Dogs can't talk."

Wickaninnish Bay was full of rocky headlands that broke the ocean spray up into a constant mist. Forms took shape along the surf, the forms becoming rocks, or disappearing, and she thought they might see the old woman again. The shoreline curved out and then cut sharply back in, and curved out again, and no one was ever there.

The night of the day of Emerson Paul's funeral, it had never gotten dark. The moon rose, almost full, misshapen and yellow, against a pewter-colored sky, and she kept thinking about him out beyond the moon somewhere, beyond the moon being as good as anywhere when it came to the geography of the dead.

She hadn't looked at the blue glass vial in a few days. She thought about him watching her, waiting for her to throw his ashes into the ocean. She thought about him being somewhere, waiting for her to do the right thing. Although she couldn't imagine why he would, why the dead would even care about the living. The dead had the secrets of the universe finally revealed. The dead would know she hadn't set any fires, that all she'd done was mouth off and not pay attention and be a fool, and that she was not full of sorrow and remorse now that she was here, but just caught by the ocean, this place and this sound and being far away.

When one of the forms did not turn into a rock or mist, it was still not the old woman. Standing still, looking out to the ocean, hands held together behind his back, it was the Chinese man from the convenience store. He didn't move as she came close, and she went behind him. But the beach was narrow along here, and Bullfrog headed toward him, wagging like the Chinese man was his old buddy.

"Bullfrog, come," she said, like he even knew that word. Bullfrog did not seem to be into commands.

The Chinese man turned around, and there were tears on his face.

"Sorry," she said. "He thinks he knows you."

Maybe his face was just wet from the mist, maybe it was raining now.

He said, "Hello," and his cheeks wrinkled into a smile and he bent and touched Bullfrog on the head. Bullfrog sat down and sniffed at his hand. The wind picked up in a gust full of heavy drops.

She said, "I didn't realize we'd walked all the way to Ucluelet."

And he straightened up, the smile there and then gone, quick, and he said, "Yep. All the way to Ucluelet."

He turned his back to the ocean and said, "There's a path, through those trees. We are both about to get drenched."

Bullfrog got up, and as they all moved to a straight path that opened right onto the beach, hard heavy drops started to hit, loud with the wind picking up. When they got to the path, the Chinese man stepped aside so she could enter the trees ahead of him. The skin of his face was deeply wrinkled, and she wanted to stare at him, but she just walked past him, into the stubby pines and straggly alders, and the salal that soaked her jeans at the knees. The Chinese man stepped to her side. He was a little taller than she was, and he walked slightly limping, his thin hair wet and stuck to his head. His skull tucked perfectly into his neck, thin curves of bone behind his ears. She was walking through the woods with this guy as if it was nothing, as if it was easy, and it was, the ease of quiet strangers.

"This dog?" the stranger said. "He cracks me up. I think he's thinking of something."

Yeah, like if there's going to be any M&M's in his near future.

The path ended at a gravel road, a repair shop, a mobile home. Up on the corner, she saw the convenience store through the rain. They left the shelter of the trees and she ducked her head, like that would keep her any drier. The Chinese man didn't duck his head, as if they weren't walking in the same rain. A German shepherd on a chain outside the mobile home lunged and snarled at Bullfrog, or maybe at her, or maybe at all of them, and Bullfrog wagged his tail a little higher. She had noticed that he was not gracious to dogs on chains.

Behind the convenience store was a wire fence, and inside it was a construction project, a square foundation hole, a stack of warped, weathered boards. The Chinese man walked past it and unlocked the front door of the store.

She said, "Do you sell coffee?"

"Yes. No decaf."

He took down a small, hand-lettered sign that said BACK SOON— SORRY FOR THE INCONVENIENCE.

"Funny," she said. "Inconvenience. Convenience store."

"Yes." He held open the door. "I found that amusing. People here, however, don't say convenience store."

She said, "Bullfrog, stay."

Bullfrog sat down, which surprised her.

The Chinese man said, "Here they say mini-mart."

"I'm from New Jersey."

He went behind the counter and shrugged out of his rain jacket, hung it on a hook there, and sat on a tall stool. He said, "I've been there. Princeton. The coffee is over there. Please help yourself."

The coffee was thick looking and very black. "You've been to Princeton?"

The pot was dark and stained. The cups were Styrofoam.

He said, "I spoke there once. You are very far from home. Fifty cents."

"You spoke at Princeton?"

"Beautiful town," he said. "Movie theater like a small castle."

"I'm from Cranbury. It's not too far from there."

She dug two coins out of her pocket and handed them to him, and wrapped her fingers around the coffee cup, holding the warmth with both hands.

He said, "Do you realize that these are nickels?"

"Oops. Sorry."

She gave him two quarters, and he gave her back the nickels, and the eagle feather fell to the floor. Guilty. She picked it up and worked it carefully back into the pocket. She couldn't tell whether he was looking at her. Bullfrog, however, was definitely looking at her. The rain blew and the wind blew, and inside the convenience store, the coolers along the walls hummed.

"So. How is it that you spoke at Princeton?"

"College of Physics. Visiting professor."

"You're a physicist?"

"I was a teacher of physics."

A pickup truck pulled onto the gravel outside, and the young man from the farmers' market hurried in, his long hair wet, his plaid shirt soaked, his cute, boyish face happy.

The Chinese man seemed to nod briefly toward the young man, who came across the floor, leaving wet footprints from his big sneakers. He said, "Pack of smokes." His back pocket had a faded white square from his wallet. He looked over his shoulder toward her. "I see your pal out there," he said. "He don't seem too happy left out."

Bullfrog watched through the door, playing up the wet hound-dog angle big time.

"Get caught in the rain?"

The coffee was bitter and burnt.

He said, "I'd be happy to give you and the little guy a ride home."

She was embarrassed in front of the Chinese man.

"No thanks, that's okay. We'll wait it out."

It was only an offer of a ride. It was raining hard.

He said, "You might have quite a wait," and he peeled the wrapper off his pack of Kools. "This is that southwest storm been moving up the coast. Crazy El Niño weather."

The Chinese man nodded.

"Come on," the young man said. "I got to go in for the mail, not even out of the way."

The Chinese man said, "A good idea."

She dropped the coffee in the trash can by the door, and she hoped the cup didn't sound as full as it was.

It was a brand-new pickup truck, and she made Bullfrog stay down on the floor at her feet. They all got in and arranged, doors shut, seat belts hooked, truck engine started up, windshield wipers going. The young man's cigarette smoke filled the air. She tasted it, liked it. It would stay in her hair and in her jacket and then she wouldn't like it, but now she did. She thought of that hard hit of smoke on the back of the throat, the release. The smoke scooted out the window as soon as he rolled it down a crack, leaving new-truck smell, wet-dog smell.

"I'm Carson," he said. "You're Bleakman's new tenant, eh? How you liking Tofino?"

"Fine." She hung on to the armrest as he pulled out onto the road. Bullfrog was looking tragic. He did not like riding on the floor. The convenience store in the side mirror made her sad, leaving the Chinese man alone in the warm, bright store in the rain.

"I'm from here," he said. "I been here all my life. Went to Port Alberni School. We got a new school here now. You're from New Jersey?"

She wanted to say *no, I'm from Kathmandu, that's in Outer Patagonia, a suburb of Tanganyika.*

Bullfrog tried to weasel his way up onto the seat.

"No," she said. "Get down, you weasel."

The young man said it was okay, but she said, "He's sandy. He's wet."

"This truck is only clean cause of being new and all," he said. "Brand-new. But don't worry, I like dogs. We got two. Mandy and Red Boy. Hunting dogs. This a hunting dog? He looks like he could flush some birds." He took the corner fast, and when she grabbed the dashboard, Bullfrog took advantage of the moment and made it up onto the seat.

"He hunts toast," she said. "M&M's. Cat food. Small game like that."

"I heard about how chocolate makes a dog sick."

"I didn't say he's a very good hunter."

"What do you call him?"

"Bullfrog."

Bullfrog leaned into her and yawned his yawn squeak, happy with the situation. And wet. And stinky, that sweet, thick wet-dog smell that she loved. How dogs knew when something was right between you, like how he knew she was glad to have him up on the seat between her and the young man, whom she could look at now and pretend to be looking at Bullfrog. The young man was really just a kid, maybe twenty-one, maybe not even that.

"Bullfrog," he said. "And what's your name?"

She didn't have one.

"Pete."

"Pete?"

"It's a nickname."

He downshifted through the highway curve. The Church of the Holy Family went by, black and hunched over itself in the blur of the rain.

He tooted the horn when they went by the farmers' market and then slowed going into the curve that led down into town. The rocks and trees closed in on either side of the road, and the storm seemed to grow quiet, although the treetops were tossing and rain bounced on the pavement. The town opened up, all on its hillside, and the ocean was a blur of storm.

"Thanks. We would've got soaked."

He stopped in front of the post office and set the brake, turned, and tugged on Bullfrog's ears just like Bullfrog liked the best, and Bullfrog gazed at him with this particularly adoring gaze he had when you tugged at his ears just right.

The kid said, "You're welcome."

On the sidewalk, she said thanks again, and Carson went inside the post office. Mr. Bleakman stood there watching out the window.

ON THURSDAY NIGHT, RUBY'S Roadhouse stayed lit up late, and cars lined the road. It wasn't raining, and once the sky was completely dark, Pattianne and Bullfrog headed down toward the beach, walking by Ruby's Roadhouse, looking in. Small folding tables were set up here and there in the lobby, and people sat, their heads bowed. Mrs. Taskey was in there. So was Mr. Bleakman, and a man in a red vest stood by the fireplace and pulled cards from a blue glass fishbowl. A woman in a huge yellow sweater jumped up and waved her arms around.

Bingo.

Father Lucke came along the road to the steps, appearing too quickly for her to pretend she didn't see him, which was something she used to be pretty good at, that disingenuous fake-out where you get to slip away by acting spaced out instead of antisocial.

He said, "Bingo," a little out of breath, smiling in the porch light, his cheeks shining like he never had to shave. He wore the canvas jacket and blue jeans and a black shirt with the collar, and Bullfrog was up and wagging at him.

"Church fund," he said. "Care to come in and contribute?"

"No." There it was again. No what? No thanks? No sir? "I was going to the beach."

He rounded out his cheeks. "At this time of night?" he said. "Pretty dark, I'd say. Why don't you come in and have some hot cider?"

"No dogs," she said. "No dogs at Ruby's Roadhouse. Says so right there on the sign."

"Ah," he said. "She does have her rules. There are always rules in life, I guess. Well, why don't I just join you out here? I'll bring you a cider." And he went past her, in the door, and he smelled like a cigarette. The guy in the red vest called out, "G-14," and then the door shut. Bullfrog went up the steps to the door and sniffed around there. She went up the steps and leaned on the railing, just out of the light of the window, and she was leaning there when Father Lucke came out with two paper cups.

"Didn't bring you one," he said to Bullfrog. "What's your name anyway?" Still talking to Bullfrog.

Go ahead, Mr. I'm a Real Guy's Dog—tell him your name if you're so friendly.

"Bullfrog," she said.

Wag wag, full circles. Bullfrog loved the sound of his name when he could hear it. Father Lucke settled himself on the long bench next to the door, stretched his legs out, and said, "So." He smiled out at the town on the hillside, lights here and there, like the light in her house. She left the light on all night, especially if she wasn't there, and especially if she was. The lightbulb had burned out again already, something wrong with the cord or connection or whatever. She didn't care. She'd bought a four-pack of bulbs.

"Low tide," he said. "It gets pretty wild out there at low tide, can't tell where it'll be coming when it turns. You go down there often?"

"Yeah, every day."

"And what brings you all the way here?" His smile was in his voice now, careful and polite and presuming in a priestly way.

She could tell him. It would be easy. Silver tide, a blue glass vial, a promise to someone who promised someone else.

"I like it here," she said. It seemed true once she said it. The wild edge of things, the ocean and the sky and the wet black rocks and the huge crows in the trees along the beach.

"Vacation?" he said, and he blew on his cider as if it was hot, which hers wasn't, and she realized that he wasn't very good at being a priest. He was uncomfortable and awkward, and she liked him a little better.

"Kind of."

"And your family? All back in New Jersey?"

"Yeah."

"Miss 'em?"

"Of course."

She missed Jen. There were two postcards that she hadn't filled out yet sitting on the windowsill. Her mother would get hers and let it sit on the hall table until she had the right moment to sit at the kitchen table with her coffee and read it. Then she'd set it by her father's plate at dinner. Jen would read hers standing at the mailbox in the lobby of her apartment building.

A woman inside yelled, "Bingo," and someone else said, "Oh, no," and Father Lucke turned and looked through the window. "Ah," he said. "A good winner, gives all her winnings."

"So, you're raising money to rebuild the church that burned down? Holy Family?"

He stepped across the porch and leaned next to her on the railing. He patted his upper jacket pocket, where his cigarettes would be if he had them. Hers were in her upper jacket pocket.

"Holy Family seems to be a church that wasn't meant to be," he said. "Got it rebuilt once before and it burned down again. Before my time."

A church burning, flames and shattering stained glass, flames and a falling steeple, flames at night.

"How'd that happen, that fire?"

"The first time they never knew," he said. "Old place, old wiring. Port Alberni Volunteer Fire Department never did much besides put it out."

His cider cup was empty now, and Bullfrog was snoozing, and letter-number bingo combinations were coming thick and fast, the game heating up inside. It sounded like a foreign language, and when she listened for the pattern in the numbers, she heard the ocean.

She said, "What about the second time?"

She wanted to edge away from him, lean somehow so that she could see him without turning her head to look right at him.

"No one really knew that time either." He set his cup on the railing, and the wind blew it off. He looked over the edge to the ground where the cup was blowing away, and he just watched it.

"Seems there was a transient living in there," he said. "May have started it accidentally."

"A transient?"

Transients in a little village like this.

"Well, that's a maybe," he said, and he went down the steps and picked up the cup.

She heard his knees crack and thought about his knees cracking when he prayed.

"There's lots of time around here to tell stories. You never know."

And he laughed, that giggly kind of nervous laugh, which didn't seem to suit a priest, although it suited him.

"You never know. My bylaw—it always ends up being true. You never know."

She tore at the rim of the paper cup, a slow, careful ruffle coming away in her fingers, working her way around the circle of it. She didn't know if he was just being New Age or if this was true and he was a weird kind of priest.

"You can only believe," he said, and a weight of anger shut her down.

"Yeah, well," she said, "I believe I'll go for my walk." She went down the steps, but she didn't know what to do with the pieces of paper cup. She ought to say thank you for the cider, but she didn't want to say thank you to this silly priest in his blue jeans and priest collar who probably prayed to an old man in a throne of clouds attended by seraphim who were in turn attended by assorted lower ranks of angels.

He held out his hand, his holy anointed fingers, bound in holy oil for two weeks so he could touch the consecrated host, if that was still true, if it was ever true, and he said, "Throw that away for you?"

"Thanks," and she put the torn pieces in his hand, careful not to touch him.

"Be very careful out there," he said. "Watch your feet. And the stars, of course. I always watch the stars. It's what I think of when I pray."

She stopped. The anger fluttered in her stomach, just above her stomach really, but not her heart, and she said, "Why'd you say that?" She wondered if it sounded as rude to him as it did to her.

"It's my job to say things like that," he said. "That and keeping the bingo games honest," and he giggled again.

She turned away and heard her own feet on the road, her breath in her ears, his voice in her ears, his voice saying, "I don't think he wants to go."

Bullfrog was watching her from his spot on the welcome mat, lying comfortably, not getting up or even looking like he was thinking about it.

Father Lucke said, "Too dark out there, eh, little fellow?" Bullfrog wagged at him.

The wind gusted at her back, cold, with an edge to it, and she hugged her arms around herself.

"Have a nice evening." He wiggled his fingers. "Whatever you two decide on."

He reached for the door. Bullfrog got out of his way, and he went in. Bullfrog settled himself back on the mat.

A shower of drops hit her face, and she looked up at rain clouds moving in, over the stars and the moon.

LATE, AFTER RUBY'S ROADHOUSE had emptied out and was dark, and only the sound of the wind or rain and the fire popping in the woodstove, and Bullfrog snoring, she thought of how to tell Jen about this crooked little town, securely balanced on the edge of the world. She went out to get firewood from the stack under the house, but she just sat in the doorway and looked down to the dark beach, for silver lights in the water.

There was a rattling down the hill by Mrs. Taskey's store. The old woman from the beach, or maybe another old woman, rattling the trash cans behind the store. She dropped a lid on the ground, turned, and looked at her in the doorway. They looked at each other, and then Pattianne was looking at the empty back of the store, the trash cans all lined up with their lids on, and Bullfrog was not snoring by the stove but standing in the doorway with her, sniffing the air. Sometimes losing time like that made her nervous. Sometimes it filled her with wonder. The world seemed to stop and start.

"Wonder," she said. "We are seeking wonder."

She wondered when a silver tide would happen. Some of the websites said bioluminescence might happen after a bright sunny day. Some said something about dinoflagellates. Nothing anywhere said anything about a silver tide, except for the four-unit motel in Nanaimo, which was closed until May. She wondered how long her money would last. And how much it would cost to fix the Fiat. And how she would find a place in St. Cloud. And what it took to get a divorce.

She laid the low table with a plate and fork and a knife, and butter in a small, crescent-shaped dish. All the dishes were some kind of green. She spooned tomatoes from a can onto toast, shook on Parmesan, and sat with her eyes shut. Bullfrog gave a low, polite moan, sitting right next to her on the floor, in front of the open door of the woodstove. He stared at the tomatoes on toast, a long, silver string of drool reaching to the floor. He hadn't eaten his dog food. Sometimes he seemed to feel that dog food was beneath him, like now, and he stared at the tomatoes on toast until he got some.

She drank red wine from a pale green coffee mug. The wine and the wood smoke made her eyes want to close, but every time she went outside to pull more wood from the pile and look down the hill at the lights of Ruby's Roadhouse, and check the surf for silver light, she got wet and cold and awake. She came back inside and loaded up the woodstove, drank more wine, and got warm and dreamy again. She stayed up, burned wood, wondered about wonder.

Wonder is a lifting in the heart.

Wonder is belief in the fleetest moment.

Time stops and starts, goes away and comes back from somewhere.

Frankie called Bullfrog the Wonder Dog.

"He wonders what's going on," he said.

It's a wonder she and Michael ended up married.

He had an orange Volkswagen when she first met him. Now he has a green one. It's shiny and wet and it's parked right in front of Ruby's Roadhouse. The same little beige Madonna had ridden her magnetic base on the dashboard of every Volkswagen he'd had since his parents bought him his first one at the age of sixteen, and also on a moped he had once.

He steps out onto the porch of Ruby's Roadhouse and looks around, shading his eyes from the sun. Then he looks right up at her, at her house. He crosses the road, disappears around the big rock, and she thinks to run, and then he comes up to her house, and she shuts the door, shuts Bullfrog inside to hide him from Michael, stands there facing Michael alone.

He makes the sign of the cross.

He says, "Are you taking your pills?"

And then she opens her eyes to being awake.

Every time.

The fire was burned to embers. Bullfrog nosed around with his front feet on the low table. The windows were no longer black squares looking back into the room, but pale and colorless, looking out to gray morning.

Her first hangover in Tofino.

She opened the door, and he headed out to do his business. It was all gusty, warm wind, smelling like candy made of pine trees, and the stink of stale wood smoke in her hair. She used to love the stink of stale wood smoke. She put an apple and a candy bar in her pocket, in with the blue glass vial and the pack of Marlboro Lights. Her head pounded.

Wickaninnish Bay was wild and white with high tide and high wind, and the daylight moon, half full, looking like a thin piece of shell. The far horizon was a black edge between the water and the gray sky, way out, and the wind from inland had an edge to it. The vial got warm in her jacket pocket, and she liked it being there. It didn't seem like she had to throw the ashes in if she didn't want to—a weird thought, creeping into her life, which wasn't even really a life right now, just this errand. This mission.

Bullfrog ran around, rock to stump to pile of kelp, his fur fluffed out. He was happy as a pinball.

She turned into the woods, and it was quieter, and bright with wet. It seemed like she was about to remember something, and then the feeling went away, and she got self-conscious. She should be thinking about guilt and lies and shooting her mouth off, Mission, and her father, Michael and his mother, her own parents, going back to St. Cloud. She came out to the highway at the church.

And it was snowing. The snowflakes were fat and falling in clumps, the snow so bright it seemed pink. She sat on the front step of the church. The snowflakes landed on her face and seemed to burn. Her eyes watered, sparks, and she just wanted to close them, so she did. She listened for Bullfrog, for his tags jingling, the wind picking up and fading, a car going by, one of the crows making its weird knocking croaking sound.

When she stood up and walked to the road, everything seemed too bright, and, at the edges of puddles, stars. Two white lights went past, a truck, and then steam pouring out a tailpipe into the cold air, the brake lights waiting for her.

"Hey! You need a ride?" and it was Carson, standing next to the truck, his door open.

She got in, Bullfrog got in, Carson was talking, and they moved through the snow that fell in sharp patterns onto a wet, black road that curved.

"Hey, Pete? Are you all right?"

"I get these headaches." It was all she could say.

He drove to the store and she got out and sank to the step, trying to shut her eyes against the sharp, bright snow. Mrs. Taskey came out.

Later, Pattianne remembered Mrs. Taskey and Carson helping her up the path to her house, one of them on each side of her, while she tried to keep her eyes shut. She remembered closing the door and falling onto the bed. She slept all day, and woke to see Bullfrog looking at her from his spot by the door, and then she slept again.

THE GIRL LAKSHMI CAME in the morning, with a care package from Mrs. Taskey. She sat in the chair and took out a small casserole dish.

"Listen. I'm fine now. I just get these headaches. You don't have to stay."

"Yes, I do," she said. "Mrs. Taskey said so. Besides, it's okay. Look, she sent cupcakes, too."

After a while, Carson came, and she couldn't look at him. He stood in the doorway in the light, and then he and Lakshmi left together, and Bullfrog sat by the woodstove and sadly watched the door.

That night Father Lucke came to the door, standing on the top step, his hands jammed into the pockets of his canvas jacket, and asked how she was feeling.

He said, "I must insist you join us." There was the giggle. "Bingo night."

She stood up straight.

"I'm fine really," she said, not feeling fine, feeling shaky and embarrassed.

"Come on, now," he said. "It will make Mrs. Taskey feel better, you know."

"Make her feel better?"

"I think she was a bit worried, you know," he said. "You being a traveler, and no people. I think she finds it a bit worrisome."

Bullfrog lay down by the woodstove and watched them. No dogs at Ruby's Roadhouse. She didn't say a word going down the path, and neither did Father Lucke. They just walked. His khaki pants dragged in the mud, too long for him.

The tall woman in her white scarf was at the desk, not cleaning, just watching the goings-on. She looked out the window to the porch when they came in.

"I left him at home," Pattianne said.

She nodded, the shells in her ears swinging, and she said, "So, you're feeling better, eh?"

"Yes. Thank you."

There were maybe fifteen people in the lobby, standing around the card tables. Carson wasn't here, but Lakshmi was, and she waved. She was with some of her sisters, or cousins, right there in the corner by the door, brushing a little girl's hair.

She said, "Where's Sugarlips?"

Pattianne whispered, "No dogs at Ruby's Roadhouse. Says so right there on the sign."

Lakshmi giggled, and the little girls covered their mouths and looked at the tall woman, who was talking to grown-ups.

Pattianne whispered to Lakshmi, "Does she live here?"

Lakshmi put her hands to her hips, shook her head as if there were shells in her ears, and whispered, "Proprietress."

Some of the people looked familiar. A young man who didn't look familiar came up to her and said he was glad she was feeling better, and she tried to smile. She sat into one of the deep soft couches and looked at the fire in the fireplace as if it were a television, as if she knew what the hell to do with her face, her hands.

Mrs. Taskey came in and hurried over and sat right next to her on the arm of the couch, patted her on the knee, a light tap she barely felt through her jeans.

She said, "Will you be taking a card, Pete?"

Pattianne hated bingo, which she didn't say, she just said no. She said, "I'll just watch."

"Okay, dear, maybe next round."

When the number-calling started, the girls all jumped up and sat at a table, and everybody else did too. They all paid close attention to the guy in the red vest, and Pattianne eased back into the pillows, almost comfortable, picturing herself as looking comfortable and at ease. She couldn't see her house out the window. She just wanted to be there, and she sent Bullfrog thoughts, forming the words clearly in her mind, one at a time: I. Will. Be. Back. Soon. The effort of thinking in sentences emptied her head, and she might as well be playing bingo.

I caused someone to die by mouthing off.

I ruined a family's life. Two families.

Three families.

I had an abortion.

She considered speaking some of these words out loud. It would be like lighting up a cigarette in church.

Mrs. Taskey caught her eye and winked.

One of the little girls at Lakshmi's table screamed, "Bingo," and Lakshmi looked over at Pattianne and rolled her eyes.

The proprietress came to her with a paper cup of cider.

Pattianne said, "Thank you."

MRS. TASKEY BENT OVER the counter, leaning on the open newspaper, doing the crossword. Pattianne said hello and kept moving, over to the rack of greeting cards. She stared for a while. Her birthday was coming up. Her father's birthday. She found a card with a sailboat on it that wasn't cutesy and walked up to the counter. Mrs. Taskey stood up and rubbed at her neck.

"So." The elbow of her pale blue sweater was black from newsprint. "How are we feeling?"

"We're fine," Pattianne said, which sounded rude, so she said, "Thank you."

Mrs. Taskey opened a cookie tin with a Currier & Ives design. "Look here." It was full of small, heart-shaped cookies.

"For your little trooper there, since he can't come in. This way he's not completely left out." And she held the tin out. "They're dog cookies, made from bone meal mostly. My little granddaughter got the recipe from the internet."

So Pattianne said thank you again, and took one, and there was an odd rush behind her eyes.

Mrs. Taskey snapped the tin shut.

"Just doing the puzzle," she said. "Makes you smart, you know. Or keeps you smart, in case you already were. Wrinkles in the brain—it's all about wrinkles in the brain. Wrinkles in the face, not good, wrinkles in the brain, good."

Pattianne put the card on the counter next to the puzzle.

"Oh, cute!"

"For my dad," she said.

"In New Jersey?" Mrs. Taskey asked. And then she said, "Well, here comes Josie—you know Josie. Well, maybe not. She drives the school bus, runs Josie House, and it's her birthday too—well, on Friday. How about that? You should come to her birthday dinner. Josie cooks the turkey, and it's potluck besides that. I'll be making apple pie. Apple with huckleberries, just a few. I sprinkle them in for color. What would you like to bring?"

A woman and two little kids came in the door. They all wore lumpy knitted scarves and caps.

Mrs. Taskey went into high gear. "Josie, Pattianne here is joining us for the Josie House potluck. It's her dad's birthday too, how about that? What should we have her bring?" She tapped the counter with her pencil.

Pattianne didn't want her to say Pattianne. She didn't want to go to dinner at the bus driver's house. She didn't know what Josie House even was, and she didn't want to know. The two kids ran down an aisle.

"Muffins! Of course!" Josie said it like it was a pronouncement, and loosened her scarf, pink and white snowflakes maybe, and unzipped her coat. "How you feeling, Pattianne?"

Josie was very pregnant.

"Okay. Thanks."

Josie rubbed her belly.

"I'm not much of a baker," Pattianne said. "I've never even lit that oven." And she held the birthday card up. "Guess I'll be off." And she escaped and tried not to let the door slam.

A short, beat-up school bus was parked outside. Bullfrog took a shot at the tires.

She wanted to write *Dearest Dad* on the card, but she didn't. They would think she was being weird. They already might. They probably all did. She tried not to think about that. She didn't think her mother and father were worried. It was surprisingly easy not to think about Michael, but she was sorry about Mrs. Bryn, and Claire, and she was too sad to think about Mr. Bryn at all. Thousands of miles, a wonderful thing, all that distance, a national border, the Strait of Juan de Fuca. A wonderful thing.

She signed the card *Love, Pattianne and Bullfrog* and put it in the envelope, and addressed it in her best handwriting, so they'd think all was well. She was just traveling, the marriage didn't work out, poor thing, she'll be fine, she'll be home soon. She held the card, knowing how far it would travel. She set it on the windowsill like a decoration, next to the big white feather.

13: SIXTEEN MILES AN HOUR

THE NEXT DAY, LAKSHMI knocked, shave-and-a-haircut, and came in with a bag, which she unloaded by dumping the contents onto the small counter. There was a carton of milk and a box of Arm & Hammer baking soda, flour in a small white bag, shortening in a squatty can. There was butter, and a red can of baking powder. There was vinegar.

Pattianna said, "What's all this stuff for?"

Lakshmi sang out, "Practice, practice, practice."

Pattianne told her she was just heading down to the beach. The rain was falling straight and steady.

"Yeah, I know," Lakshmi said. "I hate practicing anything. I used to have to practice flute but finally figured out that if I, like, practiced loud and bad, like every night, they would finally let me quit. Especially if I really practiced a lot on this one song my dad likes, like, he likes it a lot. 'Moon River'? You like banana muffins? There's some bananas down at the store that are way spotty, you know, how you use them for banana muffins. Or banana bread."

She had green glitter eye shadow today, and it had gotten on her lips. She sat down and started kissing Bullfrog, who would be glittery and green tonight.

There was another knock at the door. Pattianne pulled it open, and there stood Mrs. Taskey. A girl with pale brown braids stood behind her.

"Hello, dear. This is Barbie. Barbie, say hello. Barbie wants to help. How are you feeling today, Pattianne? Lakshmi, your father said he'd meet you at the store at five. Now you be there, down at the store," and she came in, Barbie right behind her. Barbie was maybe ten or twelve. She had small awkward breasts and a chipped tooth in front that she poked at with her tongue, staring at Pattianne, standing right there by the door.

Mrs. Taskey shook out a pink and yellow towel.

"These will look nice," she said.

The towel was decorated with ducks, or maybe teapots, and she set a folded stack of them on the counter.

Lakshmi said, "Cute," without looking up. She was actually looking closely at a single strand of her hair.

"And I brought a little hook," Mrs. Taskey said—a small, white cup hook. "How about right here, in the side by the sink, see, so handy."

Barbie moved to the edge of the bed, half sitting, half leaning. She pulled at her lower lip and didn't even look at Bullfrog, who seemed to find the wet cuff of her pants very interesting. Pattianne found Barbie's lip interesting. It seemed over-large, and it hung open, and she kept tugging at it, like maybe her lip had grown that way through years of her tugging at it like that. Bullfrog kept sniffing at her cuff, and he worked his way around her feet like he was going to lift a leg and have a shot at her.

"Now, Lakshmi, dear, do you remember how we make sour milk?"

Lakshmi was looking at her fingernail polish. Bright pink today.

"Vinegar!" Mrs. Taskey said. "Pattianne, I bet you knew that, didn't you? Barbie, don't do that, dear. Do you need a tissue? Why don't you go wash your hands?"

Lakshmi worked at her fingernail polish, chipping it off.

Mrs. Taskey said, "Let's preheat!"

Lakshmi said, "Pattianne has to do the stove," the little tick-tick of nail polish chipping off.

"We're going to make buttermilk biscuits," Mrs. Taskey said. "And we'll make sour milk with vinegar instead of buying a whole quart of buttermilk, since all we need is a half cup."

Yet another knock at the door, and Mrs. Taskey called out, "Come in."

Mr. Bleakman pushed open the door and held up two envelopes. One was long and pale-peach colored. The other was blue.

"You got to pick 'em up," he said. "No delivery, you know."

Bullfrog stopped sniffing at Barbie.

"Oh, Pattianne, you got letters, how nice. Thank you, Mr. Bleakman. Barbie, don't do that."

The envelopes were small in his big, inky fingers, and Pattianne took them out of his hand. He smelled like onions.

"While you're here, I bet you could put this nice hook into this cabinet for us, couldn't you? It's a little screw hook, but I just bet you can get it started for us, eh, girls? Please, come in. How about some tea? Should we make a pot of tea, girls?"

Lakshmi said, "Who are your letters from?"

Mr. Bleakman said, "Just work it into that hole already there."

Barbie said, "I have to go," her voice coming out low and rough.

Lakshmi said, "What kind of tea?"

Pattianne said, "I don't have a teapot."

"Here," Mrs. Taskey said, and she held the hook out to Mr. Bleakman, who was still standing with the door open. Beyond him was beautiful rain and dusk. He stepped in and pushed the door shut with one heavy, wet boot. Bullfrog went under the bed.

Barbie said, "Is that the bathroom?" pointing her finger at the open bathroom door, where the light shone on the toilet, like the toilet was just kept in there for fun and the bathroom was behind some other door that was invisible.

"You might look at the pilot light on the stove while you're here," Mrs. Taskey said. "Seems you have to light those burners with a match. Shouldn't they light when you turn on that gas?"

"Old stove," he said.

"It's number two," Barbie said.

"Is there coffee instead?" Lakshmi said. "Let's make coffee."

"You shouldn't be drinking coffee at your age, dear. How about some nice peppermint tea? Pattianne, do you have some peppermint tea?"

Lakshmi said, "Boring," and Mr. Bleakman took the hook from Mrs.

Taskey and worked it into the hole in the side of the cabinet, where it dangled.

"See, that won't do at all, will it? Let's fix it right for Pattianne as long as you're here."

Barbie said, "I have to go."

Pattianne said, "So go."

She said it a little loud maybe. Bullfrog woofed from under the bed, and the wind picked up outside.

Mrs. Taskey took Barbie by the arm and steered her into the bathroom.

"There you go," she said in a big whisper, and she came back out and closed the bathroom door very gently.

Mr. Bleakman poked his inky finger at a couple other holes in the side of the cabinet, and Pattianne slid the envelopes into her back pocket. Lakshmi unbuttoned the second button on her blouse and looked down at herself and buttoned it back up, looked at herself again. Mrs. Taskey picked up a folded pink-and-yellow duck-teapot dishtowel and fanned herself. Number two noises came from the bathroom.

"I don't have any tea," Pattianne said.

"See this nail?" Mr. Bleakman said, "Just hang what you need from this nail."

Barbie yelled, "I don't know where the flush thing is."

Lakshmi looked at Pattianne and mouthed the word *retarded*. Pattianne was shocked.

Mr. Bleakman turned to the door.

"No delivery," he said. "You got to pick it up."

He went out into the rain and dusk, and Pattianne caught the door before it shut all the way and watched him as he disappeared behind the big rock. The toilet flushed behind her.

"See here," Mrs. Taskey said. "It's a pull chain—isn't that funny. Now, let's wash our hands."

Finally, they were all gone, and it was just Pattianne and enough buttermilk biscuits to feed half the town. And they were neither ducks nor teapots, but hearts.

And the letters were not letters but cards. Another one from Mrs. Bryn. A folded note fell to the floor. She picked it up and didn't want to unfold it, but when she did, it was from Mr. Bryn.

Just come back home. Things can work out. You are united with us in the Lord Jesus Christ, who doesn't want to judge, only forgive.

The other one was from Mom and Dad. Happy birthday, with gilt and dancing parrots that seemed to be wearing top hats. *Love, Mother and Daddy*, in her mother's perfect handwriting. And below that, *to my birthday girl*, in her father's writing, thick, strong. She tried to remember ever even seeing his handwriting before. She tried not to cry. She didn't know why it should all be so sad. She didn't know why it was such a surprise.

She had never been allowed in the kitchen when her mother was cooking. Her job was cleaning up after. Her mother baked cookies every Saturday for their school lunches. She made spice cakes and angel food cakes, and she cooked dinner every night. Stuffed peppers every Thursday. Fish sticks or broiled cod on Fridays. Spaghetti sometimes, or boiled ham with green beans and potatoes, and then split pea soup with ham the next night. If Pattianne wandered into the kitchen, her mother would shake her hands and say, *I'm busy. Set the table.* Or, *You have homework to do, Pattianne.* She never liked having them in there.

Dear Mom and Dad, I'm baking biscuits with this strange Italian-looking girl who is not Italian, in a small kitchen, out here on the edge of nowhere. All is well.

THE WOMAN BEHIND THE desk in the post office took the envelope and smiled. Her two front teeth were capped and bright white in there with all her other yellowish teeth, and she smiled big, like she liked those shiny white teeth.

"Your dog out there?" she said. "He can come in here when I'm here, you know. Says 'No Dogs Allowed' and all, but I like dogs."

She dropped the envelope into a bin behind the desk.

"All the way to New Jersey, eh?"

Suddenly Pattianne wanted it back.

"Well, here," the woman said, and handed her another envelope. "He said you wouldn't be in to pick this up, but here you are, eh?" It was a long white envelope with a typed address. "So, see you at the potluck, eh? You bringing biscuits? I'm making sweet potatoes in Coke—well, RC is what she's got at the store. Sweet potatoes and yams, are they completely different? You know, I always did wonder."

Office of the Archdiocese in script in the corner.

Another woman came in then, and the woman with the teeth said, "Hey, your package is here, I was going to dial you up—well, push-button you up, I guess you should say, eh?"

Pattianne backed toward the door, ready to say goodbye in case she had to, which she didn't.

A warm, steady breeze blew in from the beach, the waves a long way out. The proprietress stood at the window of Ruby's Roadhouse, and Pattianne waved and she nodded. The sun on the water hurt her eyes, but it was just sun on the water. There was no reason to think she'd have another headache. Then again, there was no reason why she'd had the last one. She had quit taking birth control pills. The headaches should just go away.

When Jen was on the debate team, she used to go around quoting the legal definition of the word *should* whenever anyone used it: "Ought to, but not necessarily will." Great. She will not necessarily get a migraine ever again. She was just walking in the sun at the beach. The waves broke in shallow reaches on the smooth sand, and the wind smelled different somehow, like spring. Black sea grass, tangled and flat, marked high tide, and the driftwood along the back of the beach was broken and storm-beaten, bright red cedar hearts split open among the silvered logs. A half-moon, thinly white, looked like it was made of the same stuff as the high clouds. She held the blue glass vial in her hand in her pocket. Walking the beach along Wickaninnish Bay was time out of time. She never knew how long she was out here. She decided she would never check the time before and after.

Out past the foam were nets of black kelp, and around the edges of the kelp were small birds, not seagulls, smaller, and she couldn't quite see them, but she saw red and white and black stripes. Her eyes watered and everything glittered, but it was just her eyes watering. She said this to herself, to Bullfrog. "It is just my eyes watering, sun and wind," and he agreed. He thought everything was just fine and told her not to worry. Bright water, salt wind, blinking, sometimes you have to try so hard just to see. There were birds in afterimage. Dozens of birds, maybe hundreds, poking in and out of the water, with long, pointed black beaks. Here and there a single bird spinning in small circles. Yams and sweet potatoes. Turnips and rutabagas. Bird cries came over the waves, like the striking of the high keys of a piano over and over, sounding and then silenced in the wind over the water, and then she heard them again, and then Bullfrog's tags jingling. She could walk with her eyes closed.

She had come this far, the edge of the continent. She could go farther, to Alaska maybe, but this was the edge of something, and it felt safe. Nobody knew her, and she could stay here until she had just enough money left to get back to St. Cloud.

She could stay here and be quietly sorry and keep her mouth shut. She came this far to think about it all, and now she found she could be here and just not think, and just not do anything, not do anything wrong. She had run away from home. She wondered how long her money would last. She wondered if she could still get that full-time library job in St. Cloud. She wondered what it would take to change her name back.

She carried these ashes, and she would throw them into the silver tide, the first night she saw such a thing.

It was possible to run away from home. The world was a big enough place to be alone. She didn't want adventure and travel and escape. She just wanted this. An old dog, a small house. A bathtub would be nice.

Bullfrog found the path through the woods to the convenience store. She followed. The woods were still, except for two of the big crows making their strange knocking noise. Bullfrog bounced on his front feet, sniffed the air for the big dog chained up at the trailer. The air off the beach was quiet and still. The big dog wasn't there.

The air in the convenience store was dry with a cardboard smell, and something like cherry, some vague, convenience-store smell. The Chinese man sat behind the counter. His face was wet with tears, not even maybe rain this time, definitely tears. His eyes were all red. He sat behind the counter staring upward. Then he looked at her and shook his head.

"Silly Laura," he said. "She thinks Jake will never learn of her affair with William. And how is she to explain the dark skin of her child?"

"I'm sorry?"

"Jake's mother Anna will tell him, of course, she is hard-hearted and shrewd. And then Jake will have an excuse to fire William. But what is to become of William's young sister Deborah, who is, after all, Jake's half-sister? Anna does not know this. We shall see how it comes to light."

Loud, symphonic music filled the air, and the Chinese man aimed the remote at a television behind the counter, muting it.

"Next is *Young and the Restless*," he said. "Not to my liking." He wiped his face with his sleeve.

"Oh," she said. "Well, coffee? I was just out walking."

She gave him two quarters. He held them up and said, "Very good."

The coffee in the Styrofoam cup was worth two quarters just to warm her fingers.

"Cold," she said.

"And did you get to enjoy the snow?"

"No."

Her arm trembled, a small shake from shoulder to hand. She set the coffee on the counter and picked it back up.

"Crazy weather. Here," he said, pointing to another stool at the end of the counter. "Please," he said.

She sat. Her leg muscles pulsed from walking in the sand. A nice place to be. Bullfrog sat outside, looking around, his ears blowing, his nose bobbing, reading the wind. The Chinese man changed the channel and turned the sound back up. He moved the wire rabbit ears and turned the small screen so she could see it. The picture was black and white, an empty courtroom, dramatic music coming out in small, tinny tones and names appeared. *Perry Mason.* She remembered watching it when she was little, home sick from school, her mother giving her crackers and ginger ale.

"Ah," he said. "Today we get Hamilton Burger. That other DA bugs me."

Della Street walked briskly into Perry Mason's elegant office, her skirt pencil-slim, her hair sleek and bouffant.

"Ham Burger," Pattianne said. "I get it."

The Chinese man nodded and watched the screen. She scooted her stool a little closer, right next to him. He had dried shaving cream behind his ear. A large car drove up a dark mountain road, the lights of LA in the distance. The car pulled up outside a fancy house, no lights on in the house, and the music stopped when a tall man in a hat and suit got quickly out of the car. The front door of the convenience store opened, and a young man in a striped shirt pushed in a hand truck, loaded with cases of beer.

"Hmm." The Chinese man got up, still watching the screen. "Please, stay right here. Watch carefully." He followed the beer-truck driver to the back of the store. The man with the suit and hat had gone inside the house, but he didn't turn on any lights, and another car was driving slowly up the road toward the house. A gunshot rang out as the Chinese man hurried up the cookie aisle.

"I think that guy in the hat shot someone. But he hasn't come out yet."

"Not him." He looked at the Doritos clock on the wall over the door. "Too soon for the murderer to appear."

A door in the back of an office opened, and Paul Drake walked in and sat across from Perry, crossed his leg, lit a cigarette.

The Chinese man said, "Ten minutes at least before we see the face of the murderer."

She wanted to know his name. She didn't know how to ask him. She told him hers.

"I'm Pete."

He turned his face to her. He had black eyes, tired eyelids, old eyes. The whites were dim.

"Li," he said. He smiled, and his eyes disappeared for a moment, looked older. "Glad for the company." Paul Drake and Perry looked concerned.

The beer-truck driver came up the cookie aisle and looked over the counter. "Jake find out about Laura and William yet?"

Mr. Li shook his head as Della approached Perry's huge, orderly desk. Paul said, "Hello Beautiful," and Della rolled her eyes at him and announced an important phone call. The beer guy put a bill on the counter. Li looked up at the Doritos clock.

"This will be the wrongfully accused on the phone. Did you see who was in that other car?"

"No. Sorry."

He raised his hand, dismissing her apology.

The beer guy said, "I've seen this one before."

Li raised his hand, dismissing the beer-truck driver.

And there she was, in this place at the far edge of the continent, doing this ordinary thing that felt like being home from school sick when she was little. At the end of the show, all was well, and Della was perched on Perry's desk, admiring his performance in court.

Pattianne was invited back.

"Every weekday," Li said. "Two o'clock."

She and Bullfrog walked back along the highway, walking slower than on the beach. There was no wind, just easy, tired walking home, just walking, courtroom music in her head, the wonder of Della Street. The wonder of that dried bit of shaving cream behind that small ear like a shell. She came to the church. The sign by the road was grown over with sapling alders. A deserted bird nest hung in the thin branches. She walked quietly on.

When they got to the farmers' market, Bullfrog made his move, trotting right up to the wooden steps. There was an open trash can there. Bullfrog never seemed to forget an open trash can. He circled it and gave it a couple squirts. Inside, two women near the apples watched the man behind the counter, and another woman with a little kid in her arms watched him too. They all looked at Pattianne, as if they had been expecting her and she had finally arrived. She filled a paper bag with purple plums. The two women were still choosing apples when she left. Bullfrog sat on the steps, his nose working the air around the trash can.

The plum skin made her teeth shiver. She spit out a pit, and Bullfrog chased it down and carried it in his mouth for a way along the road.

Back home, she propped the birthday card with the dancing parrots in their top hats on the windowsill. Then she opened the envelope with the name there, typed, Pattianne Anthony Bryn. Her parents' names, Michael's name. None of those names was hers.

First, there would be a marriage tribunal, so Michael could receive Communion when they divorced. For an annulment, she must return to her archdiocese. As if she had one. As if she had either a name or an archdiocese. She put the letter in the second drawer, with the card from Michael's mother, with the note from his father.

She was still married. She felt around inside herself for where there was meaning in that, in her stomach, in her chest. Nana Farley had a pink glass cake cover, a round dome that closed the cake off from the world. Sometimes the inside of the cake cover got moist, like the cake was breathing.

Bullfrog was curled in a tight circle on his blanket, his chin down, his eyes open. His eyebrows were busy, keeping track of her, and she paced from the door to the window and back again, Bullfrog always keeping track of her. His eyebrows were going white with his oldness, a word her word processor once underlined with a noisy red squiggle. Not legal in Scrabble either. She always thought oldness should be a word. Jen let her use it once, and then, after Pattianne beat her by not very many points, told her that it wasn't in the Scrabble dictionary. This place had an oldness about it. She felt an oldness here, around her, in her. She could get old in a place like this. Maybe it would only take patience after all, and not years and years of struggle to do some right thing that would stay right.

She was married for all eternity. She was not married at all. She was married until she admitted that she had an archdiocese. She knew what was true, that she married within the context of a lie, and that the marriage didn't have to count. It depended on what bishop they went to. Michael said he never lied, never killed an unborn baby that he would have named for his father. For himself. How many babies there might have been, all those times they had sex, every time Michael believing, and every time her thwarting God's plans for new life.

She sat on the step eating plums, spitting the plum pits out onto the grass. Bullfrog came and sat next to her. He was still all perfumed. He watched each plum pit land in the grass and finally went down the steps, sniffed one out, picked it up, and carried it up the steps and inside. She leaned back against the doorway and closed her eyes, and thought of her father, his birthday. She kissed her parents on the cheek good night every night until fifth grade. Then one night she went to bed without kissing them. She remembered that night, being in her room, putting on purple pajamas, realizing she hadn't kissed them good night, and deciding not to go back downstairs to do it. Purple pajamas with blue hearts. She'd never kissed them good night again.

She opened her eyes to a black sky of storm clouds lit by the moon and moving fast, opening to breaks of starry patches, and then clouding over. No wind down low.

She had never been one to just doze off, and now it wasn't even weird. She just seemed to let herself drift off into some dream that was already there waiting for her. And when she woke, she felt happy.

All this space around her was like suddenly having a bed and all the blankets to herself. Until she realized she should be thinking hard about what to do with Michael. He crowded in on her. It was only right.

MICHAEL. SHE DIDN'T WANT to burn the envelopes, and she didn't want to throw them in the trash, but she didn't want them in that drawer. She went inside and took them out and put them in her pocket. She left Bullfrog curled up on his blanket, didn't even look at him, just left. There were lights on in the guest rooms upstairs at Ruby's Roadhouse, but the lobby was dark. Bullfrog would be glad she hadn't invited him to come along. She should have pointed this out to him.

It was warm and windy on the beach. She took one letter out of the bundle and tore off a corner of the envelope. It was the one with the card in it from Michael's mother. She had no feeling in her fingertips. The small piece of the envelope blew away in an instant, flying away in the dark, gone. She didn't even have to let go of it, the wind just took it.

The wind took every piece of every one.

Bright clouds lit by the moon, and black sky with stars, and wind blowing from everywhere. The tide maybe coming in, and sneaker waves that could curl over you and crash against the driftwood and rocks. Or maybe the tide was going out, with riptides that could rise slowly, and then faster and faster around your legs, and suck you down and drag you out to sea. The water was all dark noise, and if it wanted her, it could have her. She wouldn't even have to let go.

THE BLUE LETTERS OF the OPEN sign flashed, and the lights inside the store lit up the parking lot, shining on a red minivan. Everything was hard-edged with white light when she stepped in out of the darkness. Father Lucke sat in the lawn chair behind the counter wearing a red cardigan. Bright red. The television set was not turned on.

"Hello?" she said. "Hello. I mean, isn't Mr. Li here?"

He had a cigar in one hand, and in the other, he held up a china teacup with yellow roses on it. He said, "Hello to you too." His pinky finger curved above the thin handle.

Mr. Li came up the cookie aisle, carrying a teapot. "Pete," he said. "At one in the morning."

"One in the morning?"

"Not too many customers this time of night," he said, and he poured tea into Father Lucke's cup. The pot had one big yellow rose on it, and he held it up, a question.

"No, thank you," she said. "I don't like tea, but thank you." And she wished she did like tea. She wanted something from him, something his small fingers had touched. She wondered if one in the morning was either too early or too late to start a pot of coffee.

"Not tea," he said. "Bourbon toddy. A little spearmint leaf, a little lemon juice."

"And hot water, of course," Father Lucke said, raising his teacup, his fat pinky finger raised, his fat smiling face raised. He had your basic shining countenance. "It's not terribly strong." That giggle. A gust blew hard against the front of the store. "Looks like we're in for a bit of a blow. South wind."

"But with rain," Mr. Li said. "Not too bad a windstorm if there is already rain."

He turned a wire milk case upside down, pushed it against the wall, set a stack of *West Side Signals* on it. His tan loafers were side by side on the floor. He wore thick white socks. "Please," he said to her. "A seat?"

And Father Lucke said, "Doesn't look like much rain to me."

She draped her jacket over the wastebasket and accepted the seat from Mr. Li. He poured bourbon toddy into another teacup and handed it to her, and their fingers touched when she took the small cup. She couldn't speak to say thank you, leaned back against the warm, hard, solid wall.

He picked up a cigar from an ashtray and said, "It's gusting."

"Gusting counts?" Father Lucke said.

"Gusting counts," he said.

She said, "Gusting counts?"

Mr. Li lit the burnt end of the cigar with a plastic lighter, puffing the smoke gently. He said, "Of course gusting counts," and he looked closely at the end of the cigar. He looked from the cigar to her. "As rain," he said. "Gusting counts as rain."

She breathed in the steam from the teacup, the smell of bourbon, the smell of being too young to drink, too young to like the taste of whiskey, sneaking her father's bourbon, mixing it with Coke. There was maybe a little lemon in these toddies, maybe a little spearmint, but a lot of bourbon. They seemed to be on at least their second pot.

"My father used to drink bourbon," she said. He'd switched to scotch at some point. She wondered when, wondered why. Things you don't know about your parents.

Father Lucke held his cup up again. "To your father."

Mr. Li did the same. "To your father."

Her eyes watered, and sadness surprised her, frightened her. She wanted to ask her father when he'd switched to scotch, and why. She sipped the hot bourbon, noisily, as did Father Lucke, noisy also.

He said, "My mother was a bourbon drinker," and he held his teacup aloft once more. "She would have a little bourbon and White Rock ginger ale." He nodded. Sighed. Sipped. "Actually," he said, "she would have many little bourbons with White Rock ginger ale. Had to be White Rock."

"A sad story," Mr. Li said. "Please don't feel you have to retell it on our account."

"No indeed," Father Lucke said. And then they both said, "It is tiresome to be the hero of a sad story."

Pattianne understood that she was in the middle of an ongoing conversation between drinking buddies. Her story chakra engaged. She could sit back on her stack of *West Side Signals* and be the listener at the end of the bar, the sneaky kid behind the dining room door, the librarian who didn't really need to know why the book that was already checked out by someone else was so important, but would listen and understand. Stories came her way if she sat very still and didn't breathe too loud. Michael had stopped telling stories. Michael had traded in all his stories for one story.

"Now," Father Lucke said, "you are just in time, Pete." His face perked into a bright and somewhat toothy smile. "May I call you Pete?"

"Please do," she said, like they were good friends and he was funny. Then she said, "And what may I call you?" Like they really were good friends.

"John," he said.

"John?"

"No," he said. "I am not John. I am Brother Tim-Tim, actually."

"You're not a priest?"

Mr. Li snorted, and he said, "Here we go." He bent to get a Scrabble game from a low shelf.

"I am what you might call a soon-to-be-former priest," Father Lucke said. "Back to being the baby brother of five sisters who chose to name me Timothy. But really, how well do you know John?"

"John?"

"Compared to Matthew, Mark, or Luke."

The Doritos clock whirred gently, and the wind gusted significantly, and suddenly she wanted to go back out into the night. They were drinking bourbon and discussing the the apostles and trying to keep their cigars lit.

"I don't." she said. "Know John. At all." But he wore a collar. "Why are you soon-to-be-ex?" She was being brave and rude, and she wondered if Mrs. Taskey knew he was really Brother Tim-Tim.

Father Lucke waved his cigar and said, "See? The apostle John was a poet among men, and no one appreciates him." His cigar was unlit.

Mr. Li opened the ragged lid of the box and Scrabble tiles rattled. He said, "Mr. Metaphor."

Father Lucke nodded and sipped. "It is now past three in the morning in Minnesota."

Pattianne was afraid of the very word Minnesota.

"In two hours," he said, "I can call my dear old friend Brother Jude, and we can ask him his opinion."

Mr. Li loved that. He laughed a loud hoot that surprised her, made her want to stay here with them after all, and he said, "Yes, do that, Father Lucke. I want you to get another one of those official letters."

Father Lucke said, "We can call him at the seminary office."

Mr. Li stood up, his knees cracked, and he said, "Meanwhile, there is a door to lock, and then Scrabble can commence."

He went around the counter, sliding in his socks, to the front door, and if she were going to leave, it would have to be now.

She asked, "Why lock the door to play Scrabble?"

"Supposed to be locked in the first place," he said. He looked out into the dark through the windows. "Store closes at midnight. I have been remiss in my closing duties." He turned a lock. It looked like she was staying.

"Resulting in your own honored presence." Father Lucke raised his teacup to her. "Li, my friend," he said, "the sign."

Mr. Li switched off the blue neon OPEN sign. Another switch darkened the front of the store. The Doritos clock was the only hum now. A beer sign with a silver running stream caught the light from a single fluorescent light over the cigarette rack.

"A little three-handed Scrabble?"

Mr. Li slid back across the floor, and he pulled a folding table out of nowhere, unfolded the legs quick as Elizabeth making paper birds. The table took up most of the space behind the counter. Father Lucke sat back in his lawn chair, and he pulled the piece of stiff white cloth out of the front of his collar and slipped it into the pocket of his black shirt. It stuck up like a bookmark there in his pocket. He unbuttoned the top button, a plain black button-down shirt now.

Pattianne asked Brother Timothy a question.

"What's that thing called?"

He pulled it back out of his pocket and looked at it, his round face gone sad. "Collar tab."

"Oh." It seemed like such an important thing. Like it would have a more important name. Chasuble, alb, cincture, amice.

He slipped it back into the pocket, his pink hand resting there a moment, over the pocket, over his heart, the heart of a priest. Sighed. Patted his pocket. It was important to have people you don't like in your life, and she didn't want a drunk, soon-to-be-ex priest to be sad, not if they were all locked in this place playing Scrabble in a storm.

"It looks like it would make a nice bookmark," she said. He was part of her life. This was her life at the moment. Playing Scrabble with drunk old men who weren't that much older than she was.

She took pride in not being a sad drunk. Angela had been one of the perkiest, happiest drinkers she ever met. Suddenly Pattianne was a sad drunk.

Father Lucke offered the bag of tiles, a purple velvet bag with a gold drawstring, Crown Royal, and she drew an *M*. Mr. Li drew an *L*. Father Lucke drew a *B*. The wind gusted hard against the front window. The Doritos clock hummed. The Scrabble game commenced.

Father Lucke spelled out WORD and shouted, "Ha! Thirty-two!"

"In the beginning was the Word, and the Word was with God, and the Word was God," he said, and drew his new tiles out of the Crown Royal bag.

Pattiannne said, "Wait. I count sixteen."

Mr. Li leaned closer to her. "Double points if you open with something from Genesis." There was the sweet scent of tea and bourbon on his breath.

She leaned close too.

"Okay," she said. Private rules for Scrabble.

He leaned even closer and said, "He always manages to open with a word from Genesis."

Father Lucke arranged his tiles and then sat back. "The archdiocese of Prince Edward Island may not be very happy with me, but someone else is." And he rearranged his tiles.

Mr. Li had smudges of ink on his fingers. He was left-handed. He spelled out TRUTH, using the R in WORD and landing the T on a triple-letter score for ten points.

"You will know the truth, and the truth will set you free," he said. "Twenty points."

She felt the bourbon in her brain, but she still only figured ten points.

Mr. Li held up one inky finger. "One who acts on truth is happy in this world and beyond." He wrote down twenty points. "Dhammadapa," he said.

Bullfrog was a long way up the dark beach.

She said, "So, what the fuck?" and was embarrassed, and had perhaps had a little more bourbon than she'd thought.

"The Sutras," Father Lucke said. His fingers were busy clicking and rearranging his tiles on the rack.

Father Lucke stared at his letters. Mr. Li arranged his own letters and then sat back and looked at his cigar. Father Lucke spelled out WATER, and he said, "No one can enter the kingdom of God without being born of water and the Spirit."

She was beginning to get annoyed, but then she realized that she had REX, landing on a double-word score.

"Twenty points," Mr. Li said. "Very good." He picked up the lighter and puffed at his cigar, his thin fingers making shadows on his face. "There are two gifts. Carnal and spiritual. Itivuttaka."

She couldn't stand it. She didn't want to ask. Sometimes secrets like that made her not care more than she might care otherwise, but now two words were involved—*dapa*-whatever, and now this one, *itivuttaka*. She said, "What are you guys talking about?"

"Penance for the sin of racism," Mr. Li said. He laid his cigar in the dish and leaned back and steepled his fingers. He was watching Father Lucke, who stared at his letters. "We have chosen the gospel of John for tonight," Mr. Li went on. "Double points for every significant word from the gospel of John." He picked up the teapot and freshened her cup, then Father Lucke's, then his own. "However, if I can quote a parallel saying from the Buddhist tradition, he loses those points, and I get them."

"Racism?"

"Mea culpa," Father Lucke said. "Mea maxima culpa." He looked at the end of his cigar and Mr. Li handed him the lighter. Father Lucke said, "These cigars are not doing it for me," and he put his cigar in the dish and stood up, reaching across Mr. Li's head and pulling a pack of Marlboros out of the rack. "I owe you," he said. He sat back down, tore open the pack, and said, "So, to continue, I made the egregious error of assuming . . ."

"On the basis of my racial heritage," Mr. Li said.

"On the basis of Li Song's racial heritage," Father Lucke said, "I assumed he had an understanding of Buddhism."

Li Song. He hooted. "Incorrect," he said. "You assumed I was a Buddhist. Not to mention Chinese." It was a hoot like a small animal on a nature show.

Father Lucke bowed his head. "Mea culpa." He hiccupped.

"And you're not," she said to Li Song.

"Correct," Mr. Li Song said. "Was. Baptist. And Korean, not Chinese."

Korean.

"Which means he can kick my butt on the Bible," Father Lucke said.

"Okay," she said. "I think I get it. But I have one question. Well, two."

Father Lucke's cheeks were ridiculously pink now. Mr. Li Song leaned one elbow on the table, and he looked like he always did until the elbow slipped off the table and he pretended it hadn't but then said, "Damn card table."

"Why was it cheating to start with *WORD*?"

"It was not cheating, because I did not give him the double points for opening with Genesis." Mr. Li Song leaned back and gave Father Lucke, a slippery smile. "John is not the author of Genesis."

"But," Father Lucke said, holding up one finger, "he was referring to Genesis with that."

"Exegesis. Not in the spirit of the game."

Father Lucke twisted in his seat to see the Doritos clock. "We shall see," he said. "It will soon be daybreak in St. Paul." He leaned over to her, leaning dangerously sideways in the lawn chair. "The city," he said. "Not the apostle."

"Exegesis?"

"A furthering of the allegory," Mr. Li Song said, "on a drunken whim."

Both cigars were dead in the ashtray, and she played with her own pack of Marlboros, the pack that had been living so happily in her pocket for so long.

"So," she said, "you were never really Buddhist?" She tore off the cellophane, feeling reckless and thinking she was not really going to smoke one. Mr. Li Song pushed the ashtray toward her.

Father Lucke said, "That's three questions."

And Mr. Li Song said to him, "The one about exegesis was an interjection." He looked at her and said, "Correct?"

She said yes, but she was not sure why. They'd lost her.

Mr. Li Song nodded to Father Lucke, then closed his eyes and slowly shook his head no. "Never Buddhist," he said. He opened his eyes.

"You just happen to know all those sayings?"

"Berkeley," he said. "1969. I was in the physics department. But Buddhism was in the air."

Mr. Li Song young, in the sixties. She tried to do the math. Gave up.

"In Berkeley," he said. "In the sixties, if you could quote the Sutras, they saw the Spirit descending from heaven like a dove, and it abode upon you."

Father Lucke pouted. "That was a stretch," he said. "And you are a show-off."

"John," Mr. Li Song said to her, "chapter 1, verse 32." He nodded at her. "Your turn."

But she didn't know any Bible stuff, and her butt ached from sitting on the newspapers, and she hated bourbon.

"I don't know any Bible stuff."

Mr. Li Song reached out and touched her elbow. "No," he said. "We will restrain ourselves. We will simply play Scrabble. Everybody's rules. We don't want to leave you out." He untouched her. "That simply will not do."

"And this bourbon," she said. "This bourbon needs more sugar."

They both nodded, and Father Lucke said, "If I may, I have a question for you."

"As do I," said Mr. Li Song.

She waited. They both looked at each other. They both said, "Where's Bullfrog?"

"Sleeping. Home. Blanket."

Nods.

Jen once gave her a birthday gift of a calligraphed piece of legal two-letter Scrabble words, plus one which was not legal. Pattianne still didn't know which word was not legal.

By the time the teapot had been emptied and filled and emptied again, she had beaten them both. Rain gusted. Father Lucke took his leave, saying, "I must take my leave," and pushing himself up out of the lawn chair.

Mr. Li Song stood up, too, and he said, "Wait, I have that book for you," and he slid down the cookie aisle in his socks.

Father Lucke held his hand out to her to help her up, and she realized she had become one with the stack of *West Side Signals*. She took his hand, and it was cool. She expected something so fat and pink to be warm and damp. He kept her hand in his, she pulled away, and he pulled back and said, "I'm glad you came."

She didn't know if he meant to Tofino or to the convenience store.

He said, "I would be happy to offer you a ride to the village." And he returned her hand to her and took his jacket from the counter.

Mr. Li Song came sliding back up the aisle to Father Lucke and put a paperback book in his hand. Erle Stanley Gardner. Father Lucke took it and walked to the door, and he seemed steady enough at least to steer the minivan down the highway to Tofino. He turned the key in the lock and opened the door to the sound of the night and the rain.

Mr. Li Song picked up her jacket from the wastebasket and held it up. She reached for it and he reached too, around her, draping it around her shoulders. Then he leaned to her and kissed her on the forehead, one sweet, bourbon-scented kiss.

The minivan revved outside, and the headlights came on and lit up the store.

"Good night, Li Song," she said.

"Traveling mercies," he said. "Sweet dreams."

She climbed into the front seat of the minivan and buckled the seat belt. Then she had to unbuckle it to reach out and pull the door shut. "Are you okay to drive?"

Father Lucke said, "May the Lord bless us on our travels." He backed out and pulled gently onto the road, checked in his mirror, and said, "So far, so good." The speedometer indicated between 22 and 25.

"Nice van," she said.

"Western Provinces Outer Parishes Transportation Project," he said, and he patted the dashboard. "If we had more First Nation People on our list, I could have got us a full-size."

The right wheels were on the shoulder and the left wheels on the road, the gravel sound under the tires reassuring. It was steady. It was warm, and the seat was a big easy chair after the stack of *West Side Signals*. It was quiet in the van.

"So. Brother Tim-Tim."

It was drunk in the van.

He giggled.

"What kind of a priest are you?"

He was driving by the light of the brights, and the road was a lovely curve of black and white and silvery wet brush.

He said, "I'd say conservative."

"Right."

"Okay," he said. "Ultra-conservative."

"Ultra-conservative."

"Pre-enlightenment?" he said. "Pre-papal power plays? Pre-Catholic?" He was leaning over the steering wheel, and they were only going about twenty. "How about a priest who has chosen to break my vow of obedience in favor of being a follower of Christ?"

He had one eye closed.

"Are you all right to drive?"

"I am," he said. "A metaphorical priest?"

"Metaphorical?"

"I would say," he said, and then he didn't say, he drove, aiming the van carefully at the road.

"I would say," he said. "I would say that most people confuse truth with fact. This devalues metaphor."

"What?"

"Metaphoric priest."

The speedometer showed an even eighteen.

"The gospels?" he said. "The love that followed Jesus? The passion he incited with his social message? Piece of cake for God. A miracle for a man."

"So you don't believe those stories?"

"Ah," he said. The speedometer jumped back to twenty. "The stories. Well. The Bible is a source of great wonder. All you have to do is read it, and you begin to wonder. You wonder how it could possibly be true, or what if it is true, or how could anyone believe it is true. Then you find yourself wondering about the nature of belief itself. A wondrous thing. You find yourself wondering about God."

The church came up on the left, in the darkness, and she felt like she might throw up, and Brother Tim-Tim slowed down, and they both watched it go by.

"You know," he said. "Believe means 'to love.'"

She breathed in, breathed out, swallowed. She was weeping silently.

"No," she said. "I didn't know that."

"Old High German," he said softly. He touched her knee with one soft hand. "Maybe, Middle German. *Lief*, to hold dear."

He put both hands back on the wheel. They were down to sixteen miles an hour.

"I believe in those stories," he said. His voice was deeper, quieter. He was speaking carefully, speaking to her. "I love wondering about them. I believe it's terribly, awesomely important to wonder."

He didn't sound drunk anymore, and she was not drunk either, she was exhausted, and she wanted to lie awake in the dark and listen to Bullfrog snore, wait for the first cries of the five-o'clock birds, and then the sounds of Tofino waking up.

"My husband believes those stories."

Father Lucke just nodded.

"Yes," he said. "Catholic?"

They were doing about twelve now, and he turned down toward town.

"He wants an annulment," she said.

Tofino was dark, except for a light in the lobby of Ruby's Roadhouse and the light in her house behind the rock.

He smiled and turned to her, and it was a tired smile, or maybe a drunk smile.

"And you don't?"

"I don't know."

He stopped the van in front of the post office. "You know, I don't like our Holy Father very much," he said. "He seems to favor exclusionary tactics. One of them was an encyclical, 1992. Divorced Catholics may not receive communion. Although annulled marriages don't count."

So she had to do the whole marriage tribunal thing. To admit she had an archdiocese. It was the way to make it right for Michael.

14: IT SEEMED SO SIMPLE

THE SIGN ON THE back wall was black marker on bright orange paper: Rain Gear for All. Mrs. Taskey leaned on the counter, both elbows on the Vancouver newspaper.

"Good morning there," she said, looking through the top half of her glasses.

It was afternoon.

There were yellow raincoats for kids, olive-green raincoats for grown-ups, and rain hats for all, green ones that went over your head and then stuck out over the back of your neck. When Pattianne stood in front of the counter, her hands full of rain gear, Mrs. Taskey straightened herself up, and one hand went to her back down low. She poked at the puzzle with her pencil.

"Do you know a three-letter word for a river island? The middle letter might be I."

"No." Stingy with good Scrabble words, an old habit. Jen was vicious when it came to Scrabble, and Pattianne would never do a crossword puzzle in pencil. "Sorry."

The rubber rain gear was the smell of second grade.

The pencil went into an apron pocket—it was the pink rickrack today—and Mrs. Taskey said, "How's your cough?"

"I don't have a cough."

"You can't be too careful," she said. "Do you have a good wool muffler?" Wool scarves on a coat hanger hung from the cigarette rack. Lumpy and hand-knitted and quite colorful in a preschool sort of way. Mrs. Taskey stroked a yellow-and-red one with her finger. "This is Josie's work," and she turned around a paper sign pinned to a yellow-and-yellow-and-yellow-striped scarf. COMMUNITY FUN RAISER in red crayon letters, and under that, a red crayon happy face.

"I don't like wool," Pattianne said. "Itchy." And she couldn't remember which box the purple-and-blue crocheted scarf from Aunt Shirley ended up in.

Mrs. Taskey pulled a long black hair out of a pink-and-orange scarf and held it up to the light. "Lakshmi!" she said. "You know, pink is the navy blue of India. It just seems to be the basic color."

Pattianne wouldn't be here long enough to come up against her in Scrabble.

"Try *ait*," she said.

"Eight what?"

"A-I-T."

She bought the Vancouver newspaper with the crossword and went back home and waited for the night that might bring a silver tide, and while she waited, she fed the fire small sticks that popped and smoked, and worked on the crossword. And Bullfrog slept in his favorite spot of the day, which today was halfway between the bed and the door.

She had not waited for long when Lakshmi banged on the door. She knew it was Lakshmi because of her clever personal knock, shave-and-a-haircut. This time a smaller version of Lakshmi stood there too. Pattianne caught a glimpse of her as Lakshmi pushed the door open and stepped in, and the door banged against the wall and then swung shut, shutting the smaller girl out.

"Sugarlips," Lakshmi sang out, her backpack landing on the floor, and she dropped to her knees in front of him. He wagged. "I've brought you cookies," she kept singing to him. More wags, *cookie* being one of his words.

"You should open the door," Pattianne said.

"What?"

"Open the door. Your cousin-sister-friend-sidekick-whatever is still outside."

Lakshmi got up and opened the door to the girl, who hadn't moved, and said, "What are you doing out there?" She stepped aside and said, "Come on in. This is him. Sugarlips. His real name is, like, Bullfrog. Well, actually, I think his real name is Sugarlips, but she calls him Bullfrog." The girl had dark golden skin and a sweet little pointy nose. She came in and stood just inside the open door.

Lakshmi picked up her backpack and tossed it onto the bed, took the backpack off the girl's thin shoulders and tossed it there too. "I have cookies," she sang, and bounced onto the bed and unzipped her backpack, and started reaching around in there.

"You're getting my bed all wet."

"Just your sleeping bag," Lakshmi said, and to the girl, "She sleeps in her sleeping bag, like, all the time? Like she's camping out. Here, Sugarlips," and she got back down on the floor and held out a Milk-Bone. The wind got at the fire, cold wet wind, and Pattianne put down the crossword as loud as she could, which was not loud enough to do any good. "Close that door."

"Close the door, Maya," Lakshmi said. "It's really smoky in here." She let Bullfrog slobber up one of the cookies out of her hand. "Our Auntie Lovey smokes those clove cigarettes?" she said. "It gets all smoky in her room, like in layers." Maya finally closed the door.

"This is Maya," she said. "She's in second grade now."

Lakshmi got back up and fell backward onto the bed.

"That jacket of yours is all wet," Pattianne said, and Lakshmi wiggled out of it and pushed it into a pile next to the pillow. She grabbed her backpack, and she said, "Okay, now, look here, girlfriends."

It was a makeup kit, a big clear plastic purse full of bottles and brushes and nail polish and who knows what.

"Maya, let's put makeup on you." This got a reaction. Maya smiled and pulled off her own soaking-wet jacket, dropped it on the floor, and bounced onto the bed next to Lakshmi. She even spoke. "I'm not allowed," she said. "Uncle Kamal said no, not until fourteen. Not even lipstick." Her white sweatshirt had streaks of something, yellow, pink, blue, smeared down the front.

Lakshmi dumped the contents of the makeup kit onto the bed.

"Hey," Pattianne said. Besides makeup and nail polish and an enormous pink comb, there were gum wrappers, colored pencils, a can of hair spray, and what looked like a piece of Josie's knitting, pink and orange stripes, one long string of which went back inside the backpack.

"Don't you have a big mirror?" Lakshmi said.

"No. Listen, is your father coming here to get you?"

Lakshmi pulled on the long string until she got the end of it out, and she gave Bullfrog a look. "Does Bullfrog ever wear, like, outfits?"

"I want eye shadow," Maya said. "And eyelashes."

She had thick dark eyelashes that ringed her eyes like stars.

"Let's start with some lips," Lakshmi said, and she uncapped a tube of bright pink lipstick.

"What's the name of that lipstick?" Pattianne asked her.

Lakshmi looked at the bottom of the tube, looked at the top, said, "Number 651."

Pattianne hated that, when nail polish or lipstick had boring numbers instead of names. "That's boring."

Maya's delicate black eyebrows frowned for a second and Lakshmi pulled her by the chin and said, "Look this way." And to Pattianne, "So, what, are you in a bad mood?" Maya shook her head, her long black hair in its ponytail swinging back and forth, and Lakshmi said, "Not you. Her. You be still," and she carefully touched pink on Maya's lips.

Yes, Pattianne was in a bad mood. Her sleeping bag was getting all wet, and she wanted to do the crossword. She poked at the fire and smoke puffed out.

Lakshmi turned Maya around by her shoulders and pulled up the long black ponytail into a twist. Maya was facing Pattianne, who watched the long hair flip and twist, and Maya was watching her, smiling an amazing, sweet smile, this happy girl sitting on her bed, but then she squealed and grabbed at her hair. "Hey, hurting me."

Lakshmi slapped at Maya's hand and said, "Stand still."

Maya did, the sweet smile instantly back there on her face, just for Pattianne, because it didn't really hurt, because Pattianne was watching, because they were in cahoots somehow.

Lakshmi poked a long clip into the hair, and then grabbed the can of hair spray. "Close your eyes." And she fogged the whole room with the smell of cherries and flowers and some rat-killer kind of smell.

Pattianne said, "Quit spraying that stuff." Said it kind of loud.

Bullfrog headed under the bed.

Maya opened her eyes and blinked in the cloud of hair spray.

Lakshmi said, "Just a touch here."

Pattianne said, "That stuff fucking stinks."

Lakshmi sprayed Maya's bangs, and Maya, whose eyes were wide open now, squealed for real this time and knocked the hair spray out of Lakshmi's hand. It went rolling across the floor, and Maya started to cry.

"You got it all in my eyes."

Lakshmi said, "I told you to close your eyes. Why didn't you close your eyes?"

And Maya was off the bed and over to Pattianne's chair. "She got it all in my eyes." Big tears, and she wiggled in between Pattianne's legs and was practically on her lap with her face pressed against her, crying.

Pattianne went, "Shhh," rubbing her hand up Maya's backbone and down—bones like beads under the white sweatshirt. "Sh, let me see," she whispered, and Maya shook her head no and cried harder, and Pattianne said, "Don't rub your eyes."

Lakshmi sat still on the bed. Her face was one of patience. She said, "Sorry," like she was not really all that sorry, but it worked. The crying quieted a little, and Maya rubbed her eyes.

Pattianne took the small fist and held it. Small knucklebones.

"Rubbing will make it worse," she said, her face close to Maya's face, and she could taste the hair spray. "Just blink."

Maya did. Tears gathered on her thick eyelashes, and her eyes were red. The irises of her eyes were so dark they were black, no pupil, just big black eyes full of tears and red.

She said, "You said the F word."

Pattianne pulled her head close to her heart again. Holding a child, and here it is, more pain in the world. Hearts don't break. She had said the F word. She was a fuck up.

"I shouldn't have said that," she whispered. She was hiding her face from both of them. She was hiding her face from the world. Maya was so small. Pattianne was so afraid for her.

"I'm sorry," she said. She touched Maya's tears. "You want a cookie?"

"What kind?"

She had shortbread cookies in a tin and stale gingersnaps.

Lakshmi said, "We should go get chocolate-chocolate-chip cookies at Ruby's."

Maya looked hopeful. But no way was Pattianne going back out into the world. She was exhausted. She stood up tall and wrapped one of the dish towels around her head and put her hands on her hips.

"No dogs at Ruby's Roadhouse," she said, in a tall-woman, dark-skinned, singsong voice. "Says so there on the sign."

They laughed and she was redeemed for a moment, until they left and she was alone again. She cried then, for a while, wiping her face with the dish towel, crying softly.

She put more wood on the fire, built it up to a small roar, watched the fire, went back to the waiting. She got the blue glass vial from her jacket pocket and set it on the floor in front of the fire, and they waited together.

IT WAS JOSIE'S BIRTHDAY.

The place they called Josie House was behind Ruby's Roadhouse, a white cement building, long and low, the building Pattianne had seen from the beach on that first day. Now she angled across the road toward it, and what she saw was a big window that looked onto a bit of yard and a fence, to the back of Ruby's Roadhouse. An old toilet sat decoratively under the window, pink plastic flowers potted on the back of it, and she kept walking, but slower. Three cement turtles along a chain-link fence, one whose head was broken off, all headed the same way, even the one with no head. Bullfrog sniffed at them through the fence. They were bigger than he was.

"Careful of those turtles," she said.

Around the back corner of Ruby's Roadhouse, the yard turned into an L shape, and there was Mr. Bleakman and two other men, watching a skinny piece of lumber that stuck a few feet up out of the ground. Then the door opened and Josie herself came out, carrying pieces of tinfoil that blew in the wind with a sound like small thunder. One of the men took the tinfoil pieces and lay them on the ground around the stake. Mr. Bleakman sat on a shiny metal trash can that was upside-down on the ground. Pattianne stood at an opening in the fence just past the turtles. There was no gate.

Josie yelled, "Hey, you're early. Come on in."

"No, I'm not early. We're just out for a walk."

But Josie came over, a red T-shirt stretching across her pregnant belly.

"We're just about to start the bird," she said. "Come on in and have some spicy mulled wine. I'm having some myself. Just a tiny bit. Hello, Sugarlips."

Bullfrog wagged his way into the yard, and one of the men said, "Hey, Sugarlips, how's it hanging?" and they all cracked up.

Bullfrog sniffed at the trash can, sniffed at Mr. Bleakman's feet, and then headed for the piece of lumber, and all three men jumped up, saying "No, get away there," all of them shooing Bullfrog away from the stake and the tinfoil on the ground. "Wouldn't be Josie's birthday without one of the dogs getting a squirt at the two-by." And they all laughed some more. They looked like a TV commercial for Moosehead beer.

"We're really just going for a walk. Mrs. Taskey said four o'clock?"

"She's inside greasing down the bird," Josie said.

"Well, I have to take Bullfrog home anyway."

"I'm just getting started on the beans, mushed-up green beans with mushroom soup. I tell the kids that's why it's called mushroom soup, ha! Cal, weight down that tinfoil. There's the rocks, use them."

"I have to get my muffins too."

"You can smash up the almonds if you want," Josie said, heading back toward the door. "Cal, where's your hammer? Pattianne is going to help smash up almonds for the beans."

"Green beans and almonds," one man said, and the men all looked at each other. Then one said, "Hey, Pattianne, glad you can come over. There's beers over there," and he pointed to the toilet. It was full of ice and cans of Moosehead. He said, "My hammer's already in the kitchen." He seemed to be the one called Cal. He had black hair, a lot of it, on his head, down his back in a ponytail. In his ears. It seemed like she'd remember ever meeting such a hairy person.

Bullfrog joined the men staring at the stake in the ground, which was now surrounded with tinfoil weighted down with rocks. The third man, who was really just a kid, a high school kid maybe, took out a pack of cigarettes. He looked a lot like Cal. Not quite as hairy. He shook out a cigarette and offered it to Bullfrog. They all laughed, and it was easier to follow Josie than it would have been to leave.

The door was painted yellow. Instead of a doorknob there was a water faucet, HOT, which Josie yanked and then held the door open. Pattianne went in and didn't know why. She could swear she'd just said she was going for a walk. The short hallway was hung with yellow raincoats, denim jackets, sweaters, long knitted hats, a plaid wool shirt, and a pair of overalls, the paneled walls on both sides bulging with clothes. On the floor under the clothes were black rubber boots and red rubber boots and hiking boots and sneakers and one small red saddle shoe in the very middle of the floor.

Josie said, "You can hang your coat up here," and she went past, and Pattianne pressed against the wall of clothes to make room for that stomach. A red-and-black team jacket with something heavy in the pocket dropped to the floor. Josie kicked a blue high heel with a rhinestone bow out of the way. It bounced off a day-glow pink backpack and ended up in the middle of the floor next to the small red saddle shoe.

"Mary Louise," she yelled. "What's my shoe doing down here?"

"It wasn't me. It was Francie."

"That's a dirty lie. I was right here since breakfast, watching this stupid TV that don't come in."

Josie kept moving and yelled, "Turn that thing off, Francie, and get that baby dressed."

"It's Carolyn's turn. I did it yesterday."

"That's a dirty lie. Janey did it yesterday."

"Carolyn, you stick to your business," Josie yelled, and she turned a corner out of sight, still yelling. "Which I believe is rounding up all the dishes. I want every dish down here in the sink, pronto."

Pattianne thought if she lost sight of Josie, she might be stuck forever in this hallway with all this stuff falling down on her.

The kitchen was a long, wide room with an old gas stove and a counter with a deep sink, and Mrs. Taskey standing at the sink. The counter next to the sink was filled with a leaning stack of plates, rows of glasses and a mixing bowl with a blue plastic cow standing in it. A little girl in a Batman cape and underpants stood at the open refrigerator door.

"Look who came early!" Josie was not yelling now. "Tammy, I thought you were teaching Barbie how to play that card game."

Mrs. Taskey picked a turkey up out of the sink and said, "What a bird."

Josie said, "Ha!"

The little girl in the Batman cape and underpants said, "Barbie won't come out of the bathroom."

Mrs. Taskey set the turkey back down in the sink. "You tell Barbie I said come out of the bathroom."

Pattianne found her voice trapped somewhere deep in the panic in her stomach.

"My biscuits," she said. "Bullfrog. Four o'clock."

A door next to the refrigerator banged open and two, maybe three, large teenage boys with large sneakers crowded the doorway. "Okay, Ma."

"Don't yell," Josie said. "Did you hose it off?"

"Yeah, it was covered with bird you-know-what."

"Ooh." The little Batgirl slammed the refrigerator door shut. "I'm not eating off a table that has bird doots."

"Well, take it on over," Josie said. "Francie, get that baby dressed. Tammy, come help Mama."

The Batgirl ran over to Mrs. Taskey, covered her nose and most of her face with her Batman cape, and said, "Bird doots."

The boys, there appeared to be four of them now, dragged a piece of plywood through the doorway, scraping the refrigerator. A calendar and a painting of a yellow circle landed on the floor. One boy stepped on the painting of the yellow circle, and Tammy let loose a yell. "My potty picture, you wrecked it."

The boy dropped his corner of the plywood and picked up the painting and went on over to Tammy who had covered her whole face with her Batman cape and was wailing, "Ooh, ooh." He got down on his knees and said, "Don't worry, kiddy, you can make another one, I promise. Maybe we'll even add some doots." And Tammy's face came out all teary and said, "Your doots or mine?"

"Yours," he said.

"Yours are bigger," she said.

"Come on, dude, get this," one of the other boys said, and Dude told Tammy, "Okay, mine," and he dropped the potty painting on the counter and got back over to the plywood.

Mrs. Taskey was drying her hands on her apron, plaid with pink hearts along the hem.

"Now, boys, wouldn't it be smart to just drag it around the outside instead of through here?" she said. "Miss Tammy, let's go see if we can get Barbie out of the bathroom."

"I think she probably locked the door," Tammy said. "On accident probably." She followed Mrs. Taskey, who went one way, and the boys went backward out the door with the plywood.

Pattianne was suddenly standing alone in the middle of the kitchen. The TV set blasted louder and then went off. Mrs. Taskey was singing "Oh, Barbie Girl" to the tune of "Oh, Danny Boy," — *"the pipes, the pipes are calling"* — and a toilet flushed. A sharp, pinched voice in the corner of the kitchen went "Ha!"

It was a bird. A parrot type of bird, long green and red feathers, sitting on a perch. Newspaper was spread on the floor around it, covered with seeds and bird doots. It stared at her with one round yellow eye and then the other. "Ha!" It sat there on its perch, which was next to the door, which was open.

Pattianne went through the open door.

A gravel path led around to the front. When she rounded the corner, Bullfrog jumped up and came toward her, his tail all, *My god, where the hell have you been?*

"See you folks in a bit." Pattianne waved and the guys waved back. She was all perky, la la la, biscuits, four o'clock.

Ha.

A sandy trail ran behind Ruby's Roadhouse to the beach. Driftwood and small round rocks, and then the smooth sand. The wind had picked up, blowing hard and warm from the south, so they walked north. The beach didn't go very far north. She could see ahead where it cut in to an inlet with big rocks and the woods edging out to the beach. Bullfrog pranced from rock to rock.

She could see Josie House from the beach and didn't want to look back — they might be watching her escape — but she looked back anyway, and the windows that faced the beach were open and empty.

The tide was out, easy walking around tide pools, going almost in circles sometimes around clear, deep pools full of shells. She reached to get one and the water was warm. She dropped it back into the pool.

They were all in the kitchen with the parrot, or in some other room with a piece of plywood with all the bird doots hosed off. Josie seemed to think she was in charge, but Pattianne's thinking was that it was the little girl in the Batman cape. Barbie seemed to have a good deal to do with what was actually going on too.

Closer to the big rocks, tiny things lived in the pools, dark shoots and pale fleshy sea urchins caught in black strands of grass. Bird tracks circling.

Behind her, down the beach, people moved in the edge of her vision. She caught words on the wind, a laugh, a presence that anchored her. She wondered what she looked like to them—a woman with her dog on the beach—whether they were looking, whether they saw her. She wanted them to see her.

The small, thin-legged birds raced around in groups, pecking at the sand with no one in charge. She stood close to the curve of a huge rock, where water dripped down through crusted barnacles and limpets and mussels, water that made a small sound right by her ear. Bullfrog shook his head, his tags jingling, and the thin-legged birds rose, all turning on one dark wing. They vanished in the air above the surf, and then they were there again on a white wing, gliding to a spot up the beach. A limpet shell bounced down the side of the rock. The first thing she thought was *bird doots*, but then another limpet shell dropped, and a round, speckled orange bird jumped away from the rock above her, the way some birds will walk and hop and jump instead of just lifting away on their wings. She used to watch the crows in Cranbury, when they first moved there, the way they hopped around in the road, and she would think, *Just fly.*

This bird had a white face with black stripes. She walked around the big rock, following the bird, that striped face, and here were more of them, speckled birds with bright masked faces, pecking and chattering. They didn't really sound like birds, more like water on the rocks. And there, out of the wind, a rich, rotten smell gagged her. The birds scattered into the air over the rocks, one of them carrying a long, stringy piece of bloody gut. They had been swarming over a dead sea lion, the stinking carcass hopping with tiny bugs, its side pecked open. Bullfrog headed straight for it.

"No!" Loud enough for him to really hear. She grabbed his collar and dragged him back, her eyes watering, the stink, good Lord. She hooked him to his leash and dragged him back around the rock, back out into the wind. He really wanted to check out that sea lion, and she went fast up the beach to the end, to the last of the rocks, where the inlet lapped gently and prettily at the smooth sand. She breathed deep, and spit and spit, wanting the dead stink out of her nose, her throat. Her eyes were still watering.

It didn't seem very big for a sea lion. It looked like dirty melted plastic.

She climbed up on a rock, and Bullfrog sat on the sand, his leash still hooked to his collar, an insult, his nose bobbing on the wind.

"I'm watching you," she said.

The ocean was a hard, black, glittery surface, like something solid broken apart. Flocks of birds lifted into the wind, and she wouldn't look at them, hating them.

It's just death.

Ha.

Then Father Lucke and the proprietress appeared, coming toward her rock now, and there went Bullfrog, all friendly, like he was saying, *Hey, did you see that sea lion back there? Cool, huh?*

"So," he said—Father Lucke, not Bullfrog—"enjoying the sunshine?"

He said it to her, not Bullfrog, and she said, "Did you see that dead sea lion back there?"

The proprietress said, "Everybody gets a feast on Josie's birthday."

A scarf of lumpy knitted green-and-yellow stripes was wrapped around her head.

Father Lucke said, "Birds of the fields and whatnot," and he tipped a silver flask to his mouth, and then he handed it to the proprietress.

She sipped and offered it to Pattianne. "Schnapps?"

"You guys are drinking peppermint schnapps?"

Father Lucke said, "We are under the illusion that the peppermint fools the kids."

Pattianne jumped off the rock, landing hard on the sand. She took the flask and sipped. Perfect. The death was cleared from her throat.

The shell earrings swung as if they were ringing.

Pattianne said, "I don't even know your name."

"Marie."

"Thank you, Marie."

They moved toward the surf, wide around the sea lion, Pattianne holding Bullfrog's leash and Marie passing the flask to Father Lucke and him passing it to Pattianne.

When she passed it back to him he tucked it away inside his canvas jacket. He wore jeans and a black shirt with his collar tab.

He said to Marie, "So, see you in a bit?"

And Marie said to her, "I suppose you'll be bringing this dog along to dinner?"

And he said, "All creatures great and small."

Marie said, "Oh, please," and they both stood there in the sun and the wind, laughter around them like death around a rock, easy.

"So, what's the deal with Josie House?"

The wind went still, but not really, and Father Lucke said, "It's about love."

Marie said, "It's about getting that lobby ready for dinner." She nodded at Pattianne, her bells swinging, and headed up toward Ruby's Roadhouse, the wind flapping her shirt like she was a pale blue stork.

Father Lucke was not very tall, and not fat really, just one of those round people, especially in his cheeks, which made him seem rounder all over than he really was.

"Josie takes care of the folks, that's all."

His blond hair was wispy and flew all over his pink head, and he squinted at her, or maybe at the sun.

"What folks?"

"In the house."

"Are those all her kids?"

"No. Most of them, but no."

"They just all live there?"

He took her elbow and turned her south, and they walked into the wind. "Josie runs the house, does for the folks that live there. Well, there's Marilyn, and Tuck and Parker. They don't get out much. That's all for now. There have been more. There'll be others."

They stopped and looked up to the back of Ruby's Roadhouse, where Mr. Bleakman was no longer sitting on the trash can. It was now turned upright and shining silver in the sun.

Father Lucke said, "Just watch."

Mrs. Taskey was there with the pale pink turkey in a pan. One of the men took the turkey and upended it onto the stake in the ground, and its wings hung down like the limbs they were, like death, but this was too weird to take seriously. It looked like a doll with no head. Pattianne went, "Hmm."

"Hmm, indeed," he said.

"What are they doing?"

"Trash-can turkey," he said. "Now you know as much as I do."

The three men and Mrs. Taskey all stood around the turkey with their arms folded. Josie ran out of the HOT water door and Batgirl came next. She now had yellow boots on, and she stood right next to the turkey on its stake. Josie took a picture, Batgirl waving at the camera.

"Well," Father Lucke said. "If ever a bird needed a blessing, it's that one, and I'd hate to miss that." He let go of her elbow and said, "Come soon. All will be revealed," and he just stood there, looking into her face. "All creatures great and small, the bread I will give is of my flesh, whatever you need to do to be a caring person. Josie and the kids take care of the transients. They seem to need to do more than many of us. Ha!"

"Transients live in that house?"

He said. "It's all about love, especially if one avoids the trappings of Easter, or Christmas, or even Thanksgiving."

He looked at her directly for another moment, and then away. "Or the church."

"The church that burned down?"

He said, "The church is her people. Heard that one?"

She stared at his round pink face, her eyes watering a little in the wind.

He said, "We're all just people trying to live in the Word of Christ."

"And you're their good shepherd?"

He laughed, lifting his face to the wind and the sun. "I just know most of the best stories by heart. Although I must say, Tammy is running me a close second. See you at four." And he left her standing there. His footsteps ground on the gravel, and at the top, where the gravel became pavement, he turned and yelled back, "I know one. 'Every man hath his proper gift of God.'"

Then he went on, into the front door of Ruby's Roadhouse.

She could see why they wanted to kick him out of the priesthood.

Bullfrog had gone to sleep sitting in the sand. He seemed to do that sometimes, just fall asleep sitting up, and he hardly ever tipped over, although he did usually end up lying down.

Between the buildings, Mr. Bleakman had picked up the shiny new trash can, and Batgirl stuck her head up inside of it. He started to lower it over her, and her squeal came over the wind. Mr. Bleakman lifted the trash can then, and lowered it again, this time over the turkey on the stake instead of over Batgirl. He set it on the ground, and Batgirl beat on the top like it was a drum. One of the guys grabbed her, her squeal coming to Pattianne across the sand, her yellow boots kicking. Another guy wheeled a wheelbarrow over, and one of them shoveled its smoking contents onto the top of the upside-down trash can. Mrs. Taskey clapped, the sound coming to Pattianne in pops. Then the large boys came out of the "hot water" door, and some smaller kids, and they all ran around the trash can, Josie taking pictures. The man with the wheelbarrow was dumping the rest of the stuff on the ground around the trash can, on top of the tinfoil.

Father Lucke showed up. They all stood still, and then they held hands. Josie too. Batgirl broke loose from the guy holding her and ran to Father Lucke. He bent down to her, and she whispered in his ear. Then the circle slowly started to move around the trash can. The singing came down to her in bits.

"*Ring around the rosy, a pocket full of posy, ashes, ashes, they all fall down.*"

Then they all fell down. Even Mr. Bleakman. Even Mrs. Taskey. Even pregnant Josie.

"This place is weird."

Bullfrog woke up and looked back up the beach. Where the dead sea lion was, crows now hopped around on the rocks.

"Let's go," she said, and he agreed.

At home, she picked him up and put him on the bed. She crawled into her sleeping bag next to him. The warmth from his body came through the layers of down, and then his quiet snores were the only sound, and she just lay there listening. Her arm went to sleep, and she didn't move. Soon his paws would twitch and he would dream. If she moved, he would wake up annoyed and hop down. He didn't really like sharing the bed. And she really wanted him there, a living, breathing creature right next to her, warm and dreaming.

THERE WAS BANGING ON the door, and two kids were there, pushing it open, yelling, "It's turkey time! It's turkey time! Sugarlips gets to come too! There's gizzards!"

She sat up on the edge of the bed. "Is that turkey done already?"

Bullfrog jumped to the floor and wagged over to the kids. They both wore bright striped knit caps pulled down over their foreheads. They were maybe eight or nine, pretty short. One of them went to the table and said, "Are these your muffins?"

And the other kid said, "No, it's dog doots, what do you think?"

The first kid said, "I'm telling," and the other kid said, "I didn't say a bad word," and they both ran out the door. Bullfrog followed them, and they ran back in, making the floor shake with their stomping feet.

"Come on," one shouted. "Does Sugarlips have a leash?"

She said, "Is that turkey all cooked already?"

"Father Lucke is gonna pray on it."

"On the turkey."

"It's a special Josie's-birthday prayer."

"No, it isn't. It's just plain old saying grace."

"I'm telling."

Pattianne wrapped the plate of biscuits in one of the dish towels and slid them into a plastic bag.

One kid said, "I'll carry that," and the other kid said, "No, I will," and she said, "No, I will," and the one kid jammed his hands into his pockets and said, "Oh, man," and the other kid looked at her with his mouth open. He had huge front teeth.

The other kid walked around the room, stomping. He said, "How come you live here?"

"I don't. I'm just visiting."

He stopped at the bathroom door. "Don't you have a bathtub?"

"No."

"Why not?"

"Because I don't get dirty."

They looked at each other.

"Never?"

She put on her jacket and stared down the bigger of the two kids. She said, "And his name is Bullfrog."

They walked out the door, the two boys ahead of her, Bullfrog trotting along with them, his tail happy and high. The boys kept looking back at her, and one said, "I don't believe her. Everybody gets dirty." The other one said, "She doesn't look too dirty."

She looked back at the house where they thought she lived, and it was her house all right. Mr. Bleakman could probably rig up a shower easy enough. And it would be nice to have a big, thick down comforter, and there were more green dishes in the junk store in Ucluelet, and maybe Jen would come visit. She could stay at Ruby's Roadhouse. Except there was a divorce to deal with, or annulment, or whatever the fuck it was to be.

A table was set up in the middle of the lobby of Ruby's Roadhouse, and Bullfrog followed her right in. The place was full of noise and full of people, and the table was full of food. She set her biscuits on it and stood close to the wall. There were no chairs around the table, and no spaces for plates. There would be no sitting down together. She took her jacket off and held it.

Li Song was doing tricks with dominoes for three little boys. The turkey sat at one end of the table, golden brown flesh falling off the legs, the ends of the bones reaching up into the air like fists. Cal stood there with his hairy arms raised, a carving knife in one hand, a big fork in the other, and Josie took his picture.

The three big easy chairs had been pushed under the window. Two old men sat there under a lamp. One man was bald, and the lamp lit up his head. The other wore a lumpy, red knit cap. There didn't seem to be any teeth between the two of them. They were both nodding and looking around, and one of them shrank back into his chair when Lakshmi stood in front of him with a cup of coffee, or maybe tea, or maybe spicy mulled wine.

She took his hand and guided it to the cup, and said, "You got it, Tuck?"

Tuck grasped the cup with both shaking hands and shouted, "Got it."

There were other black-haired, dark-skinned girls, sisters or cousins, and there was Mr. Patel, and maybe Mrs. Patel. Pattianne tried to remember seeing her at the Pink Dolphin. She wore a sari of gauzy bright turquoise. The room was big and full of people. The other easy chair under the window in the sun was empty. Pattianne's breath was choppy, and she hated standing here like she always hated standing in a roomful of people, except when Michael was there, standing, shining, beside her, soaking up all the attention, her just warm in the glow of him.

Father Lucke stood at the other end of the table, and the room became quiet.

"Too quiet," he said, his voice full of that giggle. "God loves noise. God would want everyone to talk at once, don't you think?" and he held up a big glass of wine that sloshed down his wrist, and there was laughing all around and then quiet again. Josie took his picture, snap, flash.

Father Lucke held his wine in one hand, and with the other, he took a biscuit from the plate. It crumbled and most of it fell on the table. It was one of her biscuits. He held it up.

He said, "You are the body, you are the blood. You are all Jesus, and we are all God. We all give each other this day our daily bread, and it makes the heavens full of stars, hallelujah. At the Last Supper, Jesus said, 'This is my body.' Let's just say that's what he meant—how you eat food and it becomes part of your body. And when you love each other, that's feeding each other too, so then you are each of you like Jesus!" He popped the biscuit into his mouth and took a gulp of wine, and every-body yelled "Hallelujah!"

The biscuit plate started going from hand to hand. Broken bits of biscuit went from hand to mouth, each person feeding the next, the words, "body and blood" following the plate of biscuits around the room, and laughing and the snap and flash of Josie's camera following it too. The boys who came to get her stuffed whole biscuits into each other's mouths and then opened their mouths wide at each other. Lakshmi carefully poked a piece into the toothless mouth of one old man, then the other. Then she set a piece carefully on the seat of the empty chair. Mrs. Taskey held Barbie's arm by the wrist and guided the thick, overgrown child fingers to her own mouth.

Someone would come Pattianne's way any second, and she was in a panic, but it was Maya, who stuck a chunk of bran muffin into her mouth, and Pattianne swallowed it, whole and dry.

Maya said, "There you go," and Pattianne said, "Thanks." Maya whispered, "No, go 'body and blood.'" So Pattianne whispered back, "Body and blood." Maya nodded solemnly and said, "That's good," and Pattianne got her smile, her amazing sweet smile.

The two boys who came to get her—she thought it was the same boys—were on their knees. Bullfrog was under the table. One of the boys yelled, "Sugarlips gets some, all creatures great and small. Come here, Sugarlips."

Maya took the dishtowel off the plate. Crumbs scattered. She wrapped the dishtowel around her head and it dangled there. She put her hand on one hip and stood right in front of Pattianne, Pattianne thinking, *No, no, don't do it.*

She had a big voice for such a little thing. "No dogs at Ruby's Roadhouse," she said, loud and singsong. "Says so there on the sign."

Marie was watching.

She came over to them. She was tall, and she was not smiling.

With her big fingers, she tucked in the edges of the dishtowel with its pink and yellow hearts, one flap there, a fold there, and suddenly Maya looked just like her.

Then Marie smiled. At Maya. At Pattianne. She shook her head, and the bells rang.

The eating had begun, people lining up at the table with plates.

Pattianne lined up too. She went back to her spot at the wall, slid down to sit there, and she ate, more than she had eaten in days, weeks. Evening came on, and there were lights on in every house on the hillside and all the way up the road toward the highway. She kept looking out the window at her house and wondering why she hadn't left yet. Li Song was setting up Run Soldier Run with some small boys. They had stood the dominoes on end and lined up them under the table and around the back of the easy chairs by the window and around the corners of the lobby. Bullfrog was watching them. Paper plates were everywhere, and the girls kept rounding them up and stacking them carefully on the empty shelves. They put paper napkins in the trash. They put turkey bones in a basket. There seemed to be some kind of plan here.

One of the older boys had a guitar. There was always a boy with a guitar. Frankie probably had a guitar, and she didn't want to think of him, but there he was, and maybe somewhere in New York City, a skinny boy with a crooked tooth was thinking of her, and his boyfriend who is too old to be called a boyfriend was also thinking of her, perhaps kindly, probably not.

Li Song stepped outside and stood on the porch where she could see him. He turned in and looked at her through the window, then looked away again, so that she thought that perhaps he hadn't really looked at her. Then he lit a small cigar. Or maybe not. Maybe he was lighting a cigarette and she could join him. There were Marlboros in her pocket. There was the vial of Emerson "Bud" Paul in her pocket. There were her hands in her pocket, clenching into fists and letting go, clenching and letting go. Bullfrog, who had been watching the dominoes patiently, was now sleeping with his nose pointing toward a spot under the makeshift table. She got up, stepped over him, out the door.

It was like an evening in spring. The air was balmy and soft, and the offshore breeze was actually warm on her face. The cherry smoke of the cigar was in the air, and the pine perfume of the island. No ocean smell. She felt like she was somewhere else. It was a dark night, low clouds hiding the moon, like a careful hand was cupped over Tofino and all of them.

Li Song drew on the cigar. His face lit briefly. He said, "How are you doing here, with this crazy gathering of lost souls?"

In the darkness, she could look right at him. "Are you a lost soul?"

"Actually, my wife is the lost soul."

"Your wife?"

He said, "She was going to meet me here. I started to build us a house. She decided to remain in Korea and become my ex-wife. So I stopped. I have found being stopped to my liking."

He didn't shrug his thin shoulders, but it seemed like he did, and he said, "It is tiresome to be the hero of a sad story."

The room behind them filled with sudden laughter and a flash of light. Father Lucke held a small girl on each shoulder. They held the broken wishbone above his head, and Josie took another picture, and people were clapping. Bullfrog was snuffling around but still safely away from any turkey bones.

"So," she said. "Is he really a priest?"

"I think he is. Truly. I also think he is about to be excommunicated. And justifiably so."

She would imagine so, after seeing the sacrilege of the communion dinner inside. Then she saw what she was thinking, and beyond that, to a tall cement Jesus with tears of laughter in his eyes.

"So they'll get another priest? One who will rebuild the church?"

"They don't want a church. Or another priest. They want him. He helped Josie set her place up. She had a place like this in Alaska. He got her a grant to feed and house these people. She was doing it out of her own pocket. Now he's working on a grant for Kamal Patel."

"The Pink Dolphin?"

"Keep all those girls out of trouble. Keep them safe. Most of them are from Vancouver. The little one, Maya, is from Calgary. He and Rasa are foster parents."

"Lakshmi?"

"Foster daughter. They had another daughter who was lost to them. Their sad story."

"Is anyone here from here?"

"Of course." He tried to look stern, but he couldn't even frown. "Think of your history. We are all guests. Here by the grace of someone else's story."

They were a small crowd of strangers, here on the edge of the continent.

Then he said, "Look," pointing out toward the road, toward the dark ocean, which was not dark at all, but lit up as though a spotlight were out there on the beach, as though the moon were shining on the waves. They were bright.

"Silver tide." It was a whisper.

He turned and opened the door. "Silver tide!" It was a shout.

Father Lucke raised his tumbler of wine. Bullfrog looked straight at her through the window. The two old men in the easy chairs nodded. The soldiers ran. So did the children, out the door, Bullfrog chasing after them.

Her fingers wrapped around the blue glass vial, and her heart said it's time, her heart speaking plain English, in whispered words that she heard with her ears. Li Song's hand was on her elbow, and Bullfrog was dancing.

The beach, when they reached it, was splashing with light. The tide low, and the tide pools were rounds of dark water until small feet splashed them to life. Three big boys threw rocks into the water, and they kicked high arcs of silvery water at each other. The water splashed their faces with silver and ran in outlines of light down their bodies. Smaller children stamped the wet sand, silver spraying out around their feet.

"Is it the silver tide?"

"El Niño maybe?" Father Lucke stood near her. "It's usually a summer thing." His words were slippery with wine. A wave washed over their feet, the water actually warm, and Bullfrog backed away. He didn't go far. Everyone was here now.

Emerson "Bud" Paul was here now. She took him out and held him. The vial was black in her palm.

Li Song said, "What is it?" He was close to her, next to her.

"My sad story."

She unscrewed the tiny cap.

Maya ran up to them. "What is it?"

"A sad story," Li Song told her.

She said, "Oh," and ran away to other kids, splashing in the shallow tide.

Pattianne opened the vial, swung her arm wide. She couldn't even see the ashes that flew out into the water, and they made no silver splash, nor any sound. Then she tossed the vial into the waves, let go. A tiny silver dot disappearing.

When the end has come and also gone, there is a surprising moment left for a breath, for a person to stand alone at the edge of a continent, the waves' edges cast in dark silver light. She felt the west in her face, the east at her back, and she was so sorry.

The clouds broke apart and were lit up by the moon that she couldn't see, the clouds' edges cast in dark silver light. There were patches of stars. Sky and water, the same.

15: JUST STORIES

THE EMPTY SHELVES IN the lobby of Ruby's Roadhouse were a sign. Miss Mimi's books boxed up and stored at the Raritan Valley U-Store-It in Cranbury were a sign. The British Columbia Grant Initiative for Rural Library Projects was a sign.

She decided to use FedEx one last time, and when the big blue and white truck arrived with twenty-eight boxes of books, all the kids were lined up, waiting on the porch of Ruby's Roadhouse. Father Lucke sat at the desk. He poured schnapps into his hot chocolate, and into hers.

She opened the boxes. Marie stacked books up, certain books in front of certain shelves.

There was religion and nature and history, and a lot of books about books, and books about words. There were big books about art and architecture, and there were atlases. There were books about how to take photographs and how to grow gardens and how to drink tea and how to name the birds.

"Alphabetical by author's last name," Pattianne told the older kids. "Biography by subject."

Fiction. Easy. Poetry. Easy.

"G comes before J," she said to the smaller kids. "P comes before T."

Lakshmi passed around the stamp pads with dark green ink, and the rubber stamps—Ruby's Roadhouse Lending Library.

"Just stamp anywhere inside the front cover," she said.

Maya had her own stamp pad, in the shape of a heart, that said My Pretty Pony. "It's pink," she said. The ink was neon bright. She had it on her fingers, her pointy nose. "Please?" she said. "Can't we make some pink? Maybe this that's just stories, could it be pink?"

Pattianne said yes.

ABOUT THE AUTHOR

JOANNA ROSE IS THE author of the award-winning novel *Little Miss Strange*, which earned the Pacific Northwest Booksellers Association Award and was a finalist for the Oregon Book Award. Other work has appeared in *ZYZZYVA, Windfall Journal, Cloudbank, Artisan Journal, Northern Lights, Oregon Humanities, High Desert Journal, VoiceCatcher, Calyx*, and *Bellingham Review*. Her essay "That Thing With Feathers" was cited as Notable in 2015 Best American Essays. She established the Powell's Books reading series and curated it for fifteen years. She is an Atheneum Fellow in Poetry at the Attic Institute and cohosts the prose critique group Pinewood Table. She also works with youth through Literary Arts' Writers in the Schools and with Young Musicians & Artists. She lives in Portland, Oregon, with her husband and, at any given time, several dogs.

ACKNOWLEDGMENTS

To ALL THESE PEOPLE who picked me up hitchhiking and gave me a ride partway down the road—thank you.

Laura Stanfill, you are joy in the world. Stevan Allred—partner in story at the other end of the table. My Dreamies—Kate Gray, Yuvi Zalkow, Jackie Shannon Hollis, Cecily Patterson, Mark Lawton, fellow travelers in time and space, page after page, sentence by sentence, word by word, Thursday after Thursday. The people who have shared time and language with me at Pinewood Table and The Attic and Soapstone and Dangerous Writers. Tom Spanbauer, always. Erin Leonard for telling the important hilarious truth. Candy Mulligan, who was there that night. I wish you were here now. Geneia Jameson for your enduring presence in my life for over fifty years, and for the peace of the River Hag Ranch. And Diana Lee Latter to the east. And Terry Wolfe to the south. Debra Moser for teaching me how to be a friend. Lorraine Bahr for being my Queen of Wands. Word Sisters—Donna Prinzmetal, Penelope Scambly Schott, Andrea Hollander, Maggie Chula for the hopeful moments of Monday morning poems. Lincoln women for one quiet week each summer when I am not afraid to be afraid. Elizabeth Stewart twenty years late. Maya Myers the Scrabble Cop. Gigi Little for Bullfrog/Frisco/Rico Suave/Uncle Dog—you got all of him. Early readers—Carolyn Altman, Diane Jackson, Kevin Burke. Greg Knapp—The Keep on Truckin' Mime Troupe & Gospel Quartet is officially disbanded. I'm sorry you couldn't stay. Marie Knapp Heath and Bobby Knapp—now we are three. And Tina Knapp—we're keeping you. Literary Arts for being a beacon and a home. And every brave high school writer who looked at me like I was crazy and then did the assignment anyway.

A
SMALL
CROWD OF
STRANGERS

READERS'
GUIDE

READING GROUP GUIDE

1. Pattianne has an abortion but doesn't define herself by it. Would you call her a feminist? Why or why not? Would she ever call herself a feminist?

2. In the earliest drafts of *A Small Crowd of Strangers*, Michael Brynn didn't have a point of view. Why do you think the author changed her mind and gave him one? What context and insight does his voice bring to the story?

3. What do you think the title refers to? A particular small crowd or several of them? Have you ever felt lonely when surrounded by people?

4. As an author, Joanna Rose is known for putting humanity on the page with humor and insight. What are some of the ways she uses language to make her characters come alive on the page? Consider her use of description, dialogue, and particular objects as you answer the question.

5. Why has Bullfrog earned a prominent place on the cover of *A Small Crowd of Strangers*? Talk about his relationship with Pattianne. What does he represent in her life?